PROOF OF PASSION

"Have you forgotten that I'm a half-breed?" he asked in a low, almost threatening voice as his expression hardened.

"But you're not like them," she denied.

"How can you be so sure?"

A sudden sense of unease came over Sheri as Brand took a step toward her. "I just know it."

Driven by demons he didn't understand, Brand moved even closer until he towered over her.

Sheri stood her ground, though. She did not flinch before his obvious anger or cower before him. She bravely looked up at him with innocent, trusting eyes.

"You're living in a fantasy world, little girl. You think you know me, but you don't. Maybe I should show you just how much Indian blood I really have...."

As he reached for her, he seemed to change before her very eyes. He was no longer the scout, but was now the fierce warrior Charles had mentioned. Still, Sheri did not back down. As he pulled her close and sought her lips with his, she did not resist.

Brand did not know why he felt compelled to kiss her. It was almost as if he sought to punish her or convince her that the Brand of her fantasies didn't exist. His mouth slanted across hers as he crushed her to his chest. His kiss was savage—hard and hungry.

BOBBI SMITH

Renegade's Lady

LEISURE BOOKS **NEW YORK CITY**

*To the loving memory of Margaret Walton
and Walter Knop*

A LEISURE BOOK®
May 1997
Published by

Dorchester Publishing Co., Inc.
276 Fifth Avenue
New York, NY 10001

Printed in the United States of America.

ACKNOWLEDGMENTS

I'd like to thank Vernon Clemans and Nick Ursino of *Anderson Austin News* for their help with *Renegade's Lady*. They were true inspirations!

Thanks, also, to four of the world's greatest romance fans—Rose Wendt of Wisconsin, Darlene Hays of Missouri, Lesley Guerney of Texas and Dwylah Carpenter of Iowa, and three terrific real-life heroes—Kevin Berra, Dan Lesseg and Andrew Mitchell.

Jack Grothe of Jefferson Barracks in St. Louis, Missouri, and Odette Fuller of Fort Apache, Arizona, provided great help with research. I appreciate all their efforts on my behalf.

Renegade's Lady

Prologue

Arizona Territory—1872

Brand saw the smoke coming up over the rise, and he was filled with stark terror. He urged his horse to a gallop, desperate to get home. He'd left Becky there alone. . . .

His heart was in his throat as he charged forward. It seemed his mount couldn't run fast enough. He spurred it again and again. He hadn't meant to be away so long, but he'd had to take care of some extra business at the fort, and it had taken longer than he'd expected to finish up. Becky usually went with him on these trips, but heavy with their child as she was, she'd decided to remain behind on their small homestead.

As he reached the top of the hill, the carnage below was revealed to him. Brand jerked back on the reins.

Devastation lay before him. Smoldering ruins were all that was left of the small cabin he and Becky had called home. Rage filled Brand, and he charged forward again, clinging to the one glimmer of hope that maybe, somehow, Becky had escaped to hide in the brush until the raid was over.

"Becky!" Her name escaped him, a wrenching cry from the depths of his soul.

There came no answer. There was only silence.

He reined in before the ruins of the cabin. Dismounting quickly, he began to search for some trace of the woman he loved. He covered the area, his desperation growing with each passing minute.

And then he found her.

Brand knew he would never again in all the days of his life see anything as horrible as what had been done to his pregnant wife.

He had always considered himself a strong man, but the sight of her raped and mutilated body struck him more powerfully than a physical blow. Dropping to his knees beside Becky's still form, he gathered her to his heart. It was long minutes before he was able to move. He laid her gently back upon the ground, unmindful that her blood covered him.

Becky had always loved the view from the back of the cabin, and it was there that he scraped out her grave. With great care, he buried her. When he'd placed the last stone upon the site, he collapsed on the ground beside it. Brand remained sitting beside the grave in silence, unaware of anything save the agony in his heart. His wife and his unborn child were dead.

Hours passed. Darkness came and covered the land, yet Brand did not leave Becky's side. He remained unmoving through the long, black hours of the night.

As dawn neared, Brand rose and stared out across the land that was stained red now by the coming of the new day. The look in his eyes was deadly. He knew what he had to do.

With slow deliberation, he retrieved his horse. He tended to its needs as best he could, then mounted up. He would find the raiding party that had murdered his wife and child. They had destroyed his life. There would be no escape for them.

Brand found their trail easily. He had been trained well in tracking.

His blue-eyed gaze was filled with hatred and determination as he studied the raiding party's tracks. They had been brazen in their attack and had not worried that they would be followed. That had been their fatal mistake. Brand was not going to stop until every one of them was dead. They would pay.

Chapter One

Six Years Later
New York City

BUCK MCCADE or BADMAN OF THE
BADLANDS
by
Sheridan St. John
Epilogue

Bang!
Bang!
Buck McCade's aim was deadly. The two des-
peradoes screamed as his hot lead found its mark.
The outlaws pitched forward and lay still,
sprawled in the dust.
Buck moved to stand over his prey and prodded

one of them with the toe of his boot. When neither man moved, he nodded to himself, satisfied that the Darwin brothers had met a suitable end for their dastardly deeds. No longer would they be raping, robbing, and killing. The territory would now be safe from their evil ways.

The townspeople turned out in force when word spread that Buck McCade was back.

Lydia Whitney, the schoolmarm, heard the shouts outside in the street and told the children in the classroom to stay at their desks as she went to see what all the excitement was about.

"What is it? What's happening?"

"Buck McCade's riding into town! It looks like he caught up with them Darwin brothers!" one man called out to her as he rushed past.

Lydia's heart skipped a beat. Could it be true? Could Buck really be here?

Hurrying back inside the schoolhouse, she stayed just long enough to tell Danny Martin, the oldest boy in the class, to keep an eye on things for a minute. Then, without another thought to the lesson she'd been teaching, she ran blindly toward the sheriff's office to see if Buck really was back in town. Her pulse was racing. She'd been waiting and praying for so long. . . .

Lydia stopped, trembling, as she caught sight of him. Her beloved was back! She watched from afar as the man she had thought she'd never see again reined in before the sheriff's office.

"Sheriff Wayne!" Buck called out. "I've got the Darwin brothers, and I've come to collect the rewards on these two blackguards."

The lawman emerged from his office to get a look at the two dead men McCade had brought in, covered by blankets on the backs of their horses. "Good work, McCade. The townspeople can sleep sounder at night now, thanks to you."

"Yep," Buck answered.

"Somebody send for the undertaker," Wayne ordered as he went back inside.

Buck dismounted and followed him.

Sheriff Wayne eyed Buck with respect and a little envy as they faced each other across his office. It wasn't every man who could turn his life around so completely.

"You've come a long way, McCade. Ten years ago, the law was hunting you. Now, you're working with us, instead of against us."

"I believe in righting wrongs, sheriff."

"Buck? Is it really you? Are you really back at last?" The sound of Lydia's breathless cry interrupted them as she appeared in the doorway. Hope shone in her tear-filled eyes as she gazed at the one and only man she'd ever loved.

"Lydia . . . ?" Buck turned to stare at the woman he'd thought he'd lost so long ago.

Not another word was spoken as he opened his arms to her and she ran to him. Ecstasy was theirs as she was enfolded in his embrace.

Buck couldn't believe his good fortune. For so many years, he'd been on the run. Then, after squaring things with the law, he'd decided to live right, but in all this time, he'd never had any hope that he'd see his sweet Lydia again.

"I love you, Buck McCade! And I've been waiting for you all this time!"

"You have?" He lifted his head to gaze down at her.

She nodded, smiling. "There's no other man for me."

"Will you marry me, Lydia?"

"Yes! Yes! Oh, yes!"

And then, not caring that Sheriff Wayne was standing right there watching them, Buck McCade kissed the woman of his dreams, the woman who would soon be his wife.

"Congratulations," Wayne offered when the couple had finally moved apart. "If you're thinking about staying in these parts, I could use a good deputy."

Buck looked from Lydia to the sheriff. "Thanks, sheriff, but no thanks. With this reward money, I'm buying me a small spread and I'm looking to start raising cows and kids."

The sheriff smiled as he watched Buck and Lydia walk from the office, arm in arm.

Outside, the townspeople were waiting, and they cheered Buck McCade as he emerged into the sunlight, his lady love on his arm. McCade had saved them from the terrible Darwin brothers and brought peace to the territory!

As Buck and Lydia made their way through the crowd, they knew the future would be bright and happy for them all.

The End

Maureen Cleaver sighed as she finished proofreading the last page of the manuscript by her cousin, dime-novel writer Sheridan St. John. She had been working with Sheri since Sheri had sold her first novel to Carroll and Condon Publishers over three years before. This book was her sixth in the series and was by far the best, in Maureen's opinion.

Maureen looked up at Sheri to find her fair-haired cousin watching her, her expression intense, her green-eyed gaze clouded with what looked like worry. She thought it strange that Sheri seemed so worried. Her cousin knew she always liked her work and that she rarely found anything wrong with it.

"You can relax now. I think this story is beautiful. It's your best Buck McCade book yet!"

"You really liked it?" she asked, her gaze locking with Maureen's as she searched for the truth.

"I loved it."

She saw no deception in Maureen's eyes and, with her answer, felt relief. "Thank you. Now, I just hope the rest of the reading public does, too."

"What are you talking about? Of course they'll like it. Buck McCade is the perfect hero, and now that he's found Lydia again . . . Speaking of which, how are you going to handle their reunion in the next book? Are they really, finally, going to get married?"

"I'm sorry to disappoint you, but there aren't going to be any more Buck McCade books."

"What?" Maureen was shocked.

"I got a note from my editor last month."

"Mr. DeYoung? What about?"

"It seems the Buck McCade series isn't selling that well, so this will be the last one."

"You can't be serious . . ." Maureen looked troubled. "I thought Buck had a huge following."

"I did, too, but here's Mr. DeYoung's note." Sheri handed her the one-page missive.

"This is terrible!" she sputtered in outrage after reading the letter. "What does he mean 'your work sometimes lacks authenticity'?"

"I guess he thinks I don't know what I'm writing about. I had no idea he felt that way."

"What are you going to do? Writing is your life!"

"I don't know yet, but I will by this afternoon."

"Why?"

"I'm due at Carroll and Condon at three to turn in the new manuscript." Sheri fell silent as she mulled over her situation.

"Well, Mr. DeYoung didn't say in the note that they wouldn't buy another book from you." Maureen tried to sound encouraging.

"That's true." Even though she was agreeing, her tone was terse and troubled.

"It's going to be all right, you'll see."

Sheri managed a small smile. "I'm not going to give up my writing without a fight."

"Now that sounds more like my Sheri." Maureen saw the determination in her cousin's regard and admired her strength of will.

"I've worked hard to get this far, and I have no intention of quitting. If I have to write about something new and different, then I will."

Maureen had no doubt that her cousin would do just what she said. Sheri was a wonder. Having lost her parents to a devastating illness when she was eighteen, she'd been forced to grow up in a hurry. Now in her twenties and comfortably provided for by her father's considerable estate, she'd become an independent woman. There were whispers that she was going to end up an old maid, but Maureen knew if Sheri stayed unmarried, it was by choice.

"And you'll do a fine job, too."

"I can always count on you for moral support." She gave Maureen a quick hug.

"You don't need my support. You'd do it even without me. But will you stop by my house after you talk to Mr. DeYoung and let me know what happens?" Maureen stood to go, knowing her cousin had to have time to get ready for her meeting.

"I will, and if everything goes well, we'll celebrate." Sheri walked her to the front door.

"I'll see you then, and I'll plan on that celebration."

After seeing Maureen out, Sheri returned to her desk to straighten the manuscript. She stared down at the final page, studying the last two words she'd written—*The End*.

The emotion she'd been struggling to control finally won out, and tears traced paths down her cheeks. It was over. Finished. Buck would marry the woman he'd left two books ago and then they'd live happily ever after. No longer would he chase outlaws and bring them to justice. His days as a hero were at an end. She wondered how she was going to go on writing without him. Buck had been her one and only hero from the start.

Anger took over as Sheri realized the direction of her thoughts. In irritation, she dashed away her tears. Buck McCade was a fictional character. He didn't exist, and from what she'd learned of men so far in real life, she doubted that there was anyone like him. He was a fantasy—her fantasy. Granted, he was her idea of what the perfect male should be, but she would just have to come up with someone better—someone handsomer, someone more exciting, someone who could captivate every female as well as every male reader across the county.

And she was going to do it.

Sheridan St. John wasn't some easily defeated, mealy-mouthed little miss. She was the published author of six novels in the last four years, and she was going to keep writing no matter what. True, she wouldn't be writing about Buck anymore, but that didn't matter. Buck McCade might be literarily dead, but she would create a whole new character—someone who would catch the public's attention and capture its heart, too. Then she'd show her publisher just how good she really was!

After wrapping the manuscript in brown paper and tying it with string, Sheri left the room. It was time to pay Carroll and Condon Publishing House a visit.

When Sheri's carriage pulled to a stop before the four-story brick building that housed Carroll and Condon, she descended with her usual grace and confidence. She was more than prepared for her meeting with Mr. DeYoung.

"Good morning, Miss St. John," Joanna Cagan, the cheerful young receptionist, greeted her with a smile.

"Hello, Joanna. Mr. DeYoung is expecting me."

Sheri started toward his closed office door, expecting to go right in. She was surprised when Joanna quickly spoke up.

"I'm sorry, Miss St. John, but you can't go in there right now. He's with someone. Can you wait?"

"Will he be long?"

"He could be. The gentleman showed up unexpectedly, but Mr. DeYoung seemed really excited to see him."

Sheri was disappointed, but she didn't allow it to show. "Of course I can wait. I'll just go upstairs for a while. If you want me, I'll be with Cathy Goellner."

"I'll send for you as soon as he's done."

"Thanks."

Sheri left the outer office and went up to the third floor to visit with her friend. She'd met Cathy Goellner on her first trip to the publishing house all those years ago. Tim DeYoung had taken her on a tour of the building, and Cathy had helped to introduce her around. They had become friends right away.

Cathy, a tall, friendly, auburn-haired woman with dark eyes and an easy smile, was one of thirty women hired by the publisher to read periodicals from across the country. Her job was to find interesting articles that might translate into exciting story lines. If she found something newsworthy, she cut out the article and gave it to her supervisor. The supervisor then chose the best ones from the variety given to him and passed those select articles on to three other women, who outlined them into ideas for novels. The story ideas were given out to the various authors, and then Mr. DeYoung took over, working with the writers on completing their manuscripts.

"Sheri! I'm so glad you're here! Mr. DeYoung said you were coming in today. You must have finished the new Buck McCade," Cathy called out from her desk when she saw her enter the room.

"I sure did." Sheri made her way to her friend's side. "And I've got him right here." She patted the package she was carrying.

"I'm looking forward to reading it."

Sheri knew her praise was sincere, for Cathy had been her biggest fan from the beginning.

"Thanks. I hope Mr. DeYoung likes it, too. What have you got in your pile that looks interesting? I think I may try something different with my next book." She noticed the stack of clippings Cathy had set aside to turn in.

"You're not going to do any more Buck books?" She looked disappointed.

"No, I think it's time for something new and exciting. In fact"—Sheri lowered her voice to go on—"I'm thinking about going out West to research this one. So what looks good? I want something that's going to sell as well as *Seth Jones* did all those years ago."

Both women smiled as they remembered the outstanding numbers the *Seth Jones or A Captive of the Indians* dime novel had sold. At last count, sales were near an incredible 500,000 copies. It had been a fantastic success, and Sheri needed one of her books to sell that well if her career was going to last.

"I think I may have just the thing for you! I found it this morning. The article was in a small newspaper called the *Salt River Herald* from somewhere out in the Arizona Territory." Cathy rifled through the clippings looking for the one she wanted.

"What's it about?"

"It seems there's a half-breed scout who goes only by the name of Brand attached to the cavalry at Fort McDowell there. The wife of a captain stationed at the fort was on her way to join her husband when her stagecoach was attacked by a band of renegade Apaches. All the men on the stage were killed, and she was taken captive. Brand tracked the band for

21

days. He finally rescued her and returned her to her husband."

Sheri's eyes lit with an inner glow as she imagined the story she could weave about this man. He sounded perfect. "I don't suppose there was a picture of him?"

"No, I'm afraid not." Cathy finally found the sought-after article and handed it to Sheri.

"Miss St. John? Mr. DeYoung is ready for you," Joanna called out from the doorway.

"I'll be right there." She looked back at Cathy. "Can I keep this?"

"Absolutely."

They shared a conspiratorial smile, and Sheri hurried after Joanna to the reception area. Her rush seemed for nothing. Her editor had emerged from his office, but he was still deep in conversation with his visitor—a tall, graying, powerfully built man who was dressed like a cowboy. For a minute, Sheri thought it was a costume of some sort, but then she overheard part of their conversation.

"It's been a pleasure to meet you in person, Tex. I'm looking forward to a long and prosperous relationship with you. Carroll and Condon is thrilled to have you writing for us," Tim DeYoung was saying.

"Are you free for dinner tonight? I'd like to learn more about my new publisher."

"Of course, it would be a pleasure. Shall we say six o'clock?"

"I'll meet you here."

The two shook hands while Sheri looked on, wondering who this man could be and why Mr. DeYoung was taking him out to dinner. He had never taken her out to dinner.

When the man named Tex turned to go, he saw Sheri for the first time.

"Little lady," he said in a deep drawl as he gave her a slight nod. He disappeared out the door, putting his Stetson on as he went.

Sheri looked over at Mr. DeYoung, her expression curious. "Who was that?"

"That was Tex Bennett," he announced with pride.

"*The* Tex Bennett?" She was shocked. Tex Bennett was a very well known author. It startled her to learn that he was now writing for her publisher. Her original sense of unease about the future of her career grew.

"Yes, *the* Tex Bennett, and I just signed him on to write for us." He motioned for her to enter his office. "Come on in, and let's see what you've got."

A few minutes later Sheri was seated across the desk from him, looking him straight in the eye. The moment of truth had come. She had given him the new Buck McCade manuscript, and he'd placed it aside with little interest. Her spirits sank at his indifference, and now she knew she had to handle the situation boldly. She would not just sit there, waiting for him to tell her her writing days were over. She would take the initiative. She would seize the day.

"I realize the import of your note about the sales of Buck McCade books, and I think you're right. It's time I tried something new. I want to go out West to research my next book," she declared with passion.

"Really?" Surprise showed in Tim DeYoung's expression. This was the last thing he'd expected from someone like Sheridan St. John. She was a lady, through and through. He'd never imagined that she'd want to venture out of New York City, and that was his main problem with her writing. Her prose just didn't ring true, for she had no real-life experience. That was why he'd just added Tex to the Carroll and Condon stable of authors. He was intrigued by Miss St. John's plan, though, and wondered what she had in mind.

"Yes, and I have just the story to work on." She handed him the article about the half-breed scout and waited as he quickly looked it over. "Well? What do you think?"

"It sounds like it would make a good book, but it might be more suited to someone like Tex. Someone who knows all about the Arizona Territory and—"

"I can do it," she declared assertively, cutting him off. She wasn't about to let Tex take her story idea or her job. The half-breed scout book was her project and no one else's. Brand was hers. "I'll go to Arizona and interview him myself. What do you say?"

He silently debated the idea for a moment as he reread the article and then looked up at her. "All right. The story line is yours. How soon can you get going on this?"

"Right away."

"How much time do you need to finish the manuscript?"

Sheri's mind was racing as she estimated the length of her trip out West and back. "Six months."

"Fine. I'll expect you back here in September with the manuscript. The same terms as the Buck McCade books. Agreed?"

"Agreed."

Chapter Two

**Brand, *The Half-Breed Scout, or Trail of the Renegade*
by
Sheridan St. John
The Journey**

The ride on the stagecoach through the rough Arizona Territory was not an easy one, but Rachel Anderson was smiling as she stared out the window at the passing desert scenery. Orphaned at a young age, she'd lived in a children's home until she'd been old enough to support herself as a nanny. Her life would have continued that way, for she loved children, but then she'd met Carl. . . . Shortly after they'd met and she'd fallen in love,

25

with him, he had gone on to California to seek his fortune. He had just written to her asking her to come West to join him, and Rachel was on her way to Sacramento now to marry him. It was going to be her dream come true having a husband and a family. She was enjoying every minute of this trip that was taking her closer to him.

"You think we'll be there soon?" she asked Mercy Stewart, who was sitting across from her with her maid, Jenny. Mercy was the wife of a captain stationed at a fort here in the territory, and they'd become friends over the last hundred miles or so.

"Yes, my dear, we will," Mercy said with a smile of relief. Soon they would reach Fort McKenna, and she would be reunited with her beloved husband, Clark.

"I hope you're right, Miss Mercy. I don't know how much more of this I can stand," Jenny said with a grimace as the stage hit another bone-jarring rut in the road. *"I don't think there's an inch of me that ain't bruised!"*

"Once we reach the fort, you can rest for a week if you want."

"It may take a week to ease all that's paining me," Jenny groaned as she was thrown roughly against the side of the stage. *"But poor Miss Rachel, she's got to keep on going."*

"Don't worry, Jenny. I'll be fine. Carl's waiting for me. He makes this all worthwhile." Rachel didn't care how rough the road was as long as she got to California.

Jenny smiled at Rachel. She thought her a nice lady who deserved all her happiness. They hit an-

other bump and Jenny groaned out loud. When she'd become Mercy Lawrence's maid five years before, she had envisioned a life of comfort. After all, Mercy's father was Daniel Lawrence, a very rich man. Then, eighteen months ago, Miss Mercy had met Captain Stewart and had fallen madly in love. They'd been married in a magnificent society wedding, but after a short honeymoon, he'd been forced to return to duty, leaving his beloved wife behind. He had finally gotten quarters for them, and so here they were on their way to join him, riding in a hellish stagecoach in the middle of the most desolate landscape she'd ever seen.

"It's going to be fine, Jenny. You'll see." Mercy was gazing out the window, seemingly enraptured by the view.

"Yes, ma'am."

"I'm going to miss you both when you leave the stage," Rachel told them.

"We'll miss you, too. Maybe someday we'll meet again."

"That would be nice. Just look up Mr. and Mrs. Carl Johnson in Sacramento, and you'll find me."

"I'm so happy for you, dear. It's wonderful that all your dreams are coming true," Mercy said with heartfelt meaning.

The Apache attack on the unsuspecting stage-coach came suddenly and viciously. The Indians swooped down upon the hapless stage with murder and plunder on their minds. The sound of their war cries rent the air.

The stage driver looked back in horror to find the savages gaining on him. He could hear the screams of his passengers as he drove the horses

*to breakneck speed over the rugged terrain, but
there was no helping it. He lashed desperately at
his team, seeking to escape the blood-letting he
knew was to come. . . .*

"So you think I've captured the feel of the land and
the essence of what we've experienced on the trip?"
Sheri asked Maureen as they rode in the stagecoach
on their journey to Fort McDowell.

"I thinks it's very accurate," Maureen told her. "In
fact, I feel quite a bit like young Jenny myself, if you
must know the truth."

Both women laughed.

"I think we both do," Sheri agreed.

She had been writing without fail every night, and
Maureen had been reading her pages the following
day. Maureen knew how much Sheri wanted this
book to be accurate, and so she was watching the
details closely.

"I hope this trip is worth it for you."

"It already has been. Look how much of the country we've seen! Some of it I couldn't have imagined
even if I'd read eyewitness accounts."

"It is . . . different." Maureen was intimidated by
the raw, untamed land. She was used to living in
New York City. This wilderness was totally foreign
to her, and she couldn't imagine why anyone would
want to live out here. Cautious by nature, she never
rushed headlong into anything. Yet here she was, in
the middle of nowhere, accompanying Sheri on this
escapade. It was amazing what her cousin could talk
her into.

"I still can't believe how smoothly everything has
gone," Sheri remarked. "We're almost there, and it's

only been three and a half weeks since I spoke with Mr. DeYoung."

"James did a fine job making the arrangements," Maureen said, thinking how quickly their cousin James St. John, an attorney in Washington, had been able to arrange their visit to the fort. "Especially finding the Wallaces to chaperone us."

The middle-aged couple sitting across from them smiled.

"It's been our pleasure. It was fortunate that we were traveling to California and could arrange things this way. James is a dear friend, and we were glad to help," Fred Wallace said.

"And I find your reasons for coming here so interesting, my dear," Joyce Wallace told Sheri with sincerity. "It's unusual to find a woman involved in such pursuits."

"I know. Most people aren't as kind as you are."

"What do you mean?"

"There have been less than kind remarks made about my career, but I don't let any of it affect me. All I care about is my writing. That's why I'm going to the fort. I want to do research for my next novel."

"So your next novel is going to be set in Arizona?"

"Yes. There was an article in the newspaper about a scout from the fort who rescued a captain's wife from the Apaches. I found the story intriguing," she explained. "I made a few inquiries before we left New York, and we should be able to meet and spend time with him. I also plan to meet with the reporter who wrote the story for the newspaper."

"How exciting for you. What about the captain and his wife? Will you get to speak with them?"

"Unfortunately, no. He transferred out after his

wife's ordeal. I'm going to base the story on the scout and possibly plan a complete series about his continuing adventures."

"You have a wonderful imagination."

Sheri gave a small laugh. "That's true enough. It's amazing how my mind works. One minute, I can be carrying on a totally logical conversation with someone, and the next, in my head, I'm a thousand miles away."

Joyce looked at her in amazement. "Your writing ability is definitely a gift."

"I just feel lucky that I've been able to use it, and I want to keep using it. That's why I'm here. I want to see, touch, and feel what I'm writing about. I want to make it as real as possible for my readers."

"And I'm sure you're going to do just that, my dear," Fred said supportively, admiring her spirit. Not only was this Sheridan St. John a pretty woman, she was educated and talented, too. A rare combination, indeed.

They had just settled into a companionable silence when the driver's sudden shout filled them with instant terror.

"Indians!"

The stagecoach gave a violent lurch that sent all the occupants slamming against the walls and each other. The bone-jarring pace changed to a frantic, desperate run.

"Did he yell *Indians?*" Sheri asked, giving Maureen a look of complete incredulity as she grabbed hold of the seat to hang on for dear life.

"Oh, God!" Joyce wailed, clutching at her husband.

The stage careened eerily on two wheels as the driver took a sharp turn on his race toward the town that was still some three miles ahead.

"I can't believe this!" Maureen muttered, her teeth gritted against the pain of being thrown physically about. "We're living your story!"

"I hope not!" Sheri returned, thinking of how her stage attack was going to end.

Desperate to see what was going on, Sheri managed to stick her head partially out the window to get a look around. A frisson of fear shot down her spine as she caught sight of them—a group of warriors atop a rise in the distance. It was the first time she'd ever seen Indian warriors. They looked forbidding and dangerous and deadly. Sheri went pale, and she jerked her head back inside. She had never thought her escapades would actually be dangerous. She had come West to further her career, not to end it by being killed.

Suddenly, the murder and mayhem she'd been writing about all these years struck another chord within her. Real people were fighting and dying out here. Not just cardboard figures she made up in her head and wrote about. Distantly, she wondered if that was part of what Mr. DeYoung had been talking about when he'd told her her writing had lacked authenticity. She suppressed a shudder. She had wanted to do research, but there were limits to what she wanted to experience firsthand.

Sheri had never before been really terrified. She'd been afraid and uncertain when her parents died, but that was nothing compared to the stark horror of knowing death could be imminent.

Will Sparks, the driver, cast a worried glance back over his shoulder to find that the warriors were giving chase. He leaned low and whipped the horses again and again. He'd heard talk of what the Apache did to captives, and he had no desire to find out if the tales were true.

Desperately, frantically, he drove on. Phoenix was just a few miles ahead, and he prayed that they would make it. The stage rocked wildly beneath him. Several times he feared that they were going to overturn, but somehow, each time, the stage righted itself. He concentrated only on his goal—reaching town. He tried not to think about the death-dealing redskins who, he had no doubt, were gaining on them. Safety lay just ahead. If only he could get there! His arms ached from controlling the team. Sweat poured from him, yet he struggled on.

Will never knew how he managed to make it into Phoenix without being killed. As they finally reached the outskirts of town, he nearly collapsed in relief, only to have his horror return full-force when he glanced back one last time to find that the Indians were still behind him. Only then did he realize that they weren't shooting, but were slowing their frenetic pace, too. He finally reined in and watched cautiously as one man separated himself from the Indians and rode toward them.

"Are you all right?" the man asked Will. "We saw the way the stage was running and thought renegades were chasing you."

"Who are you?" Will stared at him, shocked to find that he was a white man in a cavalry uniform.

"We're scouts from the fort. You looked like you were in trouble. That's why we followed you into town."

The townspeople came out to see what all the excitement was about. They quickly recognized the scout detachment from the fort and showed no surprise at their presence.

"No, we're fine . . ." Will didn't know which emotion was more powerful within him—the feeling of stupidity he felt because he had panicked at the sight of Indians, or the relief that pounded through him over realizing that they were safe.

"We'll be on our way then," the man said. With that, he wheeled his horse around and started off, calling out to the other scouts as he did so.

Sheri heard their conversation, and, sore though she was, she threw the door wide and climbed out. As she started to step down, she lifted her head to look around and it was then that she saw him. He wore a red headband, fringed buckskin pants, and high moccasins, leaving his broad, firmly muscled, sun-bronzed chest completely bared to her gaze. Though he was dressed as an Indian, there was no doubt in her mind that white blood ran in his veins. His hair was black and worn long. His features were cleanly cut, his nose straight and strong, his mouth firm, as if unused to smiling. He rode confidently, as one with his horse.

Sheri stared openly, mesmerized. She had never seen a real, live, half-naked man before. Oh, she'd seen statues in museums, but this was very different. Her breath caught in her throat. She didn't understand why, but she couldn't take her eyes off him. There was a wild and untamed quality about him, something almost predatory.

He must have sensed her gaze upon him, for he looked her way, and across the distance their eyes met. His expression was proud and arrogant—and dismissive. He turned away, and putting his heels to his horse's flanks, he rode off. He did not look back.

Sheri's gaze remained fixed on the scout until he had ridden from sight. She watched him go, entranced by the realization that he'd had blue eyes.

"Sheri? What is it?" Maureen asked from behind her in the stage.

"Oh, nothing."

Jarred back to reality, she descended the rest of the way to the ground. Every inch of her body was aching from the abuse of the last twenty minutes. She had no doubt that she would be black and blue in various unspeakable places the next morning.

"What happened? Who were those Indians?" Sheri asked Will, who'd just climbed down from the driver's seat. She noticed he looked ragged and more than a little exhausted.

"I thought we were going to be attacked. I thought they were renegades. . . ." He paused to draw a deep breath. "Turns out they were scouts from the fort."

"They were?" Sheri's bruises and weariness were immediately forgotten as she stared after them. A mental image of the blue-eyed warrior stayed with her. "Why did they chase us?"

"They weren't chasing us. They were escorting us. I didn't know it, and I sure as hell . . . er, heck . . . pardon me, ma'am, I wasn't going to wait around out there on the trail to find out."

"I'm sure we all appreciate your discretion," Sheri said, exhilarated to think that she'd already come face-to-face with scouts from the fort and wondering at the identity of the blue-eyed man. She grew even more excited about what the next days and weeks would bring.

"Indeed, we do, sir," Fred said as he climbed down

and then turned to help his wife and Maureen out of the vehicle. "And there was no harm done. If anything, we've probably arrived ahead of schedule."

As the tenseness of the situation eased, the townsfolk who'd come out to see what was happening shifted away. Maureen was shaken and a bit unsteady as she went to stand with Sheri.

"Nothing like making an entrance, is there?" Maureen quipped, her voice quavering.

"I wonder . . ."

"What?"

"Did you see that one scout? The one with the blue eyes?"

"Blue eyes? No, I didn't. Do you think it might have been him?"

"I don't know, but I plan to find out. I need to find Charles Brennan. He's the reporter who wrote the article. He'll be able to tell me. I wrote and let him know that we were coming, so he should be expecting us. I wonder where the *Salt River Herald*'s office is?" She looked around, hoping to spot the newspaper office.

"Can we look him up a little later?" Maureen asked, her knees still shaking.

Sheri cast a glance at her cousin, saw how shaken she still was, and smiled. "This evening will be fine. I'll send a note over to the newspaper office as soon as we get settled in."

"Come, ladies, let's see about getting us rooms for the night. First thing in the morning, we can head out to the fort," Fred said. He took charge, ushering them down the street toward the hotel.

When Sheri and Maureen finally reached their rooms, Sheri dropped her things in her own room and went to talk to Maureen in hers. She walked to the window and stood there staring down at the street below. As she paused for a moment, she realized what she'd just lived through. Her pulse was still racing from the excitement of it.

"You know, I think I can write about real terror now," she said slowly, turning to look at her exhausted cousin. "I never knew how horrible it was to face certain death before, but I do now."

"You're not the only one," Maureen agreed, sitting down heavily on the bed. "And it wasn't fun."

"No. It wasn't."

"How do I let you talk me into doing these things? We could have been murdered today! Scalped! Or God knows what else . . ." She trembled visibly, repulsed by what her imagination was conjuring up.

"But we weren't," Sheri pointed out logically. "You know . . . I need to get this down on paper while it's still fresh in my mind. I'll be in my room writing, if you want me."

"Enjoy yourself," Maureen said as she lay down to rest and recover from the excitement of their ordeal.

Sheri returned to her own room and dug through her traveling case to find her foolscap paper and pencils. Dragging a chair over to the one small table in the room, she began to write.

"Dismissed!" Sergeant Mike O'Toole called out to his scouts.

It wasn't a minute too soon as far as the men were concerned. After a two-week trek through the surrounding mountains looking for Apache, they were more than ready to relax for a while.

"Brand, wait a minute. Lieutenant Long wants to see the both of us."

Brand was curious at the summons. It wasn't often that the officer wanted to see them. He followed his friend to the lieutenant's office.

"You wanted to see us, sir?"

"Yes, Sergeant O'Toole. I especially want to see Brand, here."

"What about?"

"It seems any day now, we're going to be having a visitor here at the fort."

"We are? That's unusual, isn't it, sir? Is it someone important?" O'Toole asked.

"Let me put it this way—the orders relating to this 'visit' came directly from Washington."

"Who's coming?" Brand asked. He couldn't imagine what someone from Washington wanted with him.

"A novelist from New York City, a certain Sheridan St. John, is interested in meeting you, Brand, and interviewing you. Mr. St. John read an account of how you saved Mrs. Garner, and he wants to write a book about it."

"I'm not interested," he said tersely.

"Well, Washington is interested. St. John has already published a number of books. This could be good publicity for us and for our campaigns out here. We've been instructed to welcome Mr. St. John and to accommodate him in any way. Who knows? Maybe this writer could make Fort McDowell and the 6th cavalry household names."

"Then we're being ordered to cooperate, sir?" Brand asked.

"If I have to make it an order, I will," Long replied

tightly, although he realized that he should have anticipated just such a reaction from the half-breed. Personally, he was looking forward to the visit. He thought, perhaps, he could convince St. John that he had a story of his own to tell that was far more fascinating than anything the half-breed had to offer. He certainly wasn't averse to seeing his own name in print. In fact, he rather relished the idea. "Do we understand each other?"

"Yes, sir," both men replied.

"Fine. You're dismissed."

As they left the office, O'Toole smiled wryly. "This should be interesting."

"For you maybe."

"You read. Wouldn't you like to see yourself immortalized in a book?"

"No."

"Well, it looks like you don't really have much choice. Washington's involved."

Brand grunted in disgust. All he wanted to do was track down renegades, not waste his time with some greenhorn from back East. He was not looking forward to meeting St. John.

Chapter Three

**Brand, The Half-Breed Scout, or Trail of the
Renegade
The Chase**

*But there would be no escape for the ill-fated
stage driver and his passengers this day. A deadly
arrow pierced his heart, ending his valiant attempt to save the lives entrusted to him. Thrown
from the careening stage, the driver's life's blood
spilled out into the Arizona dust.*

*The Indians closed in, snaring the lead horses
and bringing the team to a stop. The prize was
theirs!*

*Within the confines of the stagecoach, the pas-
sengers looked at each other in horror. Rachel had*

gone pale, and Mercy and Jenny were clinging to each other in frantic desperation.

"What's happening?" Rachel asked, her eyes wide with fright.

"Indian attack. . . . The driver's dead," Gus Jones, the only other passenger on the stage, replied tersely as he drew his gun. He knew their ultimate fate, but he was determined not to die without taking a few of these damned savages with him. "Get down and start praying, ladies!"

The three women huddled on the floor. Both Mercy and Jenny screamed as Gus started shooting wildly out the window. His defense was short-lived. Another arrow found its mark, and he collapsed, dead on the seat near Rachel.

"Oh, God!" she screamed.

The door was thrown open then, and three ghoulishly painted warriors stood staring into the stage. With cruel, harsh hands, they grabbed for the three white women. . . .

"That must be Charles Brennan," Sheri told Maureen as they sat at a table in the restaurant that evening.

Maureen looked up to see an attractive, bespectacled, dark-haired young man of medium height speaking to the waitress. As the woman pointed in their direction, a look of surprise showed in his expression. He said something more to the waitress, then walked toward them.

"Mr. Brennan?" Sheri asked, smiling as he approached their table.

"Miss St. John?" Charles Brennan countered with a grin.

"Sheri to my friends." She rose and extended her hand to him.

Charles's gaze swept over her appreciatively as they shook hands. "It's a pleasure."

"And this is my cousin, Maureen Cleaver." She made the introduction.

Charles greeted the other woman with equal appreciation. Though not as strikingly beautiful as her blond-haired, green-eyed cousin, Maureen Cleaver had a gentle, almost serene loveliness about her. Her hair was a shade darker than Sheri's, and her brown eyes were warm and friendly. He smiled at her, liking her immediately.

"It's nice to meet you, Mr. Brennan. We admire your work," Maureen said.

"Please join us, Mr. Brennan," Sheri invited him as she sat back down.

"Call me Charles, please," he said, taking the seat across from her. "I've been looking forward to meeting you ever since I received your letter, but I have to admit, I honestly thought you were a man. How is it that such a lovely lady as yourself came to be a published author? It's an unusual occupation for a woman, isn't it?"

"My parents died a few years back, and though they left me comfortably well off, I knew I had to do something more with my life. I had always loved books and writing, so when I read my first Carroll and Condon dime novel . . . well, I just knew that that was what I wanted to do. Luckily, my own name is not very feminine, so I was allowed to use it for my pen name."

He looked at her with even more respect. "I'm impressed. How many books have you published now?"

"I've just turned in my sixth, but I think it's time for a change. That's why I'm here. I want to research a story that I think would make a great novel."

"And that has something to do with me and the article I wrote on the rescue of the captain's wife from out at the fort?"

"Yes. I want to do a book about the half-breed scout who saved her."

He stared at her in amazement. "I'm still surprised that you heard about it. How is it that you read about Brand in New York City?"

She quickly explained how things were done at Carroll and Condon Publishing House. "I have the clipping right here."

Sheri took the carefully folded article out of her small reticule and handed it to him.

"I always wanted a large readership, but I never thought what I was writing for the *Salt River Herald* would make it all the way to New York City."

Sheri smiled at him, understanding completely his feelings. She felt the same way when her novels were published. There was no way of knowing who was reading her work or how it was affecting them. "Believe me, I appreciate your writing. I think this Brand has the potential to be the hero in a continuing line of Western adventures. That's why I wanted to meet with you first and talk with you about him."

"So you haven't met Brand yet?"

"No. We'll be traveling out to the fort tomorrow. I thought you could provide me with a little more insight into his character before we go."

"I'd be delighted to help you, but it will be interesting to see how Brand reacts to your idea of featuring him in a book."

"I hope he'll be pleased."

"Most men would be, but . . ." Charles paused. "Brand's a difficult man to figure. I'm not sure what kind of reception you'll be getting from him."

"Tell me about him," Sheri encouraged Charles.

"He's a half-breed, as you know. His mother was a white captive, his father Apache."

"Do you know how his mother was taken captive?"

"No, I didn't ask, and he never offered. Although I did interview him at length for the article, I can't claim to be his friend. Brand's very much a loner. I do know that he was orphaned at twelve and that Sergeant O'Toole at McDowell, who was Trooper O'Toole at the time, took him in. Evidently Brand's mother had schooled him in white ways. When he moved to the fort with O'Toole, he tried to fit into the white man's world."

"And?" Sheri was growing even more excited. This Brand sounded perfect—*no*, she thought, *he sounded better than perfect*.

"He did fine from what I could find out, working around the fort doing odd jobs. He even married a white girl a few years back. She was the commander's daughter, actually."

"Oh . . ." This surprised her. For some reason, Sheri hadn't even considered that he might be married.

"Quite a few white people were put out by their union. Her father wasn't too happy about it in the beginning, either, but things worked out . . . for a while. Then there was an Indian raid one day on their small ranch, and she was killed."

Sheri and Maureen gasped in horror. "That must have been horrible for him."

43

"He tracked down the band that had murdered her and exacted his own revenge."

"What did he do to them?"

"You don't want to know."

Both women paled slightly, their imaginations working overtime.

Sheri swallowed nervously. "So that's why he was so relentless in finding that captain's wife."

"The poor man," Maureen sympathized. "First, his own mother was a captive, and then his wife was killed . . ."

"It was nothing short of a miracle that he found Mrs. Garner. He's very good at what he does."

"He must be magnificent," Sheri breathed, in awe of him already.

Charles couldn't help chuckling at her reaction. "I'm sure he wouldn't describe himself that way."

Sheri turned serious. "How do you think he would describe himself?"

"A few years ago, I'm sure his answer would have been different. But right now, after all he's been through, my impression of him is that he thinks of himself as a warrior."

A shiver of anticipation went through Sheri at his words. "I see."

"When he came back to the fort, O'Toole almost didn't recognize him. He'd gone back to his Indian ways to do his tracking. He signed up to be a scout then, and that's what he's been doing ever since."

"He sounds fascinating."

"So you're going to McDowell tomorrow?"

"Yes, first thing in the morning. Would you like to accompany us?" Sheri asked.

"We'd love it," Maureen spoke up. She'd taken an

instant liking to Charles and wanted to get to know him better. There was something about him . . . a certain twinkle in his eyes that denoted a keen intelligence and a quick wit that attracted her.

"I'd like that. I'll plan on it."

"Tell me, Charles," Sheri asked, "how did you end up here in the Territory? You're not a native. Your accent seems more Eastern."

"You're very perceptive," he told her with an easy grin. "Actually, I'm from Cleveland, but I went to Boston College before heading West."

"But what brought you here?" Maureen was curious. As a college-educated young man back East, he could have gone anywhere and done anything. Instead, he'd ended up here, in the middle of a desert filled with cactus and murderous Indians.

He was thoughtful for a moment. "I'm not sure. I was passing through a few years back on my way to California, and this is as far as I got. Something inside of me said 'stay', so I did."

"But it's such a harsh land."

"It is harsh. Sometimes it's even deadly, but it's also beautiful."

"So you're happy? You've never regretted it?"

"I love being a part of something that's new and growing. Phoenix may not be a big town yet, but I predict that some day it will be. I want to be around to see it."

"But what about the Indian trouble?"

"They're mostly confined to the reservations now. The depredations aren't nearly as serious as they were a few years back. The cavalry's been doing a fine job. I think you'll be impressed by the fort."

Bobbi Smith

"I'm looking forward to seeing it and meeting Brand."

"What time were you planning on leaving?"

"A little after nine. Would you like to meet us in the hotel lobby right at nine? The Wallaces are traveling with us, too. They've been chaperoning us for the trip."

"I'll be there. It's been nice meeting you both." He stood to go. "I'll see you in the morning."

Charles left them, and after a few minutes, they started back to the hotel to retire for the night.

"What an interesting man," Maureen remarked thoughtfully as she joined Sheri in her room for a minute.

"Yes, Brand is," Sheri replied. "I can't wait to finally meet him face-to-face."

Maureen smiled. She'd been talking about Charles Brennan, not the scout. "It should prove interesting."

"He is going to make the most wonderful hero. You know how readers love heroes with tortured pasts. This man is perfect."

"I hope he goes along with your plan."

"So do I. I'll be very circumspect. I won't annoy him in any way. I just want to find out what the real Brand is like, so I can make him come alive for my readers. I also want to learn everything I can about the way he lives, from the food he eats to the clothes he wears."

"For some reason, I have the feeling that this isn't going to be as easy as it seems."

"That doesn't matter. I'm going to make this my best book ever. Carroll and Condon are going to be so proud of me. Once they see the sales on *Brand, the Half-Breed Scout*, they're going to discover they don't need Tex Bennett any more. They've got me—Sheridan St. John." Sheri's pride had been badly damaged, and she was bound and determined to prove her worth.

"You'll do it. I know you will."

"All I have to do is write the rest of the book." She grinned ruefully.

"Well, at least you're all the way up to the kidnapping."

"But I don't know any of the rest of it. I won't be able to write much more until I've met Brand."

"The good news is, you're going to do that tomorrow."

A short while later, after Maureen had gone on to her own room, Sheri lay in bed trying to imagine what the next day was going to bring. An image of the blue-eyed warrior she'd seen earlier that day played in her mind, and as she drifted off, she wondered. . . .

The ride to Fort McDowell was long, hot, and dusty, but there was never a lack of conversation. Charles regaled Sheri, Maureen, and the Wallaces with interesting stories about the Territory.

Sheri listened attentively to his tales as she watched the passing scenery out the window. She had her paper and pencil handy and took notes whenever she saw something she thought she might be able to use in her work.

"You're really serious about this, aren't you?" Charles asked, noticing how intense her expression was as she studied the landscape.

Sheri looked up at him, her regard steady. "Very. I've traveled over a thousand miles for this moment.

I don't intend to waste a second of it."

"What do you think of Arizona so far?"

"I think it's exactly the way people back East envision it—a vast, untamed wilderness, just waiting for heroes like Buck McCade and Brand to civilize it."

"It would be wonderful if real life was as easily dealt with as fiction, but I'm not sure you're going to be finding a happy ending here."

"You're concerned about Brand?"

"Not concerned . . . just cautious. As I told you last night, he's a hard man. There's no scout more loyal or trustworthy, but remember, for all that he's learned the white man's ways, Brand is still half Indian."

"Don't worry. I won't do anything to offend him. I just want to get my story."

"I'm looking forward to reading it when you're through. Make sure you let me know when it's published," Charles told her.

"Us, too!" Joyce Wallace put in. She had listened to their conversations about this upcoming book and was growing excited about it. She found she was almost as anxious as Sheri and Maureen about meeting this famous scout. "When do you think it will be released?"

"If my writing goes well, it should be out some time next year. I'll be sure to let you know."

"Look!" Maureen interrupted as she caught sight of the fort in the distance. "Is that McDowell?"

"It is," Charles answered. "We should be there in just a few more minutes. You did say that you were expected?"

"Yes. Our cousin had contacts in Washington who

helped set this up for us. We're to meet with a Lieutenant Long."

Charles looked less than enthusiastic. "You're dealing with Long, are you?"

"Yes, why?" Sheri asked perceptively.

"No reason."

"You don't like him?" She sensed some disapproval in his tone.

"I don't know him well enough to like or dislike him. I've only had a few passing dealings with him."

"And?"

"And he's been unremarkable." He tried his best not to prejudice her against the pompous, arrogant ass. "I think you'll find Sergeant O'Toole more to your liking. He's a good-natured, down-to-earth man."

"Meaning this Lieutenant Long isn't?"

"I'll leave you to form your own opinion."

The stage rumbled into the fort then and drew to a stop before the commander's office. Fred and Charles climbed out and then turned to help the ladies down. Joyce and Maureen descended first, followed by Sheri.

Sheri gazed out across the parade ground at the neatly appointed officers' quarters and thought it quite a nice place, considering its location in the middle of nowhere.

"Good afternoon." A tall, blond-haired, slickly handsome lieutenant emerged from the office.

Instinctively, Sheri knew this was Long, and she immediately understood Charles's reaction to him.

"Lieutenant Long," Charles said as he stepped forward to greet him.

"Brennan," he said with less than enthusiasm. "What brings you here?"

"These ladies are anxious to meet you."

Long looked curious. He couldn't imagine who these young women were, but he was eager to find out. It wasn't often that pretty women came to the Territory.

"Welcome to Fort McDowell," he said courteously. "I'm Lieutenant Long, at your service."

"It's a pleasure to meet you, Lieutenant. I'm Fred Wallace. This is my wife, Joyce, and these two lovely young ladies are Miss Maureen Cleaver and Miss Sheridan St. John from New York City."

Long had been listening attentively, and at the news that this striking beauty was Sheridan St. John, he was shocked.

"You're Sheridan St. John?" He stepped nearer and peered at her in disbelief, then smiled widely. "We were all under the impression that you were a man."

Sheri smiled blithely. It certainly wasn't the first time the mistake had been made and it wouldn't be the last. "I'm sorry to disappoint you, lieutenant."

Long hastened to correct his faux pas. "No . . . no. Trust me when I tell you that I'm not in the least bit disappointed, Miss St. John. In fact, the truth of your identity is a delightful surprise."

"Why, thank you." She turned her charms on him, yet even as he melted before her flirtatious look, she sensed something very oily about the man. She didn't know why she didn't like him. She just didn't. She was beginning to respect Charles Brennan's opinion more and more. "Charles has been telling us all about you and the fort. The Territory is so fascinating."

"I'm glad you think so. Please, come into the office." He gestured everyone inside.

Sheri and Maureen led the way as Charles spoke to the lieutenant.

"Is Brand at the fort?"

"Yes, he just got back yesterday from scouting with O'Toole."

"I'll go find him. Miss St. John's very eager to meet him."

"Later," Long said in terse tones. "There's no rush. Why don't you come inside and join us? The breed's not going anywhere, and I'd like to take the opportunity to show Miss St. John around a bit before we bring him into it."

Charles stared at the officer coldly. "She made the trip to meet Brand."

"And she will. In time. Come, let's go inside and relax, perhaps have a drink. I'll send word to Colonel Hancock and Captain Whitmore that you're here, so introductions can be made."

Charles relented, but he resented the lieutenant's taking charge of Sheri and Maureen this way. Knowing Long as he did, he was beginning to wonder just how much time Sheri would actually have with the scout.

When they were seated in the office, Sheri was the first to speak.

"Tell me, Lieutenant Long, when can I meet Brand? I'm anxious to get started on my interview with him."

"We'll send for him shortly," he answered evasively. "For now, relax and enjoy a cool drink. Your trip from town must have been a hot one."

"It wasn't too bad. I was so eager to get here that I hardly noticed."

"We've chaperoned Miss St. John and Miss Cleaver all the way from Washington, D.C.," Fred Wallace said, "and, I can tell you, Miss St. John has thought of nothing else but meeting your scout since the beginning."

"It's good to know that you're excited about joining us here at Fort McDowell. I take it this is your first trip west?"

"Yes, and I'm loving every minute of it."

"It's certainly a far cry from New York City."

"And that's precisely why I'm here. I wanted to experience the wild West for myself. I want to know exactly what my characters are seeing and feeling when I write about it."

"Then it will be my pleasure to assist you in any way I can," Long said ingratiatingly.

"I appreciate your thoughtfulness, and right now, the only thing I want to do is to meet Brand. Charles has told me all about him, and I think it's time I met him face-to-face."

"I'll go find him," Charles offered, heading out the door without waiting for Long's approval. As he stepped outside, he met Colonel Hancock, the commander of the fort, and Captain Whitmore.

"Brennan, what brings you to McDowell?" Whitmore asked.

"Sheridan St. John has arrived, sir, and I came along on the trip to help with the introductions. I'm on my way to find Brand now."

"I saw him a short time ago by the corral, working

with the horses," the captain offered.

"I'll look there first."

Brand was never particularly glad when they returned to the fort from scouting. His life was tracking renegades, and he felt at loose ends and bored when they came back from a trek. The search they'd returned from yesterday had been frustrating. There had been no sign of the Apache who had been raiding nearby. He knew they were out there. He just hadn't found them yet. But he would.

He had just finished working his horse when he glanced up to see Charles Brennan coming toward him. He wondered what had brought the newspaper reporter out to the fort.

"Brennan, why are you here?"

"I've got news for you. Sheridan St. John's arrived and is waiting in Lieutenant Long's office to meet you."

"Tell them I'll be right there." Inwardly he grimaced, but he revealed nothing of what he was feeling as Charles walked away.

Brand was not looking forward to this encounter. His feelings hadn't changed since he and O'Toole had learned of the writer's imminent arrival the day before. He had little use for this St. John person and would be glad when the whole ordeal was over. He and O'Toole had already discussed what should be done, and they'd agreed that they would be cordial, but offer no unnecessary information. If they had to, they would take St. John on a short, staged 'scout', then return to the fort as quickly as possible so the man could be on his way. They both realized that Lieutenant Long was enamored of the idea of finding himself immortalized in print, but neither of them harbored any such fantasy. They only wanted the aggravation of someone from back East disrupting their lives to be over as quickly and painlessly as possible, so they could get on with what they did best—hunt renegades.

Brand finished working with his horse and followed Charles toward the office. He crossed the parade ground, lost in thought.

When he reached the office, Hancock and Whitmore were on their way out.

"Brand, we expect your full cooperation in this venture. Do you understand?" Nelson Hancock said.

"I understand," he answered. He and Hancock had managed to get along while Becky was alive, but since her death they'd had little to do with each other.

"We're counting on you," Whitmore added as they moved off.

Brand went inside to find Charles standing with the lieutenant, an elderly man, and three women. He immediately assumed that the man was St. John.

"Ah, Brand, you're here." Long said with artificial enthusiasm. "Sheridan St. John has been looking forward to meeting you."

Brand turned toward the man and eyed him skeptically, wondering why the lieutenant was so taken with this whole idea. "Mr. St. John," he said with a slight nod.

Fred smiled at his misunderstanding. "No, I'm afraid I'm not Sheridan's father. I'm Fred Wallace. This is Sheridan St. John." He gestured toward Sheri.

Brand frowned as he turned to find himself face-to-face with the same green-eyed beauty he'd seen getting off the stage in town the day before.

Chapter Four

Brand, the Half-Breed Scout, or Trail of the Renegade
The Confrontation

"No!" Rachel screamed as she was dragged from the stage.

Painful hands pawed at her, tearing her clothing and yanking her hair free from its neat constraint. Cruel laughter surrounded her. The warriors were speaking, but in a guttural tongue that she didn't understand. She cast a desperate glance around, praying for rescue, but saw only cacti and Joshua trees and miles of endless desert. She fought to break free, frantic to avoid their violating touch, but to no avail.

A bloodcurdling scream rent the air, and Rachel looked over to see Jenny collapsing to the ground. Her clothing was half-ripped from her body and Mercy was fighting desperately to save her. Mercy was dragged off by another warrior, leaving a lone, grinning, evil-looking renegade, his eyes shining with feral hunger, standing over Jenny.

The warrior who was leading the raid claimed Rachel as his prize. She continued to fight him, but he only laughed at her efforts as he picked her up and threw her, face down, over the back of his horse. He mounted behind her and rode quickly from the scene. Rachel did not know what had happened to her friends, and she worried about them as she was taken away to whatever horrid fate awaited her.

The rest of the raiding party hurried to strip the stage of all valuables. That done, they rode from the site of the attack, victorious. They had taken captives, whiskey, and gold. There would be great stories to tell around the campfire that night. . . .

"Hello," Sheri said as a shiver of anticipation went up her spine. Brand was the blue-eyed scout she'd seen in town, and up close, he was an even more magnificent specimen of manhood. Dressed in a loose-fitting shirt, buckskin breeches, and moccasins that laced to his knees, he was every inch the untamed scout she'd imagined him to be and more. She knew instantly that he was the man who was going to save her career.

Brand had thought it was going to be difficult enough dealing with the writer when he'd believed St. John to be a man, but now . . . Sheridan St. John was a woman—the same one he'd seen descending from the stage in town! His gaze raked over her insolently, missing nothing. She was beautiful, there was no denying that, and he felt a stirring of pure animal attraction for her, but he quickly dismissed it. She was an Eastern miss, a lady who didn't know one end of a horse from the other. She had no business being there. His job was to track renegades, not to cater to spoiled females who happened to have friends in high places in Washington. He was going to look forward to putting her on a stage heading back east.

The look in his eyes was cold as he addressed her. "Miss St. John."

Sheri saw the iciness in his regard and realized that Charles had been right in cautioning her about the reception she was going to receive. Brand wasn't pleased to see her. Still, she wasn't about to give up. She hadn't traveled all this way for nothing. She was going to write this story with or without his help. But she really hoped he would help her. There was so much she had to learn.

"I've been looking forward to meeting you. It isn't often that I get to meet a real live hero."

"What can I do for you?" he asked, ignoring her remark. He knew he was expected to cooperate. He would do it, but he didn't have to like it.

"Well, first, I'd like to interview you at length. I need to learn everything there is to know about you and scouting." Sheri's mind was racing as she imagined Brand walking through the pages of her book. He was going to be magnificent—fighting, winning, rescuing damsels in distress. This was going to be one fantastic book! She couldn't wait to see Carroll

57

and Condon's reaction to the manuscript when she sent it in.

"Why?" Brand's tone was terse.

"It's important I find out everything I can about you so I can make your character more realistic in the book. My plan is for you to be the continuing hero in a series of novels about the Territory. I thought I could title the first one *Brand, the Half-Breed Scout,* or *Trail of the Renegade.* Just think! There will be books about you everywhere."

"Miss St. John, why did you think I'd care about any of this?"

Lieutenant Long cleared his throat as he cast a quick, irritated look at Brand. He wondered if the man had forgotten that he was supposed to cooperate in this venture.

Sheri was stunned by the harshness in his voice. Then she realized that this was a man who'd been through hell and who no doubt relived it every time he went out to track down murderous renegades. What she did for a living probably seemed ridiculously frivolous to him. "Mr. Brand . . ."

"No 'mister', just Brand."

"Brand," she began again, steeling herself against the nervousness she was feeling. "I'm very serious about my work. That's why I'm here. I could have written your story without ever leaving New York City, but I wanted the book to be realistic. I want this novel to be special, and to do that, I need your help."

He glanced toward Lieutenant Long and, seeing the officer's expression, realized there was no escaping the situation. "What exactly did you want to do?"

"As I said, we need to talk. I want to learn your routine, what your average day is like, what riding on a scout is like." She hastened to reassure him even more. "I am more than willing to do whatever you think is necessary to get this story."

"I'll see what can be arranged."

"I'd also like to see the place where Mrs. Garner's stage was attacked and, if possible, the site of her rescue, too."

Lieutenant Long spoke up quickly. "That might prove dangerous. Why don't we leave the plans for your scout to Brand and Sergeant O'Toole's discretion?"

"Whatever you say, Lieutenant Long," Sheri replied. "I just want to get a real feel for the area I'm going to be writing about."

"I understand, and I'm sure Brand will take that into consideration when he's planning the trek. Brand, why don't you talk to Sergeant O'Toole and then let us know what you have laid out? Miss St. John and her cousin, Miss Cleaver, will be staying on with us in the officers' quarters until she's finished her research."

"Yes, sir. Ma'am." Brand nodded curtly in Sheri's direction and left the office.

Sheri was sorry when he'd gone. She had been watching his every move, mentally taking note of the way he walked, the way he held his head, the look in his eyes, and how carefully he guarded his expression. Brand was not a man to be trifled with, and she now understood what Charles had been trying to explain to her about him.

She tried to imagine what it would be like to be a renegade and know that Brand was the scout coming after you. 'Unnerving' was the word that came to mind. She sensed there was a savage edge to him, and she knew he would be relentless in his pursuit. Accustomed as she was to civilized New York gentlemen, she realized that understanding Brand was going to be a real challenge. But challenge though it might be, she was up to the task. He was her new hero. There was no doubt about it.

"Miss St. John, Miss Cleaver, allow me to show you to your quarters," Lieutenant Long offered. He was glad that the breed was gone. "We'll get you settled in and then have a relaxing dinner this evening with Colonel Hancock, Captain and Mrs. Whitmore, and the other officers and their wives."

"And Brand?" she added.

"Of course." He hid his disapproval. "I'll let him know of the arrangements."

"Thank you. We're looking forward to meeting everyone."

"Mr. and Mrs. Wallace, are you planning to stay with us long?"

"We'll just be staying on for tonight. We're on our way to California, and we'll be returning to Phoenix tomorrow so we can continue our trip."

"Fine. I'll make sure we have comfortable accommodations for you, too. And Mr. Brennan?"

"It isn't every day that a famous author comes to the Territory." Charles flashed a grin at Sheri and Maureen. "I want to cover this for the newspaper, so if you have no objections, I'll stay on for a while."

"All right. Well, if you'll follow me, I'll introduce to you Cecelia Whitmore, the captain's wife. She'll help you get settled in."

Lieutenant Long offered Sheri his arm and she took it, allowing him to guide her from the office.

* * *

Brand sought out O'Toole near the stables.

The sergeant saw his scowl and wondered what had happened. "What's wrong?"

"The author's arrived."

"Well, we knew he was coming."

"What we didn't know was that Sheridan St. John is a woman."

O'Toole stared at him in amazement and then threw his head back and laughed. "A woman writer? If that don't beat all! I guess we're going to have to take things even easier than we'd planned."

Brand's annoyance was obvious, and he didn't take kindly to his friend's sense of humor.

"A whole lot easier," Brand agreed. "She's quite the Eastern lady." His tone was not complimentary.

"Can she ride?"

"Maybe sidesaddle."

"We'll keep the scout short and simple. She'll have the taste of the wild West she's after and then we'll send her on her way. She'll never know the difference."

"Good. The less I have to do with this, the better."

"Don't let it bother you. It's not that important. We'll lose a day or two, and that'll be it."

"You don't understand."

O'Toole frowned as he glanced at his friend.

"I just talked to her. Her whole point in coming out here was to meet me. She wants me to become the hero in a series of books she's going to write."

"Are you serious?" O'Toole couldn't help chuckling. "I can see you now, immortalized forever in a dime novel."

"I'm not interested."

"But she is. I don't know how you're going to discourage her, or even if you should try. You know what the lieutenant said about us cooperating. Washington's behind this, so it's our job to make her happy. We can do it willingly or under orders."

"I know."

"Cheer up," O'Toole told him with a grin. "It's not every scout that gets to escort a real live author around the territory. Some of the other troopers would give their eye teeth for the chance."

"They're welcome to it."

"But she wants you, so there's no getting out of it. You may as well relax. When are you going to talk to her again?"

"Some time tonight. I need to tell them our plans."

"We'll ride out at dawn and stay out for the day. That will give her one meal on the trail, and a good look at the lay of the land. Maybe that will be enough to satisfy her."

"I hope so."

"I'm looking forward to meeting your author." O'Toole grinned at him. "She must be some woman."

"She's not 'my' anything." Brand's expression turned black, and he walked away.

O'Toole agreed that it was distracting to have this St. John woman at the fort, but he believed Brand was overreacting. They dealt with murderous Apaches on almost a daily basis. One lone female writer from New York City wasn't going to give them any trouble.

Sheri and Maureen were given a room to share that was spartan, but comfortable, with two single beds and a small dresser. They took some time before the evening meal to rest and freshen up.

"What do you think, Maureen? My blue gown or the green one?" Sheri asked as she smoothed the wrinkles from the two most fashionable gowns she'd brought along.

"Hold them up and let me see," her cousin suggested.

Sheri did, and Maureen quickly chose the green one.

"It brings out the color of your eyes."

"Not that it matters. There's no man here I'm trying to attract."

"That handsome lieutenant seems quite taken with you," Maureen pointed out, remembering how solicitous Long had been.

"Maybe, but he's not my type."

"What is your type, Sheri? You've never been in love, have you?"

"No . . . well, once . . . maybe."

"Oh, really? Who was it?"

"I thought I was in love with Gerald Ruskin in grade school, but he quickly disabused me of that idea."

Maureen was smiling. "What did Gerald do?"

"He stuck my pigtail in an inkwell!" Sheri was still righteously indignant when she remembered his meanness all those years ago. "I had to get some of my hair cut off because of him. It was awful."

"Well, I think you're safe here tonight. Brand may not be a charming, debonair gentleman, but I don't think he's as mean as Gerald Ruskin."

"Good thing, too," Sheri countered, her eyes alight with good humor. "Because I'm ready for the Gerald Ruskins of the world now."

She was still smiling as she slipped into the emerald gown. It was long-sleeved and high-necked, a sedate, demure creation that somehow emphasized her femininity more than if it had been low-cut and revealing. She always felt confident and in control when she wore it. She added earrings and then styled her hair up away from her face.

"There. I think I'm ready for Mr. Brand, the half-breed scout."

"No 'mister', remember?" Maureen corrected.

"For being the quiet one of the two of us, you're developing quite a sharp wit."

"I guess being around you is starting to rub off on me. Pretty soon I'll be ready for the Gerald Ruskins of the world, too."

"I hope not. I like you just the way you are—sweet and innocent of the ways of the world. Now, what are *you* wearing tonight?"

Less than an hour later, they were being ushered into Captain Whitmore's quarters.

"It's so wonderful to have you here visiting us," Cecelia Whitmore told them after she'd introduced them around the room.

Sheri had been pleased to meet all four of the officers and their wives. Colonel Hancock and Lieutenant Long were there, as was Charles, but there was no sign of Brand yet. She was disappointed.

"Is Brand coming late?" she asked her hostess.

"Brand . . . Yes, he will be joining us," Cecelia answered, keeping her expression carefully guarded. "Although some of the ladies are a little uncomfortable with the idea."

"But why? He saved Mrs. Garner. I thought everyone would be singing his praises." Sheri was confronting the prejudice against Indians for the first time, and she wasn't liking it.

"He's part Apache, my dear," Cecelia replied.

Sheri wanted to argue that Brand was a scout for the U.S. Army and risking his life tracking and fighting the renegades, but she avoided the issue. She'd wanted to learn the truth about the West, and she was learning—even though some of the lessons were coming as a shock. She remembered Charles's words on the trip out, cautioning her about Brand, reminding her that he was half Indian, and now she was beginning to understand far more clearly just what that meant in this part of the world.

"What do you think of our fort so far, Miss St. John?" Reginald asked as he came to stand with them.

"Everyone has been very helpful, but there is one thing troubling me."

"What's that? Perhaps I can help."

"If the Indian problem is so bad here in the territory, why doesn't Fort McDowell have walls?"

"Spoken like a true Easterner." He smiled at her.

Sheri thought he sounded a tad condescending, but she wanted an answer to her question. Every fort she'd ever seen a picture of was a stockade. "I doubt my being from back East has anything to do with it. If all those wild Indians are out there just waiting for the chance to murder white people, it would seem to me that safety would be one of your top concerns. The way McDowell is built, there's little to protect you. What's to stop the Apache from just sneaking in, stealing all your stock and killing everyone?"

Lieutenant Long stepped in, wanting to calm her fears. "Many Western forts lack walls. Nature provides much of our protection. As flat as the desert is, we can see for miles, and we're heavily garrisoned. We try to keep the hostiles on the run so much that they don't have time to mass an attack against us here."

"So we're safe?"

"Absolutely," Cecelia replied with confidence.

"You need have no fear," Reginald added.

"I'm here to do research, but there is a limit to how much I actually want to experience," she told them with a smile.

"The Apache are ruthless. Why, when I think of what could have happened to Melissa Garner . . ." Cecelia shuddered.

"They're more than ruthless—they're savages," Reginald said. "Some of the things we've witnessed . . ." He glanced toward the colonel to make sure he was a distance away and couldn't hear what he was about to say. "It was terrible what was done to the colonel's daughter."

"You mean Brand's wife?" She thought it odd that they referred to her as the colonel's daughter and not Brand's wife.

"Yes. Becky was a dear girl, and it was all so tragic," Cecelia put in.

"It's hard to imagine how one human being could do such things to another," Reginald went on.

"There are ladies present, my dear," his wife admonished gently, afraid of just how much he might say in delicate company.

"But if I'm going to write about these things accurately, I need to know the truth," Sheri interrupted, wanting to learn more.

"I'm not sure that's a good idea," Charles spoke up. He knew the truth. He had seen the results of Indian attacks several times himself.

Long was tempted to join in and tell her tales of the Indians' torturous ways to impress her, but he did not want to risk offending Mrs. Whitmore. There would be time later for him to describe some of the depredations to her, and once he did, he was sure it would influence her thinking about the half-breed. "I know it's important to you to understand how vicious the renegades truly are, but some things are better left unsaid."

Sheri was left to imagine the horror Brand had faced in having his wife murdered that way.

"Just trust us when we tell you that the Indians are untamed heathens," Cecelia said. "This is why we're always careful, even around the scouts."

"You can never know what viciousness lurks within them," Colonel Hancock finished as he walked up.

She heard the disdain in his voice and realized that he despised the very men who worked for him, including the man who had been his son-in-law.

There was a knock at the door then, and Sheri glanced over to see Brand enter the room. He was dressed as a white man this night in boots, dark pants, and a white shirt. Even across the room she could feel the power of his presence. She watched with interest as the ladies moved as far away from his path as they could. The men merely nodded to him as he passed by. Only Charles and Maureen went forward to speak to him, then walked with him to where Sheri stood with Hancock and the Whitmores.

"Good evening, Brand," Sheri said, trying not to sound too excited about seeing him again. He had been handsome as a warrior, but he was devastatingly good-looking dressed in the clothes he was wearing now. She understood completely how Becky had fallen in love with him.

"Miss St. John," he said curtly, making it clear he had no desire to be there.

"Please, call me Sheri," she invited. She was so caught up in talking to him that she didn't see the quickly masked looks of outrage from the other ladies.

He only nodded in response.

"We were just discussing scouts and their value to the cavalry. From the accounts I've read, General Crook's soldiers wouldn't have fared nearly as well without the scouts' help tracking. Isn't that true?"

"Their talent is amazing," Captain Whitmore said. "I've seen some Indian scouts follow trails over solid rock."

"That's what I've been wondering about in connection with your rescue of Mrs. Garner," she said to Brand. "From what I've seen of the territory so far, you must have made an incredible effort to find her."

Long grew irritated that she was praising the half-breed. "It's his job."

"But surely not just anyone could have found her, considering the circumstances."

"He's paid to track down renegades, and that's what he did. He deserves no extra glory or praise for doing what he was supposed to do," Long said stiffly.

"If the damned Apache stayed on the reservation, Mrs. Garner would never have been taken in the first place," the colonel said with a savage note to his voice.

"But Brand is by far your best scout, wouldn't you say, Colonel?"

The fort commander looked at the man who had been married to his daughter. "He is a good scout."

At his words, Brand met his gaze, but he found no warmth there. There never had been, not even when he'd been married to Becky. The colonel's statement was just that—a statement of fact.

"I think it's very heroic of you to work with the cavalry to keep the territory safe from renegades." Sheri wanted him to know just how much she thought of him, in spite of the way Lieutenant Long tried to minimalize his work.

"I don't do it to be heroic," he answered, and then turned to Long. "Lieutenant, if I could speak with you for a moment? There was something I needed to discuss with you."

Long was glad to get him away from Sheri. "If you'll excuse us for a moment?"

Sheri was disappointed when they moved off, and she wondered just what they were going to talk about.

Brand was eager to tell Long what he and O'Toole had arranged for the following day and then leave the party. He had no desire to be a part of this world. He was a loner, a solitary man, and he liked it that way. He didn't need anyone. He definitely didn't want to spend any more time than was absolutely necessary with the St. John woman. It was going to be difficult enough being stuck with her from dawn to dusk tomorrow.

"Have you talked with O'Toole?" Long asked.

"Yes, we'll be riding out at sunup. We're going to keep it simple—just one day, out and back."

"That sounds good."

"She can ride horseback, can't she? She's not planning on going out in a carriage in one of those fancy gowns, is she?"

"I most certainly can ride," Sheri said from behind them, surprising them both. Neither man had noticed that she'd maneuvered herself closer to listen to their conversation, and she was proud of herself. If they were talking about her, she was entitled to know what was being said.

When Brand turned to look at her, she met his mocking gaze with a defiant lift of her chin.

"I'll be ready to go whenever you are," she told him with confidence.

"Good." Brand stared at her, seeing the fire in her eyes. He had to stop himself from smiling, a rare occurrence for him. He had to admit to himself that she was a beautiful woman. Sleek and sophisticated. He doubted seriously that she'd last ten minutes on the trail. He felt a stirring of admiration for her, and his resolve to get the next day over with as quickly as possible and be rid of her hardened even more. "Meet us at dawn near the stables. We'll be riding out then."

"Fine." She responded to the unspoken challenge in his words and in his regard. "Maureen and I will be there."

Chapter Five

**Brand, the Half-Breed Scout, or Trail of the
Renegade
The Hero**

*Some said Brand, the half-breed scout, was a
dangerous man—a savage—and they were right.
Naked to the waist, wearing only buckskins and
moccasins, he looked every bit the savage warrior
as he moved silently among the boulders above the
renegade camp. His hair shone blue-black in the
glinting late afternoon sun, and his darkly tanned,
heavily muscled chest glistened with sweat from
the ordeal of his two-day relentless search. He was
a sleek and deadly predator, and he had cornered
his prey at last.*

71

Brand smiled grimly to himself as he found the vantage point from which to launch his ambush on the murderous raiding party below. They had attacked a small ranch outside Phoenix two days before, killing all of the family who lived there, and Brand had been on their trail ever since. He settled into position and lifted his rifle to take aim. The renegades thought they were safe. They thought no one had followed them. They were wrong.

Brand was ready. Though he was outnumbered twelve to one, he felt no fear. He knew only a driving need to avenge the deaths of the innocent. His blue-eyed gaze narrowed in concentration as he took careful aim at the leader. . . .

"Sheri . . ." Maureen breathed her friend's name as she looked up at her, wide-eyed. It was late and she had been ready for bed when Sheri insisted she read the pages she'd been laboring over for the past few hours. Now she understood why.

"What?" Sheri had been waiting for Maureen's opinion, and she was worried by her reaction.

"I didn't know you felt this way. . . ."

"What way?"

"This description of Brand. It's so . . . uh, so . . ."

"Realistic?"

"Yes," Maureen quickly agreed, reading over the handwritten pages one more time. "This is wonderful. Are you going to let him read it?"

Sheri looked unsettled by her cousin's question. "Not right away."

"Why not? You might impress him with your style. This is really good. You are definitely improving."

"If I let him read it, it just might send him running for the hills."

"Run for the hills? Your predator? Your savage warrior?" She said the phrases with emphasis. "You think he'd run from a little old dime novelist?"

"No, but he's reluctant enough to help me now. I don't want to make things any worse. Let's see how our scout goes in the morning, and then I'll think about letting him read it."

"It is going well. You're almost up to thirty pages."

"I know. I can't believe how much I love this story."

"How gruesome are you going to get?"

"It depends on what I can find out from Brand. Captain Whitmore and Lieutenant Long refused to discuss the depredations with me. They said I was a lady and ladies shouldn't hear such things. I said I was a writer and that I needed to know, but it didn't seem to matter to them."

"I've got the feeling that Brand's not going to hold anything back from you. He'll tell you whatever you want to know, whether you really want to know it or not."

"Good. That's all I want from him. Total honesty."

"I guess we'd better get some sleep. It's late and we're supposed to meet Brand just before dawn."

"I'll try, but the writing's been going so well, I don't know if I can. I might just keep working."

"Please do if it's going to be this good. This book is going to be something special. I just know it."

"I hope you're right."

The hour before dawn came far too soon for Maureen, but Sheri was so excited that she was already up and just about dressed when she woke Maureen.

"Why are you up so early?" Maureen asked in a voice that was husky and confused by sleep.

"I didn't get much rest. I guess I'm just too excited about going out with Brand today."

"This is what we made the trip for." Maureen slowly sat up, trying to get her bearings. "Did you get any more writing done?"

"Just a page or two."

"That's better than nothing. I guess I'd better get dressed."

"Yes, we have to meet Brand and the others at the stable in about twenty-five minutes."

Maureen gave a groan of weariness as she rose and went to the clothes she'd laid out the night before.

"Thank heaven for Cecelia and Laura, the other lieutenant's wife," Maureen said as she began to dress. "They certainly came to our rescue giving us these clothes."

"They sure did. I wasn't about to let Brand know that he was right about the type of clothes I'd brought along. What was I thinking of when I packed those riding habits?"

"Neither one of us has ever been West before. We didn't know what to expect." Maureen smiled wryly. "Who would have dreamed it would be so . . . rugged out here? As far as we knew, our habits would have worked just fine."

"And they still might, judging from what I overheard last night," Sheri said a little angrily, "not that I'm going to take the chance of being laughed at, though."

"What are you talking about? What did you overhear?"

"Only that Brand has deliberately made today's

trek an easy scout for us. I'm sure it's because he thinks that we'll be satisfied with just a glimpse of the surrounding desert and mountains."

"He's probably right."

"Speak for yourself," Sheri countered as she finished tucking her blouse into her split leather riding skirt and then picked up the Western hat Cecelia had given her. "I came here to experience the real West. I don't want to be patted on the head like a good little girl and treated as if I don't have any sense."

"That is probably what they're all thinking. After all, we are two women alone in the middle of the Arizona Territory."

"Precisely, and contrary to your way of thinking, the fact that we are here on our own should tell them right from the start that we are not a pair of simpering females. I came here to get a story, and I'm going to get it."

"You're right. I have to be braver. Keep reminding me that I'm no simpering female, all right?"

"I will. Are you about ready? I don't want to be late and give Brand any reason not to go with us." Sheri picked up her small bag and stuffed a pencil and a pad of paper into it. She intended to take notes all day about the sights, sounds, and smells of the area.

"I'm ready." Maureen finished buttoning her last button.

"Then let's ride." Sheri put her Western hat on and grinned as she turned to Maureen for approval. "What do you think? Do I look like a female Buck McCade?"

"I think you look better than Buck. You look like you belong out here."

"Good. That's exactly the impression I want to give

Brand. He thinks I'm helpless. I'm going to prove him wrong."

"How do I look?"

"Wonderful," Sheri told her, admiring her split riding skirt, boots, and blouse.

"Then let's go get 'em," Maureen declared as she put on her own hat.

Satisfied that they would show Brand a thing or two, Sheri led the way from their quarters.

It was still dark as they headed to the stables. Sheri was not surprised to find that Brand was already there. He was wearing a loose-fitting shirt, buckskin pants, and moccasins that came up to just below the knee. A single lamp was burning, and the horses were saddled and ready to go.

"Good morning, Brand," Sheri said sweetly. "Is there anything we can help you with?"

"No."

His gaze swept over her, but Sheri couldn't tell if there was a change in his expression in the dimness of the half-light. She'd expected him to notice and comment on her attire. After all, he had been concerned about it the night before. His lack of reaction irked her for some reason.

"Shall we mount up?"

"The horses are ready, but we're still waiting for the lieutenant and Brennan."

O'Toole came out of the stable just then leading his own horse. "Good morning, ladies. I'm Sergeant O'Toole."

Sheri and Maureen quickly introduced themselves.

"It's a pleasure to meet you," Sheri said as she went to shake hands with him. "I've heard a lot about you."

"Oh?"

"All good, I assure you."

"That's a relief." He smiled at her.

He was a bear of a man, standing well over six feet tall. His hair was dark, his eyes brown, his manner friendly. Sheri liked him immediately.

They heard the sounds of a conversation in the distance and looked up to find Charles and Lieutenant Long coming toward them.

"You ladies are up bright and early," Long commented.

"We're excited about the ride today," Sheri answered. "I'm looking forward to spending this time with Brand learning what a scout does."

Brand said nothing, but swung up into the saddle and waited for the others to follow his example.

"Allow me to help you," Long said as he went to Sheri. Putting his hands at her waist, he helped her to mount.

"Maureen, do you need a hand up?" Charles asked.

"If you don't mind," she said. The horse they'd given her was a tall one, and she'd been wondering if they had a block she could stand on to take her seat. Charles's hands at her waist were strong and sure, and soon she was comfortably seated. She rewarded him with a bright smile as he looked up at her.

"You comfortable?"

"I'm all set."

"Let's ride," Sergeant O'Toole announced.

Charles quickly climbed on his own horse and they were ready to go.

The small party rode slowly from the fort, heading toward the Superstition Mountains. Brand and

O'Toole were reasonably certain that they would be safe and the trip there would be uneventful, which was just what they wanted.

Brand had to admit to himself that he was surprised by the women's riding ability. He'd expected them to ask for sidesaddles and riding crops; instead, they were wearing practical riding clothes and had mounted without complaint. They were keeping up without incident and both seemed adept at controlling their horses. He cast a glance back toward Sheri and saw that she was deep in conversation with Long, which was just fine with him.

"Seems like our fine upstanding lieutenant has taken a liking to Miss St. John," O'Toole remarked after catching Brand looking back their way.

"Maybe she'll make *him* her hero."

"I think he'd like that just fine."

"Good. Then I can head back to the fort right now."

"Don't get your hopes up. She's heading your way. Get ready." O'Toole was grinning at Brand's discomfort as he kneed his horse and distanced himself to give them time to talk.

"Brand?" Sheri reined in beside him. "Do you mind if I ask you some questions while we ride?"

"What do you want to know?"

He was abrupt, but from the way things had been going between them she'd expected no less.

"First, tell me about a normal day in the life of a scout." She was ready. She'd been waiting for this time with him since she'd read the article in New York. She hoped she could remember everything he was about to tell her, and hoped they would stop for a while so she could take notes on what she remembered.

"If we're tracking renegades, we ride as soon as it's light."

"Are there troops with you?"

"Usually. We're always ahead of them, though, checking the trail, watching for trouble."

"How long do these scouts last?"

"As long as it takes."

"So you never give up?" She looked over at him.

He turned a piercing gaze on her. "No."

"But aren't there times when you lose the trail and are forced to turn back?"

"Not often," Long interrupted as he rode up to join them.

Sheri almost groaned out loud. It seemed there was no escaping this man. Every time she turned around, he was there. She'd wanted some time alone with Brand, and here was Long again. As solicitous as he was, she was certain that he wanted to be included in her book, and with his vanity, there was no doubt that he wanted to be more than just a minor character. He'd asked her to call him by his first name, Philip, and she'd agreed, even though it implied an intimacy and friendship that she didn't feel.

"So the scouts of Fort McDowell are the best?" she asked.

"The men of Fort McDowell are the best," Philip corrected, giving her a winning smile.

Refusing to be deterred from questioning Brand, Sheri turned back to him. "Where did you learn to track so well?"

"I was raised by my father's people. One of the first things an Apache boy must learn is tracking."

"Can you show me how to do it? Is there a trail around here we could follow for a while?"

Bobbi Smith

Brand reined in and dismounted. He moved a short distance away and hunkered down to study the rocky ground.

"Why did we stop?" Maureen asked, looking puzzled as she rode up next to Sheri.

"Brand's going to show me how to track," she said excitedly.

Sheri quickly grabbed her bag off the saddle horn and slid down off her horse's back. She tugged her paper and pencil out of the bag and immediately went to stand beside Brand, taking notes describing everything he did.

Brand was hard pressed not to scowl as she trailed after him.

"What are you looking for?" She could see nothing indicating that any creature, human or animal, had passed this way.

"Signs," he replied as he concentrated.

"What kind of signs?"

"A broken twig. A partial print in the dust. A grain of barley. Anything that would indicate that someone or something has traveled through here." He studied the ground again, then slowly stood looking off toward the mountains. "They headed this way."

Sheri noticed that his expression had changed. He looked more serious, more thoughtful. There was a sudden tension about him.

"Who?" she asked, confused. She could see no sign whatsoever that anything had passed this way.

"Apache." Brand frowned. There was no mistaking the signs. "At least three of them."

"How can you know that?"

"There's a moccasin print there near the brush." He pointed to the nearly invisible track in the dust.

Sheri was amazed. She knelt down to try to get a look at it, but could barely make it out. "Where?"

"Here." He knelt beside her and showed her where a small patch of the desert grass had been pressed down and was discolored.

"How can you tell that's an Indian footprint?"

Sheri turned her head to stare at him in amazement. He was close. Too close, almost, and when he glanced over at her, their eyes met and locked. Suddenly, she felt off-balance, lost somehow in the intensity of his blue-eyed gaze. She stared at him, committing to memory the dark slash of his brows, the strength in the hard line of his jaw and the firm line of his lips. Her gaze lingered on his lips for a moment, and she wondered how handsome he would look if he ever smiled . . . wondered what it would feel like to press her lips to his. At the realization of her thoughts, she mentally jerked herself back to reality and looked away, trying to hide the blush that threatened at her runaway musing.

"How can you tell?" she asked again, forcing herself to stare at the ground.

"A boot would have made a heavier imprint, so this was no white man. And see here?" He pointed to the slightly irregular pattern that was revealed for only an inch or two in the dust. "I can tell by the stitching which tribe they're from."

"That's amazing," she breathed, in awe of his abilities. She would never have seen the print to begin with, let alone be able to identify the Indian who'd made it.

"They came through here some time last night."

"How do you know that?" Sheri stared down at the imprint, then drew a quick sketch so she'd remember everything he was telling her.

"By the color of the grass. It's been dead for a while, more than four hours, so they're far ahead of us."

"And that's good?"

Brand gazed off into the wilderness, wondering. "That's good . . . unless I was tracking them."

"You said you were raised by the Apache. . . . That's how you came to learn all this," she said thoughtfully. "Doesn't it bother you to be hunting down your father's people now?"

Something in Brand's expression hardened as he glanced sharply back at her. "I hunt down murderers and thieves. The Apache who kill so freely are not my people."

"Who are your people?" Her question was innocent.

Before he could answer, Philip and O'Toole strode up to them.

"Trouble?" the lieutenant asked. He had seen the way Brand was studying the ground and wondered what he'd found.

Brand glanced at the two men and nodded in the direction of the footprint. "Take a look."

O'Toole studied the ground and then stood, his gaze sweeping the craggy landscape. "It's been hours."

"We'll just have to keep a lookout," Philip said. In a way he was glad for the unspoken danger for it made him look even more heroic.

"Is there a problem?" Charles asked as he rode up closer with Maureen.

"Nothing to be too concerned about. There were Apache here overnight, but there are no fresh tracks.

82

We'll just have to keep an eye out."

As the men talked, Sheri walked over to Maureen. "Brand just showed me how to identify tracks."

"Do you understand it well enough to write about it?"

"Yes," she said proudly, then she lowered her voice. "Will you do me a favor?"

"You know I will," Maureen said. "What is it?"

"Try to keep the lieutenant busy, will you? It seems like every time I start to get Brand talking, Long interrupts."

"So I've noticed." Maureen looked to where the tall, fair-haired officer was conversing with his scouts. "I think he wants a major role in your book."

"I hate to disappoint him, but he's no half-breed scout."

"So change your hero. He'd definitely be more agreeable to work with," she teased, knowing full well how her cousin was coming to feel about Long.

"Absolutely not. This is Brand's book. No one else's."

"Just trying to help."

"Well, you can help the most by keeping him busy. Ask him questions, distract him. I need some time alone with Brand to try to feel him out and learn everything I can about him."

"I'll do my best."

"Thanks. I knew I could count on you."

"If not me, then who?"

"Exactly."

Charles came to join them then. "What do you think about our trek so far? Have you seen anything you can use in the book?"

"A lot. Brand was just showing me how to track

and the terrain is like nothing I've ever seen before."

"I'm glad it's helping you. Long just suggested that we ride on for about another hour, then break for the noon meal. Are you up to a few more miles in the saddle?"

"I'm ready for anything today." With a confident grin, she put away her paper and pencil and returned to her horse to mount up.

When everyone was ready to ride, Sheri managed to maneuver herself next to Brand again.

"Please tell me about your rescue of Mrs. Garner. How did you hear about it? Did it take you a long time to find her? If the Apache are so bloodthirsty, why hadn't they killed her?"

Brand turned to look at her as they moved off down the trail. "Have you ever heard of torture?"

Sheri paled a little. Her voice was a little unsteady as she asked, "Did they torture her before you got there?"

"No, but they would have. That raiding party enjoyed it."

"What would they have done?"

Brand wasn't sure he should tell her everything, but he thought he might as well scare her a little bit. "They've been known to shoot their victims with arrows, taking care not to hit anything vital. One unlucky man was wounded over a hundred times before they finally put him out of his misery."

"Would they do that to a woman?"

"Worse."

"It could be worse?"

"There have been times when they've tied a hostage to a tree and then set the tree on fire."

Sheri made a strangled sound.

"They've also staked men out naked on anthills in the direct sun and cut off their eyelids."

She fought down a shudder of revulsion. "Creative in the use of pain, aren't they?"

"You can use your imagination to figure out what they do to women."

"Then how did you manage to get to Mrs. Garner in time?"

"She was physically unharmed, but I don't really know how lucky she was. She might have been better off dead."

Sheri gasped. "How can you say that?"

Brand's expression turned hard. "By the time I got to her . . ."

"But I thought they hadn't tortured her in any way."

"There are many kinds of torture. They don't all have to be of the flesh. When I rescued her, she had already seen so much. Experienced so much. I don't know that she'll ever be the same again."

"You mean what she lived through when they attacked the stage?"

He gave a terse nod. "Have you ever seen or heard what the victims look like when the Apache get through with them?"

"No." Her voice sounded small.

"The men are maimed before they're killed, and the women . . ."

"Yes . . . ?" she urged, hanging on his every word.

"Death is a welcome release for them when it finally comes." He was deliberately trying to make his tale shocking, hoping it would discourage her in her effort and she would quickly go back East.

"And Mrs. Garner saw it all?"

85

"She saw it all."

Sheri swallowed and offered up an unspoken prayer that the poor officer's wife was recovering from her ordeal. "No wonder they left the Territory."

She remained quiet as she tried to visualize the horrors he'd described to her. She silently thanked Maureen for keeping Philip at bay.

As if by just thinking of him, though, it seemed she conjured him up. The next thing she knew, Philip was once again at her side.

"Enjoying yourself?"

"I'm certainly learning a lot."

"Good. I know that's what you wanted to do. So Brand is helping you?"

"Very much. He's being very cooperative."

"Good." Philip smiled, but in truth, he wasn't pleased. He had wanted to be the one to answer her questions. After all, he came from a fine, upstanding military family back East. Who better to help her research? If only he could convince her of that.

Behind them, Charles and Maureen rode together. Charles had been quietly watching the interaction between Sheri, Brand, and the lieutenant with growing amusement. He couldn't hold back a chuckle when Philip broke off the conversation Maureen had initiated and went to speak to Sheri.

"A valiant try," he said with a mocking grin.

"Excuse me?" She acted innocent.

"Your attempt to keep our lieutenant occupied so Sheri could have a few minutes with Brand uninterrupted. I'm afraid Long has other ideas, though."

"I'm sure I don't know what you're talking about."

"There are times when playing innocent works,

but this isn't one of them. Your questions to the fine, upstanding officer were a trifle contrived."

"Excuse me?" Maureen managed a wounded, out-raged look.

"Like 'Oh, Philip, how do you manage to keep this territory so safe? It must be such a difficult job, and yet things are so peaceful' . . ." Charles chuckled again. "Good try, my dear."

"If you say so." She was embarrassed that she must have been so obvious, but Long hadn't seemed to notice.

"Relax, I'm on your side," he told her in a more confidential tone. "Remember, I'm the one who wanted you to form your own opinion about our il-lustrious officer, and now I think you have."

"Sheri and I both have, and you're right. She asked me earlier, when we stopped to look at those tracks, if I would keep him occupied so she could interview Brand. I think the lieutenant wants her full and un-divided attention on him."

"I'm sure he does. We'll have to work together to see if we can help her."

"A conspiracy of sorts?" She slanted a sidelong glance at Charles as she smiled. "You'd do that?"

"I love rescuing damsels in distress. I don't get the opportunity very often. And who knows? Sheri just might make me a character in the book." He grinned wickedly at her.

"You help me with him, and I'll make sure she puts you in the story."

"As the hero?" he teased.

She laughed. "You're as bad as the lieutenant!"

"You wound me sorely."

"You're right. You couldn't possibly be that bad."

"Thank you."

Chapter Six

Brand, the Half-Breed Scout, or Trail of the Renegade
The Challenge

Brand returned to the fort weary but victorious. Yet he took no glory in the triumph of his surprise attack on the raiding party; there was only the satisfaction of knowing that by defeating the renegades he had prevented further slaughter. Still, the innocent were dead. He could not bring them back.

"Brand! Thank God you're back! They've taken the captain's wife!" Sergeant Lowery, the chief of scouts, shouted when he saw him ride back into the fort.

*Brand was instantly alert as he dismounted.
"What happened?"*

*"Captain Stewart's wife was due to arrive yes-
terday, but the stage was attacked by renegades!
We need you to head out as soon as you can." He
quickly told Brand everything he knew about the
attack.*

*Captain Stewart heard that Brand had returned
and he came out to speak to his best scout. "Find
my wife, Brand. Find her for me." There was agony in his voice.*

*Brand knew that with the headstart they had on
him, it would be difficult tracking, but he would
do his best. If her body hadn't been found at the
site of the attack, there was a very good chance
she was still alive.*

*Within an hour, Brand had a fresh horse and
provisions, and was ready to be on his way. It
would be a rugged chase, but he would do everything he could to see Mrs. Stewart returned unharmed. He only hoped he found her in time. . . .*

They stopped for the noon meal, then continued
on the scout. They had about reached the farthest
point from the fort and were almost ready to turn
back to be sure that they would reach safety by night-
fall.

Craggy, jagged mountains loomed over them and
cacti abounded. Sheri and Maureen were fascinated
by the landscape. There was a terrible beauty about
it that mesmerized them. But where Sheri grew excited about it, Maureen felt only a terrible sense of
dread.

"I don't like this place," she told Charles as they

rode together behind the others.

"Why not? It's so wild and untamed . . ." He looked around, his love for the land showing in his expression.

"Precisely. What if you needed help out here? What would you do? There's no one around for miles."

"You hope," he returned.

"That's not amusing, especially after finding those tracks back there."

"I can't imagine living anywhere else," Charles said. "The freedom of it—"

"There's freedom and then there's dangerous wilderness. This place seems very dangerous to me."

"Only if you get too close to a cactus," he teased, wanting to lighten the discussion.

"You don't have to worry about me doing that. I'm going to give them a wide berth."

"Then you'll have nothing to fear."

She grinned at him. "I wish I could see the beauty as you do, but something about this place makes me very uncomfortable. I don't know how to describe it. I just feel uneasy."

"Well, you're new to it. It'll grow on you. Just give it a chance."

"We'll see."

"How's Sheri doing with the lieutenant and Brand?"

"Lieutenant Long's been riding right between them since we broke from lunch. Do you suppose it's time I try to talk to him again?"

"It sure couldn't hurt."

They shared a smile as Maureen quickly invented a good question to distract the officer.

Sheri had been having the time of her life. It would have been absolutely perfect if Philip hadn't been there, but there was little she could do about that. She was stuck with him and would have to do her best in spite of him. When Maureen called out to Philip, Sheri almost let out a cheer of relief. Brand remained quiet when the officer was around, and it was his opinion she wanted the most, his expertise she wanted to plumb.

"So a normal scouting expedition could go on for weeks?" Sheri asked to open the conversation between them again.

"It could. Usually there are troops and mules carrying the supplies, so travel isn't fast, especially when you're in the mountains."

Sheri looked up at the harsh peaks near them and was impressed by their beauty. "It's a shame we didn't make this a two-day scout. I'd like to know what it feels like to camp out here. I'd like to listen to the sounds of the night and sleep under the stars."

"It can be beautiful, but it can also be deadly. There are rattlesnakes and scorpions around, not to mention the other more dangerous predators."

"You mean like coyotes and wolves and mountain lions?"

"I mean men. Mankind is more dangerous and deadly than anything else ever put on earth."

"I had no idea you were a philosopher." She was surprised by his statement and chilled by it, too.

"I just say the truth."

"Well, I'm with you, so I'm safe from all harm. You're my new hero."

Brand looked over at her, his expression stony. He didn't know what he had to do or say to discourage her, but he was growing even more annoyed with every passing mile. "I'm no one's hero." His words were hard.

"Don't you understand how wonderful you are?" she countered, thinking of him gracing the pages of her novel. "You saved the captain's wife. You help people all the time. You're perfect."

Her words lashed at him. If there was one thing he wasn't, it was perfect. She might think he was some kind of savior, but he knew the truth. When his protection was most needed, he had failed miserably. The one person in the world he'd loved, he'd let down. He would spend the rest of his days making up for it.

"I'm no one's savior, and I'm no hero. I have a job to do and I do it. That's all."

His tone was so flat that Sheri glanced over at him. His expression seemed almost bleak for a moment before he resumed his usual indifferent look.

"There are those who would argue the point with you."

He shrugged.

She quickly went on, wanting to explain to him why she was doing what she was doing. "My readers want a bigger-than-life hero. They want to believe that good can conquer evil. They want to believe in happy endings."

"Life isn't that way."

"That's why they read my books," she argued. It was all quite logical to her. "Look, I know you're spending this time with me practically under protest. I know you think you have more important things to do. And you do. But Brand, I respect you and your work. I just want the rest of the world to have a hero

92

to look up to, so that for just a little while, they can pretend that things really will be all right in the end. Don't you see?"

"You live in a fairy-tale world, little girl."

"I'm not a little girl, and, believe me, I do not live in a fairy-tale world. I may create one for my readers, but I certainly don't live in one," she fired back, growing more and more annoyed with him. "If I did, you'd be cooperating fully with me on this novel."

She sounded so irritated with him that Brand finally smiled. His smile caught her unawares, and she stared at him in amazement. She'd thought him devastatingly handsome before, but now . . . He was magnificent.

"So, you do know how to smile!" She sounded triumphant.

He quickly sobered. He scowled at her and gave a grunt of dismissal.

O'Toole joined them just then. "Think we should rest the horses for a while before we head back?"

"It's time," he agreed, glad for the interruption. He was finding it more and more difficult to ignore Sheridan St. John. Not only was she beautiful, which was hard enough to ignore, but she had shown up at dawn, dressed like a woman who understood the West, and she was handling her horse with skill. Before they'd started out, he'd expected her questions to be annoying. Instead, she was asking him intelligent, thoughtful ones, and paying full attention to his answers. Too, she wasn't afraid of him, and white women usually were. She was surprising him in every way. Trouble was, he was a man who didn't like surprises.

As everyone dismounted and relaxed for a while,

Brand felt the need to escape. He walked his horse to the top of a ridge a distance away, wanting some peace and quiet.

"He just went off by himself—why don't you go after him?" Maureen whispered to Sheri as they shared a drink from a canteen.

"I don't think he likes me very much."

"He's a man. Of course he likes you."

"I don't know. It's almost as though he thinks I'm useless or something. He told me a few minutes ago that I live in a fairy-tale world."

"Well, compared to life out here, I guess New York does look pretty tame."

"That's beside the point. He doesn't respect what I do."

"Then you're just going to have to prove to him that you're different from every other woman he's met."

"That's true enough. He's never had to deal with the likes of Sheridan St. John before."

"Remember Tex Bennett."

"Is that going to be my battle cry?"

"Did it work?"

"Yes."

"Then what are you waiting for? Go interview your scout."

"When did you become so insightful?"

"I'm not. I just know you're frustrated, but you shouldn't be. Look how far you've come. You're not going to let a little thing like a reluctant hero stop you, are you? You're Sheridan St. John. You're on a scout in the Arizona Territory with the man you've been wanting to meet. You can't quit now."

Sheri gave her cousin a quick hug. More determined than ever, she took her bag with her paper and pencil and, leaving her horse with the others, made her way up to join Brand.

Philip started to follow her, but Maureen grabbed him by the arm and distracted him by asking him more questions about himself. It was the one subject that he just loved to talk about.

Sheri watched her cousin in action and was relieved to be free of the lieutenant for at least a few minutes. She approached Brand where he stood alone at the top of the rise, looking very much the solitary scout. She wanted and needed to know more about him.

Brand groaned inwardly when he saw her drawing near. He had come up here to get away from her distracting presence. It seemed there would be no escaping her until he put her physically on the stage for home.

"If I'm going to be accurate in my writing, what else do I need to know about a successful scout?" she asked, determined to get everything out of him she could.

"It's mostly good tracking and luck."

Sheri sat down on a rock nearby, gazing up at him as he stood before her. Outlined against the bright blue sky as he was, he appeared the fearless warrior, battle-hardened and fierce. There was no doubt in her mind that he was the stuff of which legends were made.

"How did the cavalry fare before they started using scouts with your qualifications?"

"You mean before they hired Indian scouts?" he asked sarcastically as he turned to look down at her.

Her temper flared. She had been nothing but enthusiastic and honest with him from the moment they'd met. Yet, he continually belittled what she was doing.

"Mr. Brand," she bit out hotly, deliberately using the 'mister', "I do not know why you find it necessary to be so sharp with me, but let me assure you, I do not think less of you because of your Indian blood. I am certain that there are many people in the Territory, including one Mrs. Garner, who are very impressed with you and your work. I cannot control what other people think, and you would do well to remember that yourself. Do not project upon me prejudices that I do not share. If you find yourself criticized or ostracized because you are part Indian, then cooperate with me more fully and through the Half-Breed Scout series of books, we can educate people."

She didn't know where the thought had come from, but she was pleased with it once she'd expressed it in words. She was challenging him to ignore his prejudice against her. She wondered if he would take her up on it.

She looked away from him, staring down at the ground, while she awaited his answer. But silence was his only reply for a long minute. It was then, as she was studying the rocks and grass, that she noticed the track. Her worry about his reply vanished as she stared down at the footprint only a short distance ahead of them.

"Brand . . ."

He grunted, his irritation obvious.

"Brand, look!" She leaned closer, studying the track, looking out beyond to see if she could see anybody. "This was made recently. The grass hasn't yellowed yet."

He glanced down and muttered a curse as he quickly bent to inspect the trail. His irritated expression turned to one of caution as he quickly stood and looked off into the distance.

"Go back down to the others and—"

Before he could finish his sentence, the first shots rang out.

They had been watching and waiting for the chance. They did not know what the two bluecoats and their scout were doing with the two white women, but they were not going to pass up this chance to ambush them. There were ten of them and they had the element of surprise on their side. They would not wait. They would take care of the larger group first and then go after the scout and his woman.

"Get down and stay down!" Brand snarled, physically pushing Sheri to the ground.

"What is it?" she whispered as she heard more shots and screams echoing around them.

"A raiding party. Don't move!"

Creeping among the rocks, he tried to position himself to get a shot at the attackers, but they were chasing O'Toole and the others, who had already mounted up and were riding at breakneck speed for the fort.

"Damn . . ." he muttered, quickly returning to Sheri's side. "We have to get out of here now."

"What happened? Is Maureen all right?"

"They managed to get on their horses, but the Indians are chasing them. We've only got a few minutes to hide before they come back for us."

She looked up then and saw the sun glint off something high in the rocks behind him. "Look out! There! By that rock!"

He turned and fired, his aim accurate and deadly. The brave who had hoped to pick them off fell mortally wounded.

"Let's go!"

Brand grabbed Sheri up and all but threw her on his horse's back.

"Wait! My bag! Don't forget my bag!"

He growled something under his breath as he snatched up her bag, then he mounted before her and put his heels to his horse's sides.

"Hold on and keep quiet!"

Sheri could do nothing else. She was all but in shock. She had found the trail! She had discovered the presence of the Indians before Brand. She would have trembled, but she was hanging on to him too tightly.

Brand turned his horse in the opposite direction from the fort and charged as quickly as he could down the craggy hillside. He didn't know how the others were doing, but he would worry about that later. Right now, the only thing that mattered was getting Sheri someplace safe. There was a deep, partially hidden cave several miles farther down the canyon, halfway up a nearly sheer mountainside. If they could get there, he knew he could protect her.

Guiding his horse with a trained hand, he maneuvered carefully across the rocky terrain. The distant sound of shots kept coming to them, and he hoped O'Toole and the others were faring well. They'd been taken by surprise, but had at least had enough time to mount up and ride. It was a long trek back to the fort, but he doubted the raiding party would give chase the entire way. Once O'Toole found a place to fight back, he'd do it. He was not a man who gave up without a fight. Brand just hoped no one had been seriously wounded.

"Where are we going?" Sheri asked long minutes into their flight.

"There's a cave a mile or so up ahead. If we can get there, we'll be safe."

She nodded against his back and hung on, her arms wrapped tightly about his waist, her cheek pressed to his back. She could feel the power and the tension in him. This was no game. This was a life-or-death run to safety. Oddly, though, she truly believed that she would be all right. Brand was taking care of her. Certainly, if she had to be trapped by the Apache out in the middle of nowhere with any man in the world, she would have picked Brand hands down. She closed her eyes and tightened her grip on the solid strength of him.

Brand concentrated only on reaching the haven. The feel of her pressed so tightly against him, her breasts against his back, would have aroused other feelings in him had the circumstances been different, but right now there was time only to think about surviving. He had his rifle, canteen, and enough ammunition to hold off the renegades for a day or two, but after that it would be difficult to say how long they could hold out. He only hoped that he managed to lose them, heading through the canyon with its rocky floor. One way or the other, he was going to be alone with Sheri for some time. The prospect was troubling, but more troubling was the thought of her being shot or taken captive.

Brand felt mortified that he hadn't seen the tracks. Sheri had been the one who'd found them. Her perception and quick learning impressed him even as he guided their mount toward the cave. Because of her, they'd had at least that one moment of warning before the first shots had been fired. She had listened to his earlier instruction in tracking and she had learned from it. Much as he wanted to deny it, his estimation of her rose even higher.

The last thing he wanted was any involvement with her. The whole point of this trek had been to show her the countryside, give her a taste of what a scout was like and then send her back East innocent, happy, and smiling. It wasn't working out that way, though, and he doubted things would ever be the same. Soon, she would learn the truth of terror. She would see what it was like to live in the wilds. To fight the elements and the Indians, to survive by one's wits and little else. He hoped she was woman enough for it.

Somehow, he already knew she was.

And that troubled him.

"It's there," he said to her after a long silence.

Sheri had been thinking of nothing but holding on and not losing her precarious seat behind him, but at his words she looked up. There, high above her, was the opening to the cave in the rough-hewn rocks. It was virtually invisible unless someone knew where to look for it, and she prayed the Indians who'd ambushed them did not know of its existence.

"We'll be safe here?"

"As safe as I can make us. They aren't after us yet, so if we can get in there before they return, I should be able to hold them off until help comes."

"So you think they'll be back?" There was unmistakable fear in her voice.

"We'll know soon enough. Hang on, this is going to be a steep climb."

Though his mount was weary, it was used to such runs. Under Brand's skillful guidance, the steed carefully picked its way up the mountainside. Though it seemed an eternity to Sheri, they actually reached the cave quickly.

Brand swung down first, then reached up and helped her down. She rested her hands on his shoulders as he lowered her to the cave floor. When her knees almost buckled beneath her, Brand was forced to hold on to her for a while to make certain her legs would support her.

"Are you all right?"

She gave him a quavering smile as she looked up at him. "Just a little frightened, I guess. What can I do to help?"

Brand looked into the depths of her eyes and saw the fear she was valiantly struggling to control. It made him even more determined to protect her from harm.

"Just stay down and stay quiet," he ordered harshly. "It won't be dark for hours yet, so we have to keep out of sight. You just find a seat toward the back where it's protected and keep low, while I set the horse loose."

"You're turning it loose?"

"If they come after us, I want them to have a false trail to follow."

"Oh." The idea of being on foot in the mountains intimidated her, but she trusted that Brand knew what he was doing. She nodded and started to go sit down. Then she turned back to him. "Brand?"

He glanced up at her, thinking something was wrong.

"Thank you," she said simply.

Brand stared at her. For the first time since he'd met her, she looked vulnerable. He knew a great urge to go to her and hold her, to reassure her that everything would be all right, but he fought it down. He would not allow himself to feel these things. Never again. The pain when he'd lost Becky had been too terrible. He'd vowed then never to care for another person again. He would not forsake that vow. Sheri was proving too dangerous for his peace of mind. He had to concentrate on getting them out of there. He had no time to be comforting women.

"It'll be all right."

"Is there anything I can do?"

"Just stay out of my way." He deliberately made his words cold, wanting to distance himself from her.

Sheri heard the change in his tone and recoiled from it. Without another word, she retreated. Judging from his mood, she believed he was blaming her for their predicament. If she hadn't come to the Territory to go on a scout, they wouldn't be trapped in this cave in the middle of the desert, all alone, without any help. Recalling all the resentment he'd shown toward her since she met him, she felt miserable. Somehow, she was going to have to help him, but she didn't know how. The only way she could help right now, was to do as she was told and watch for the opportunity later to prove her worth to him.

Brand took up his vigil behind a boulder at the front of the cave. It appeared quiet for as far as he could see, but he knew that could change in the blink of an eye. He checked his rifle and waited. It was going to be a long afternoon.

The shots had taken O'Toole and the others by surprise, and they had only time enough to throw themselves on their horses and race off. Charles had stopped to help Maureen and, as he had lifted her to safety on her horse's back, a shot had rung out and he had been thrown forward.

"Charles!" Maureen had screamed, unable to help herself as she watched crimson blood stain his shirt. She'd started to dismount to help him, but O'Toole had been there, half-carrying, half-dragging Charles to his own horse.

"Can you ride?"

"If I can't, we're dead," Charles had ground out from between clenched teeth. "Get me the hell up there. . . ."

O'Toole had helped him and then they'd been off, racing out across the desert, back the way they'd come.

"What about Sheri?" Maureen cried out.

"She's with Brand," O'Toole answered, whipping her horse to an even faster gallop as they tore away from the attackers.

The renegades gave chase, firing wildly. O'Toole turned on them and covered for the others as they rode. He was pleased to see that Charles was handling his horse well in spite of his wound. Lieutenant Long was staying with Maureen, but when she was a distance away, he turned back to help O'Toole. Together, they fired heatedly at the attacking renegades.

It was a bloody exchange. At least four warriors fell before their fire. The Indians regrouped and came at them again, only to be driven back once more. When it had quieted, O'Toole and Long mounted up and followed quickly after Maureen and Charles. They found that they had reined in and dismounted behind a rocky formation that offered protection from the gunfire.

"I'd always heard the pen was mightier than the sword, but they didn't say anything about guns." Charles tried to laugh, but he could only groan in agony. The bullet had slammed into his shoulder, but had not exited. It would have to be taken out when they reached the fort.

Maureen tried to staunch the bleeding by using her handkerchief, but it did little to stop it.

"Here," O'Toole growled, taking off his neckerchief and pressing it firmly against his wound. "We've got to get him back to McDowell."

"Do you think it's safe?" Maureen asked. "What if they come back?"

"That's what we're here for," Philip said with confidence. "We killed at least four or five of them. I don't know if they'll try again or not."

"They might," O'Toole said worriedly. "We'd better travel while we can. He needs a doctor. We'll stay close to the rocks and keep moving. It'll be dark before too long, and they rarely attack after sundown."

Maureen nodded, feeling safe in O'Toole's care. No wonder she'd felt so uncomfortable all day. Who knew how long those Indians had been watching them? "What about Sheri and Brand? Do you think they need our help?"

O'Toole looked up at her and smiled grimly. "If there's a man alive who can avoid being taken by the Apache, it's Brand. If there's any way out for them, he'll find it. My guess is, they might beat us back to the fort."

Maureen wanted to believe him. "I hope you're right."

"Let's get moving. The quicker we get him back, the better." He shared a concerned look with the lieutenant, and they helped Charles back on his horse.

"Are you going to be able to handle this?"

White-faced with pain, Charles nodded. He didn't argue as O'Toole took his reins to lead his horse.

"All right. We'll keep you between us, just in case. Hold on."

It seemed the ride back to McDowell would take forever, and Maureen wondered if they'd ever reach the fort. The terror she'd felt on the stage coming into Phoenix when they believed they'd been under attack by Indians faded before this true horror. She had just seen men killed and a man wounded. She swallowed against the bile that rose in her throat. She would not disgrace herself or Sheri. She would be brave. She would be strong. She had to be—she had to help Charles.

Chapter Seven

Brand, the Half-Breed Scout, or Trail of the Renegade
Danger Threatens

Rachel and Mercy had grown numb with the passage of time. There had been no rest for them since they were taken from the stage. Their captors had not physically harmed them yet, but they knew it was just a matter of time.

"We have to escape," Rachel whispered to Mercy.

"Escape?" Mercy turned terrified eyes to her. "How can we escape these devils? They are Satan's spawn. . . . They are hell's demons. . . ."

"Keep your voice down," Rachel cautioned.

106

Though she realized the warriors couldn't under-
stand English, she didn't want them to figure out
that she was planning something.

Mercy trembled visibly and tears filled her eyes.
"How in heaven did I ever come to this? They're
going to kill me. I just know they are."

"Not if we don't let them!" Rachel hissed. She
had been through a lot in her life, and now that
she was this close to happiness, she was not go-
ing to lose her dream of marrying and having a
family! She'd been afraid before, but she'd al-
ways found some way to save herself. There had
to be a way to escape from the renegades. There
had to be. . . .

Darkness claimed the land, and only then did
Brand allow himself to relax his vigil. He had heard
shots in the distance, but had not seen any sign that
the raiding party was returning for them. Still, he
knew better than to believe they were completely out
of harm's way. He would watch and wait. By dawn,
he would know if it was safe to attempt a return to
the fort.

Brand hoped that O'Toole and the others had managed to get away. All he had for evidence one way or
the other was the sound of shots and the memory of
Maureen's scream. It didn't look good for them, but
he wasn't about to say anything to Sheri. There was
no telling how she'd react if she thought her cousin
had been killed or taken hostage.

At the thought of Sheri, Brand glanced back to
where she was sitting, still clutching her bag to her
breast. She had remained silent just as he'd told her
to do, and he was glad. The one thing he hadn't

needed was a distraction, and she was definitely that. Hell, if she hadn't been up there talking to him and aggravating him when they stopped for a rest on the scout, they wouldn't be in this fix right now.

"Are you all right?" he demanded.

"I'm fine . . . I think," she answered. "Is it safe? Can we leave now?"

"No, and it won't be until at least morning. Maybe not even then."

"You mean we're going to have to spend the night here?" For some reason, Sheri had imagined that the renegades would just disappear and that they would return to the fort as they'd originally planned. She'd thought this was just a temporary distraction from their original purpose that could easily be rectified.

"Yes." His answer was terse. He didn't like the idea of spending the night out here any more than she did.

"Oh."

"You sound unhappy about it. I thought this would fit perfectly into your plan." There was an edge of sarcasm to his tone.

"What plan?"

"You did say you wanted the scout to be realistic."

She grimaced. "Not this realistic."

Brand looked impatient. "You should have thought about that before you insisted on coming."

"But I overheard you last night talking to the lieutenant. You said this was going to be an easy scout. One day on the trail, just out and back, I believe is the way you put it."

"You're right. That's exactly what it was supposed to be, and that's what it would have been if you hadn't had me so distracted with all your questions that I missed the trail."

"If I hadn't distracted you?" she countered, outraged. "I'm the one who found the tracks!" Fire flashed in her eyes, and she forgot all about being afraid. "Shouldn't you be thanking me for saving you, instead of criticizing me for asking pertinent questions about how you do your job?"

"If it wasn't for you, I wouldn't have needed 'saving' in the first place!" he roared. "If it wasn't for you, I'd be back at McDowell right now, eating a hot meal and relaxing. I wouldn't be stuck in this cave with you, surrounded by who knows how many Apache looking to take our scalps!"

They glared at each other, neither giving an inch.

"You're no hero!" she snapped.

"I never wanted to be!" he snarled back. "That's your fantasy, not mine, and right now, you'd do well to forget all about it. This isn't a fairy tale. No prince is going to come charging up this hillside on a white horse to rescue you. You are trapped in a cave in the middle of the desert surrounded by bloodthirsty Apache who'd like nothing better than to kill you or take you captive!"

They stood eye to eye, neither giving an inch. Finally, Brand spoke.

"Do you know how to use a firearm?"

"I took some lessons at the hunt club back home. Why?"

He looked skeptical as he drew his gun and handed it to her. "Well, just in case, here's my pistol. It's loaded, so be careful, and only use it if I'm dead. All right?"

Her eyes widened at his words. A new, numbing

terror began within her. She stared down at the revolver in her hand as she repeated, "If you're dead?"

"That's what I said."

"Do you really think we're going to die?" There was a sudden vulnerability in her voice.

"I think I'd better get back to keeping watch."

"The Indians truly are nothing but savages, aren't they? To kill for no reason . . ."

Her generalization stung him as a long-buried memory of his life with his father's people surfaced. "They have a reason," he told her tersely. "They think the white man is stealing what is rightfully theirs. The Indians were here long before any whites showed up."

"How can you defend them when they're so brutal and vicious?"

"Have you forgotten that I'm a half-breed?" he asked in a low, almost threatening voice as his expression hardened.

"But you're not like them," she protested.

"How can you be so sure?"

A sudden sense of unease came over Sheri as he took a step toward her. "I just know it."

Driven by demons he didn't understand, Brand moved even closer until he towered over her.

Sheri stood her ground, though. She did not flinch before his obvious anger or cower before him. She bravely looked up at him with innocent, trusting eyes.

"You're living in a fantasy world, little girl. You think you know me, but you don't. Maybe I should show you just how much Indian blood I really have. . . ."

As he reached for her, he seemed to change before

her very eyes. He was no longer the scout, but was now the fierce warrior Charles had mentioned. Still, Sheri did not back down. As he pulled her close and sought her lips with his, she did not resist.

Brand did not know why he felt compelled to kiss her. It was almost as if he sought to punish her or convince her that the Brand of her fantasies didn't exist. His mouth slanted across hers as he crushed her to his chest. His kiss was savage—hard and hungry.

Then, suddenly, an awareness jolted through him. Suddenly, he became aware of everything about her . . . the sweet scent that was only hers, the lush softness of her womanly curves pressed against him, the way her body molded to his. She wasn't fighting him or trying to escape his embrace, and amazingly, kissing her wasn't punishment anymore. It was wild and wonderful. He gentled his hold on her as he realized how delicate she was . . . how special . . .

And he knew this had to end—now.

With all the fierce resolve he could muster, Brand tore himself from her, taking a step back to put some distance between them.

Sheri was stunned. She gazed up at him, her eyes wide and questioning in the wake of the feelings his embrace had aroused. She had never known a kiss like his before. Her heart was racing, and she longed to be back in his arms again.

"I have to keep watch," he said tersely, coldly. He turned his back on her and walked away.

Maureen had been right when she thought that the trek back to McDowell would seem endless. It did. Charles was weak, and eventually O'Toole was forced to ride double with him to keep him in the saddle. They were constantly on watch, expecting the raiding party to come back after them again at any time, while Maureen looked continually and hopefully for some sign of Sheri and Brand.

But there was nothing. It was eerily quiet, and with every passing mile that took her farther away from Sheri, Maureen grew more and more upset.

"I feel like I'm abandoning her . . ." Maureen agonized.

O'Toole could see how desperate she was. He wished he could promise her that everything would be all right, but until they were safely back at the fort, there was no way to be absolutely sure. "We'll send out troops to look for them as soon as we reach McDowell," O'Toole told her.

"And I'll personally lead the search," Philip added.

His offer didn't necessarily reassure Maureen, but she didn't say anything. She needed all the help she could get and couldn't risk offending anyone.

"It's getting dark. What if she needs us now? What if something's happened to Brand, and she's all alone?" Maureen cast an anguished glance back toward the wilderness they'd just fled.

"Even if it was safe for us to go back right now, there's no way we could track them at night."

Maureen gave a strangled sigh. "I know you're right. It's just that I feel so helpless."

Charles managed to speak. "Brand will take care of her. He's her hero."

His hard-fought words made Maureen smile. If Charles could feel optimistic in as much pain as he was, she certainly could. She fell silent, concentrating only on the ride and praying that they would soon reach McDowell.

It was hours later when they finally made it to the fort. They'd traveled after dark, moving slowly but steadily to safety.

Philip had ridden ahead to announce their return. He was waiting for them with several troopers to help when they arrived. With their aid, they got Charles down and rushed him off to the hospital, where the doctor had already been awakened and was ready to treat him.

"He's in good hands now," Philip said confidently as he went to Maureen and helped her down.

"I hope so." She tried to stand, but found her legs were weak after so many hours in the saddle.

Philip noticed her unsteadiness and tightened his supportive hold on her. "Are you all right?"

"Don't worry about me. You go ahead and do what you have to do. All I care about is that Charles is all right and that you find Sheri and Brand."

"We'll be heading out again shortly. Orders have already been given. Let me help you back to your quarters."

"Thank you, but I think I'll go with Charles. I have to find out how he is."

"I can have one of the men report to you, if you'd like," he offered, trying to discourage her.

"No. It's all my fault that this happened to him. He only got involved in this because of us. I want him to know that I'm worried about him."

"There is a small waiting room. Doctor Aldridge probably won't mind you waiting there."

She nodded and moved off in the direction O'Toole had gone. Her emotions were turbulent. She was torn between concern for Charles and her fears for Sheri. No matter what, it was going to be a long night.

Sheri sat watching Brand as he stood near the cave entrance. He was a tall, lean, broad-shouldered silhouette in the soft moonlight, and she shivered as she remembered the power of his touch. Strange feelings besieged her. For that one breathless moment in time when his lips had been on hers, she had been in ecstasy, and now . . . Sheri didn't know what to think. His abandoning her without so much as a backward glance had left her feeling unsure, confused . . . and a little angry.

"Is there anything I should do?" she finally asked when she found her voice. "Do you want me to help you keep watch?"

"No. Just stay there, where you'll be safe," Brand told her, knowing the last thing he wanted or needed was to have her anywhere near him.

His grim rebuff left Sheri's thoughts in turmoil. She'd been kissed by a few men in her lifetime, but those chaste pecks had been nothing like Brand's embrace. His kiss had stirred her to the depths of her soul, yet he had been able to turn his back on her and walk away as if it had meant nothing to him. Sheri didn't know whether to break down and cry or hit him. At the moment, neither option seemed like a good one. Instead, she sat stoically in the darkness, wondering how she'd come to be there, and wondering, as memories of the renegades intruded on her thoughts of Brand, if she was going to be alive at sunrise.

Brand stared out into the night, forcing himself to

concentrate on keeping watch. He had to ignore the woman behind him. He knew now that he should never have kissed her. He regretted it more than he could say. His original intention had been to scare her. His plan had gone completely awry at the first touch of his lips on hers. Her kiss had stirred feelings in him that he'd thought long dead, and that troubled him.

Brand wished there was some way to get her back to the fort tonight so he would be rid of her. The sooner he was away from Sheridan St. John, the better. He didn't want to be anywhere around her. He didn't want anything more to do with her. He wanted her to pack her things and go back to where she came from. She should just go away and write her books—and leave him alone.

Alone . . . He liked being alone. Then he had no one to worry about except himself.

He glanced back at her, and again, emotions he had long been denying tore at him. They were under attack by renegades, and she was depending on him to keep her safe. He had failed Becky He would not fail again. He would keep Sheri safe from harm or he would die in the effort.

Brand hardened himself again against the emotions that threatened his concentration. He had to keep watch. He could allow himself no lapse. There was little chance that the renegades would come after them at night, but he had to be sure. He'd made two mistakes that day already—missing the renegades' tracks and kissing Sheri. He wasn't about to make another.

Sheri glanced askance at the revolver where she'd laid it on the ground beside her, and she swallowed uneasily. Just the sight of it brought home the reality that this was no dream, no fantasy she could write her way out of. She was truly caught up in an adventure, and it wasn't one that she particularly delighted in.

With a sigh, she decided to try to get some rest. Since Brand had made it clear he didn't need or want her help, she would sleep so she would be alert and possibly of some help to him in the morning—if he let her help. She felt useless, and it made her angry. Sheri wasn't used to being told to sit down and be quiet. She was a woman of action. She liked to be in control of her life, and right now, control was the one thing she didn't have.

Frustrated, Sheri curled up on her side on the cave floor and murmured no complaint as she sought some form of comfort on the rocky, unforgiving ground. She kept the revolver Brand had given her and her bag with her writing materials close at hand.

The minutes seemed like hours as Maureen waited for the doctor to finished treating Charles. She had caught a glimpse of the doctor only once, and his expression had been so solemn that she'd begun to fear Charles was gravely wounded. She'd known it was a bloody wound, but she hadn't thought he was in mortal danger. Now, worry and guilt consumed her.

"How is he?" O'Toole's voice cut into her thoughts as he came into the small confines of the waiting area.

"I don't know yet. The doctor's still with him," she supplied wearily, glancing anxiously toward the private area where they'd taken Charles.

"I hope we got him here in time. I didn't think it looked too bad, but sometimes it's hard to tell."

"I hope he's all right, too." A great sadness filled her. Nothing was turning out the way it was supposed to. She feared their big adventure had turned into a tragedy. If Charles died . . . The thought horrified her. She had only known him a few days, but she liked him a lot and couldn't bear to think of him dying.

"I came to tell you that we're getting the men ready to ride. We'll be heading back out at first light."

"Thank you."

"We'll find them," he told her.

"Soon, I hope."

"We'll do our best."

Maureen smiled wearily. "Sheri's certainly getting all the research she'll need for her book, isn't she? Attacked by renegades, disappearing with the half-breed scout, then being rescued by the cavalry . . ." She added her own happy ending to the sequence.

"That she is." As he turned to go, her call stopped him

"Sergeant O'Toole?"

When he looked back, all her fears and worries were plain on her features. "Good luck."

He nodded, his expression solemn, then disappeared out the door.

Maureen settled back to continue to wait. Her vigil was rewarded a few minutes later when the doctor came to her.

"Miss?"

"Yes, sir?" She jumped to her feet, thrilled to see him, yet fearful of what he might be about to tell her. "How is Charles? Is he going to be all right?"

"Are you a relative of Mr. Brennan's?" he asked, wondering at her relationship to the young man.

"No . . ." she answered hesitantly.

"Well, then . . ." He paused, unsure of whether to continue or not.

"What is it?" Her eyes widened with worry.

"My dear, it's highly unusual for anyone outside of family to be involved this way."

"I could lie to you and tell you I'm his sister," she retorted quickly, "but I won't. He's my friend, and it's my fault that he's lying in there right now. So just tell me the truth. How is he?"

"I got the bullet out . . ."

His expression was so guarded, his words spoken with such care that Maureen couldn't stand it. She thought he was going to announce that Charles was dead.

"Is he . . . dead?" she choked over the last word.

Aldridge looked at her, stunned. "Dead? No. He's lost some blood, and he's going to be sore for a while, but he will definitely recover," he explained.

"Really?" It was as if a thousand-pound weight had been lifted off her.

"Really," he repeated, smiling at the joy he saw on her face.

"Thank, God. I'm going to him. I've got to see him." She started past the doctor.

"Miss, this is highly unorthodox," he protested. She was a single lady; he was an injured young man.

Maureen did not know where the words came from, but she whirled on the doctor, glaring at him. "If you think, after everything I've been through today, I'm going to let something as ridiculous as society's dictates keep me from seeing Charles, you are sorely mistaken."

The physician was shocked by her display of temper and immediately backed down. "Well . . . er, all right, my dear. Let me show you where he is."

"Thank you." Her words were terse. She followed the doctor without further comment as he led the way.

The hospital was not a large facility. It had only six beds, and Charles was the only patient. He was pale and he looked unconscious. Maureen approached the bedside slowly. He didn't open his eyes, so she stepped back and turned to the doctor.

"I'm going to stay with him."

"But Miss Cleaver . . . That just isn't done. You're a lady and he's . . ." He looked distressed by the thought, until he saw the warning glint in her eye.

"And he's wounded because of me." She lowered her voice to a commanding tone. "Bring me a chair. This man almost lost his life because I convinced him to go along with Sheri and me. If I had just stayed in New York where I belonged and hadn't let my cousin convince me to come on this hellish nightmare of a trip to this godforsaken country, none of this would have happened. Charles would be fine, minding his own business, writing his newspaper columns in town. I am not going to leave him by himself at a time like this."

The doctor didn't even try to respond. He just rushed off to get a chair.

Maureen suddenly felt helpless and drained by the force of the emotions that were wracking her. When the doctor returned with the chair, she sat down with all the elegance of an Eastern lady.

"Thank you."

"I'll be nearby if you need me."

She could tell he was uncomfortable with her being there, but she didn't really care. Charles had become her friend, and she took care of those she loved.

"Quite a display for a quiet little lady." Charles's soft chuckle surprised Maureen.

"You're conscious!"

"I was just sleeping, but who could sleep with you ordering the doctor around like that?"

Tears burned in her eyes. "Thank heaven. I was so worried about you . . ."

"You were?" He turned his head so he could look at her, and he could see her torment in her expression.

"Yes. He's been in here with you for what seemed like eternity. I was afraid you were going to die. . . ." She admitted the truth, and there was a catch of emotion in her voice.

"You can't get rid of me that easily," he countered, then gave a slight cough and groaned.

"Are you all right?" She was instantly anxious, and she reached out to touch his arm.

"I'll live," he said in a painful rasp. "Could you hand me my glasses?"

She quickly picked them up off the bedside table and gave them to him.

He had to shift positions to put them on. "Damn . . . Oh, sorry . . . I didn't mean to swear, but I've never been shot before."

"Don't worry about that," she said, unable to believe that he was still being the gentleman even after all he'd been through that day. "I'm the one who's sorry."

"You? What for?"

"This is all my fault. If I hadn't convinced you to come along with us, none of this would have happened to you."

"Maureen, there's one thing you're going to have to learn about me." His gaze caught and held hers with serious intent.

"What's that?"

"I never do anything I don't want to do."

"Oh . . ." A great sense of relief washed over her.

"I wouldn't have missed that scout with you and Sheri for anything. I just hope they get back here safely and soon."

"Me, too."

"I think I need to rest for a while. . . ." A great weariness suddenly came over him, and his eyes drifted shut. He fell back asleep almost immediately, their conversation having taken its toll on him.

Maureen slipped his glasses off, but he did not stir. She did not leave him, but stayed by his side all through the night.

It was long hours before Brand stirred. It would be dawn soon, and he was worried about what the new day would bring. Needing to move around a little to keep himself alert, he stood and walked back into the cave to check on Sheri. She'd surprised him when she'd done exactly what he'd told her to do, and he wanted to make sure she was all right now that he had his control back.

Brand found Sheri asleep on her side, her arms wrapped around herself as if she were cold. Without thought, he stripped off his shirt, and, taking care not to waken her, he covered her with it. He was glad that she'd gotten some rest. The day to come was going to be long and dangerous.

As Brand stared down at her, he realized that some of her papers had fallen out of her bag where it lay beside her. He reached down to pick them up, meaning to put them back, but as he held them he glanced down at one page. It was dark, but he could make out a few words.

Brand returned to the fort weary but victorious . . .

The sight of his name so boldly written in her handwriting intrigued him. Quietly retrieving the whole bag, he returned to the front of the cave and settled in to keep watch again—and to read.

He was surprised to find that she was carrying all the pages of her book with her. He sorted them, putting them in order, then began to read—from the beginning.

Brand quickly realized that, contrary to his original thoughts about her, Sheri did have talent. As he went through page after page of handwritten manuscript, he found himself caught up in the drama she was creating. He knew this was a rough draft, but it was good. She had cleverly woven the facts she'd learned since being there into the story. She was a wonderful storyteller.

And then he reached the page with his own description on it.

Brand read it once, then stopped and read it again. *A dangerous man . . . darkly tanned, heavily muscled . . . a sleek and deadly predator . . .* He had never thought of himself in the terms she'd used. Over and over, he had told her that he was nobody's hero. Yet, he was mesmerized by the images she was creating with her words.

Looking up from the pages, he glanced back to where she was resting. She had not yet stirred, and he was glad. He knew he should have asked her first if he could read her work, but it was too late now. He was caught up in the story and wanted to know more of what she'd done.

Brand turned his attention back to the pages and kept reading, following the adventures of Brand, the Half-Breed Scout, as he continued his brave exploits. When he'd finished all the pages, he slipped them back into her bag and moved quietly to return it to her side so she wouldn't miss it. He was surprised to find that he wished she'd written more. He wanted to know what was going to happen next.

The faintest light of dawn was painting the eastern horizon as he reached her side. The soft glow gave him just the light he needed to study her while she slept.

Brand had tried to deny the softer feelings she stirred within him. He did not want to care for anyone that way ever again. The pain of losing a loved one was too terrible. Since Becky's murder, there hadn't been a day when he hadn't thought of her. Some nights he dreamed of her dying, crying out to him for help, and always in his nightmare he was bound and held helpless, unable to reach her, unable to save her from her terrible fate.

And now . . . This woman, this Sheridan St. John had appeared out of nowhere and believed, just from reading Brennan's newpaper article, that he was someone special. . . . Her unwavering belief that he was good and kind and brave touched an emptiness in his soul. But he knew it wasn't true. He was no hero.

Since he'd come to the fort as a child, no one but O'Toole and Becky had ever truly believed in him. He stared down at Sheri, wondering why she felt that way, why she had chosen him. And as he watched her, he remembered her description of him and he remembered her kiss.

In that moment, as if by magic, Sheri stirred and came awake. Her eyes drifted open to find Brand standing over her, bare-chested. For a moment, she wondered what had happened to his shirt, then realized that he had covered her with it.

"Thank you . . ." she said in a sleep-husky whisper as her hand touched his shirt.

She looked up at him, her eyes locking with his. They studied each other in the muted half-light.

Brand had been watching over her, guarding her, keeping her safe, keeping her warm. His thoughtful gesture touched her more than any gift of great value. As much as he tried to convince her that he was heartless and cold, a 'savage', she still believed that her instincts about him were right. Unable to help herself, she smiled up at him. It was a tender, inviting smile, and as she remembered the touch of his lips on hers, her body warmed to his nearness.

Brand could not move away, although he knew he should. He was mesmerized by her sleep-flushed loveliness. His gaze traced over her perfect features and visually caressed the silken, golden beauty of her hair. She was a very desirable woman, and he felt the heat of his need for her flame to life within him. No matter how much he'd fought to put her from him earlier, he wanted her now.

The sound was faint, distant, almost indistinguishable, but Brand immediately tensed. He looked back toward the cave entrance, all physical desire vanishing as reality returned with a vengeance.

Chapter Eight

Brand, the Half-Breed Scout, or Trail of the Renegade
Fearless Courage

The warriors had gathered around the campfire and were taking turns drinking straight from the bottles of liquor they'd stolen from the stage. They grew drunk and unruly. As the night aged, they became louder and more savage, even began fighting among themselves.

Rachel and Mercy were filled with dread as they cowered in the shadows away from the warriors. They prayed for rescue, but knew they had only themselves to count on. They had to escape or their lives would be over, possibly by dawn.

"We have to do something." Rachel told Mercy in a desperate whisper.

"But what?" Mercy asked, trying to control her fear.

"Anything's better than just sitting here waiting for them to kill us. If I turn my back to you, do you think you could untie me?" She had been twisting and turning her hands, trying to work loose the rawhide thong that bound her.

"Maybe . . . But what if they see us?" Mercy worried.

"We'll just move slow and keep inching farther back away from them. With any luck, they'll get drunk enough that they won't notice . . . not even when we make a run for it."

"But . . ."

"But what? Stay here and die? At least, if we try to escape, we have a chance."

Mercy was frightened, but she knew Rachel was right. "All right. I'll try."

"Just move carefully, and pray like mad that they don't plan to come for us any time soon."

Mercy shifted so they were back-to-back. Her fingers sought the tight knot in the rawhide that bound Rachel's hands. Hope stirred in her breast for the first time since she'd been dragged from the stage. Maybe Rachel was right. Maybe they would be able to get away. . . .

"What is it?" Sheri whispered.

But Brand only shook his head in response, silencing her, as he raced back to the opening.

Brand reached his vantage point and picked up his

rifle. He wasn't certain what the noise had been, and for that reason, he was all the more cautious as he took up his position. His gaze swept the area, searching each rocky outcropping for some sign of the raiding party. The sun had just cleared the horizon, bathing the mountains in its harsh brilliance.

It was then that he saw the signs of their approach—a faint reflection, a distant glimmer, a subtle movement among the rocks. They were coming—four of them.

Brand had two choices. He could try to pick them off now from a distance and let them know for certain that they had located him, or he could wait quietly, unmoving, until they reached the cave and then attack.

Brand thought of Sheri and knew he would wait for them to come to him. It might be bloody, but at least he'd have a fighting chance. If he tried to shoot them now, it would be simple for them to out-wait him, to starve them out. It was far better to lure them in. Then he would be the one in control of the fight.

He waited.

Sheri saw the change in him and how fierce he suddenly had become. Something was wrong. She snatched up the revolver he'd given her and got up to go to him, but he silently signaled for her to stay where she was. Gun in hand, she watched and waited for what was going to happen next.

Brand sat unmoving, in total silence, waiting, listening. He heard the distant sound again, and he knew they were drawing closer. It wouldn't be long— just another minute or two—and then he was going to have to shoot fast and straight.

He deliberately shifted back farther into the darkness of the cave. The renegades would be partially blinded by the daylight when they first entered, and that would give him the advantage he needed. It would only last for a moment, so he had to be ready.

Sheri saw his movement away from the entrance, and a chill shivered up her spine. Someone must be coming. She drew a ragged breath and waited, hoping she would be able to shoot when the time came. She'd never had to shoot anything live before, and she wondered if she could.

After turning back from their running attack on the other whites from the fort, the four remaining Apache warriors had hunted for the scout and his woman until sundown the day before. When they'd finally discovered Brand's horse's trail, they'd known they were close. At first light, they began to move in. They were angry that their original attack had failed, and they were determined to make these two pay for the deaths of the other braves.

The Apache closed in, cautiously, warily. They knew there might be trouble, but they also believed in their superior fighting ability. Their tracking had led them here. They were certain that their prey was within reach.

Slowly, silently, they approached the cave. When one of their number dislodged a small stone, they stopped, waiting to see if anyone or anything came out. There was no movement, no response, but they knew better than to believe no one was there.

The leader of the party neared the cave from above. He jumped lightly down at the entrance, crouching low, his rifle in hand, ready to kill. Peering into the darkness, he could make out little, so he ventured forth.

Brand remained frozen in place. He had backed as close as he could to the wall, trying to blend in, trying not to be seen. He wanted the others to come in, too. Killing only one of them would do little to gain their freedom. Knowing he had only seconds to act, he drew his knife, and as the warrior stepped nearer, Brand lunged forward, throwing the Apache to the ground and ending his life with a swift stab.

The warrior's blood covered Brand, but he had no time to think. Just as he drew away, another brave appeared and immediately fired at Brand. He dodged the shot, diving behind a boulder, firing back. He prayed that Sheri was hidden away farther back out of the line of fire.

Another Indian joined him and the fourth followed. He could hear them talking as they maneuvered themselves to get closer in.

And then they attacked. All three at once, darting among the rocks near the entrance, making sure that they were safe from any return fire.

Brand fired wildly, shifting positions as best he could, but when he ran out of bullets and had no time to reload, he knew he would have to do more. In one brazen lunge, he threw a rock at the Indian closest to him, knocking his weapon from his hands. They grappled on the ground, rolling over and over as each man fought for supremacy.

Sheri saw the battle and felt a scream rise in her throat as the other two braves descended on Brand. She knew she had to take action. She could not just hide there and watch him be murdered. As one renegade prepared to fire point-blank at Brand, she lifted the revolver and, without thought, pulled the trigger.

The Apache fell, mortally wounded by her shot. The other two were shocked by her sudden appearance.

Her timely interruption gave Brand the edge he needed. With brute force, he threw the warrior off him and, grabbing the Indian's rifle, shot him, then quickly turned on the other man, who was about to shoot back at Sheri.

It all took place in less than a blink of an eye, yet it seemed an eternity to Sheri. She felt as if everything was happening in slow motion. Sheri knew she should fire again. The other warrior was taking aim at her. She needed to save herself. Yet the horror of realizing that she'd just killed someone held her immobile. Across the distance of the cave, her gaze collided with the savage's. She saw the blood-chilling hatred in his eyes. She realized that she was facing certain death. The Indian's finger closed on the trigger. . . .

It was then that Brand rose from his mortal combat and shot the Apache. With an agonized, pain-filled cry, the warrior fell dead.

Brand got to his feet and stood over the dead Apache. Echoes of his gunshot rang around them.

The four Apache were dead.

It was over.

The silence was overwhelming. Where moments before shouts and shots had echoed through the cave, now there was nothing. All Sheri could hear was the tortured rasp of her own breathing.

"Are they dead?" she asked. Though she was trembling violently, her grip on the gun was as fierce as ever.

At her question, Brand turned toward her. He was still tense, still ready to do battle. He looked wild and untamed. Blood streamed from a knife wound high on his arm. His expression was brutal, remorseless. And then he saw her, standing like an avenging angel, gun in hand.

If he'd been asked the day before what he'd thought she was capable of, he would never have imagined this. She looked proud and fierce, braver than many men, and she had saved his life by her quick action.

"They're dead." He felt some of the tension ease from him as he glanced down at their bodies. "That's all of them. There were only four."

At his statement, all the fury and fear that had driven Sheri drained away, and she suddenly realized what she'd done.

"Oh, God . . ." she whispered, swallowing tightly. Her knees grew weak and she sank down on a rock, the revolver still clutched in her hand. "I killed a man. . . ."

Brand cast one last glance at the dead warriors and then went to her. The bloodlust that had filled him eased as he knelt before her. "Sheri, if you hadn't killed him, he would have killed us."

"But . . ." She looked up at him. "I've never killed anyone before. . . ."

"There aren't many women who could have done what you just did. You were wonderful."

"I don't feel wonderful," she said miserably.

"If it hadn't been for you, I'd be dead right now."

"I know. . . ." She lifted her gaze to his, glad that she'd saved him. "And if it hadn't been for you, I'd be dead right now, too."

They regarded each other steadily, Brand seeing her with a new respect.

"We've got to get out of here," he said, urgency in his tone.

"If they're all dead, why do we have to keep running?"

"There may be others coming after them. We need to leave now while there's time."

"All right. Let's go." She trusted him completely.

"Good. There's no time to waste." He started to rise; then, unable to help himself, he reached out and gently touched her cheek. "Thank you."

She managed a tremulous smile as she found herself lost in his fathomless gaze.

Brand wanted to take her in his arms and kiss her and hold her to his heart, but that would have to wait. The only important thing right now was to get as far away from the cave as fast as they could. He had to keep her alive.

He stood and held out his hand to her. She took his hand and allowed him to draw her to her feet. Before he could lead her from their hideout, she stopped him, though.

"What about your arm? You're bleeding. Let me see if I can stop it. I've still got your shirt. I could tie it around the cut. . . ."

He had been so caught up in the moment that he hadn't realized until then just how deep the cut was. He flexed his arm and knew she was right. It needed to be wrapped. "All right, but hurry."

She quickly snatched up his shirt and tore a large bandage from it. She wound it around his arm, staunching the bloody flow. She tied it as tightly as she could.

"There. That should hold it at least for a while."

He tested his arm and found she'd done a good job. "Don't forget your bag. I'd hate to have to come back for it." He nodded toward her writing materials.

She smiled at him and ran to get the bag.

"I'll go out first to make sure it's safe," Brand told her quietly. "Then once we're out of here, I want you to stay close behind me."

"Do you want this back?" She held out the revolver to him.

"No, you keep it. Better that both of us are armed."

He grabbed up the canteen, and as he started past the dead attackers, he picked up his rifle. He paused only long enough to reload.

"I'll be right back. Stay out of sight." He left the cave and disappeared from view.

"I will."

Sheri was nervous as she awaited his return. Then suddenly, as quietly as he'd left, he was back.

"Let's go."

She picked her way past the dead warriors, trying not to stare at the carnage. And then she was free of the bloody confines of the cave and out in the sunlight. She paused, wanting to savor the moment and draw a deep cleansing breath, but Brand didn't wait for her. He immediately moved off, making his way up the mountainside.

She wondered why he didn't head back the way they'd come, but said nothing. She trusted him. He'd kept them alive this long. He knew what he was doing. He was the scout.

The trek was rugged, each step an effort as they slowly made their way up the steep maze of rocks, cacti, and scorpions. Sheri was amazed at how little she jumped now whenever one of the nasty little creatures scurried unexpectedly out in front of her. She dodged them agilely, uttering no sound.

Neither Brand nor Sheri spoke until they had reached the top. Sheri was thrilled when she saw two Indian ponies waiting there for their masters. She thought that they would simply mount up and ride back to McDowell.

She thought wrong.

Sheri watched in horror, disbelief showing plainly on her face, as Brand sent both mounts running off.

"Are you crazy?" she demanded, thinking he'd surely lost his senses. "Why did you do that? We could have ridden them back to the fort!"

It was hot and rocky and downright miserable out there. With the horses, they could have made the fort by late afternoon, but now they were stuck on foot out in the middle of the desert with only one canteen of water and no food. And she was getting hungry. Earlier she'd been too scared to think about food, but now her stomach was definitely feeling a lack.

"If others are following, it will take them longer to find their friends if their horses are running in the opposite direction. Far better that they track them riderless, than trail us riding them."

"Oh." That was all she could say to his perfect logic. She reminded herself once again that he was the scout.

"Let's keep moving. We won't be able to stop for any length of time until late this afternoon when we're well away from here. I know of a water hole that we'll head for."

Sheri hoisted her bag onto her shoulder and tucked the revolver into the waistband of her skirt.

"All right. But do you think they've sent anyone out from the fort to look for us?"

"If the others got back, then yes, help is on the way. But until we meet up with them, we're on our own."

"Do you think we're still in danger?" she asked, gazing around at the endless miles of wilderness.

Brand went perfectly still as their gazes met. "There can always be danger here."

Certain that he was issuing some kind of unspoken challenge, Sheri did not look away. She would not back down. Having come this far, she would not fall apart now, even though she was wracked with worry about Maureen and the others. "Then let's keep moving. I don't want to be the reason any more Apache find us."

"Do you need a drink?" He offered her the canteen.

"Not yet. We don't have that much water, so I'll wait until later."

"That water hole is a few miles ahead. We'll stop there." He started off again.

Sheri followed in his wake, amazed at his ability to find a trail where there seemed to her to be none. They walked at a steady pace, pausing only briefly so she could catch her breath every mile or so. It was a strenuous trek, but Sheri did not lag. She endured even though the heat of the day grew oppressive. Occasionally Brand would stop and hunker down to read signs along the trail, but each time his concern was for naught. And she was glad.

When they finally reached the water hole, she was more than ready to rest. She thought briefly about food, but she was past being hungry. Traveling as far as they could as fast as they could was all that mattered.

"Do you think any of them are coming after us?" she asked.

"No, not yet."

She started to kneel down and get a drink of the water.

"Don't drink anything." It was a harsh order.

Sheri glared at him. They'd just walked miles to get here. She was thirsty, and she didn't understand why she couldn't have a drink.

"Why not?" she asked sharply, suddenly weary and needing a simple drink of water to ease her anxiety. That wasn't too much to ask, was it?

Brand circled the small natural basin, studying the land as if searching for something. Then he knelt down and scooped up a handful of water and drank it himself.

"All right. You can drink now."

"What was that?" she demanded, her mood testy. "Some kind of Apache ritual where you have to circle the watering hole and then be the one to take the first drink?"

He looked up at her strangely, wondering where she could ever have gotten an idea like that.

"No," Brand answered. "I was looking for dead animals or insects to see if the water was bad. I took the first drink to make sure it was safe for you."

Sheri was suddenly humbled and embarrassed by his explanation. Her irritation vanished. "So that's how you do it. . . . Look on the ground for dead animals and insects. I'd never thought of that." She made a mental note.

"And neither do many others of your kind. That's why they don't last long out here."

"How is it you know this land so well? Have you

137

traveled these mountains a lot with the cavalry?"

Brand paused to look around him, trying to see the mountains through her eyes. They were harsh in their glory, but they were a stark, mighty reflection of his Indian heritage. "My people often crossed these mountains when I was a boy."

"So that's why you know them so well." She was amazed by his unerring sense of direction. There was no doubt in her mind that she was lucky to be with him. Without him, she would have been lost forever in this jumble of rocks that the people from the Territory called mountains.

She had always thought mountains were supposed to look like the pictures she'd seen in books—snow-capped and covered with thick pine forests that harbored wildlife like deer and antelope and harmless creatures of beauty. Clear, rushing, sparkling streams were supposed to tumble down the mountains' sides, feeding a multitude of cool, beautiful lakes. Instead, here she was hiking through something she was sure had a lot in common with hell—it was hot, dry, and miserable, with people trying to kill you at every turn. She smiled wryly at the thought.

"Something is funny?" he asked, seeing her smile.

"Not really. I was just thinking how much these mountains have in common with hell."

He looked at her expectantly, waiting for her to go on.

"They're hot, dry, and downright miserable, and there's someone just waiting for the chance to kill you at every turn."

"Legend has it that all the Indians climbed to the tops of the mountains at the time of the big flood. When the waters receded, the bad Indians had turned to stone, so you're not far wrong."

Sheri stared up at the jagged peaks again and studied them in the light of his story. She could almost make out what looked like faces, frozen in the rocky landscape. She was beginning to understand why the Apache often hid there. It would be easy to blend in as you lay in wait and not be seen until it was too late for your hapless prey to escape. Brand had done that exact thing in the cave.

She took a deep drink and grimaced. It was far from the sweet-tasting water she was accustomed to back home, but at this point, she was just thrilled that it was wet and not going to poison her.

Seeking a bit of shade in the shadow of a boulder, she sat down for a while. She smiled again as she thought about all that she was learning, whether she wanted to or not. Unable to help herself, she took out her pencil and paper and started to write, quickly jotting down everything they'd done that day.

In detail, she described the assault on the cave and Brand's valiant defense of her. She wrote of binding his wound with his shirt and of how it had felt to touch him and nurse him. Description after description followed as fast as she could record them, for she sought to commit to paper all the things she was experiencing. There were so many details she wanted to remember, so many things that would prove to Tim De Young that she did know what she was writing about. She'd show them all, and in the end it would all be worth it—providing she found that Maureen was safe at the fort.

Brand had replenished the canteen and was keeping watch. He noticed how quiet she'd become, and he glanced over at her to find her bent over her papers, writing diligently. The memory of what he'd read that morning returned, and he found he was curious to know what she'd written.

"What are you doing?"

"I want to write down everything," she replied. "So much has happened today. I want to make sure that I get it all down on paper while it's still fresh in my mind. My readers will be fascinated to learn how you make sure the water is safe and they'll want to know the story about the flood."

"You'll have to finish later," he said with little emotion. "We need to move on."

"Is something wrong?" She was instantly worried again.

"Not yet, but we're in the open. It would be easy to spot us here if someone is after us. We'll find a place farther on to hole up for a couple of hours. You can write more then."

Sheri thought it was odd that he was suddenly being so solicitous of her craft. It was strange, but she was glad of the change. He was almost being nice. She put her things back in her bag and stood up, ready to follow him. The revolver she was carrying seemed to grow heavier with every step, but she wasn't about to complain. She had helped save them once by using it, and she would do so again if she had to.

They traveled on, past the greasewood and palo verde, past the saguaro and barrel cacti, past the Joshua trees and ocotillo. The trek seemed endless. Sheri almost asked him where exactly they were bound, but she knew what his answer would be—they were heading for the fort. She just didn't know if they were going there by way of China or if he knew a secret passage that would bring them safely back to McDowell.

Again they moved in a steady rhythm, and Sheri found herself becoming almost numb to the harshness of it. When, at long last, Brand found a suitable place for them to rest, she was more than ready. Though she was fully clothed and was wearing her hat, the hot Western sun was baking her. She wondered how it was that Brand did not burn, traveling shirtless as he was, but then remembered his Indian blood. The only happy thought she could come up with as she trudged on was that she was glad it wasn't August.

When they finally found a suitable place to rest for a while, she all but collapsed on the hard ground. There was shade, but it didn't offer much in the way of relief from the heat. Trying to distract herself from thoughts of her physical discomfort, she took out her paper and pencil again and once more set to work.

Sheri knew she had to use this trek of theirs in the book. She wasn't quite sure exactly how Rachel and Mercy were going to end up lost and wandering alone in the wilderness, but they were. Brand the Half-Breed Scout would have to rescue them, of course. That was what heroes did, but she was going to enjoy writing the Eastern women's reactions to the wilderness as she was experiencing it right now. She could just imagine how she would be reacting if she were out here alone without Brand's guidance and protection, and it was those thoughts and feelings that she needed to capture in the book. Her readers had to believe that it was all really happening.

Brand was growing annoyed when he found himself continually looking over at Sheri as she busily wrote down all her thoughts. He needed to rest and to keep an eye out for trouble, but he was having little success doing either with her sitting so near. It irritated him that he found his gaze drawn to her over and over again. He studied the slight tilt of her head, the way her eyes lit up when she thought of a new idea, and the way she frowned in concentration when she was writing a lengthy passage. He wondered what was in her notes, then grew even more angry with himself for the thought. He shouldn't want her. He shouldn't be attracted to her. He shouldn't care about her book. It troubled him that he was losing his objectivity where she was concerned.

"It's hot," she declared, unbuttoning a button high on her blouse to try to cool off a little.

Brand's gaze traveled the path of the vee of pale flesh she'd just revealed to him by that simple move. She hadn't meant it to be a seductive action, but the way the soft, white material clung to her in the heat, revealing the fullness of her breasts, created a heat deep within him that had nothing to do with the weather. He frowned, his expression turning black.

"Is your arm hurting?"

Her question surprised him, and he shrugged in response.

"You look like you're in pain. I'll be glad to take another look at it, if you want me to."

"No." His answer was sharp, encouraging no discussion. He did not want her anywhere near him. He did not want her hands on him. His temper was sorely stretched as it was, and he didn't need any further contact with her. That would only make things more difficult.

"When are we going to get back to McDowell?"

"On foot, it could be days."

Sheri groaned inwardly. "I don't suppose there's any hope that we could find a horse out there somewhere, is there?"

"Only in your book."

"It's a shame that reality isn't as convenient as fiction. If I had my way, the cavalry would come charging over the hill right now with Sergeant O'Toole in the lead and rescue us from our plight."

"O'Toole would be your hero then."

"Anybody would be my hero who showed up right now with a horse."

"Even Lieutenant Long?"

"There are limits to the lengths I'll go to get rescued." She slanted him a smile.

Her smile jarred him. He stood up abruptly and asked in a hard tone, "Ready?"

"Do I have a choice?" she asked with a weary half-grin.

"Not if you're coming with me. You can stay here if you like, waiting for the cavalry, but I think it might be a very long wait." He moved off, scowling, not waiting for her.

Sheri quickly stowed her things in the bag and rushed after Brand. She kept up, following in blind obedience, saying very little and concentrating only on matching his longer strides.

As the hours passed, she let her thoughts drift to the night to come. It promised to be even more interesting than the day had been, though she wasn't sure that 'interesting' was quite the right word.

True, she would be sleeping out under the stars. The trouble was, as much as she'd wanted to experience a night out on the trail on a scout, she was enough of a city girl to have wanted at least the comfort of a bedroll, a campfire, and a hot meal to go along with it. She stifled a sigh and kept walking.

Chapter Nine

Brand, the Half-Breed Scout, or Trail of the Renegade
The Escape

Rachel led the way as she and Mercy slipped out of the Indians' camp. They crept from shadow to shadow until at last they were far enough away that they could run. It was a dark night with no moonlight to guide them, and that cover of darkness was both a blessing and a curse. It helped them elude detection, but hampered a quick escape.

Mercy followed Rachel without making a sound. She had always considered herself a prim and proper lady, a teetotaler who disdained the *use of liquor for any reason save medicinal, but not anymore. As the two of them disappeared into the night, she was praying silently and fervently that every last Apache warrior would get knock-down, falling-over drunk. She wanted them all to pass out and not wake up until late the next morning, and they seemed to be well on their way to making her prayer come true. Mercy hated to admit it, but she supposed demon liquor did have a useful purpose after all.*

"Are you doing all right?" Rachel whispered as she stopped behind a huge boulder and waited for Mercy to catch up with her.

"Yes. The farther away from them I get, the better!"

They moved onward as quietly as they could over the rough terrain. Slowly but surely the sounds of the warriors' revelry faded away and they were alone in the night. Both women almost felt like celebrating, but they knew the terrible truth. If they weren't many miles from there by dawn, the renegades would be able to find them easily. They could not stop their flight. They had to keep moving.

And then it happened. . . . Just as they thought they were nearing safety. . . . A man stepped out of the shadows before them.

Mercy couldn't help herself. . . . She screamed.

It was near sundown when Brand finally reached the site he'd been heading for.

"We'll camp here," he announced, looking back the way they'd come to make sure no one was following.

All was quiet, save for the rustle of a roadrunner hurrying through the brush.

"Here?" Sheri looked at the rocky setting in disbelief. Though the view of the canyon was good and no one would be able to sneak up on them, she saw absolutely nothing about the place that looked as if they could lie down comfortably here, let alone get some sleep.

"Duck down and follow me in."

Sheri couldn't figure out what he was talking about, and then he disappeared right before her very eyes. Startled to think that there was more to this site than just the outcropping, she stooped down and crawled after him.

Though sometimes she did question him, she'd always believed he was good at what he did, and he reaffirmed that belief yet another time. Following his lead, she found herself inside a small, cool, low-ceilinged chamber just big enough for the two of them.

"Good. No one's been here."

"You've been here before? How in the world did you ever find this place?"

"When I was young, my friends and I used to come here to hunt and track. We found it by accident one day, and it became our secret place." He looked around, satisfied that they would be able to sleep there safely. And he did need some sleep, not to mention some food.

Sheri looked around the dimly lit hole in the rock that would be her bedchamber for the night, hoping to find a place to sit down. The low ceiling was annoying, and she wanted to relax . . . as much as she could relax considering their circumstances. She gave a deep sigh and started to sink down in one corner near a small pile of rocks.

"Don't move!" Brand's order was abrupt and harsh.

"Why? What is it now? Do you have to check for dead animals to see if this is a safe place for me to sit down?" she asked sarcastically. She was tired, more tired than she'd ever been in her life, and she wanted—no needed—to rest.

She looked up at him to find him coming toward her, his knife drawn, a murderous look in his eye. She swallowed and almost took a step back, thinking that she had pushed him too far, that he was coming after her. "Brand? What—?"

And then she heard it—the unmistakable sound of a rattlesnake.

Sheri gasped in understanding and stood stock still as, with one fluid motion, Brand threw his knife within inches of her leg. She heard the impact, and the ominous sound of the rattle instantly died.

"Oh, God," she breathed when she looked down to see the snake curled up within striking distance. "How did you even see it?" She backed away, horrified.

He ignored her question as he moved forward to retrieve his knife. He picked up the dead rattler and held it up for her to see. It was nearly four feet long and as thick as her arm.

"It's huge. I didn't know they got that big."

She watched as he sat down and began to skin the snake.

"What are you doing? That's disgusting. Aren't you just going to throw it away, so it doesn't start to smell?"

He looked up at her. "This, Miss St. John, is our dinner. Unless you don't want to eat tonight."

"Dinner?" The word was a horrified squeak.

"As soon as I finish cleaning it, I'll cook it. Then I'll be able to put the fire out before it gets dark."

Sheri swallowed nervously, testing her stomach's readiness for snake meat. Her stomach did roil uncomfortably, but she wasn't sure if that was from the thought of eating the snake or from the fact that she was very, very hungry.

Again, she told herself that this was a learning experience. She was doing research, but she still dreaded taking the first bite. Then logic asserted itself, and she realized that it was far, far better that she was biting the snake than that it was biting her.

That rationalization settled it for her. She was hungry. She would eat.

Still, once the decision was made, her mind started playing jokes on her, conjuring up such gourmet titles for her soon-to-be entrée as Roast of Rattler, Filet of Fang, Sidewinder Scallops, and Breast of Reptile. *Breast of Reptile?* She repeated that one in her mind, wondering if a snake had a breast.

Dinner. Ummmm.

Sheri thought about writing down her entrée names, but didn't. She didn't think her book was going to be particularly funny. In fact, there wasn't a whole lot that was funny in her life or in the book right now.

"Can I sit down now?" she asked almost timidly.

"You're safe," he told her, still concentrating on preparing the food.

Sheri dropped down on the hard cave floor and sighed. A feeling of despair threatened. So far, she'd managed to keep her spirits up, but exhaustion and hunger were taking their toll. She tried to draw upon that inner spirit of hers that always egged her on to try to do more, to try to be the best. She reminded herself of why she was there—to show Carroll and Condon that she could write "real" Westerns.

At the thought of her publisher and New York City and her friends there, a deep melancholy settled over her. She tried to think of one solid reason why she shouldn't have a good cry. After all, she'd survived an Indian attack, she'd killed a man in self-defense, and now she'd lived through almost being bitten by a rattlesnake. She definitely thought she was entitled.

The trouble was, Brand was there with her. Through this whole ordeal, her motivating force had been that she wanted him to have a good opinion of her. She wanted his respect. If she broke down like a senseless, helpless female right now, she would lose any credibility she had with him, and she'd fought too long and too hard to ruin it all now.

"Here."

Sheri jumped as something thudded at her feet. "What's that?"

"A present for you," he told her without a smile.

She started to pick it up, then bit back a scream. It was the rattle from the snake. He'd cut it off. "That's disgusting."

"It's the other end. It won't bite."

"No, thanks." She delicately shoved it away from her with the toe of her boot.

"You don't want a keepsake of your trip to the Territory? Some people take snake skin and make hat bands out of it."

"That's quite all right. I don't think rattlesnake would be all that popular in New York."

"Missing home, are you?"

"There are moments," she sighed honestly. "Dinner in a restaurant would taste really good right now."

"Well, some folks say snake tastes like chicken."

"Some people lie a lot, too."

He picked up the cleaned meat and left their safe haven to build the fire and quickly cook the meat. When he returned some time later, he handed her a stick with chunks of meat roasted on it.

"So this is dinner?"

"I set a snare for overnight, so we might have rabbit for breakfast, but for now this is all there is."

Ravenously hungry, Sheri took a small, tentative bite of the meat. Though it wasn't delicious, it wasn't horrible either. She surprised herself by taking another bite, then another.

Brand watched her for a moment, enjoying her expressions, then he ate his own portion. It wasn't enough to fill him, but it was better than nothing.

"How was your food?" he asked when he'd finished and looked up to see that she, too, was done.

"I suppose the old saying is true—a starving man will eat anything."

"You may as well bed down."

"I'd love to, if you'd produce a bed," she said with an exhausted smile.

He shot her a look that wasn't marked by humor.

"I know, I know," she responded quickly before he could say anything. "Don't say it. I wanted to be on a real scout, so now I am."

She looked around at the ground and sought the

least hard-looking spot. Using her bag as a pillow, she lay down and groaned.

"What's wrong?"

"This is hard."

"Think of it this way—the sooner you get to sleep, the sooner it will be morning and we'll be on our way again."

"I'm not sure which is more fun—sleeping on solid rock or hiking in the desert heat. I'll sleep on it before I make my decision."

She turned on her side away from him and closed her eyes, hoping she really could drift off.

Brand crept outside to take one last look around. The night was clear, and there was no sign of any other living creature. Satisfied that they were safe and undetected, he climbed back inside. He stood, looking down at Sheri as she sought rest, and he felt a stirring of admiration for her. In spite of all the hardships they'd endured on this trek to safety, she'd uttered not one word of complaint. She had been braver than many of the men he knew back at McDowell. She was one special woman.

As he lay down, Brand knew that if things were still quiet in the morning, they could change direction and head straight toward where the troops would be looking for them. That was, providing O'Toole and the others had made it back. He refused to consider the possibility that they hadn't. His friend was too good a soldier not to have survived that ambush. He closed his eyes, willing himself to sleep. He had to rest while he had the opportunity. Tomorrow might prove to be another long day.

Sheri did not know why she woke up. It could have been for any number of reasons—most of which had something to do with being completely and totally miserable. She tried to stretch, but her every muscle felt cramped. Shifting carefully so as not to disturb Brand, who was sleeping close by, she rolled to her back and stared up at the rock ceiling in the darkness. All was quiet.

There was nothing she would have liked more than to fall back asleep, but her mind had other plans. As she courted sweet dreams of forgetfulness and home, her thoughts conjured up a continual vision of all the horrors she'd been through in the last two days. Everything she'd planned for this trip had seemed to turn into a nightmare. She thought of how excited she'd been to meet Brand and of how he hadn't wanted anything to do with her. Images of the attacking Apache were seared into her mind, as was the sound of Maureen's scream echoing through the canyon. She had seen men killed today, and, most devastating of all, she had killed a man herself.

A tremble shook her as she remembered the fight Brand had put up to defend them. She had a faint and confused memory of the incident, of aiming the gun and firing just as the warrior would have slain Brand. She bit her lip as the terror of the moment returned full blast. She didn't want to think about it. She didn't want to relive the horror of it all, but lying awake, all alone in the silent darkness, there was no escaping it. The memories would not be suppressed. Image after graphic image flooded her thoughts, and the tears she'd been fighting for so long could no longer be denied.

Sheri refused to make a sound even though she wanted to sob her heart out. She didn't want to disturb Brand, slumbering as he was beside her. She didn't want him to know of her weakness.

Brand was resting next to her, but he was not asleep. He had come awake as soon as she had shifted position. He was a light sleeper, a quality that had always served him well through the years. Usually, once he'd made certain that everything was all right, he could drift off again. But not tonight. He sensed something was wrong. Sheri's breathing was strangely ragged and she seemed tense. He rolled to his side and leaned up on one elbow so he could look down at her.

"Sheri . . . Are you . . . ?"

It was then, in that barest of light, that he saw the crystalline tears that traced paths down her cheeks. She was crying.

"Are you hurt?" His voice was gruff with concern.

Sheri had given an inward groan when Brand stirred and rose up next to her. She had tried not to disturb him, and she had failed even at that. It seemed she couldn't do anything right anymore.

"I'm sorry," she said in a choked whisper.

"For what?" Brand was confused.

"I didn't want to wake you."

"What's wrong?" he pressed her. If something was bothering her, why hadn't she wanted to wake him?

"It's just that . . ." She paused to draw a deep, strangled breath. "As I was lying here . . . I realized what happened today. I killed a man . . ." The last came out in a sob, and finally she began to cry in tortured agony.

"Sheri . . ." He touched her cheek, cupping her face with his hand. "It's all right. You did what you had to do."

"But . . . I shot him . . ."

"If you hadn't, I would be dead and so would you. You were very brave."

"But I didn't want to kill anybody. I just wanted to come out here to Arizona to meet you. I just wanted to learn all about the West so I could write books about it. That's all . . ."

"You saved my life today. On top of that you've also been through probably the hardest day of your entire life. I pushed you hard, and you kept up. You moved at a trooper's pace. I wanted to keep you alive, so I forced you to do things no other woman's ever done," he said seriously, responding to the abject misery in her voice. "You did everything I asked of you, and more."

"It was that or die," she said softly, a warmth radiating through her from the simple touch of his hand on her cheek. She lifted her gaze to his and saw actual concern and kindness in the depths of his eyes. She managed a small smile. "I'm sorry I've caused you so much trouble. I didn't mean to."

He found himself smiling back at her as he leaned closer and in a tender gesture, pressed his lips to her cheek where the tears had left their trace.

"Oh, Brand . . ." she sighed.

He had kissed her with the most noble of intentions. He had meant to ease her worry and her fears. But somehow that simple kiss stirred him more deeply that he'd ever dreamed it could. And he was lost. . . .

His lips traced a path down her cheek to her mouth and settled there in a passionate, long-denied exchange. He had fought against his desire for her, but now her tears and gentleness had conquered him. He had lost the battle. She was beautiful, and

155

she wanted him as much as he wanted her. When her arms came around him, drawing him down to her, he savored that intimate contact, holding the slender length of her body against his.

His mouth left hers to explore the sweet curve of her neck and to trace that enticing vee of her blouse that had driven him to distraction earlier that day. She gave a small moan of wonder at the feelings he was arousing in her, and he could no longer resist touching her. His hands sculpted her body, tracing each curve with loving excitement. She was silken and irresistible, and he wanted her desperately. He rose up over her to kiss her again, and she met him fully in that fervent caress. Her own hands moved restlessly, tracing paths of fire over the broad, hard-muscled width of his back and shoulders.

His hunger driving him, Brand unbuttoned her blouse and slipped the garment from her shoulders. Brushing aside the straps to her camisole top, he bared her full breasts to his touch.

Sheri arched in wonder at the heated caress of his mouth against her. She had never known such ecstasy, and she moved restlessly against him as he pressed hot kisses to her tender flesh.

Sheri was caught up in a firestorm of arousal as he moved over her. The weight of his body upon her was erotic. She shifted her hips, wanting him closer, seeking some unknown fulfillment that only he could give. Brand fitted himself to her, savoring the closeness, needing her, wanting her . . .

"Brand . . ." Sheri whispered his name, reaching for him, desperately wanting what only he could give her.

Her voice was heavenly, her soft touch his undoing. It had been so long since he'd loved and been loved. Not since Becky had he felt this way. Not since . . .

Becky . . .

With the memory of his dead wife came the return of reality. He had been caught up in a dream world. He had been drugged by Sheri's beauty and lost in the wonder of her kiss.

Jarred back to the reality of where he was and what he was doing, Brand suddenly stilled. No matter what ecstasy and joy might be his for this short period of time, in the end, it would be the same. He would not, could not, let himself feel again. Becky had suffered and died because of him. He would never put another woman in that position.

Sheri had never been so intimate with a man. When he stopped so suddenly, she was still caught up in a passionate haze, wanting him to continue kissing her.

"Brand?" she whispered as she reached for him.

"No, Sheri. Stop." His tone was emotionless. "I don't want this to happen."

Jolted from passion's delight to cruel reality in one quick moment, Sheri stared up at him in confusion. "I don't understand. . . ."

"There's a lot you don't understand." Without another word, he moved away from her.

Her bare flesh was touched by the cool air surrounding them then, leaving her shivering. She quickly covered herself, embarrassed by his rejection and by what she had almost done. She had almost given herself to him. But the coldness of the air was nothing compared to the chill in his voice.

"What do you mean?" She looked up at him, her

eyes wide and pleading for understanding.

"I mean, the only reason I'm here is on orders from the captain." He was determined to be cruel. He had to distance himself from her.

"But . . ."

He cut her off before she could say more. "I don't care about your writing. My job is to track renegade Apache, not provide you with research for your book. And I kinda figured that that's what this was all about."

"Why . . . you . . . ! What a horrible thing to say!"

"Maybe it's time your heroine—what's her name? Rachel? Maybe it's time Rachel got her first kiss, and you wanted to do some research on that, too."

She glared at him. "I thought I was coming to know you, but I wasn't. I don't know you. I don't know you at all."

"You're damned straight you don't know me, lady. Do you still think I'm a sleek and deadly predator?"

She gasped. "You read my work!"

He shrugged indifferently at her outrage, knowing that that would make her even more furious. He wanted her mad. He wanted her to hate him. This would be much easier for him if she hated him.

"You are absolutely right. You are no hero!" Fire was flashing in her eyes as she shrugged into her blouse and clutched it together over her breasts.

He smiled at her in grim satisfaction. "Just so you understand that."

With that, he left her, disappearing out into the night.

In a huff, Sheri quickly buttoned her blouse, then angrily lay back down. Sleep was lost to her for the rest of the night, though. Where before she'd felt only like crying, now she felt complete and total fury. She couldn't wait to be away from him. Why had she ever thought a . . . She stopped herself, for she had almost called him a half-breed. His being a half-breed had nothing to do with what had just happened between them. She had offered herself to him like a wanton, and he had walked away. The humiliation stung, along with the realization that she truly had wanted him to make love to her. What was happening to her?

As she asked herself that question, she suddenly had her answer. She'd made one fatal mistake. It was the Brand in her book she'd loved and wanted. She'd gotten the real Brand confused with the hero she'd created out of her own imagination. This Brand was a far harder, more complicated man. He was not her hero. Her anger sustained her through the rest of the night.

Shortly before dawn, she emerged from the hideout to find Brand cutting up some kind of strange-looking, pear-shaped fruit.

"I didn't snare a rabbit, so you'll have to be satisfied with some prickly pear."

Sheri didn't say a word. She took what he handed her and ate in silence. When he announced that it was time to go, she gathered up her bag and followed him. There was no point in talking. There was nothing left to say.

Charles was up and dressed and moving gingerly about the hospital, testing his own strength. The pain from the wound was not as bad as it had been, and though he was still a little weak, he was getting better. He wished he could will himself well. He wanted to be out helping O'Toole and the others search for Sheri. It had been almost two days now, and there had been no word. It troubled him to sit with Maureen and listen to her voice her concerns about her cousin, and know that there was nothing he could do or say to make things any better.

"What are you doing up?" Maureen asked as she arrived at the hospital. She was surprised to find him out of bed, half dressed in trousers with a loose robe about his shoulders.

"I thought it would be nice if you got to see me in some position other than on my back," he told her with a grin as he moved slowly back toward his bed.

"As long as you're feeling better, I don't care what position you're in."

Charles reached the bed and sat down gingerly on the side. If he moved too easily or too fast, his body quickly reminded him of his limitations.

"There," he sighed. "Now, has there been any word from Long or O'Toole?"

"Nothing," Maureen answered, the light that had been glowing in her eyes at finding him improved dulled. "Not a word. I'm really getting worried. I would have thought they would have found them by now."

"Maybe they had to hide from the raiding party and are making their way back by a longer route. You heard O'Toole. There's no better man for Sheri to be out in the desert with than Brand."

"I know, but some of the talk I've been hearing hasn't been pretty."

"What are they saying?"

"Some of the women think Sheri's reputation has been ruined because she's been out there all alone with Brand for two nights."

"Sometimes I don't understand how people think. Those women should be praying like mad that Sheri and Brand are safe. They should be glad that Brand is there to protect her, and not let their small minds create trouble where there is none. Sheri certainly didn't ask to be attacked by renegades and then be lost in the desert."

"That's true enough, but Sheri has always been a woman who does exactly what she wants. It's just never gotten her into this kind of trouble before."

"She's not in trouble. It's going to be all right."

"I hope so. I mean, she's my inspiration. She's the one with the great ideas and wonderful imagination. I'm the timid one. I would never have come out here in the first place if it hadn't been for her."

Charles smiled at Maureen. "Then remind me to thank her when she gets back."

"Thank her? For what?" She looked at him, a bit confused.

"For convincing you to come to the Territory. If she hadn't, I would never have gotten to meet you."

Maureen was caught off-guard by his remark. "That's a nice thing for you to say, but you ought to remember that it's because of me you got shot."

"I thought we'd settled that already."

"I remember what you said, but I still feel guilty about it."

"Don't. I'm getting the story of a lifetime out of this. What other reporter has been through what I've been through in the last few days? I got to ride on a cavalry scout. I was attacked and almost killed by renegades, and am now being nursed back to health by the prettiest woman I've ever seen."

Maureen blushed prettily. "I didn't know you felt that way. Sheri's the pretty one."

"Trust me, my dear, you are not hard on the eyes."

"Thank you."

"There's no need to thank me. I'm a reporter. I always tell the truth."

"And you honestly don't think the talk about Sheri's reputation will matter?"

"People talk. But you and I both know that Sheri's a lady who's been caught up in circumstances beyond her control."

"I know. She was so excited about coming here and meeting Brand. She's always daring me to try new, exciting things. She'd be the first one to say it's not important what other people think—it's only important what you think."

"She's definitely a woman ahead of her times."

"And I just want her to stay alive long enough to get to those times."

"I'm sure if Brand has anything to say about it, she'll be fine."

The fear that she'd been trying to control overwhelmed her again and tears filled her eyes.

"I hope you're right." She drew a ragged breath. "I really hope you're right."

There came the sudden sound of shouting from outside on the parade ground, and Maureen and Charles exchanged puzzled looks.

"I wonder what's happened?"

"Maybe they're back!" Maureen ran for the door to see, while Charles waited where he was.

"What is it? Can you see anything?"

There were troopers milling around in a crowd near the center of the area.

162

"I'll go check. Wait here. I'll be right back. I can't tell from here what's going on."

Charles wanted to tell her to wait for him, that he'd go with her, but he knew that would only slow her down. She was excited, thinking something good had happened. Slowly and painfully, he got to his feet and started after her. He hoped all the shouting was good news about Brand and Sheri, but just in case it wasn't, he wanted to be there for Maureen.

Maureen ran toward the spot where the troopers were gathered. She kept looking for some sign of Sheri, but saw none.

"What is it?" she asked anxiously as she reached the first of the soldiers. "Did you find them?"

A sudden hush fell over the men as they realized she was there. A sergeant who'd been at the center of the throng of soldiers stepped forward to talk to her.

"We didn't find any sign of them, but we did find Brand's horse." He nodded toward the exhausted-looking steed.

Maureen heard one man mumble to another. "You know how much the breed loves that horse. There's no way it would get away from him unless . . ."

When she looked his way, her expression filled with sudden terror, he shut up.

"They had to be somewhere close to where you found the horse! Why did you stop looking for them? You can't just quit. You have to go back . . ." She was growing hysterical at the thought of Sheri on foot in the desert with the Apache after her.

"Ma'am, the horse found us. He was running free and had been for God knows how long."

Maureen began to cry, and she turned away from

the soldiers. Charles had been right to go after her. He slipped his good arm around her shoulders in a supportive gesture.

"Let's go back inside," he said softly, drawing her away from the crowd. He could do little to relieve her fears, but he could stay with her and help her keep up her courage.

Chapter Ten

Brand, the Half-Breed Scout, or Trail of the Renegade
The Rescue

Mercy's scream was instantly cut off when a powerful, ruthless hand clamped down firmly over her mouth.

Rachel could barely make out the man before her, but in the darkness he looked like one of the Apache. She reacted instinctively. She was beyond caring as she threw herself at the warrior in a desperate attack.

"You savage!" she cried.

"Are you trying to get us all killed?" the man demanded harshly as he warded off her blows. "If

165

Bobbi Smith

I was one of them, you'd already be dead."

The meaning of his words finally penetrated her fury.

"What? Who are you?" she asked in a strangled whisper.

"My name's Brand. I'm a scout from the fort. I've been sent to find you and bring you back. Which one of you is Mrs. Stewart?"

At his words, Brand felt Mercy relax in his grip.

"You are?" he asked, and felt her nod in affirmation. "Are you going to scream any more?"

When she shook her head, he released her.

"Follow me. We haven't got a lot of time. If they heard you, they'll be coming after us right now."

The walk that day seemed interminable and infinitely more difficult than the day before. Sheri told herself she felt that way only because they weren't speaking, but in truth, they did climb many steep hills on their way out of the mountains. It seemed to her that Brand was much more lax in watching for the Apache, but after seeing no trace of them for two days, he probably knew they were safe. Whatever the reason, the trek grew tedious, hot, and miserable.

Sheri could not think of words that would be good enough to describe how she was going to feel once she saw some sign of civilization. Thrilled, ecstatic, excited . . . She only hoped that that moment would come soon.

Philip was disgusted and growing more and more fearful as he and O'Toole began retracing their route in hopes of finding some trace of the vanished Brand and Sheri.

"I don't understand how they could just disappear this way without so much as a trace," Philip complained in frustration.

"I know. I only hope that they weren't taken captive. I hope they're out there somewhere, making their way back toward us."

They rode on, seeking and not finding any clues to the pair's disappearance.

"If you were Brand, which way would you have headed?" Philip asked, trying to second-guess the scout.

"Away from the raiding party for a day or two and then circle back around. He's got to have a good idea of where we'll be looking for them. If they're still alive and free, he knows where to head. If it's at all possible, Brand will bring Sheri back here."

"I hope you're right. She's been through enough already without being subjected to any more living in the wilds than she has to."

They fell silent as they concentrated on watching the surrounding hills for some sign of Sheri and Brand. Philip's resolve was firm. If they were out there alive, he would find them.

As Brand and Sheri topped one hill, he caught sight of the cavalry's dust in the distance, and he was glad. Rescue hadn't come a minute too soon. He held up his rifle so the sun glinted off the metal, using it as a signal to those below.

O'Toole had been keeping careful watch over the craggy hills. When he saw the momentary flash, he reined in hard.

"There!" he shouted excitedly, pointing toward the rugged hillside.

167

The entire column wheeled around, and with O'Toole and Philip in the lead, they spurred their mounts to a run in the direction he'd indicated.

"What's that?" Sheri asked, finally seeing the dust.

"That is your lieutenant, coming to your rescue."

"They found us!" she cried, ecstatic at the thought of finally being rescued. "That must mean that Maureen and the others made it back to the fort!"

Her happiness was boundless at the thought that her cousin was uninjured and safe. She started to run toward the cavalry. In her wildest dreams, she had never thought that seeing Philip again would be such a thrill.

Brand watched without emotion as she charged ahead of him down the hill toward the coming troops. He preferred to think that they had found the cavalry, not the other way around, but it really didn't matter. Soon, they would be back at McDowell. Soon, he would be done with her.

Brand had expected to be pleased at the prospect of being free of Sheri's presence. He had had little to say to her since the night before, and that was just fine with him. There was really nothing more to say. She had her life to go back to, and he had his—and his didn't include any emotional entanglements. He had made a vow to himself never to care for another woman, and he had meant it. Still, as he watched her racing toward the cavalry, he knew a longing that things could be different. But when he saw the lieutenant dismount to greet her, a pang of a very different emotion stabbed at him.

Brand ignored it as best he could. He told himself he was glad that this was over. She had her life back East to return to. And that was what he'd wanted all along. She'd had no business being out here doing her research. She was a woman, innocent of the ways of the West. He was just glad that no harm had come to her while she'd been with him.

"Brand!"

He heard O'Toole's shout and lifted his arm in greeting. He watched as his friend separated himself from where the others had gathered around the lieutenant and Sheri, and rode straight for him.

"How the hell are you?" O'Toole asked, smiling broadly.

"Fine, now," Brand answered simply.

"What happened to your arm?"

"The raiding party decided to come after us, after they'd finished with you."

"Where did you fight them?"

"The cave."

O'Toole nodded. "Good place to wait them out. Anywhere else and they would have had you."

Brand grunted in agreement. "What took you so long to find us? Are you slipping in your old age?"

O'Toole shot him a look of mock outrage. "We've been out every day. What took you so long to hike out of the mountains? Did she slow you down that much?" he teased, nodding toward Sheri. "She doesn't look too much worse for the wear, though. How did it go?"

"Not bad. Not many women could have put up with what she just went through."

O'Toole knew Brand, and he knew what a high compliment his friend had just paid Sheri. "She held up well? No hysterics?"

"No. She kept her nerve. The only thing that scared

169

her was worrying about her cousin. She was afraid you'd all been killed."

"They tried damned hard, I'll tell you, but we managed to get away. I guess that's when they decided to double back and go after you."

"I figured they'd come looking for us. That's why I sent the horse on. Did he make it to the fort?"

"Yep, but I'll tell you what—when he came back in, Maureen thought for sure you were both dead."

"I guess we'd better head back, so we can put her at ease."

O'Toole held out his hand and, clasping Brand's forearm, helped him swing up behind him. They joined the others.

Brand displayed no emotion at the sight of Sheri mounted behind the lieutenant, her arms wrapped around him to hold on. Long seemed to be preening at having her so close.

"Well done, Brand. Sheri looks wonderful. You took good care of her."

Brand only nodded in response.

"Sheri tells me you fought off four of them?"

"Yes, sir, but she did her share, too. I'd be dead now if it wasn't for her straight shooting."

Philip twisted in the saddle to look at her in surprise. "You can handle a firearm?"

"Some." She did not want to go into detail or talk about the killing. She just wanted to get back to the fort and see Maureen. "It was luck mostly. Brand did all the fighting. He's the one who kept me safe."

Sheri wanted to deflect any questions about her using the gun. She wanted to forget all about that if she could. She wanted to forget all about the time that followed, too.

"Then we're doubly grateful to you, Brand," Philip said. "Sheri's back with us safe and unharmed. That's the most important thing. Shall we ride for the fort? Are you ready to see your cousin? I know she's anxious to see you."

"More than ready," she replied quickly, looking forward to a warm bath and clean clothes. She avoided Brand's unfathomable gaze as he watched her.

"We'll see you back at McDowell."

The lieutenant put his heels to his horse and headed off toward McDowell. He left the others to follow.

"I don't know what I'm going to do if something terrible has happened to Sheri," Maureen said solemnly to Charles as she sat with him in the hospital.

It was late in the afternoon, almost sundown, in fact, and there had been no new information one way or the other about Brand and Sheri since his horse had returned earlier that day. Her nerves were stretched taut as she imagined all the terrible things that might have happened to her cousin if she had been taken by the Apache.

"Try not to think about it," Charles said. "It will only make things worse if you let your imagination run wild."

"I know, but it was easier to pretend that we were going to find her and that she was fine and unhurt before they found Brand's horse."

Charles understood and knew there was little he could say to ease her concern. All he could do was hope to distract her.

"Well, if you're looking for a way to pass the time,

171

I could teach you how to play poker," he offered with a grin.

"Poker?" She blinked, surprised by his offer. "You mean gamble?"

His smile turned even more rakish. "All in the name of helping you stay busy so you don't have time to worry."

"I've never played poker." Maureen was pondering the idea. "I mean, my father always said ladies shouldn't play such games."

"Ah, but your father's not here, and I promise I won't write and tell him."

"Well . . ."

"We won't bet anything too outrageous."

"I do have a little money," she said thoughtfully, intrigued by the idea.

"We don't have to play for cash."

"What would we play for then?" she asked.

"We'll think of something. We'll worry about that later, once you understand the game."

Then, when Maureen realized what she was considering doing, she smiled widely at Charles. "I can't believe I'm going to do this, but I am. If Sheri's taught me nothing else, she's taught me to not be afraid to try something new. Where do they keep the cards around here?"

"I played with some of the troopers last night for a while, and they left a set here with me." He took them out of the drawer in the small table beside his bed, then pulled the table over between them.

Maureen watched as he shuffled. He seemed to be quite good at it. "Are you a card sharp?"

Charles just smiled. "I played my share of poker in college."

"Am I in danger of losing my entire fortune?"

"No . . . Just a portion of it." He laughed and dealt her a hand, explaining the rules as he did.

Maureen was a quick study and caught on right away. Glad for the distraction, she concentrated on the cards and played a mean hand. Charles was glad that she was proving to be so adept at it. After she'd soundly trounced him on two consecutive hands, he decided to make the stakes interesting.

"All right," he said in a serious tone. "I think you've figured out how to play."

"What makes you think that? I'm just an innocent beginner." She tried to keep her expression sweet as she spoke, but her eyes were twinkling as she looked at him across the small table.

"An innocent beginner who's very good."

"No wonder Sheri always says to try new things. This is fun."

"I wonder what you're going to say when you start losing."

"Hah!" she scoffed. "You just told me I'm good. I'm not going to lose."

"Good, now you're over-confident. I've got you right where I want you. It's time to start playing for big stakes."

"Oh?"

"Yes. If I win this next hand, I know exactly what I want from you."

"What? Lots of money?"

He gave her a leering grin. "No, not this time. If I win, you'll have to pay up."

"Pay up, with what? I don't like the look on your face," she said astutely.

He gave a low chuckle. "A kiss."

She stared at him, amazed by his suggestive wager. Heat crept into her cheeks as she imagined herself kissing Charles. What surprised her even more was that she found the idea quite intriguing. "Oh."

"Are you ready for such a wild proposition?"

"You have to beat me first to claim your prize," she said with mock intensity. "I'm ready."

"But what do you want for your prize if you win the hand?"

She gave him a daring look. "You'll just have to wait and see. I'll name mine when we're through. I wouldn't want to make you so nervous you couldn't play."

He laughed out loud and got ready to play. Maureen dealt him a hand that was a definite winner, and he was glad. The more he was with her, the more he liked her. She was witty and bright, not to mention beautiful. He'd been wondering what it would be like to kiss her for some time now, and at last he was going to find out.

Charles kept his cards close to his chest. He studied them and decided the best way to play the hand. He took two cards, and knew fate was on his side when Maureen dealt him exactly what he needed.

"I call. What have you got?" he asked when the time was right.

"Nothing," she said. "I was going for a straight, but I didn't get it."

"Pity. It looks like I win."

"Yes, it does." She tried not to smile. She didn't want to let him know that she'd deliberately discarded two of her three kings in order to let him have this hand.

"What shall I do about collecting my winnings?" he asked.

"I'm not sure."

Their gazes met across the table, and time seemed to stand still. Awareness faded until it was just the two of them, alone.

Charles might have brazenly kissed her right then in the middle of the hospital, if the shout hadn't come from outside.

"They're back!"

They heard the call distantly, and all thoughts of the poker hand and its enticing stakes were instantly forgotten.

"Thank God. They're back!" Maureen cried, running to look out the window.

In the distance, she could see Philip riding in. As he dismounted, she saw that Sheri had been riding double with him.

"Charles! Sheri's here! Philip's found her!" She couldn't hold back her cry of joy. "Come with me?"

She turned and waited as he rose to accompany her. He was moving slowly, but steadily, and they went outside to greet Sheri together.

Sheri had never thought Fort McDowell would look this good to her. She was thrilled to be back. The only thing that might have looked better would have been her own home. The troopers and their wives came out to welcome her.

"Where's Maureen?" she asked as she climbed down from the lieutenant's horse.

"I'm right here, Sheri!" Maureen called out in excitement as she charged through the milling soldiers to get to her cousin.

Charles stayed back, following the last short distance a bit behind her.

"Maureen! Thank God you're all right!"

"Me?" Maureen replied as they hugged each other tightly. "You were worried about me? I've been going crazy worrying about *you*. Just ask Charles." She nodded toward where he stood close at hand.

"Oh, no . . . Charles, Philip just told me on the ride back that you were hurt . . ." Sheri looked up from hugging Maureen to see him standing there.

"I'll be fine. The doctor and Maureen have been taking good care of me."

"Thank heaven. I can't believe everything turned out so well . . ."

"But where's Brand? I thought he would be the one to bring you back in."

"Brand did keep me safe. He's riding in with Sergeant O'Toole. They should be along any time now."

"I see you've still got your writing materials," Maureen laughed, seeing how Sheri was still clutching her bag. "I should have known that you'd never lose that."

"You're right, and have I learned a lot more." She silently added, *more than I ever wanted to know*.

"Where were you all this time?"

"I'll tell you all about it later. Right now, I just want something to eat and a hot bath."

"Come with me. I'll see what I can do for you."

"I'm glad you're safe. We've all been very worried about you," Charles told her.

"Thanks. Brand deserves all the credit. He protected me. He saved my life that first morning out."

"So he turned out to be a true hero, just like in your book?" Maureen was thinking that everything couldn't have worked out any better. Brand had proven himself to be just as wonderful as Sheri had believed he was.

At her cousin's comparison, some of Sheri's happiness faltered, yet she hid it well. Only Maureen noticed the fleeting look of some strange emotion—sadness, maybe—that shone in her eyes for a moment.

"The Brand in my book is certainly going to be the perfect hero," Sheri managed, avoiding answering her directly.

"Well, let's go to our quarters and see about getting you that bath," Maureen suggested.

She could tell Sheri needed some time alone. She turned to Charles.

"I'll see you tomorrow?"

"You can count on it," he replied. Then in a voice meant just for her alone, he added, "I still have my winnings to collect."

A small thrill of anticipation ran through Maureen at the intimacy in his voice and the knowing twinkle in his eyes.

"I'm looking forward to it," she said in low tones, surprising herself again. "I'll see you then."

Charles watched the two women make their way toward their quarters. He was glad that they had both come through the ordeal unscathed. He was glad, too, that he'd had this time alone with Maureen to get to know her better. He couldn't believe she'd just said what she had to him. He grinned as he thought about it, and he knew he was going to be smiling for the rest of the night in anticipation of the day to come. He returned to the hospital to find the doctor there waiting to examine him.

"This will be your last night here," the doctor informed him after removing his bandages and checking his wound. "You're healing nicely. How are you feeling?"

"Better, but I'm still a little weak."

"You will be that way for a while. You just have to take things easy and not push yourself. Give your body the time it needs to heal."

"So I can return to the regular quarters they gave me in the morning?"

"That'll be fine. I just want to keep an eye on you one more night. Right now, it seems to me that you are healing well. I'll see you one more time tomorrow. How soon are you planning on returning to Phoenix?"

"It will depend on the ladies. I'll know more after I talk to them tomorrow. I traveled out here with them and had planned to stay as long as they did. I'm not sure if they're ready to leave yet or not."

"I certainly wouldn't blame them if they packed up and took the first stage out of here. They got more than just a taste of the real wild West, that's for sure."

"I know. It wasn't supposed to be this way for them."

The doctor applied a new bandage to his shoulder and left Charles alone to retire for the night. Charles's thoughts were on Maureen as he stretched out on the bed and started to relax. A smile curved his lips as he thought of her response to him, and he went to sleep that night looking forward to the next day with more enthusiasm than he'd felt in a long time.

Chapter Eleven

Brand, the Half-Breed Scout, or Trail of the Renegade
The Awareness

Mercy was nearly hysterical, but Rachel tried to reassure her.

"It'll be all right now, Mercy. We're not all alone anymore. We've got help."

"Let's go. We've got some ground to cover." Brand said no more, but led off.

When they reached the place where he'd left his horse, he let them rest for a moment. He'd been thinking about the fact that they'd escaped on their own and wondering how they'd done it.

"How did you get away? I thought I was going

to have one bloody fight on my hands getting you out of there."

"It was Rachel's idea," Mercy told him as she looked over at the younger woman with pride.

Brand glanced at the female who'd attacked him with such fury earlier. "That was a very brave thing for you to do, sneaking out of camp that way."

"We were going to die one way or the other. I didn't see that we had any choice."

"But we're going to be safe now, Rachel," Mercy said in a tear-choked voice as she impulsively hugged her. "Thanks to you and to Brand."

"I hope you're right. . . ." Rachel looked at the man who was going to lead them out of there.

Sheri sat in the portable tub that was provided for bathing, scrubbing every inch of her skin until it glowed. She almost wished she was back home, for if she had been she could have soaked herself in a tub of pearl water. She loved the scent of the orange essence, Castile soap, and rosemary that went into that bath, and she looked forward to the day when she could enjoy the luxury again.

She'd caught a glimpse of herself in the mirror before she'd sunk down into the hot water, and she knew that her pale complexion, so sought after in her social circle back East, was lost now. In spite of the fact that she'd worn her hat the whole time they were outdoors, she had tanned. Sheri found it wasn't an unattractive look. It was just that ladies were supposed to avoid the out-of-doors, and that was one thing she hadn't done.

Finishing off the bath by washing her hair, she finally wrapped a towel around her head like a turban and then used another to quickly dry off. That done, she pulled on her dressing gown and called out to Maureen.

"It's safe to come back in. I'm all clean again."

Maureen had been waiting patiently in the other room for her to finish. When she went in to join her, she found Sheri sitting before a mirror, a towel draped around her shoulders as she tried to work all the tangles out of her hair.

"A bath certainly makes you feel better," Sheri sighed as she smoothed out her mane.

"And look better. You seem far more relaxed now."

"I am. I think . . ." Sheri paused, searching for the best way to talk to Maureen about all that had happened.

"Now, tell me everything," Maureen encouraged her, sensing that her cousin wanted to talk about her ordeal. "While you were out there alone with him, did Brand teach you all kinds of things you can use in the book?"

"I learned a lot," Sheri said quietly, thinking of his kisses and his rejection of her when she would have offered him her most precious gift.

Maureen waited a minute for her to go on, then said, "Like what?"

Sheri lifted her troubled gaze to her cousin. "I learned that I can survive just about anything."

"I'll say," Maureen agreed. "It was difficult for us, and we were only on the run for that one afternoon. The Apache were after you for two days."

"I never dreamed I could do some of the things I did." Sheri gave a disbelieving shake of her head as she thought of the last few days. "It's hard to believe that any of it was real."

"Tell me everything from the start. Where did you go? How did you lose his horse?"

Sheri began slowly, reliving in her mind the first attack. "It was terrible for me. I heard you scream, but we had to ride in the other direction or we would have been killed right then."

"Charles was shot right in front of me. I was so afraid that he was going to die . . ."

"No wonder you screamed. I thought that you'd been shot. I wanted to go back to you, but Brand knew we had to ride in the other direction or we would be killed. So I spent the last few days thinking you were hurt. It was awful."

"I was afraid you were dead," Maureen told her. "I didn't lose hope until Brand's horse returned without you, and then I really got scared. I hadn't dreamed that anything like this could happen to us."

"I know, and I'm the one who talked you into coming."

"Don't worry about that. I'm glad I did."

"You are? But the whole trip has turned into a nightmare."

"I can't believe you just said that. Are you an impostor? What happened to my Sheri? Is she still lost out there somewhere in the desert?"

Sheri managed a weary smile. "No, the real Sheri is here. She just never thought researching the wild West would be so wild."

"I've been enjoying a lot of the wild West," Maureen told her with a sly smile.

"You have?" Now, it was Sheri's turn to be surprised. "You were the one who didn't want to come.

I thought you'd be more ready than I am to head back East again. What exactly have you been enjoying so much? Or should I say 'who'?"

"It's Charles, Sheri. When he was shot and I thought he might die, I realized that I've come to care about him. The last few days, I've been staying with him as much as I could at the hospital. I know a lot of people don't think it's proper for a single young lady to do that, but I didn't care. I wanted to be with him, so I stayed."

A slow, triumphant grin spread across Sheri's face. "If nothing else comes of this trip, it will all have been worth it just to hear you say that."

"What do you mean 'if nothing else comes of this trip'? Isn't your research going well?"

"I'm just not sure of anything right now," she said slowly.

"Well, you know that Brand is the perfect hero. What else is there to be sure about?"

Sheri sighed heavily. "I was so naive when we came out here. It's hard to believe that was less than a week ago."

"Naive about what? You're a published author. You knew that you wanted to learn all about scouts and what they did with the cavalry. That's what you've been doing."

"Yes, but I've also been learning a lot about myself. I expected everyone else to be as excited about my book as I was. But Brand couldn't care less. He told me last night that the only reason he was with me, trapped in the mountains, being chased by Apache, was because he'd been forced into it by his commander. If it hadn't been for me, he wouldn't have been wounded in the fight or forced to walk all those miles through the desert."

"You had to walk through the desert, too," Maureen argued.

"Yes, but I wanted to be there. It was a big adventure to me. To Brand, I was just a nuisance he couldn't wait to be rid of. Well, he took me on the scout. Now he can go about his own business."

"But I thought you liked him."

"I do like him. . . ." Sheri paused, remembering. "But it's pointless. He made it quite clear that he's glad he's done with me."

Something in her voice told Maureen that there was more she wasn't telling.

"What is it, Sheri? What happened between the two of you?"

"Nothing," she denied quickly, almost too quickly, and the stain of a blush colored her cheeks. "And that's the way it has to stay."

Maureen was not as knowledgeable in the ways of the world as Sheri was. Still, she understood that something had happened between Brand and her cousin while they were alone in the wilderness. "You don't want to talk about it?"

"There's nothing to talk about," Sheri admitted. "Brand is a solitary man, and he plans to remain that way."

"Did you want it to be otherwise?" Maureen prodded gently. "Are you coming to care for the man?"

"No. He won't let me."

"I don't understand."

"We camped last night in a small cave that only he knew about. I was doing fine until I woke up in the middle of the night, and I couldn't get back to sleep.

All the horror of the Indian attack came back to me. I hadn't meant to cry, but I couldn't stop myself."

"You were entitled," Maureen told her defensively. "After all you'd been through, I'm amazed you lasted as long as you did without breaking down."

"Well, I was so worried about you. I didn't know if you were dead or taken captive." She shuddered. "I accidentally woke Brand up when I was crying, and he tried to comfort me. But then . . ."

" 'But then' what?" Maureen asked, seeing the confusion on her cousin's face.

"He kissed me."

"Oh." Maureen's eyes widened at the news. She was quiet for a moment, and then she smiled delightedly. "This sounds just like one of your books!"

"It's not amusing," Sheri said flatly.

"You don't think so? Listen to what's just happened—you came out here to meet your 'hero' and got attacked by Apaches. You were stranded in the wilderness with a handsome man, and then you were rescued by the cavalry and a certain lieutenant, who'd searched for you for days." She was smiling broadly now. "Now the heroine has to choose between the two heroes. This is great!"

"My life is not as simple as a book plot."

"The only tough decision you've got to make is, do you want Brand or do you want Philip?"

"Maureen!" Sheri was exasperated by her cousin's simplistic logic. "Brand doesn't want me, so it wouldn't matter if I wanted him or not."

"What are you talking about? Of course he wants you. He wouldn't have kissed you if he didn't want you."

"I wouldn't bet money on that."

"I don't know," Maureen said. "I've turned into a pretty good gambler."

"When have you ever gambled in your life?"

"Earlier today, Charles was teaching me how to play poker, and I was beating him quite soundly up until the last hand."

"Beginner's luck."

"No, I planned to lose that last hand."

"Why?"

"Because of what I was going to win, if I lost."

"You're confusing me."

"Charles wanted a kiss if he won the hand." Maureen smiled coyly at her cousin. "I threw away two kings, just so I could lose."

"Maureen!" Sheri wasn't sure whether to laugh or be outraged.

"You're the one who taught me to try new things and be daring. So I took your advice. Trouble is, you returned to the fort just when he'd won the hand, so he hasn't had the chance to collect his winnings yet."

"It's hard to believe this is sweet, little, innocent Maureen talking to me."

"I'm still sweet and innocent. I just wanted to kiss Charles, and this seemed like the perfect way to do it. Now, back to you and Brand . . ."

"There is no 'me and Brand'."

"I say the man's attracted to you."

"Hardly. He made it very clear that he was sorry he'd ever kissed me."

"I'm sure he was sorry. You've probably got him all confused now. He's never met anyone like you before. He thought you were a simpering little Eastern girl who didn't know a thing about the real world, and here you matched him mile for mile on the trek and shot an Indian dead to save his life. He's probably thinking he can't wait until you leave, so he can get back to his normal life."

"I'm sure he is. Your Charles may be the perfect gentleman, but Brand only cares about tracking down renegades. As far as I can tell, he doesn't want to get involved with anybody or anything. It seems O'Toole is his only friend."

"Well, it does make sense that he's a solitary man. Life hasn't been easy for him."

"I know." Sheri fell silent as she thought about everything Brand had lived through. "Maybe I've done enough research here at the fort. What do you say we go back to Phoenix and stay at the hotel for a few days?"

"Won't Philip be disappointed if you go?"

"I don't know, and I don't care."

"Well, if your life is like your books, then it's obvious your decision is already made."

"What decision?"

"Whether you want the scout or the lieutenant," Maureen said with a grin. "It looks like the scout won."

"Oh, you . . ."

"What kind of happy ending are you going to give Rachel? Who's she going to marry? Brand or the man she's engaged to?"

Sheri paused to think about it. "I'm not sure yet. I've still got a long way to go in her story."

And in your life, Maureen added to herself. She knew the next few days were going to be very interesting—very interesting, indeed. "We can leave for Phoenix whenever you want."

"I'll tell Philip in the morning. He's breakfasting with me, so I'll be able to arrange our departure."

Philip was more than pleased with himself. Sheri was back and appeared to be unharmed. Things had turned out very well. At breakfast in the morning, he would find out what more she needed to know for her book and see if he could help her with it.

Sheri was proving to be quite a lady. He was most taken with her. He had spoken to the colonel and to the captain's wife, and they had agreed to have another party in Sheri and Maureen's honor, now that they were safely returned. If Sheri approved, it would be held the following evening. He would discuss that with her in the morning. Until then, he just had to bide his time and enjoy the fact that she'd returned safely from her escapade.

Morning came far too early for Sheri. The bed felt luxurious after two nights of sleeping on the rocky ground, and if she hadn't already made arrangements to see Philip, she would have stayed in it until well past noon. As it was, she dragged herself out early and got ready for her eight o'clock breakfast with the lieutenant.

"You know, Maureen, I must have been having a weak moment last night to have agreed to this."

"I'm sure you were not at your best."

"Do you know I was actually glad to see the man when he came riding up to me?" She shook her head as she smiled wryly. "It's amazing what desperation will do for your outlook."

"He's not a bad person," Maureen pointed out. "He's just . . ."

"Egotistical?"

"Yes."

"Arrogant?"

"Yes."

"Condescending?"

"Yes, and more."

"Exactly," Sheri agreed. "I'll just have to be nice and make sure I thank him graciously for everything he's done. Then we can leave here as quickly as possible."

"What about Brand?"

"What about him?"

"Have you thought about what you're going to say to him when you see him again?"

"I don't know if I will see him again."

"I'm sure you will. You can't leave the Territory without saying good-bye to the man who saved your life."

"I suppose."

Sheri tried to sound indifferent, but Maureen knew better. "If you don't tell him good-bye yourself, I'll find him for you and make you talk to him. He's the hero of your new series of books. You ought to part as friends."

"All right," she agreed. "But we'll worry about that later."

A knock at the door interrupted them, and Maureen opened it to find Philip waiting there.

"Good morning," she greeted him. "Sheri's all ready to go."

Sheri appeared behind her. "Hello, Philip."

His gaze was warm upon her. She was wearing a fashionable day gown and looked quite the lady. "You look lovely this morning."

189

"Why, thank you." She laughed lightly. "It's certainly an improvement over the last time you saw me, that's for sure."

"You will never look better to me than you did last night when I saw that you were alive and well," he said earnestly.

"I must admit, I was very glad to see you, too. Maureen, I'll see you a little later."

"Would you care to join us?" Philip offered, less than enthusiastically.

"No, but thank you for the invitation. I have a few things to take care of here." She didn't really, but anything would be better than putting up with him for a few hours. Sheri could go alone and enjoy herself. Maureen was sure that when her cousin returned, she would really be looking forward to seeing Brand again. The thought brought a smile to her face. "Have a good breakfast."

Philip offered her his arm, and he escorted her to the dining hall.

Sheri was greeted by the others who were eating, and then Philip directed her to a table off to one side, so they could speak quietly.

"So, how does it feel to be back in civilization?" he asked, once they'd settled in.

"It feels marvelous. I never dreamed life could be so harsh, but I really learned a lot. You soldiers certainly earn your pay."

"It's not an easy job, but there are rewards. . . ."

She looked up at him questioningly.

"Like meeting you," he said with a smile. "It has indeed been a pleasure. I'm looking forward to the book. Have you been able to write at all?"

"Oh, yes. I've gotten a few pages done here and

there. Mostly, though, I've been taking notes on everything that's happened so I won't forget anything once we head back home."

"And when will that be?"

"Maureen and I had talked about traveling back to Phoenix tomorrow and staying there a few days to get an accurate look at living in a Western town."

"So soon?" It distressed him to think that she would be leaving that quickly.

"I do need to get the book written, and I can best do that back home. Will there be a stage tomorrow?"

"Yes, there's one at midday. I had spoken with Cecelia about having another party for you tonight in celebration of the fact that you're safely back. But now, it seems, we'll have to make it a going-away party."

"That's so sweet of you. It would be wonderful to visit with everybody again before we have to go."

"We'll plan on it, then. Shall I call for you and Maureen at, say, seven o'clock?"

"That would be wonderful, thank you."

Maureen couldn't imagine who was knocking on her door so soon after Sheri had left with Philip. She had had her morning planned: As soon as she finished eating breakfast, she was going over to the hospital to visit with Charles and make sure he was all right. But now, it looked as if her plans were already being changed.

"Yes?" She opened the door to come face-to-face with Charles. He was up and fully dressed, and though still a bit pale from his ordeal, he looked quite fit. "Good morning," she said sweetly, her mood of agitation immediately disappearing at the

191

sight of him. "You're better . . ."

"Much," he answered. Then, glancing past her and seeing no one around, he added, "Now that I'm with you."

"I was planning to come to the hospital and see you in just a little while." Maureen smiled up at him. "Would you like to come in?"

"It's hardly proper, Miss Cleaver," he reminded her. "It might cause gossip."

"What can we do about that?" she teased.

"Nothing, I'm afraid. It's one thing for you to flout convention and visit me in the hospital. It's another for you, as an unmarried woman, to have me in your home unchaperoned."

"But I was hoping you'd come to collect your winnings," she said flirtatiously, looking up at him with open longing.

Charles bit back a groan that had nothing to do with pain from his injuries. "There is nothing I'd like more than to claim what is owed me, but I must protect your reputation above all else. Would you care to take a walk with me?"

"Are you strong enough?" She was still worried about him, though obviously, he had to be recovering or the doctor would not have let him go.

"Absolutely."

"Then there is no one I would rather walk with than you, sir."

She closed the door behind her, and together they strolled around the grounds.

"Sheri and I are planning on leaving the fort tomorrow and spending some time in Phoenix before we head back home."

"You're going home soon?"

"In a few days. I know there are still some things she wants to learn about in town."

"I'll be glad to show you around."

"I'd like that." She lifted her gaze to his.

"Whatever you need, just let me know." Charles stared down at Maureen, thinking of how lovely she looked and how much he was going to miss her when she was gone. She was a delightful companion, witty and intelligent, soft-spoken yet articulate. She was everything he'd ever wanted in a woman, and . . .

The realization struck him like a lightning bolt, mentally staggering him. He had only known her a few days. Granted, they'd been some of the wildest days of his life, but just in that short span of time, Charles knew that he had fallen in love. The idea was so new to him that he said nothing, wanting to take time to analyze it and understand it before he declared himself. But he did care for this woman, and he hadn't even kissed her yet. That was something he was going to have to remedy very soon.

"Is something wrong?" Maureen noticed his strange expression, a rather bemused one, and wondered at it.

"No . . . no . . . Everything's fine." He quickly changed the conversation as they continued on their walk.

As Sheri allowed Philip to escort her back to her quarters, she kept a lookout for Brand, but could see no sign of him. It didn't surprise her. From the way things had ended between them the day before, she was afraid now that she would never see him again. Later, once Philip was gone, she was going to look for him. If for no other reason than just to thank him

193

for his help and to tell him that she would be leaving the following day.

"I'll speak with Cecelia and tell her of your plans. Then I'll be back for you this evening."

"That will be fine. I'll look forward to seeing you then."

She waited a few strategic moments until he'd gone, then left to seek out Brand. Her efforts proved futile, though. Finally she saw Sergeant O'Toole and went to speak to him.

"I was hoping to speak to Brand today, sergeant. Is he around?"

"No, ma'am. He rode out early this morning, and I don't expect him back for some time." At her fleeting look of disappointment, he quickly asked, "Is there anything I can do to help you?"

"No, but thanks. I just wanted to talk to him again. Maureen and I will be heading back to Phoenix tomorrow, and I wanted to thank him for all his help."

"I'll relay the message when I see him, but I'm not sure when he'll be back. As a scout, he can come and go pretty much as he pleases, unless the captain needs him."

"Well, thank you for all your help. It was wonderful getting to know you."

"It was my pleasure. I hope your book turns out great."

She smiled at him. "It will. How can it not, when I had all your help?"

They shared a warm look of respect, and she returned to her quarters. She wondered if she would ever see Brand again.

Chapter Twelve

Brand, the Half-Breed Scout, or Trail of the Renegade
A Conflict of the Heart

Brand helped the two women onto his horse and led the animal over the treacherous, mountainous terrain. Several times in the dark of the night, he stopped to listen. His instincts were telling him that all was not as it seemed, but he could detect no one near. He started forward on again, cautiously, anxiously, eager to be away from the area.

And then it happened. . . .

Two braves who'd discovered that Rachel and Mercy were missing had given chase. They spotted

Brand as he started up a steep incline leading the horse. One tried to shoot him, but in his drunken stupor, he missed. The other drunken warrior drew his knife and charged, ready to kill Brand and reclaim his white captives.

The first shot alerted Brand to their presence, and he'd just started to turn around when he heard Rachel yell.

"Look out!"

The other warrior threw himself upon the scout, trying to slit his throat as his friend rushed to join the battle.

Rachel grabbed Brand's rifle from its sheath as she dismounted.

"Get out of here now, Mercy!" she ordered.

"But . . ."

"Go!"

Rachel slapped the horse hard, and as the other woman galloped away, she turned on the two attackers who were trying to kill Brand. She had fired a gun only occasionally in her life, but tonight it didn't matter. If she didn't help Brand, he would be dead.

She held the heavy weapon to her shoulder and aimed point-blank at the warrior who was running to help his friend. She squeezed the trigger, knowing this was a matter of life and death. . . .

The ladies of the fort were not quite sure what to make of all that had happened. They were attending the party that evening because they were pleased that the two visiting women were safe. However, they still had serious reservations about the state of Sheridan St. John's reputation after two nights and three days alone in the wild with the half-breed. They stood in one corner of the room watching Sheri as she made the rounds, speaking with everyone while Philip hovered solicitously over her.

"Miss St. John certainly seems to have weathered her adventure quite well. She looks lovely tonight."

"I don't know, Cecelia," Dora Lawson said snidely. "How can she even hold her head up? I mean she slept with that . . . that man! How could she stand it?"

"I hope you mean 'slept' with and nothing more, Dora," Laura Walker put in sternly. "She appears unharmed, and she has certainly been singing Brand's praises ever since they got back. He did save her life, you know. I think you're being quite catty and tasteless with what you're implying."

Dora looked huffy. "I'm just commenting as any good-living person would."

"Are you saying, because renegades attacked their party, she's no longer a good woman?"

"I'm merely saying that she should, perhaps, be a little more reserved in her celebrations, that's all. God only knows what happened to her during that time with him."

"I assure you, she knows and so does he, and neither of them is talking. So why don't you just be kind and believe that he was a gentleman and did protect her virtue and her honor?"

"The breed was a gentleman?" Dora exclaimed in low, outraged tones. "Don't you think that's asking a bit too much?"

"You're impossible."

"No, I'm realistic. She just spent two nights alone with a man who's more Indian than white."

"Dora!"

"It's true! Don't you ever look at him? He dresses like an Indian and he acts like one, too!"

"In case you've forgotten, he was married to the colonel's daughter. He is not a heathen."

"So you say," she replied in a huff. "We shall see. I say she's leaving the fort so soon because she's afraid we'll all figure out what really happened while they were alone out there. Face it, ladies, if it had been one of your daughters who was lost in the wilds with him, you'd be reacting quite differently."

"You're right, Dora, but it wasn't one of our daughters. Miss St. John chose to go of her own accord. It was her decision. She alone will live with the consequences."

"Her 'adventure', as you call it, doesn't seem to have affected Philip's regard for her. He still seems quite taken with her—in spite of everything," Laura pointed out.

"I think Philip is most taken with the thought of seeing himself as a hero in one of her books," Dora said knowingly. "You know how highly he regards himself."

The other two women laughed lightly.

"I think you're right about that."

"Then we do agree on something tonight?"

"We do."

Sheri was enjoying the party more than she'd thought she would. She kept watching for Brand, though, and there had been no sign of him. It distressed her to think that she would leave the fort and never get to see him again. If nothing else, she did want to tell him good-bye and thank him once more for saving her.

"Good evening, Cecelia. Dora. Hello, Laura," Sheri greeted the women as she came to speak with them. "Thank you for the party tonight. It's wonderful to see everyone again."

"What's wonderful is that you're back, safe and sound."

"I know," Sheri said with a smile. "No one's happier about that than I am. It was an adventure."

The ladies shared a private knowing look at her use of the word.

"I'll say," Dora said primly. "How did you manage, my dear? I doubt I would have lived through it."

"It was difficult and frightening at times, but with Brand there, I knew everything was going to be all right."

"Yes . . . Brand . . ." The disapproval was plain in Dora's voice. "I still don't know how you slept, knowing the breed was right there next to you. . . ."

Sheri glanced at the portly, gray-haired matron, taken aback by her venom. "I wouldn't have slept at all, if 'the breed', as you call him, hadn't been there beside me. I would have been dead."

"I just wouldn't say that too loudly, if I were you."

"Say what too loudly?" She couldn't imagine what this vicious little woman was getting at.

"About sleeping with him, dear. Your reputation, you know . . ."

"My reputation? My reputation is just fine. I'm alive and well thanks to Brand's bravery."

"If you say so."

"I do." Fire flared in her eyes as she regarded the women. "Brand is a wonderful scout and a good man. There aren't many like him. I respect and admire him. He deserves no less."

"I'm sure you're right, Sheri," Cecelia interjected, wanting to calm the discussion. "Dora was just concerned about you, that's all."

Sheri doubted that. She knew better. She'd dealt with small-minded women like Dora all her life, and she didn't have time to waste on them anymore. She was barely in control of her temper as she said, "I appreciate your concern, but there's really no need for any of you to be worried. Brand is an honorable man, and I trust him implicitly."

"Of course, my dear," all three women quickly responded.

"If you'll excuse me?"

With that, Sheri turned her back on them and walked way. She was furious with them for their small-minded ways, but she knew she shouldn't have been so surprised by it. She'd been dealing with this kind of thing from other women ever since she'd started her writing career.

Their criticism of Brand, though, had really angered her, and she was glad she'd defended him. She now understood why he hadn't come to the party tonight. Why would he want to subject himself to people with that kind of attitude? Obviously, they were never going to let him forget that he had Apache blood in his veins, no matter how much they needed his talent for tracking when the time came.

Sheri was glad to see that Philip was deep in conversation with one of the other officers. If he was distracted, it would be easy for her to slip away outside to get a breath of fresh air—and to calm down.

As she left the house and moved a short distance

away from the lights, the night sky sparkled above her. She stared up at it, remembering her desire to spend a night camping out to get the real flavor of a scout. She'd gotten her wish all right, and then some.

Her smile was sad, and she walked a little farther, wanting to separate herself from the ugliness she'd just experienced inside. She had wanted to enjoy this last night at the fort, not spend it worrying over what everyone was saying about her and Brand.

Sheri never knew what it was that drew her attention across the parade ground, but she found herself staring into the shadows at the barely visible image of the man who stood there. She didn't speak but walked toward him, knowing it was Brand even before she could clearly see him.

"It's a pretty night out," she said softly as she came to stand before him. She gazed up at him, studying his chiseled features, softened now in the moonlight. He was handsome, magnificently so, and she could sense the barely leashed power in him. Yet his expression was shuttered, revealing no emotion. She couldn't tell whether he was glad to see her or not. "You like being outside better than being at a party?"

"Don't you?" he countered.

"Tonight, yes." She tried to forget how angry she'd just been with the narrow-minded women. "How's your arm?"

"It was only a scratch." He did not want her concern.

"Well, anyway, I'm glad I found you. I wanted to tell you good-bye and thank you again for all you did for me. You were a great help."

"You're leaving." It was a flat statement.

"Tomorrow. Maureen and I are going into Phoenix. We're planning to stay there for a few days and take a look around town. Then we'll be heading back to New York."

Brand stared at her, knowing what a rare woman she was. He had not forgotten her kiss or her touch. He couldn't. It had been for that very reason that he'd stayed away from her since they'd been rescued. She was beautiful, soft, and sweet; yet she had enough spirit and strength of will to make her a match for any man. She had suffered his worst temper and had not flinched before him. He admired her, and more. . . .

And it was for that very reason that he had to let her go.

But she was lovely. As he looked down at her, he tried to resist the temptation to kiss her just once more. He remembered far too clearly how her last kiss had affected him, and he knew it was dangerous. But after tomorrow, she would disappear from his life and he would never see her again. He wanted . . . no, he needed, just one last fleeting taste of her sweet innocence before she was gone. . . .

"Sheri . . ." He said her name softly.

"Oh, Brand . . ." Sheri looked up at him and saw the flaring emotion in his shadowed gaze. She was leaving. They would never be together again. She knew in that one fleeting instant that she had to have the memory of one more kiss to take with her. Sheri forgot all the harsh things he'd said to her in the cave. She remembered only the pleasure of his embrace and how much she'd come to care for him.

Taking a step nearer, she stood on tiptoe to press her lips to his. Her kiss was sweet and gentle, but she knew it could be so much more.

Brand's control was iron; he would accept her kiss and no more. Then he tasted the sweetness of her, and her heady scent surrounded him, and his rigid control snapped. His arms came around her, crushing her to his chest as his mouth plundered hers with passion's intent. He wanted her . . . damn, but he wanted her. . . .

Sheri responded fully to his heated embrace. She had wanted this, had longed for this. She gloried in the feel of his hard body against hers, and she wanted to know more. Even as she thought it, though, she knew she had to stop. Though he might want her for a moment, now, in the shadowy moonlight, she knew the truth of his feelings. This wasn't the Brand of her imagination. This was the real, live Brand who was so much more exciting and intriguing and dangerous to her sensibilities. With all the willpower she could muster, she drew away from him, stepping free of his embrace. She gazed up at him in the moonlight, her heart breaking.

"Good-bye, Brand," she said in a whisper.

And then she was gone.

Brand stood unmoving as he watched her go. He was tempted to go after her, to stop her and ask her to stay. But he didn't. He couldn't. He kept watch over her until she disappeared back inside the party; then he turned and walked off into the night. It was better this way. She would be safe and happy back East writing her books.

"There's Sheri," Maureen said to Charles as she caught sight of her cousin coming in the door. "I guess she just needed a breath of fresh air."

"I could use one, too . . . if you're in the mood to

accompany me for, say, a stroll in the moonlight?"

She glanced up at him archly. "Are you planning on making me pay up tonight?"

"It had been on my mind."

There was an intimacy to his smile that sent a thrill coursing through her.

"Mine, too," she said, sounding slightly breathless.

"Shall we go outside?"

She nodded and took his arm as he led her out into the night. They moved a little away from the lights and noise of the house, wanting a moment or two alone, just the two of them.

"Beautiful," Maureen said, gazing up at the star-spangled sky.

"Yes," he agreed.

She cast a sidelong glance at him to find that he wasn't looking up, but was looking straight at her.

"Oh . . ."

Charles gently took her in his arms and drew her to him. "I've been wanting to do this for days now . . ."

There, under the stars, he kissed her.

Maureen didn't know why she was surprised by the passion in his kiss. Perhaps it was because he was always so logical and controlled in everyday dealings. But there was nothing logical or controlled about his embrace, and she loved it. His mouth slanted over hers with heated possession. She looped her arms around his neck, wanting to be even closer to him. Encouraged by her move, he deepened the kiss.

The sound of distant voices intruded as someone left the party early, and Charles was forced to release Maureen. He moved a respectable distance away, so no one would suspect that he had just been collecting his "winnings."

Maureen felt almost bereft when he released her so suddenly.

"We have company," he said quietly.

Had there been more light, Charles would have seen that Maureen was blushing quite prettily.

"I was so busy worrying about paying off my gambling debt that I completely forgot myself."

"I'm glad you did. I certainly enjoyed myself."

"I'm just glad your hearing is better than mine." She slanted him a smile that promised much.

"We'd better go back in, don't you think?"

"I'm afraid so. Who knows? Sheri may be needing us to rescue her from Philip."

"I wonder where Brand is?"

"I don't know, and that's too bad. I know she wanted to tell him good-bye before we left for town tomorrow."

"Maybe she'll get to see him in the morning."

As the evening came to a close, Sheri found the ever-attentive Philip at her side.

"May I escort you back to your quarters?" he asked gallantly.

"Thank you. I'd like that," she answered, silently giving thanks that after tomorrow she would never have to deal with him again.

She thanked Cecelia and the captain for hosting the party, and they left with Charles and Maureen following.

"It was a lovely evening. Thank you for thinking of it," she complimented Philip.

"It was my pleasure. I'm just glad that everything turned out so well."

"It has."

"Is there anything more I can help you with? Anything else you need to know about the workings of the fort or about the cavalry?" he asked chivalrously.

"I believe I've got everything, but I'll be sure to write you if I think of something else I need to know."

"It would be my pleasure to help."

She smiled up at him. "You've been a big help already. I know this book is going to be wonderful."

"I wish you every success with it."

"Thank you."

"Who knows? Maybe you'll want to come back again and research another."

"You never know. Charles is going to help us in town when we go to Phoenix for a few days," she said, encouraging the other couple to join in the conversation.

"I thought I'd show them how the newspaper office runs and a few other things around town."

"I hope it all goes well for you."

They reached their quarters, and Charles bade them all good night.

"I'll see you in the morning. The stage leaves about one o'clock, so we'll have to be ready by then."

"We'll be ready," Maureen told him. "And thank you for a lovely evening."

"It was my pleasure," Charles told her with a slight bow, meaning every word. "Good night."

Maureen went on inside after telling Philip good night, too, but she left the door ajar so Sheri was not forced to be totally alone with him.

"Well, I'd better go inside now. Again, thank you for all that you've done."

"I'll see you in the morning?" he asked hopefully.

"I'm sure."

He started to move toward her as if to kiss her, but Sheri was too quick for him. She stepped through the door and effectively cut him off.

"Good night."

Philip understood her reluctance and attributed it to her being a lady. Still, he would have liked to kiss her. He thought her quite attractive, and he was more than eager to earn a place in her book. He was, after all, the dashing cavalry officer who'd rescued her from almost certain death in the desert mountains. He felt confident as he swaggered back to his own quarters smiling.

Brand had not meant to watch, but when he saw Sheri emerge on the lieutenant's arm, he couldn't look away. He had stayed out of sight, feeling a little like a renegade before a raid as he'd watched the officer take her home and then attempt to kiss her. He couldn't believe how much it had pleased him when Sheri effectively out-maneuvered the lieutenant. He had stayed there until she was safely inside with the curtains closed, and then he disappeared into the darkness.

Brand knew he should never have kissed her, but there had been no helping it. The finality of realizing that she was leaving and he would never see her again was haunting him. He told himself that it was what he wanted. He wanted her out of his life. She'd caused nothing but chaos since she'd shown up. Yet a part of him wanted to spend more time with her, wanted to get to know her better. It was not to be.

Agitated and knowing he wouldn't be able to sleep, Brand saddled his horse and rode from the fort. As a scout, he had more liberty of movement than the regular troops. He knew that as long as he returned before the next scout went out, no one would care that he'd gone.

Surrounded by the night, Brand rode aimlessly across the land. At first, he hadn't been sure where he was heading, but as the night aged, his traveling took on purpose and direction. It had been a long time since he'd returned there, but he knew he had to go.

The wee hours of the morning found him back at his old ranch, still deserted and forsaken. He had not visited Becky's grave in several years. There had seemed no point. For all that her body might be there, she was not. She was gone from him forever.

Brand dismounted and made his way to the grave site. He found it easily and stood over it, thinking about Becky and the love they'd shared. It had been an idyllic time for him, and it had ended far too soon. But that had been years ago. He had carried the pain of her loss with him every day since. It would never go away, but it seemed to be changing. He wondered now, as he thought of Sheri and the feelings she aroused in him, if he just might be able to come to care for someone again.

The idea was foreign to him. He had vowed never to let that happen; yet somehow Sheri had slipped passed his guard. He didn't know how she'd done it, whether by pure grit and determination or what, but she had.

An image of her danced in his thoughts and surprised him. He had expected his thoughts to be filled with Becky, yet Sheri was the woman whose face was mirrored in his mind's eye, whose kiss he longed for, and whose smile touched his heart.

He turned away from the grave and slowly mounted up again. He sat on his horse watching the sunrise. It was a new day, but could he start a new life? He had no answer.

Chapter Thirteen

Brand, the Half-Breed Scout, or Trail of the Renegade
The Plot Thickens

The force of the gunshot sent Rachel staggering backward. She looked up to find the warrior wounded, but still on his feet. He was advancing on her, knife in hand. Rachel lifted the rifle to fire again, but he attacked before she could pull the trigger. Brand was fighting the renegade who'd attacked him when he heard the gunshot. In a burst of fury, thinking something had happened to Rachel and Mercy, he overpowered and killed the warrior, then charged to his feet, gun drawn to go to their aid. He saw the brave lunge at Rachel and

wanted to shoot, but he couldn't get a clear shot.
He was there in an instant, dragging the warrior
away from her. When the renegade turned on him,
Brand shot him dead.

"Rachel . . ." he said her name in a strangled
voice as he hurried to her side to find that she'd
been stabbed.

He tore a strip of cloth from her gown to fashion
a bandage to stop the bleeding. There were still a
few hours left until daylight, but he needed to get
a better look at Rachel's wound. She gave a moan
of pain as he gathered her up in his arms.

"Brand?" she asked as she opened her eyes to
find herself in his arms. "Are you all right?"

"You saved my life," he told her.

She smiled weakly. "I'm glad."

"I'll get you out of here," he promised.

"I know," she sighed.

Carefully carrying her, he headed for a small
cave he knew was close. He could keep her safe
there and better tend to her wounds.

As he moved off slowly through the night, Brand
worried about the captain's wife. She was on
horseback, alone in territory she didn't know. He
knew the dangers that could befall her and knew
he had to find her fast, before anything happened
to her. . . .

Sheri watched out the window of the stage until the
last vestige of Fort McDowell was lost from sight.
Brand had not appeared that morning to say good-
bye, and as she settled back into her seat, she was

careful not to let any of her disappointment show in her expression.

"Well, we're finally on our way back to civilization," Maureen said lightly, looking forward to being back in town. "Are you going to miss the fort?"

"Not after last night," Sheri replied, still remembering the wives' comments at the party. "It will be nice to be in town." She looked at Charles, who was recovering very nicely from his wound. "I'll bet you're going to be glad to be back in your office."

"It's got to be safer for me, that's for sure," he answered with a smile.

"You are feeling better, aren't you?" Sheri asked.

"My shoulder's still very sore and I'm sure it's going to be stiff for a while, but yes, I am much stronger."

"Good," she said with a smile. "I expect the forty-cent tour of Phoenix from you as soon as you're up to it."

"We can start tomorrow. Tonight, however, I'd like to take you both to dinner, if you'd honor me with your presence?"

"Why, Charles, that's so nice of you."

"We'd be delighted," Maureen answered without hesitation.

They fell into a companionable silence, suffering the jostling of the stage as it traveled the distance to town.

Sheri stared sightlessly out the window. Memories of the last week played in her mind—of Brand the first time she'd seen him in town, looking very much the warrior, of Brand's surprise at her finding the renegades' tracks and of how he'd saved her life that day. She thought of their first night in the cave and of how he'd kept watch so vigilantly to keep her safe from harm. She recalled far too vividly for her peace of mind the fighting and how she'd shot the renegade to save Brand's life. She remembered, too, his tenderness that night in the darkness of the cave . . . and the glory of his touch. For as long as she lived, Brand would always be in her thoughts and in her heart. She knew the difference now between the Brand of her story and the real Brand, but it was too late. She was leaving, and he didn't care.

Sheri was so lost in her memories that she did not see the lone rider who sat atop a hill in the distance, watching the stage's passage. She did not know that Brand had come to say good-bye.

Phoenix was alive with activity, and Sheri, Maureen, and Charles were glad when they arrived at the stage office. Charles was favoring his injury a bit as he descended, the jarring ride having taken its toll on him. He made sure Maureen and Sheri were safely at the hotel before retiring to his own home to get some much-needed rest and to begin writing his column for the paper.

Charles met them, and they dined early that night. When they returned to the hotel, Maureen stopped with Sheri outside the door to her room. Maureen sensed something was wrong, and she wanted to help if she could.

"You're going to miss Brand, aren't you?" Maureen asked perceptively.

"I thought you were going up to your room."

"I am, just as soon as I'm sure you're going to be all right."

"I'm fine."

"Are you sure?"

"Of course. When haven't I been fine?"

"But with Brand, it seems different somehow."

"He was different. I've never met anyone like him before. He was honest and brave and . . ."

"Do you love him?"

The question surprised her. "I don't know, but even if I did, what would it matter? He has his life here." There was a weary acceptance in her voice. "What about Charles? How do you feel about him?"

"We weren't talking about me, we were talking about you."

"Then there's nothing more to say. I'm going to go home and write my *Brand, the Half-Breed Scout* book, and live happily ever after, just like my heroines."

"And your book's going to sell better than Carroll and Condon ever dreamed!"

"You always say just the right thing."

"I like to make you happy."

Sheri lifted her gaze to her cousin's. "I don't know if I'll ever be happy again."

"Sure you will. You'll see." Maureen hugged her impulsively.

"I hope you're right, but right now, I'm not sure."

Maureen went on into her room. Sheri reached her own room, but instead of sleeping, she got out her paper and pencils and stayed up until the wee hours of the morning writing. She wanted to get down on paper all the turbulent emotions that were tearing at her heart. She could use them in her work. She would make this her most powerful book. She wanted the hero to be bigger than life, and he would be. This was Brand's book. She would make sure it was perfect—for him.

The next day, Charles met them at mid-morning and gave them a tour of the *Salt River Herald*'s office. He introduced them to his boss, Jeremy Davis. Jeremy was an older, silver-haired man, who was quite taken with Sheri and her career, and he plied her with many questions about the publishing industry. Afterward, they walked the streets of Phoenix, stopping at the blacksmith's and the dry goods store, and even peeking in the window of a saloon, just so Sheri could get the feel of a real Western town. The oil portrait of the robust, naked, reclining woman over the bar brought a blush to her cheeks. She took a lot of notes that day, intending to use most of the information in one way or another in the story. It was mid-afternoon when they stopped at the jail to meet the sheriff.

"Sheriff Warren, this is Miss Sheridan St. John and her cousin, Maureen Cleaver, of New York. Miss St. John is a novelist, and she's in town doing research for her next book," Charles explained as they stepped inside the office.

"I've been hearing talk that you were in the area," the sheriff said as he rose from his desk and went to greet them. "Would you like to see the jail?"

"If you wouldn't mind," Sheri said sweetly, intrigued by the thought.

He guided them through the small office area, showing them where he kept his weapons, ammunition, and keys, then on into the back room, where there were two cells. Each cell was furnished with only an uncomfortable-looking cot. They were stark, cold reminders of what the lawless had to suffer. A double-locked door at the end of the walkway in front of the cells gave access to the alley.

Sheri was glad to get out of there. "Do you have much crime in Phoenix, sheriff?"

"Nothing too exciting, but we're ready if anything ever does happen."

"I appreciate you showing us around," Sheri told him as they started from the office.

"Any time. Say, Charles, what happened to your shoulder?" Sheriff Warren asked, noticing how he was favoring it.

"We had a run-in with some renegades out at the fort."

"You hurt bad?"

"It wasn't fun, but I'm going to live."

"Well, that's good to hear."

They headed back toward the hotel.

"Is there anything else you wanted to see?" Charles asked.

Sheri had been quiet and thoughtful for a while, and she surprised him with her answer. "There is one more place I'd like to visit, but I'm not sure if it's possible."

"What's that?"

"You had mentioned to me that Brand's wife was killed at their ranch. Could we possibly ride out to the homestead and take a look around?"

"We can do that if you want."

"Is it very far?"

"It's an hour or two ride, so it's too late to go today. Why don't we go in the morning? That will give us the whole day."

"Are you sure you're up to it?" Maureen worried.

"I'll be fine," he assured her. "I'll see about getting us horses. Shall we meet at the stable at eight-thirty? Will that give you time enough in the morning?"

"That'll be fine."

"Would you like to have dinner tonight?"

"I want to work, but . . . Maureen?" Sheri looked at her cousin.

"I'd love to have dinner with you," Maureen said, smiling at Charles.

"I'll see you a little later then."

Maureen and Charles spent the evening together, sharing a quiet dinner. His feelings for her were growing ever stronger, yet he held himself back from saying anything. They had only known each other for the better part of a week, and he knew it would be far too bold to speak of his feelings just yet.

Still, Maureen would be leaving soon, and Charles couldn't let her go without telling her how he felt. He would bide his time and wait for the right moment—if it ever came. He had some doubts about that. She was an Eastern lady, who'd made it clear from the first time they'd met that she missed her home in New York and couldn't wait to get back. He was a small-town newspaperman, and he was happy there in the Territory. The pay wasn't good and he would never have a lot of money, but if love was counted as riches, Maureen would be a wealthy woman.

Charles gave her a perfunctory kiss on the cheek in the hotel lobby when they parted company, and he watched until she was upstairs before going home for the night. He found himself imagining what it would be like to take her home with him. He liked the thought.

The following morning they met at the stables and rode for Brand's long-deserted ranch. It was a warm day, but not overly so. Charles told them more history of the area and of the Indian fighting as they made the trip.

"We're almost there," Charles announced when they started up the low rise. "It's just on the other side of this hill."

As they topped it, Sheri reined in to stare at the scene below. All that remained of Brand and Becky's shattered dream was the burned skeleton of their house. In Sheri's imagination, she could see and hear and feel all that had happened that night. The attack, the terror, the fire . . . and finally death. She let her gaze sweep over the area, studying the landscape with a writer's eye, seeing the desolate miles of desert with no sign of life or hope. Then, slowly, she urged her mount forward, leaving Charles and Maureen to follow.

Sheri dismounted and with quiet intent approached what little was left of the house. She tried to imagine what Brand had experienced when he'd returned to find the life he'd worked so hard to create for himself and his wife destroyed. Remaining silent, Sheri listened for the sound of the wind and the call of the birds. She told herself she was paying so much attention to detail, because she wanted to be realistic when she wrote about the fictional Brand's background. But, in truth, she had come here today not so much to research the book, but to try to find answers that would help her understand the real Brand.

Making her way around the site, Sheri found the grave by accident, and it startled her. She hadn't considered that Brand might have buried Becky there, but there was no denying that the mounded rocks definitely marked a grave site.

"Maureen . . . Charles . . ." she called out to them softly.

They came to her side.

"This must be Becky's grave. It must have been so terrible for Brand, coming home to find everything destroyed and his wife murdered."

"Did you know that she was pregnant at the time?" Charles asked, recalling more of the tragedy.

"No . . ." Sheri was aghast at the thought. She stared down at the grave, wishing there was some way she could erase all the tragedy, and knowing there wasn't.

Maureen paled at the revelation. "No wonder he's so driven to hunt renegades."

Charles and Maureen moved off to look at something else, and Sheri remained standing there over the grave, thinking of the handsome young man who'd lost his love that day all those years ago. She knew Becky had been a very lucky woman to have had Brand's devotion.

Driven by some emotion she couldn't name, Sheri knelt down beside the grave and touched the rocks that covered it. She prayed that Becky was happy in a better world than the one she'd left and that Brand would somehow find happiness again. Rising slowly, she turned and walked back to where her horse was tethered.

"Are you ready?" Charles called out.

"When you are."

They made their way back to the horses and mounted up for the return trip to town.

Brand told himself he was crazy. He told himself it was ridiculous that he was doing this, that he was

219

asking for trouble, but he couldn't help himself. Sheri was haunting him. Her spirit . . . Her intelligence . . . Her tears . . . Her kiss . . . He had dressed as a white man, and he was riding into Phoenix to see her one last time.

The trip seemed to take longer than it ever had before. Mile after endless mile stretched out before him, and by the time he reached town, it was dark.

He wasn't sure exactly what he was going to say once he found her. He just knew he couldn't bear to let her go without seeing her again.

Reining in near the hotel, Brand tied up his horse and mentally girded himself to meet her. He started toward the main hotel entrance, then changed his mind as he heard the music from the Gold Bar Saloon down the street. The thought of a whiskey right then appealed greatly, so he altered his course and went into the saloon to get a drink before going on to see Sheri.

It was crowded, and quite a few heads turned as he walked in. He might be dressed as the other men were, but he was still part Indian. They never let him forget it.

"Whiskey," Brand ordered as he took a place at the bar.

The barkeep set a shot before him, and he paid for the drink. He took one appreciative sip, savoring the power of the liquor, then quickly downed the rest. It burned all the way down, and he was glad. He needed the power and fearlessness whiskey would give him tonight.

"You want another?" the bartender asked, seeing how fast the first one had disappeared.

Brand nodded and waited while the man poured

more of the potent liquor into his glass. Logic told him he should get back on his horse and ride out of town. He had no business seeing Sheri again. Beautiful though she might be. Drawn to her though he was. If he truly cared about her, he should leave and never look back. Trouble was, a part of him ached to be near her, to see her smile, to hold her and kiss her once more.

He picked up the glass and took a deep drink. He stared straight ahead, not paying attention to anyone or anything. He was too caught up in deciding what to do. She was close. Just a short distance away. All he had to do was go to her. He wasn't sure what he would say once he was there, but he had to do it. . . . Brand finished the shot and pushed the glass toward the barkeep for one more refill.

It was about fifteen minutes and two more drinks later that the sound of the drunken man's voice rose above the regular noise of the crowd in the saloon.

"It's him, I tell you. He's the one from the fort."

"Shut up, Hale."

"I ain't gonna shut up. Somebody needs to set the bastard straight. With what he's been gettin' away with all these years . . ."

"I came out for a drink, Hale. Not for a fight."

"To hell with you then. I'll tell him to his face what I think!"

The man named Hale separated himself from a knot of drunks at the end of the bar and staggered toward Brand. The look in his beady black eyes was mean as he stared at Brand.

"You're that breed scout, ain't ya?" he demanded, stopping about three feet from where Brand stood at the bar.

221

Brand had heard the sound of their argument, but had ignored it. He had other things on his mind . . . more important things. He didn't care if these people liked him or not. They meant nothing in his life. All that mattered was finding Sheri.

"You! Breed! I'm talkin' to you!" Hale shouted.

Brand turned his head to look at the man. He kept his expression carefully guarded. "You want something, mister?" He remained calm and cool, not wanting to provoke the drunk in any way.

"Yeah, I want something. You're the one from the fort, aren't you? Your name's Brand, ain't it?"

"That's right."

Hale looked over at his drunken companions and smiled broadly. "Told ya it was him. Told ya it was the one keeps makin' whores outta white women . . ."

Brand stiffened at his statement, and the expression in his eyes turned deadly.

"What'sa matter, injun? Cat got your tongue? Don't ya like hearin' the truth?" he sneered, then looked over confidently at his companions. "He ain't got nothing to say for himself, 'cause he knows it's the truth. He likes them white women. . . . He likes that white meat. First, you put it to the colonel's daughter, and now this little gal from back East—"

He got no further.

"I'm going to kill you, you son of a bitch," Brand seethed, the liquor having eroded his usual rigid self-control. This man was talking about Becky and Sheri! He wasn't even good enough to be in the same room with them, let alone call them whores! He lunged at the drunk in a move that was so swift and so deadly, none of those around could believe it.

Chaos erupted as Brand fought with the man. The drunk put up a good fight, but Brand was beyond fury. He wanted the man dead for the things he'd said. He would have continued to throttle him, possibly even killing him bare-handed, had not strong hands torn him from his bloody retribution.

"Brand! Stop it!" Philip ordered as he and Colonel Hancock got a grip on him and dragged him away.

It had been pure coincidence that they had walked into the Gold Bar at that particular moment and heard the exchange between the two.

"Let's get him out of here!" Hancock snarled sternly, furious over the situation.

Together, they all but dragged the still struggling Brand from the saloon. They forced him down the sidewalk away from the entrance, wanting him as far away from the troublemaking drunk as possible.

"Brand! Get yourself under control!" Hancock ordered.

Philip had always known that Brand would be a vicious enemy, but he'd had no idea the scout was such a powerful man. He seriously doubted that he could have controlled Brand had the colonel not been there to help. Not that he blamed Brand for his anger. He, too, had been outraged by the drunk's ugliness.

As his bloodlust eased, Brand slowly stopped fighting them. When he had calmed, he shook himself free of their restraining hold and faced them. His expression was still murderous, for he had not forgotten the insults the man had cast upon Becky and Sheri. In the semi-darkness, he glared angrily at the two officers who'd stopped him. They regarded each other in silence for a long, tense moment; then he turned and stalked away.

Philip had been tense and ready for trouble. He breathed a little easier once Brand had gone. "I'm glad we broke that up. I was afraid he might actually kill the man."

"He was angry enough," Hancock agreed. "Are you still ready for that drink?"

"I think I could use a double now."

They went back inside.

It was some time later when Hale staggered out of the Gold Bar Saloon. He was drunk, mad, and sore as hell after his fight with the half-breed.

"I coulda beaten the bastard if they'd just let me alone with him," he snarled out loud, talking to himself. "They shoulda let me kill him while I had the chance . . . The way he's always after white women . . . 'Course, any white woman who'd have him is a slut, but that don't matter none . . . No breed should be touchin' a white woman . . ."

There was no one to hear his drunken ramblings. The streets were deserted. All was quiet. Lurching unsteadily, he started toward home. He angled down an alley that was a short cut, unaware of anything save the need to reach his own bed.

A shadowy figure stalked Hale at a distance, taking care to avoid notice. The wicked blade of the lethal-looking knife he carried glinted in the pale moonlight. When Hale ventured into the seclusion of the alley, he knew it was time to strike. He was cautious in his attack. Surprise meant everything. Silently, he closed on the drunk, and in a swift and deadly assault, he ended the man's life. The only sound was that of his lifeless body collapsing to the ground, his throat slit.

Satisfied that Hale had gotten what he'd deserved, his murderer wiped the blood from his weapon onto the dead man's shirt and then backed away, disappearing into the night, leaving no trace of his presence.

Chapter Fourteen

**Brand, the Half-Breed Scout, or Trail of the Renegade
The Return**

Mercy had heard the gunshot and had ridden as fast as she could in the opposite direction to escape. But then when silence fell like a pall over the area, she knew she had to go back. She couldn't just ride off and leave them behind. She was a cavalry captain's wife. She owed allegiance to the man who'd tried to save her and to the woman who'd bravely stayed to fight. Mercy headed back. She might be signing her death warrant, but it didn't matter. All that mattered was helping the others.

Riding slowly and as quietly as she could, Mercy neared the site of the attack. She reined in and dismounted. After tying the horse to a bush, she traveled the rest of the way on foot. She wanted the element of surprise on her side. The night was dark. As silently as possible, she moved among the rocks and cacti vigilantly searching for some sign of her companions, some clue as to their fate. . . .

Sheri was irritated. She had retired early again just so she'd have some time to write, but for some reason her characters weren't talking to her tonight. The book had been moving along so smoothly for a while that the story seemed to be telling itself. Now, for some reason, she couldn't think of a thing for them to say or do. In frustration, she threw down the paper and pencil and stood up to stretch. She was tired, but it was more emotional than physical. Visiting Brand's ranch that day had touched her deeply.

Brand . . .

An image of him seared through her thoughts, and she felt a great sadness in her heart. She would be leaving Phoenix soon, and they would never meet again. He was gone from her life, just like Buck McCade. The trouble was, Buck had been a fantasy and Brand was real. Too real for her own inner peace . . .

Sheri moved to stand at the window, hoping for a cool breeze to refresh her. The night was still, though. Nothing was stirring. She parted the sheer curtain to look out into the darkness, and it was then that she saw him—a shadowy figure across the way, watching her.

"Brand . . ." she said his name in a breathless invitation as her soul instantly recognized him. He was there. . . . He had come to her. . . .

Sheri let the curtain fall and backed away from the window, unsure of exactly what to do next. She was dressed for bed in her nightgown and wrapper, but if Brand was there and wanted to see her, she would certainly put on a daygown and go downstairs to meet him. Rushing to her trunk, she hurried to open it and pull out a suitable gown. She had just started to untie the sash of her wrapper when a feeling came over her that she wasn't alone, and she stopped. Slowly, she turned to find Brand standing in her room just inside the window.

"You came. . . ." she said in soft amazement. His presence seemed to fill the room.

"I had to see you again," he said with an intensity that came from the depths of his soul. His gaze was warm upon her. Silhouetted as she was by the lamp on the table behind her, he could see the outline of her lush curves through the silken garments she wore. A tight ache grew within him.

Sheri let the daygown drop from her hands as she took a tentative step toward him. He had come to her because he'd wanted to. No one had forced him or ordered him there.

"I'm glad," she said gently. Then she noticed a slight cut near his left eye and a little swelling. She reached up to gently touch the injury. "You're hurt. . . . What happened?"

"Nothing. That's not important." He trapped her wrist in a gentle hold as he gazed down at her. She was beauty and innocence and fire and spirit. She had matched him in every challenge and had torn down the walls he'd built to shield himself from the pain of feeling again. He knew it was crazy. He knew he shouldn't be here, but sometimes logic failed. His heart told him this was right, and that was all that mattered.

"What is important?" Sheri asked breathlessly as she gazed up at him. She could see the heat in his blue-eyed gaze, and she felt an answering fire flame to life within her.

"This . . ."

His mouth swooped down to claim hers in a passionate, long-denied exchange. He had ached for her. He had wanted her for so long. He needed this. He needed her. . . .

Brand crushed her to him as his mouth claimed its plunder. He could very well have closed his eyes and forgotten everything, but he had to be sure that this was what she wanted, too.

"Sheri . . ." His voice was hoarse with passion as he fought for control. He drew slightly away, still holding her by the shoulders, his eyes boring into hers. "If you want me to go, say so now."

"Stay with me, Brand. . . ." She whispered her most fervent dream.

It was all the invitation he needed. His control shattered and with a low growl of desire, he clasped her to his heart as their lips met. The moment was pure ecstasy.

Sheri lifted her arms and looped them around his neck, drawing him even closer. She had never known such rapture. His kiss in the cave had been powerful and stirring, but this tenderness and passion he was showing her now were even more exciting. When she wrote her books, she'd always described the hero and heroine's kisses as passionate, but she'd never known the true meaning of the word until now. Now, she understood the driving desire that could make a woman forget who she was and what she was doing. She wanted Brand . . . had wanted him since he'd first touched her in the cave, and she could not get enough of being close to him. The heat of him . . . The hardness of him . . . Caught up in a firestorm of desire, she felt an aching yearning coiled deep within the womanly heart of her.

Brand felt the eagerness in her and he began to caress her. When he'd been standing in the shadows of the alley and had seen her in the window, he'd known he wanted her more than he'd wanted any woman. She had been a silken silhouette with the filmy wrapper offering her her only protection from the searing heat of his gaze. Her hair was down, flowing about her shoulders in a tumble of pale curls, and he lifted his hands now to rake them through the silken tresses. She was beauty and fire and all woman, and he needed her. He wanted to bury himself within the heated sheath of her body and know the pleasure of being one with her.

His hands caressed her, skimming over her full curves, coming to rest on her rounded hips. He held her tightly to him, letting her feel the power of his need for her.

Sheri felt the strength of him pressed against her, and she instinctively moved against his hardness, innocently enticing him and encouraging him.

"Are you sure you want this to happen?" he asked as he pressed heated kisses to her throat.

"I want you, Brand. That's all that matters."

He lifted her up in his arms then, and carried her to her bed. Gently laying her upon it, he followed her down. Brand stretched out beside her so he could study her. His gaze raked hungrily over her. High color stained her cheeks at his bold assessment.

"What are you looking at?" Sheri asked, a little embarrassed to find him staring at her so intently.

"You," he said, leaning over to press a hot kiss to her throat.

Sheri murmured a welcoming sound as tingles of delight coursed through her. She had never been in bed with a man before, and she was as excited as she was frightened. Common sense dictated that she get up and send him from the room now, while there was still time to save herself. But Sheri had no desire to save herself from Brand. He was the man she'd waited all her life to love. She wanted to give him the gift of her innocence. Driven on by the arousing touch of his lips at her throat and then lower, she began to caress him, unbuttoning his shirt and running her hands over his chest. He felt good to her . . . so good. When he untied the sash to her wrapper and slipped the garment from her shoulders, she helped him. She felt a little shy as he brushed the straps of her gown down, baring her breasts to his gaze.

"You're beautiful," he told her in a husky tone.

Then, with great care, he caressed her. His lips followed the path his hands had traced, stirring fires to a fever pitch within her. As his mouth sought the crest of her breast, she cried out in ecstasy. She clung to him, moving restlessly beneath his caresses. Never had she known such pleasure.

Brand moved over her, his body a fiery imprint

upon her willing flesh. The intimacy of their position shocked her, yet she could not stop moving, could not stop urging him nearer. Brand continued to caress her as he rose to kiss her. It was a devouring kiss that spoke of need and desire and overwhelming passion.

Then he moved away from her to shed his clothes. When he came back to the bed, she stared at him with open interest and a little embarrassment.

"You're beautiful . . ." she said, her gaze tracing over the ridges of hard muscle and sinew that were his chest and hips. When her gaze dropped to the proof of his desire for her, her blush deepened.

Of all the things she might have said to him, that was not what he'd expected. Suddenly, he was aware that she was an innocent, unknowing of the ways of men. He came back to her then, helping her to strip away the last of her garments, so at last they were flesh-to-flesh.

Brand moved over her, searing her with the heat of that intimate contact. She opened her legs to him and shifted her hips to accommodate him. He pressed against her, seeking the heat of her, the core of her innocence, and he found it. With utmost care, he began to caress and kiss her again. He wanted her ready for him. He wanted her to enjoy the night as much as he knew he would.

Tomorrow, she might walk out of his life forever, so they had to grab what happiness they could, while they could. Carefully, he positioned himself to possess her. As his mouth claimed hers in another passionate exchange, his body slid into the heat of her, past the barrier that proclaimed her untouched, and made her his own for all time.

Sheri tensed at this invasion, so foreign to her. She clung tightly to his shoulders as she waited for the burning agony to pass. And pass it did, as Brand began to arouse her again. She relaxed beneath his expert ministrations, coming slowly to enjoy the melding of their bodies.

Now, at last, she understood the mystery of lovemaking. But there was no time for reason. She was caught up in a wildfire of excitement that burned hotly within her. Brand's enthralling touch stoked the fire of her desire ever higher, until all thought of the pain of his possession faded away. She was lost in the splendor of being one with him, giving and taking, caressing and holding, until delight burst upon them.

Brand had meant to go slowly with Sheri. To savor each kiss and touch, but when she'd begun to move with him, his good intentions had been lost. He had thrust deeply into her welcoming warmth, losing himself in the glory of loving her, forgetting everything but the moment and Sheri.

They crested together, reaching the heights of ecstasy and floating back to reality locked in love's embrace. They clung together, their bodies still one.

Safe in Brand's arms, Sheri drifted off to sleep. The rapture that had burst upon her was new and exciting. She had never known she could feel that way. As she lay close to his chest, she could hear the sound of his steady heartbeat and knew that everything was going to be all right. She was with Brand. He would protect her with his life.

It was a long time before she stirred and opened her eyes. Brand was resting beside her, so she took the time to study him. He was handsome, magnificently so. Her gaze traced the strength of his features, the strong line of his jaw, the firm line of his lips. She smiled as she remembered the pleasure those lips had given her. She let her gaze sweep down his body, across the hard plane of his chest, and then lower. A faint blush stained her cheeks and she quickly averted her gaze. She was surprised to discover that she wanted to kiss him again . . . to see the passion in his eyes that was just for her. He was everything she'd ever dreamed of in a man. Besides being good-looking, he was strong, intelligent, and determined. She wondered how she was ever going to be able to leave him now. . . .

As she continued to gaze at him, Brand sensed that she was awake and opened his eyes. His blue-eyed gaze burned hotly as he stared at her. Her golden mane tumbled about her in a riot of soft curls; her eyes were aglow as she met his regard and the softness of her slightly parted lips stirred the heat within him again. His body hardened in response to the memory of loving her, and there was no denying he wanted her again.

Brand gathered her to him. Without saying a word, he kissed her. It was a gentle exploration, a far cry from the explosive need that had swept them away earlier. This time, they came together slowly, sweetly, taking the time to cherish each touch, each kiss. They learned how to pleasure one another, seeking those most sensitive places with caresses and kisses designed to rouse one another to mindlessness, until nothing mattered but their coming together, sharing love's most precious embrace. They rocked together in the age-old rhythm, thrilling in the closeness, enthralled by the gift of their loving.

They spiraled to the heights, perfect in their mating. Ecstasy claimed Sheri, and she clung tightly to Brand as rapture's tempest burst around her, taking her to forgetfulness and beyond. Brand held her close as he joined her in that shimmering splendor. They were one as they collapsed together, limbs entwined.

After a moment, Sheri rose above him, her hips still pressed intimately to his. She gazed down at him lovingly. Seeing the cut near his eye again, she leaned forward, her bare breasts brushing against his chest, to press a soft kiss to the wound.

"Who hurt you?" she asked.

"A drunk at the saloon was looking for a fight, that's all."

"And you obliged?" She gave a half-smile.

He shrugged, not wanting to think about what had happened. "Hancock and Long came in and broke it up."

"What was it about?"

"What is it always about? The man took a dislike to me because I'm a half-breed."

"I'm glad I've got better judgment than he does," she said in a throaty voice. "Brand?"

She waited to go on until he'd lifted his gaze to hers.

"Why did you come to me tonight? All along, you made it clear that you wanted nothing to do with me, and yet now. . . ." She was at a loss for words to describe the wonder of what had just taken place between them.

"Life is much easier when you're alone."

"It's also much lonelier."

He lifted one hand to trace a path down her cheek. "It's very lonely."

Sheri dipped her head to brush a gentle kiss over his lips, determined to make sure he was lonely no longer.

It was several hours later when Brand quietly got up and began to pull on his clothes. Sheri had been sleeping when he'd left her side, but she soon awoke when she realized that he was gone from her.

"Brand?" She said his name sleepily, as she sat up clutching the sheet to her breasts "Where are you going?"

"It will be dawn soon. I have to go. I don't want to be seen leaving your room."

She knew he was only thinking of her and her reputation, but she hated the fact that he had to sneak off like a thief in the night. "You could just stay," she said with a devilish smile. "I could tell Maureen that I'm not feeling well and won't be out today. Then we'd never have to leave the room."

He pulled on his shirt and fastened it, then started to tuck it into his pants. "The idea is tempting. . . ."

Sheri was slowly learning how provocative she could be and how much power that gave her. She did not want to be parted from him yet, so she let the sheet fall away as she rose to her knees before him. "Kiss me once more before you go. . . ." she invited him.

Brand stopped in mid-motion to stare at her. She was perfection, and she was offering herself to him. Unable to resist just one last kiss, he moved to the bedside. Sheri lifted her arms to him.

"Are you sure you want to leave me already?" she asked huskily.

Brand wasn't sure of anything right then, except that he needed to have her in his arms again. With a growl of need, he pulled her against him, ravishing her mouth with a devouring kiss. He'd meant to let her go, but Sheri had learned much about how to please him these last, long, hot hours. She slipped her hands beneath his shirt to push it up, then she bent to press a searing kiss to his chest.

Brand felt as if lightning had jolted through him at the intimate touch of her mouth. Caught up in a frenzy of undeniable need, they fell together upon the bed. They strained against each other, each seeking the release that only the other could give. Brand freed himself from his pants and Sheri eagerly guided him to her. Their joining was fast and powerful. Their passion was fiery and explosive, and when it had been spent, they lay beside each other, panting and breathless.

The faint hint of light in the eastern sky drove Brand from her bed. His expression was intense as he quickly finished dressing, then leaned back down to press one last kiss to her lips.

Sheri wanted to deepen the kiss. She wanted him to stay. Though she knew what damage it would do to her reputation if they were found out, right then it didn't matter to her. All she wanted was to be in Brand's arms, to have him love her as she loved him.

She realized then for the first time the full extent of her feelings for him, and her heart swelled with the knowledge. She did love him. How else could she have given herself to him so freely without any regret or hesitation? She loved Brand, but he didn't love her. She wanted him to never leave her, but it was no good if she had to beg. He had to be with her because he wanted to be, and for no other reason.

Brand was filled with regret as the common sense urge to leave in order to save her reputation battled with his need to stay and make love to her yet another time. He knew she would not deny him if he went to her. He knew she would welcome him back to her bed with open arms. But he had to protect her. He was no good for her. They had had this one night, but it must end here . . . now. There could be no more to their relationship.

"Sheri, I . . ."

"Don't . . ." She cut him off, knowing what he was about to say. She looked toward the window and saw the dawn. "You have to go."

Sheri looked up at him once more, their eyes meeting in a poignant moment. Then she looked away, fearing she would betray her own feelings for him, fearing that he would see everything she felt for him there in her expression.

After a long moment, Sheri looked back, thinking he was still there, but as noiselessly as he'd come to her, Brand had gone. She wondered in silent anguish if she would ever see him again.

Getting up from the bed, she donned her nightgown and lay back down. It was still early enough that she could get some sleep before she was to meet Maureen for breakfast.

Try as she might, though, rest would not come. Memories of the night's heated splendor and the glory of Brand's loving played in her mind. Haunted by the possibility that she might never see him again, she tossed and turned for over an hour. She tried to come to grips with what had passed between them. She had given herself to him freely, without reserve.

As brazen as it was, Sheri would never be sorry for as long as she lived.

Brand moved quietly down the back alley, heading toward the main street where he'd left his horse tied up all those hours ago. The last thing he wanted to do was draw any attention to himself. It was important that no one find out where he'd been. He would not allow anything to harm Sheri in any way. He would get out of town as quickly as he could and take his time riding back to the fort. He had some serious thinking to do. As he stepped out into the main street, though, he saw a crowd of men gathering down closer to the saloon where he'd tied his mount.

"Look! There he is! I told you this was his horse! I told you he'd be back for it!" Shouted the man who'd been with Hale as he caught sight of Brand.

Brand stopped. His instincts told him to run, but he stood his ground. He had no idea why everyone was so concerned that the horse was his. Cautiously, he ventured forth.

"There he is! That's him!" said another man who'd been in the saloon the night before.

Sheriff Warren saw Brand coming and waited for him to approach. This was ugly, but he had to do it.

"Sheriff," Brand said, nodding toward the lawman. All he wanted to do was mount up and get out of there, but somehow he knew it wasn't going to be that simple.

"We been wondering where you were," Warren told him curtly.

"Why? Is something wrong?"

"Yes. You're under arrest," he announced, drawing his sidearm in anticipation of trouble.

Brand was shocked. "For what?"

"The murder of Marcus Hale."

Chapter Fifteen

Brand, the Half-Breed Scout, or Trail of the Renegade
The Turmoil

Brand's touch was gentle as he checked Rachel's wound. She gazed up at him, focusing only on him, studying his handsome features as she tried to distract herself from the pain of her injury.

"The bleeding's stopped. You're going to be all right."

"Thank you," she said softly, giving him a slight smile. She was amazed that such a big, strong man could be so kind.

Brand heard something outside the cave just then, and, worried, he got up to investigate. Gun *in hand, he prepared for the worst as he crept out-side.*

Mercy had been searching the area for what seemed like hours, hoping for some sign of her friends. She'd found the dead Indians, but saw no trace of Brand or Rachel. She was almost in tears, for her terror was great.

"Here!" Brand called out to her in a low whisper. Mercy spun around to find Brand emerging from hiding. "Thank heaven I've found you! Where's Rachel?"

"She's been wounded. She's here in the cave. Where's the horse?"

She quickly told him where she'd left it tied.

"Stay with Rachel while I go get him. We have to move and we have to move fast."

He rushed off to get his mount and was soon back.

Rachel was in pain, but did not complain as Brand helped her onto the horse's back. She had to get through this. She had to get to Sacramento. Carl was waiting for her. . . .

"You're crazy," Brand ground out as the sheriff advanced on him. "I didn't kill anybody!"

"We heard you threaten him, breed!" yelled the man who'd been in the saloon. "We heard you say you were going to kill Hale, and now he's dead."

"And injun style, too!" another man added.

"I don't know what you're talking about," Brand countered.

"Hale was found in an alley behind the saloon. His throat was slit," Sheriff Warren informed him. "We have multiple witnesses who heard you threaten to kill him last night. I'm taking you in."

"But I'm innocent."

"That'll be for a jury to decide. Let's go." He gestured toward the sheriff's office with his gun. "You can come along peaceful-like or I can recruit some deputies. Which way is it going to be?"

Brand was furious, but there was little he could do right then. If he tried to make a run for it, no doubt they'd shoot him down like a dog. He was innocent, so he saw no reason why he shouldn't just go along with the sheriff and wait for things to work themselves out.

"All right, sheriff. I'll go with you."

Warren was surprised by his cooperation, but figured it was just because Brand was outnumbered. He felt great relief that things had worked out so well. It never occurred to him that Brand might be innocent. He was a half-breed, who'd been heard threatening to kill Hale by a saloon full of people only a short time before. And now Hale was dead. It didn't get much simpler than that. The case was already solved. All that remained was a trial, and that would be in just a few weeks.

"Good! Take the bastard in, Warren!" another of the men shouted as the sheriff took Brand's gun and knife and directed him toward the jail.

"He's just a breed! We know how they are! We ought to string him up now!"

"There'll be none of that!" Warren warned them as he started off toward the office. "We're going to do things by the law here. We're going to have a trial."

The men were angry. Hale was dead, murdered in a bloody crime, and they were determined that somebody pay for it.

"Sheriff, there are two witnesses who can tell you that I didn't kill Hale."

"Who are they?"

"Colonel Hancock and Lieutenant Long from the fort. They should still be in town. They can tell you that I left the saloon after the initial fight and never went back."

"Just because you never went back inside the saloon doesn't mean you didn't kill Hale. Now, get on inside and head for the back room. I want you all locked up, good and tight, where I can keep an eye on you."

Brand was furious, but did as he was told. This was not the time to cause trouble. He was innocent, and surely the colonel and the lieutenant would get him out of jail quickly.

Sheriff Warren unlocked the cell door and held the door wide for Brand to enter. When he'd gone in, the lawman slammed it shut behind him and turned the key.

"You won't be causing any trouble in there," he announced triumphantly.

"I wasn't causing you any trouble, anyway," Brand told him fiercely. "Get Hancock and Long. They'll vouch for me."

"Yeah, yeah," Warren sneered, believing he had the right man and that there was no need to investigate further. "I'll talk to them as soon as I find them. You just settle in and shut up. The less I hear out of you, the better."

The sheriff went back into the outer office and sat down at his desk. He'd go look for the officers later. Right now, he wanted to get some rest. It had been a long night.

*   *   *

Sheri never fell asleep. Her emotions were in too great a turmoil for her to rest. Finally giving up the effort, she rose and dressed for breakfast. When Maureen knocked on her door a little after eight, she was more than ready to go eat.

"Did you sleep well?" Sheri asked her cousin as they headed toward the restaurant.

"Like a baby," Maureen assured her. "It was wonderful to get a good night's sleep again. What about you?"

"I didn't sleep much."

"Were you worrying about something? Brand maybe?"

She nodded. "I never dreamed he'd become so important to me, but he has."

"I understand. He's a wonderful man, and the more we learn about him and everything that's happened to him, the more I respect him."

"I love him," Sheri admitted quietly.

"I thought so," Maureen said with a warm smile.

"Am I that obvious?"

"Only to me. I know you, remember?"

"Well, just because I love Brand doesn't mean anything is going to come of it, especially with the way he feels."

"What are you going to do about it? Are you just going to leave? Can you go home and write your books about Brand, the Half-Breed Scout, and never look back?" Maureen was deliberately forcing her to think about a future without Brand. "Or do you want to stay here and fight for what you want?"

"I'm not sure it would make any difference. I can't force him to love me."

"Maybe not, but if you leave too soon, you'll never know what could have been."

They settled in at the restaurant and had just been served their meal when they saw a man rush in and start talking excitedly to the waitress.

"It looks like he's all in an uproar about something," Sheri said, watching the animated way the man was going on.

"I wonder what happened? It must be important for him to come running in here like that."

"We'll ask the waitress when she comes back," Sheri told her, only a little curious. She had too much on her mind to worry about town gossip.

A minute or two passed and then the waitress approached them.

"I suppose you know the news already, don't you? What with being friends with that breed and all," she said to them, a slight sneer in her tone.

Sheri and Maureen stared at her in confusion.

"What news?" Sheri asked, sensing suddenly that something was very wrong.

"Why, there was a murder in town last night! That's what Jones was just telling me about. They found Marcus Hale in an alley with his throat cut."

"Who's Marcus Hale?"

"Mostly a drunk and a troublemaker, but he ain't going to be causing any more trouble for anybody now that he's dead. Seems the breed killed him."

"You mean Brand from Fort McDowell?"

"That's the one. They had a fight in the saloon, and everybody heard the breed tell Hale he was going to kill him. They found Hale's body just before dawn. Looks like he'd been lying there most of the night."

245

"No . . ." Sheri went pale, thinking of Brand's injury, of the blood on him and his evasive answer about how he'd come to be hurt. Could Brand possibly have killed a man and then come to her? For an instant she considered that he might have done it, and the thought was chilling. She had seen Brand fight. She knew what he was capable of in the heat of a battle. But no matter what other people thought of him, she knew in her heart and in her soul that Brand was no cold-blooded killer.

"The sheriff has already arrested him. I don't think it will take too long for justice to be served this time. Everybody in town's wantin' a lynching."

"Brand is no murderer," Sheri retorted.

"Lady, he's an Indian. They're all murderers." The waitress dismissed her as a half-witted Easterner and moved away, confident that her own assessment of the breed was right.

Sheri had gone pale at the news, but her expression was determined. "I have to go to Brand. I know he didn't do it."

"Of course. I'll go with you," Maureen said.

The two of them quickly paid for their half-eaten meal and left the restaurant. Sheri all but ran to the sheriff's office. She entered without pausing to find Sheriff Warren sitting at his desk. He rose as they came through the door.

"Ladies . . ." He was surprised by their appearance. "What can I do for you?"

"I need to speak to Brand, please," Sheri told him.

"That's not a good idea, my dear. He's a vicious killer, you know," he said, trying to discourage her. It was unseemly that a lovely young woman like this wanted to speak to the scout.

"Brand saved my life when we were ambushed by the Apache. The man is not a murderer," she declared with conviction, her eyes flashing fire. "I want to see him now."

"Well . . ." The sheriff looked doubtful, but as he stared at the determined young woman, who showed no sign of relenting in her request, he backed down. "All right, but just for a few minutes."

"That'll be fine," Sheri said with dignity. "Maureen, why don't you wait here for me? I won't be long."

She followed the lawman into the back room.

"You got a visitor," Warren announced flatly.

Brand had been sitting on the cot, biding his time when he'd heard Sheri talking to the sheriff. Her spirited defense of him had touched him. It had been a long time since anyone had truly believed in him that way. When he saw her come through the door, he was surprised by the feelings that surged through him. She looked like an avenging, glorious angel coming to his rescue.

"If you'll allow us a moment, please, sheriff?" She looked at him with a disdainful expression.

Warren looked from Brand to Sheri and then nodded. "I'll be right outside if you need me. If he tries anything, all you have to do is yell, and I'll come running."

"Thank you. You're very kind, but I'm sure I'm in no danger."

She couldn't wait for the man to leave so she could talk to Brand alone. She didn't speak until she was sure the sheriff was in the outer office talking to Maureen.

"What happened?" She turned to him quickly, her

proud demeanor fading before the reality of his imprisonment.

"I was heading out of town, and the sheriff arrested me for murder."

"Maureen and I heard about it from the waitress in the restaurant, so I came right over. We have to get you out of here. You didn't kill anybody last night. You were with me."

"I don't want you to tell the sheriff that we were together last night." His expression was serious as he spoke in low tones, wanting their lovemaking to remain private. "I didn't do it, and once he talks to Hancock and Long, he'll probably let me go."

"What do they have to do with anything?"

"They can tell the sheriff that I left the bar after the fight was broken up and that I didn't come back. They're the ones who pulled me off Hale and got me out of there. If they hadn't, I damned well might have killed him. . . ." He shook his head slowly at the memory. "But I didn't."

"What did he do to make you so angry?"

The look in Brand's eyes could only be described as deadly as he remembered their encounter the night before. "I'd had a few whiskeys at the saloon. Hale was drunk and talking to another man across the room." The scene replayed in his mind with graphic intensity. The other man's words had the power to anger him even now. "He said things about Becky and about you. . . ."

"About me?" She stared at him in shock. She had worried about his injuries last night, and now she discovered that he had gotten them defending her honor. Her heartbeat quickened at the realization.

"It was ugly, and I went after him. That's when

Hancock and Long walked in and broke it up. They got me out of there, and I never went back."

"Has the sheriff sent for them yet?"

"I don't know. I told him to when he brought me in. I think they went back in the saloon after I left. They probably know more about what happened to Hale than I do, so I don't want you to put your reputation at risk because of this. We'll just wait it out. It'll be all right."

"You're sure?" she questioned, hating the fact that they'd locked him up and he was innocent.

"Yes. Now, go on. This is no place for a lady."

"It's no place for you, either," she returned.

"I know." He grimaced.

She started to leave, then paused to look back at him. "Thank you, Brand."

"For what?"

"For defending my honor."

Their gazes met and locked for a moment as sweet memories of the night just passed swirled around them. She turned away and went back to where Maureen had been keeping the sheriff occupied.

"I'm ready to go now," she announced. "Have you spoken with Colonel Hancock and Lieutenant Long yet?"

"No, not yet. The lieutenant headed back to the fort early this morning, but Colonel Hancock is still here on business. I've left word that I need to speak with him."

"I'm sure you'll be releasing Brand as soon as you do."

"We'll see," he said evasively. He didn't know why she was so sure the breed was innocent. Everybody knew the damned half-breed had killed Hale. Talk-

249

ing to Hancock wouldn't do Brand any good unless he'd been with him the entire night.

Sheri had an uneasy feeling as she left the office with Maureen.

"How was he?" Maureen asked once they were outside.

"He seemed fine, but I'm sure he'll be much better once he's been released. I wish the colonel would get here."

Hancock had heard the talk of Brand's arrest, but he had not rushed to rescue his scout. He had completed his business dealings in town and then headed toward the sheriff's office.

"Sheriff Warren? I understand there was some trouble in town last night involving one of my men," he said as he stepped into the office.

Warren rose and shook hands with the officer. "Yes, sir, Colonel Hancock. Thank you for coming in. Brand has been arrested and charged with the murder of Marcus Hale."

"Hale? The drunk who was causing all the trouble at the Gold Bar last night?"

"That's the one. We have at least five witnesses who heard Brand threaten to kill him when they were fighting last night. Your man swears he's innocent and that you can prove it."

"Well, it's true that Lieutenant Long and I broke up the fight in the bar and separated the two men, but I did not see Brand again that night after he left. Long and I had a few drinks, and then we went back to our hotel."

"So you have no personal knowledge of Brand's whereabouts at the time of the murder?"

"No, I don't, and if he is guilty, I want to see him punished to the full extent of the law. I do not take kindly to men who bring shame upon the military. I expect this to be dealt with quickly and fairly."

"We're working on it. With all the witnesses hearing him make the threat and then the way Hale was killed . . ." The sheriff remembered his first look at the body.

"How was he murdered?"

"His throat was slit."

Hancock nodded. "May I see Brand for a few minutes?"

"He's in back." The sheriff gestured toward the closed door.

The colonel went to seek out Brand.

Brand had heard the sound of voices in the outer office, but with the door closed it had been difficult to make out who the visitor was or what was being said. When it opened and Hancock appeared, he was actually glad to see the man. The colonel closed the door behind him.

"Thanks for coming, colonel," Brand said as he rose to speak to him. "Are they letting me out now?" He looked past him to see if the sheriff was following.

"I'm afraid not," Hancock answered coldly. "Though I can testify to your actions up until you left the saloon, I can't really say what you did after that. So until you can prove where you were, you are the primary suspect."

"I didn't do it!" Brand said, angry and frustrated. He knew that Sheri could clear his name, but in doing so she would forever ruin hers.

"You know me. I wouldn't do anything like this."

251

"Know you? I know nothing about you. You're a half-breed."

"But I'm innocent!" Brand protested, looking up at the colonel and seeing the unmistakable hatred in his eyes.

Hancock smiled a feral smile at the man who'd been married to his daughter. "I'm sure you are, but how are you going to prove it? Do you have any witnesses who could testify as to what you were doing for all those hours?"

When he didn't answer, the colonel shrugged.

"I wonder what Becky would think of you now, locked up like an animal after spending the night with another white woman."

"Wait a minute . . . You saw me last night?"

"Last night was interesting. I saw a lot of things. But today . . ." He chuckled. "Today is most satisfying."

He walked out without another word.

Brand stared after him, shocked by what the man had just revealed. The colonel knew he hadn't done it, yet he was refusing to tell the sheriff. He'd always known the man didn't like him, but he'd never realized just how much he hated him until now. He sat back down on the cot and rested his head in his hands, wondering what he could do to prove his innocence.

Hancock found Sheriff Warren waiting for him in the outer office.

"I've spoken with Brand, but I don't think there's much more I can do to help. I'll speak with the lieutenant when I get back to the fort and see if he's aware of anything that can help you."

"That'll be good. There was talk earlier of a lynching, but I think folks have calmed down for now."

"We'll wait to hear from you."

Hancock left the office and decided to stop by the Gold Bar before starting back to the fort. He was surprised to find Charles Brennan there sitting at a table, deep in conversation with the bartender and several of the customers.

"So, is that all you remember from last night?" Charles was asking, taking notes as they responded. "Did anyone else leave right before Hale or just after him?"

The three men frowned and tried to remember exactly what had transpired the night before.

"People were in and out all night. I didn't see any sign of the half-breed again, though." The barkeep was frowning in concentration. "And good thing, too, after trying to bust up the place. The colonel left, and so did the lieutenant, close about the same time as Hale, I believe. But the rest of the regulars stayed on. It was late when I closed up." The barkeep looked at the others to see if anyone could think of anything else.

"So no one heard anything unusual or saw anything out of the ordinary?" Charles questioned.

"Not after the fight. Hale kept mouthing off about the half-breed, but that was about all."

Charles waited a moment to see if anyone had anything to add. When they didn't, he thanked them and got up to leave.

"Colonel Hancock, it's good to see you," Charles said in greeting. "I've been interviewing everyone for the paper, and I wondered if I might talk to you for a minute?"

"Of course. This is all so tragic and senseless."

"Murder is. I don't know if you heard what the other men were saying, but they didn't notice anything unusual after Brand was taken from the saloon. Did you?"

"No. It was pretty quiet. I just spoke with the sheriff and couldn't help him much either. He was hoping I could tell him of Brand's whereabouts after the fight, but I didn't see him again that night."

"So while you were here in the Gold Bar, Hale's ramblings didn't bother you?"

"No, I don't pay much attention to drunks, although I have to admit the man did have a point with his views on Indians. From what I've seen of them, they're little better than filthy predators."

"Do you include your own scouts in that assessment?" Charles pressed.

The colonel pinned him with an icy, furious glare. "If Brand is the one who slit Hale's throat, then he deserves whatever he gets."

"But isn't Brand your son-in-law? Don't you know him well enough to know whether he's guilty or not?"

"My daughter's long dead. He's no relation of mine," Hancock said venomously, the look in his eyes growing wilder. "I don't care if they string him up today! It's what he deserves!"

A rumble of agreement came from the others in the saloon.

"But what about justice?" Charles insisted.

"Did Hale have any justice?" one of the others yelled, interrupting. "The hell with justice—we want what's right!"

"Yeah!" another man called out, inciting the others further. "Let's get a rope and string him up!"

"You're supposed to be the civilized ones," Charles

said, trying to calm them. "There's nothing civilized about a lynching."

"Except maybe the outcome," the barkeep put in, his eyes glowing at the thought of seeing the half-breed swing.

Charles started from the saloon, hoping that once he was gone, everyone would calm down. He returned to the newspaper office to find Sheri and Maureen waiting for him.

"What did you find out?" Sheri asked the minute he'd come inside.

"Nothing that's going to help us. I did run into the colonel, and he'd already been to the jail to talk with the sheriff."

"So, Brand's free now?" Sheri said excitedly.

"No. According to Hancock, he had no contact with Brand after they broke up the fight. That leaves the night unaccounted for and no witnesses to back up Brand's claim of innocence." Charles looked tired. "I don't know where to look next or who to talk to, but I can tell you one thing—the colonel is a frightening man."

"Why?"

"He hates Indians, and Brand in particular, with a passion. He doesn't even claim him as kin, despite the fact that Brand was married to his daughter. He's over there now, saying that Brand deserves whatever he gets and that it wouldn't bother him if they went ahead and strung him up."

"Do you think they will?" Sheri felt panic rise within her.

"I don't know. It's hard to tell what men will do if they get too much liquor in them."

"Maybe I'd better . . ." Sheri was looking desperate. If they formed a mob and set out to hang Brand, it would be too late for her to do anything. She had to help him now.

"You'd better what?" Maureen asked, frowning at the look of distress on her cousin's face. "What are you thinking about doing?"

She straightened her shoulders as she stood up to leave the newspaper office. "I have to talk to the sheriff again."

"Why?"

"Because I know Brand is innocent."

"So do we, but we have to prove it."

"I can." She met the looks of surprise and confusion they gave her calmly.

"How?"

"There is a witness who knows exactly where Brand was until dawn."

"Who?" Maureen was shocked at this information.

"Who?" Charles parroted. "I want to interview him."

"It's me. Brand was with me all night."

Chapter Sixteen

Brand, the Half-Breed Scout, or Trail of the Renegade
The Getaway

The warriors found their dead friends and were furious. The women had escaped, but they were not capable of killing this way. Someone else had done the killing. The renegades would track them down and make them pay for what they'd done!

Brand, Rachel, and Mercy had been traveling continually since leaving the cave. Even though Rachel was in pain, Brand knew it was not safe to rest. More of the raiding party could be coming after them. He would take no chances with their safety.

Bobbi Smith

"Is it far to the fort?" Mercy asked.

"It will take us another day, if we keep moving the way we are."

The women were relieved to hear that there was only one more day of travel. They could make it. They were with Brand.

They camped that night in a secluded spot, high in the mountains. Rachel was feeling weak and feverish, but she said nothing. She would not hinder their rescue. Brand was counting on her to be strong. At dawn, they moved out again.

It was near midday, just as they were about to leave the mountains, when Brand sensed that all was not as it should be. He kept a wary watch on the hills behind them, hoping for some hint of the raiding party's location, but saw nothing.

The attack came suddenly and viciously. Brand knew just what he had to do.

"Rachel! Mercy! Ride due west and don't stop or look back!"

"Brand!" Rachel cried out as Mercy kicked the horse into a run.

The mount charged forward, and Brand was left alone to fight the renegades. . . .

"You?" Maureen was shocked as she stared at Sheri. "He was with you?"

Sheri nodded. "That's why I've got to go to the sheriff now and tell him the truth. I can't let anything happen to Brand. I'd never forgive myself." She paused as she looked at Charlcs and Maureen. They were staring at her as if she were crazy.

"You're making this up, right?" Charles asked, still stunned by her revelation.

"No, Charles, I'm not," she answered, meeting his regard squarely and without embarrassment. "I love Brand."

"Enough to lie for him?"

"I'm not lying," she protested in frustration. "I was standing at the window of my room and I saw him in the alley below. He came to me then, and he stayed because I wanted him to."

"Oh, my," Maureen said, trying to decide whether to smile or be shocked. She had waited all these years for Sheri to fall in love, and now that she'd really done it, nothing was working out right. She looked at Charles. "We need to go with her."

"No!" Sheri said sharply. "I'll be all right."

"Are you sure?" Maureen went to her and hugged her supportively.

"I'm sure." Her expression was troubled. "I'd better hurry. I don't want to take the chance that something might happen to him. I can't risk it."

"We'll wait here for you."

She nodded; then, girding herself for what was to come, she marched from the newspaper office. She would do whatever was necessary to save Brand. There was no doubt in her mind.

Sheri swallowed nervously as she neared the sheriff's office. She'd had to pass the Gold Bar Saloon on her way there, and she had heard the shouting and swearing as the men inside talked of stringing Brand up. Their threats only quickened her pace. She wiped her hands nervously on the skirt of her gown and then walked right in to face the lawman.

Sheriff Warren almost groaned when he saw it was her. One of the deputies had told him there was trouble brewing down at the Gold Bar, and the last thing he needed right now was this lady back aggravating him.

"Miss St. John," he greeted her. "What can I do for you now?"

"Sheriff Warren, I need to talk to you. It's important."

"If it's about the officers from the fort, I've already talked to Colonel Hancock, and he was unable to help with an alibi for Brand."

"I heard that, and it's for that reason that I came back to talk to you again. I need to tell you the truth. I know where Brand was all night, and he wasn't out murdering Marcus Hale."

"Where was he?"

"Brand spent the night with me." She all but blurted it out.

Sheriff Warren stared at her, amazed at the lengths she was going to, to save the half-breed. "You're saying Brand was with you?"

"Yes, sir. He was with me in my room at the hotel." She was firm and unwavering.

Sheri wasn't sure what she expected from the man—scorn, maybe. Sneering condemnation. Those she could have handled. What she got outraged her.

"Little lady," he said condescendingly. "I got big trouble brewing here over this killing. I know what you're trying to do, but it doesn't do any good to lie about such things."

"But it's the truth."

"I don't know what it is about this half-breed that makes white women go so crazy about him. I mean, first Becky Hancock and now you, but I'm telling you, he ain't worth lying about and ruining your reputation."

"But . . . !" She could not believe he was scoffing at her.

"Miss St. John, you Easterners come out here thinking you know everything about everything, and you don't. For sure, you don't know a damned thing about the Apache or about half-breeds. You ain't never lived with them. You don't know how they think or act. So you ought to just pack yourself up and head on back where you belong. This ain't one of your books, lady."

Sheri was beyond furious as she glared at him. "If it was one of my books, you can be assured that I would have written in a smarter sheriff!"

He tensed at her insult, his patience with her at an end. "I got a job to do. I don't need you here getting in the way if things turn ugly. Now, go on back to your hotel and stay there."

"If anything happens to Brand . . ." she threatened.

"It will be because you kept me from doing my job," he snarled at her.

Sheri was ready to scream in frustration. She glanced toward the closed door to the cells and wondered what to do next. She had been Brand's only hope. She'd been telling the truth, yet the sheriff didn't believe her. There had to be some way she could help Brand. She would not stand idly by and watch the man she loved be hanged for a murder he didn't commit.

The sheriff turned his back on her to get a rifle out of his rifle case, and it was then that Sheri saw them. . . . His extra set of keys were lying on the desk beneath a few sheets of paper. She knew he kept one set on him at all times, for he'd told her so that day he'd given them the tour. Without making a sound, she snatched up the keys and started from the office.

"I'm holding you responsible for Brand's safety, sheriff. He's an innocent man."

Warren didn't respond, but took out his rifle, checked to make sure it was loaded, and then closed and locked the case. He set it next to the desk as he sat back down.

"It's been real interesting visiting with you, Miss St. John. I do not plan on repeating that little story you made up just to save the breed. I suggest you don't either." His words were terse as he watched her walk from the office, her head held high.

Sheri might have lost this round, but somehow, some way, she was going to save Brand. She did have the keys.

Maureen and Charles were waiting for her in the newspaper office. They both looked up when she walked in.

"Where's Brand? Is he coming after you?" Maureen asked, trying to read her cousin's strange expression.

"The sheriff didn't believe me," she told them in disgust.

"He didn't?" Maureen knew she sounded like a simpleton, but she couldn't believe what Sheri was saying.

"He said he didn't know why white women wanted half-breeds. He said I shouldn't repeat my story again, and that he wouldn't repeat it either. I don't know what to do next." The look she gave Maureen and Charles was worried. "He said there was trouble brewing down at the saloon, and he's concerned about what might happen. So . . . when I had the chance, I took these. . . ."

She opened her hand to show them the keys she'd been clutching.

"You didn't!"

"I did, but I don't know what to do. Do I wait and make sure that there's not going to be a mob going after Brand to hang him, or do I break him out now and make sure he stays alive?"

"You're really thinking about a jailbreak?" Charles was astounded at her daring.

"I will not sit by and watch Brand die for something I know he didn't do. If I can save him, I will."

"You're one hell of a woman, Sheri," he said with respect.

"Well, I haven't done anything yet. Let's see what happens next. Do you have horses we could use?"

"They put Brand's up at the stable, and you can take mine."

"What about supplies? If I get him out of there, we're going to need a gun, ammunition, food, and canteens."

" 'We'?" Maureen went still. "What do you mean 'we'? You're not thinking of doing anything crazy, like going with him, are you?"

Sheri looked her straight in the eye. "If you think I'm going to break him out and then stay behind while he runs alone, you're wrong. I'll be as wanted as he is. They'll be after me, too."

"This is insane."

"This whole situation is. If I wrote it in one of my books, Tim DeYoung would probably tell me that it was too far-fetched and that it lacked authenticity!"

Maureen and Sheri both laughed at how ridiculous everything that had happened in New York suddenly seemed. Charles only stared at them, confused.

"Who's Tim DeYoung?" he asked.

"My editor," Sheri answered, still managing a smile.

"Sheri . . ." Maureen turned serious. The time for laughter was over. "For God's sake, be careful."

"I will. You know I wouldn't do this if it wasn't a matter of life or death. They want Brand dead, and I'm the only one who can save him."

Maureen had always respected Sheri's courage, but never more so than she did now. She hugged her impulsively.

"What can we do to help you?"

"The big thing will be distracting the sheriff so I can go in through the back door and break Brand out."

"I can help with that," Charles offered. "I'll go down to the saloon and see what's going on. I'll send word to the sheriff to get down there, that there's trouble brewing and he needs to calm everybody down."

"Thanks, Charles. I don't know what we would have done without you."

"I'm glad you didn't have to find out. You be careful, though. This may not work, but if it does, they'll be coming after you as soon as they realize he's gone."

"I know, but Brand's good. If anybody can escape and hide his trail, he can."

"If it works and you two get away, how will I know how you are? What should we do?" Maureen asked.

"We have to find out who really killed Marcus Hale. Until we know that, Brand doesn't have a chance."

"We'll keep working on it," Charles said. "If we find

out something, how can we get in touch with you?"

Sheri was quiet for a minute. "There's only one person Brand trusts, and that's O'Toole. Tell him whatever you can find out. He'll know what to do."

"We will. I promise," Maureen told her.

"Go back to your room and get what you need to take with you. I'll go see about the horses for you and tie them up somewhere back behind the jail where they're not too obvious. Then I'll head down to the Gold Bar. Where will you be?" Charles asked.

"I'll keep watch from down the street. When I see the sheriff leave the office, I'll go in after him."

"I'm going with you," Maureen volunteered.

"No, you're not," Sheri returned immediately. "I won't have you in danger because of me. This is my plan, and I'll live with the consequences. You stay here out of trouble or go up to your room. I can't be worrying about you, too. Right now I have to save Brand."

"All right, but I want to help."

"Then find the man who killed Marcus Hale."

With that, they put their plan into action.

"Sheriff! They sent me down here to get you. There's trouble brewing down at the saloon!" A young boy stuck his head in the jail and yelled at the lawman.

"What kind of trouble?"

"They said it looked like some of the men are trying to form a lynch mob and you'd better hurry!"

Warren muttered vilely under his breath as he stood up and got his rifle. If Sullivan wanted him, there was something going on. "Let's go."

He stopped only long enough to lock up the office,

then followed the boy down the street. He'd been worried that something like this would happen all day, and now that it was almost dark, it sounded like all hell was about to break loose.

Sheri had been watching and waiting for the chance to make her move. She'd changed into her riding clothes and had packed the few things they'd need while on the run. She didn't know where Brand would take her, and she didn't care as long as he was safe from the hangman's noose.

The minute Sheriff Warren had gone, Sheri made her way to the back of the jail. She said a silent prayer that she had the keys she needed as she started to unlock the alley door. Her prayer was answered. She had the door opened in no time.

"What the . . . ?" Brand was startled and jumped to his feet when the door swung open. "Sheri!" he whispered her name in shock. "What are you doing here?"

"I'm breaking you out!" She wasted no time talking, but quickly unlocked his cell and threw the door wide. "Let's go! There isn't much time."

"I can't run. It'll just make me look even more guilty." He remained standing in the cell.

"There's a mob forming down at the saloon that wants to see you hang. Do you plan to wait around and see if the sheriff can control them or do you want to get out of here?"

"But I didn't do it. If I break out . . ."

"Brand, I told the sheriff the truth this afternoon. I told him you were with me all night, and he didn't believe me. We have to get you out of here! We're never going to find Hale's murderer with you locked up!"

He knew she was right, but he hated to do it. He was innocent.

"All right. Let's go."

Sheri hurried to replace the keys where she'd found them earlier that day. Then they went out the back door and shut it tightly behind them. As she led Brand to where the two horses were tied, he frowned at her.

"You're not coming with me," he stated flatly, fearing she would be hurt.

"I'm not staying here and getting thrown in jail for breaking you out. I'm just as wanted by the law as you are right now, so you'd better get me out of town and keep me safe. Come on! We haven't got much time!"

He swore under his breath as he helped her up on her horse, then mounted his own. "We'll walk them out. It's quieter. Stay right with me. If there's any trouble, any trouble at all, I want you to surrender. I don't want you hurt."

She nodded, and when he led the way, she was by his side.

Marcus Hale's friends were in a fury as they sat drinking together in the saloon. They even had a rope and were practicing making a noose.

"I say we hang the bastard right now! Who cares about a trial? We know he did it! Look at the way Hale's throat was cut!"

"Let's go get the breed and be done with it!"

"That's what that colonel said before he headed back to the fort! He said we should hang him and save the court the trouble!" another man added.

"I don't give a damn what anybody said," Sheriff

Warren announced as he came through the swinging doors, his rifle resting in his arms. "There ain't going to be any trouble here tonight."

"That's what I was telling them, sheriff," Deputy Sullivan said nervously. He'd been listening to the level of anger growing and knew he needed help. One man alone against all these men wouldn't be able to hold them back. When Charles Brennan had volunteered to send somebody to the sheriff for help, he'd let him.

"Why don't you boys just all go home and sleep it off? If the breed is guilty, he'll be convicted and then we'll see about a hanging."

"But Hale's dead! He ain't getting no justice! He's six feet under already! Ain't nobody thinking about poor Hale."

"If an innocent man is wrongly hanged, then there would be two dead men to mourn. We wait for the trial," Sheriff Warren dictated. "Now, if I hear any more talk about this, I'll close the place down and send you on home. Understand?"

A grumble of discontent went through the drunken crowd, but they did not threaten the lawman in any way. He stayed around a little while longer to make sure everything was quieting down, then he headed back to the jail.

Brand and Sheri reached the outskirts of town without incident and then urged their mounts to a gallop. They rode like the wind into the night. The farther away from town they got, the better. Brand was glad for the cover of darkness. They would need all the help they could get escaping the posse he was sure would follow. He knew where he was going.

They needed a place to hide out until he could find the real murderer, and the small cave was just the place.

The jail looked peaceful and undisturbed, and that was just the way Sheriff Warren wanted it. He didn't bother to check on Brand right away. He put the rifle aside, but within arm's reach, and then locked the office door from the inside. He was just about to settle in at the desk, when he thought he'd better take a quick look at his prisoner.

The explosion of profanity that followed reflected his fury as he found himself staring at the empty cell, its door standing wide open. He shook his head in disbelief, trying to figure out how Brand had escaped. He checked the back door and found it unlocked. It made no sense. If someone had come in the back door, they would have had to break it down, but the locks were intact. Then he remembered the extra set of keys. He ran back to the front office to check on them, and, to his surprise, they were right where he always left them on his desk.

Warren tried to remember all the people who'd been in the office that day who could have taken them and then left them after the jailbreak. He grew even more frustrated, for there were any number who could have done it. The more he tried to narrow it down, the more he focused on the St. John woman. She had been the one most concerned about Brand. She had been the one pressuring him to release Brand with that story she'd made up to get him out of jail.

Storming from the jail, Warren headed out to find Deputy Sullivan. He would search the town from one end to the other, and then, at first light, if they hadn't found Brand yet, he would get a posse together and track him down.

Night had just fallen, and O'Toole was working with his horse when he heard someone call his name. He looked up to see the lieutenant coming toward him.

"Yes, sir?"

"I need to talk to you for a minute. I have some news. . . ."

At his uneasy expression, O'Toole frowned. "Is something wrong?"

"I'm afraid so. The colonel has just returned from town. It seems a man named Marcus Hale was murdered in Phoenix last night." He paused, then added solemnly, "Colonel Hancock just informed me that Brand has been arrested for the crime."

"Brand?" O'Toole was shocked. "I didn't even know he'd gone into town, but why the hell would he kill anybody?"

"The colonel and I broke up a fight between them earlier last night. Brand threatened to kill Hale. Everyone who was in the saloon heard him."

"But why? It's not like him to lose control like that."

"This Hale had made some remark about Brand making whores out of white women, and that set him off. They didn't find Hale's body until after I'd already left town this morning. That's why I just found out."

"What can we do to help Brand? We gotta get him out of there."

"Colonel Hancock visited him in jail, but he says

there's not much we can do, what with the witnesses to his threat and all."

"I can tell you right now, Brand didn't kill the man," O'Toole stated firmly.

"Then who did?"

"I don't know, but I've got to find out. I can't just leave him there to hang. You know what kind of justice he'll get, being a half-breed and all."

"I'll talk to the colonel first thing in the morning and see if I can get us permission to go into Phoenix and check on him."

"Good. Let me know right away. I can be ready to ride in a few minutes."

The two men parted, each concerned in his own way about the fate of their scout.

Sheriff Warren and Deputy Sullivan were frustrated. Their search of the town had turned up nothing. There was no sign of Brand anywhere. He was gone and so was his horse. The sheriff had questioned the hand at the stable about who'd come for the mount, but he'd sworn that he hadn't seen or heard anything unusual that evening.

"I've got a strange feeling that I know who's involved in this. Come with me. We're going to pay a call on one Sheridan St. John."

They got Maureen and Sheri's room numbers from the hotel desk and went upstairs to knock on their doors. No one answered, and Warren was angry. He returned to the desk.

"Where are Miss St. John and Miss Cleaver?"

"I don't know, sir. I haven't seen them for some time."

He was about to leave when he saw Maureen entering the hotel on Charles's arm.

"Miss Cleaver, I want to talk to you."

Maureen looked shocked at his fierce attitude. "Of course, sheriff. What is it? Is something wrong? Has something happened to Sheri?"

"That's what I was just about to ask you. Where is your cousin, Miss Cleaver?"

"Why, she decided to retire early rather than go out to dinner with Charles and me. I last saw her about an hour or two ago. Did you try her room?"

"Yes, we did, and no one answered."

Maureen looked worried. "I'd better check on her. It's not like Sheri not to answer the door if someone calls."

"There's more to my wanting her than just to check on her, ma'am."

"Why? What is it, sheriff?"

"There's been a jailbreak, Miss Cleaver. Brand's been broken out of jail and I have an uneasy feeling that your cousin might have had a part in it."

Maureen managed an outraged look. "How can you even think such a thing? I'm sure she's up in her room, sleeping soundly. You'll see."

With righteous indignation, Maureen marched ahead of him up the steps to Sheri's door. She knocked several times herself; then, when the manager came up with another key, he unlocked it for her.

"There must be something gravely wrong with her, not to answer me," she told them worriedly as the manager swung the door open.

They stepped forward to find the room deserted, and some of Sheri's clothes thrown haphazardly about.

"Dear God . . . Something's happened to her."

"Just as I suspected!" Sheriff Warren thundered. "She's gone! She must have been in on it."

"In on what? Freeing Brand?" Maureen and Charles looked at him in outraged innocence.

"Yes," he told them coldly. "Be warned, your cousin is now accused of helping a murderer escape justice. We won't go easy on her when we find her—and we will find her."

Maureen saw the fury in his gaze and moved closer to Charles. He put a supportive arm around her.

"I'll be sure to cover this for the newspaper," he told him.

"You do that, Brennan. An accused murderer has been broken out of my jail and is on the run. There'll be a bounty on him in the morning." With that, he stalked out of the room.

Maureen was trembling as she realized just how much trouble Sheri was in.

"She's going to be all right, isn't she?" she asked, turning her desperate gaze to Charles.

"Yes, she'll be all right, but we're going to have to do our part."

"What can we do? You've already interviewed everybody who was there that night."

"Everybody but the lieutenant. I think I want to go back out to the fort and have a talk with Long. Do you want to come with me?"

"Absolutely. I have to help Sheri in any way I can. This is serious. She's in trouble and so is Brand."

"We'll go back tomorrow. Maybe the lieutenant saw something that nobody else did. You never know. The least that will happen is we can set up

273

contact with Sergeant O'Toole and let him know what's going on."

"I'll be ready whenever you are."

Charles started to leave. Then, unable to help himself, he turned back to Maureen and took her in his arms and held her close. "We'll figure this out. I know we will."

"Thank you."

She looked up at him, her eyes glowing with her feelings for him. Charles could not resist the invitation in her eyes. He bent to her and kissed her. "I'll see you in the morning."

"Good night," she breathed as she watched him go.

She went to her own room, after locking Sheri's door behind her. She hurried to the window and watched Charles as he left the hotel and headed off down the street. She stayed there watching until he had moved out of sight. Only then did she undress and retire for the night, but sleep did not come easily. Thoughts of Sheri on the run with Brand stayed with her, and she hoped they would find the real killer soon.

"Sullivan, I know it's late, but I want you to ride out to the fort and tell Colonel Hancock what's happened here. Tell him to keep an eye out for Brand and the woman. I'll form up a posse first thing in the morning, and we'll be heading out then."

"Shall I meet you on the trail and ride with you?"

"No. You come back here and keep an eye on things in town for me. I have no idea how long this will take, but I am not letting that breed get away with murder."

"Yes, sir. I'll leave for McDowell right now."

Chapter Seventeen

**Brand, the Half-Breed Scout, or Trail of the
Renegade
The Pursuit**

*Terror filled their hearts as they raced across the
desert. Behind them, they could hear the sounds
of the battle raging, and they worried that Brand
would be killed. He had saved them, and now he
was sacrificing himself for them. . . .*

*The troopers, with Captain Stewart in the lead,
were returning from a short scout when they saw
the single horse charging toward them. They recognized it as Brand's and rode out to intercept it.
When they realized there were two women riding
the horse, they urged their mounts to a gallop. One*

of the men grabbed the reins and slowed the exhausted animal to a halt.

"Mercy! Thank God, it's you!" Captain Stewart dismounted and rushed to his wife's side, taking her down from the horse's back and clasping her to him.

"Oh, Clark! I can't believe you've found us!" Mercy cried, collapsing in her husband's strong arms.

"You have to help Brand!" Rachel managed. Pain was searing through her from her wound, but her only thoughts were of Brand, the brave scout who had rescued them from certain death.

"Where is he?"

"Near the mountains . . . The renegades attacked us there, and he stayed to fight them on foot!" Rachel pointed out the way.

"Three of you men, see the women safely to the fort. The rest of you, ride with me!"

Clark kissed Mercy tenderly, then rode off to help Brand. The scout had risked his life to save Mercy. The captain could do no less for him.

Brand and Sheri rode through the night, stopping only to rest the horses. He knew that the best way to avoid the posse that would be coming after them was to head back to the mountains. Silence was essential, so neither spoke unless it was necessary. They kept up their steady, ground-eating pace, and when the sun lightened the eastern horizon, Sheri could see the craggy peaks looming in the distance.

"We made it," she said triumphantly, gazing up at them. She had never thought she would think these mountains beautiful, but they were to her this day.

"Not yet, we haven't," Brand told her, watching for some sign that they were being followed. "I don't know how close they are behind us. We might have half an hour on them or we might have six or seven. There's no way of knowing."

"Then we keep riding?"

"We keep riding."

They continued on, desperation driving them toward their only haven.

Colonel Hancock stared at the deputy, his expression one of disbelief and loathing. "You let the damned half-breed murderer escape?"

"No, sir. We didn't let anybody escape. Someone broke him out."

"Who?" Hancock thundered.

"We're not sure, colonel. It could have been anybody. Maybe even that woman—you know, the writer? She was in the office with the sheriff twice yesterday trying to get him released."

"You and the sheriff let some female from back East outsmart you?" Hancock sneered. "I can't believe your incompetence! You had a cold-blooded killer locked up, and now he's on the loose again! Is anyone safe in this territory?"

Deputy Sullivan had suffered many tongue-lashings in his time, but this man sounded crazy. "We'll catch him again, colonel. Sheriff Warren's riding out with a posse at sunup. They'll find him and bring him in."

"You hope. The man's half Apache, or have you forgotten that? He's a scout! You'd better hope your trackers are as good as he is, or you'll never see him again!"

"We'll find him."

"Let's just hope you do, deputy. Killers shouldn't be running free. He deserves to be hanged for what he's done!" He was ferocious in his tone. His face was red, and veins bulged in his neck.

Sullivan was glad to get out of there. He'd done what the sheriff had told him to do. He had delivered the message. But something about the colonel scared him. He had expected the man to be upset. *They* were upset! Brand had broken out of their jail. But he had never thought the colonel would be as furious as he was. That was strange.

"I expect full reports from you on the status of your search," the colonel yelled after him. "Notify me immediately when you have him back in custody."

"We will."

Hancock was glad to see the deputy go, and as soon as he had left his office, he got up and began to pace the room. He had planned everything so carefully. It would have worked, too, if it hadn't been for that damned interfering St. John woman. It made sense that they suspected her of helping Brand get away. She had followed Brand around worshipfully from the first, believing he could do no wrong. She had been nothing but trouble since she showed up. He regretted now that he had accommodated her in her request to research her novel. True, the orders had come from Washington and it had been exciting at the time to think of themselves portrayed in a novel, but that was before she had caused such an uproar around the fort—first, with the raid and, now, this. . . .

He swore loudly at the thought that she might have been the one who'd helped Brand escape. He had finally had the filthy breed right where he'd wanted him—ready to hang. Now, everything had gone wrong, and it was all because of Sheridan St. John.

A sudden shaft of fear shot through him as he thought about his visit with Brand in jail. He realized that he might have revealed too much. A terrible feeling of unease overcame him, making his fury even greater. He would do whatever was necessary to see that Brand was caught and hanged. Brand deserved to die . . . for what he'd done to Becky. . . .

It was morning before Hancock finally ventured outside. He had remained locked in his office, desperately seeking a plan to deal with Brand. As he made his way across the parade ground, the lieutenant approached him.

"Sir, I spoke with Sergeant O'Toole about Brand last night. He was concerned about him."

"He was concerned about a murderer?" Hancock sneered in wonder.

Philip ignored his comment. He'd long recognized that there was no love lost between the colonel and Brand. "We were wondering, sir, if you would give us permission to go into town, so we could talk to Brand and find out how he is?"

Hancock fixed him with a deadly glare. "There's no need for that. I spoke with him yesterday."

"Colonel, there's every need. He's one of our men. I want to make sure he's being properly treated."

"He is a half-breed!"

"Yes, sir, but Brand is the best scout we've got. I believe he's innocent. I want to help him."

"Lieutenant," Hancock sneered. His tone was cold. "This just shows how sadly lacking your judgment is."

"Sir?" Philip was shocked and almost took a step backward at the venom in the colonel's words.

"Your wonderful, innocent scout is a renegade! He broke out of jail last night."

Philip stared at him. "When did you hear that?"

"Deputy Sullivan rode out with the news in the middle of the night. I spoke with him at length, and he's already returned to town. The posse was leaving from Phoenix at sunup."

"Why would he run?" Philip was confused.

"Why, indeed, lieutenant." Hancock was scathing. "He's guilty. Why else?"

"But . . ."

The colonel interrupted him. "I've given the matter much thought, and I've decided that you, O'Toole, and several of the other scouts should find the posse and help track the breed down. It's the least we can do to help. After all, as you say, he is one of *our* men."

"Yes, sir."

"Tell the sheriff that the man is to be considered a murdering Apache renegade. I wouldn't blame any of them if they shot him on sight!"

"But he could be innocent!"

"Innocent men don't run," Hancock snarled. "I will be waiting to hear from you. Don't disappoint me, lieutenant. It's humiliating enough to learn that one of our men is a cold-blooded killer. I want you to find him and see that he pays in full for his crimes."

"Yes, sir." Philip started away, shocked and worried. "We'll be riding out as soon as I can get the men ready."

Hancock merely nodded. His cold expression did not change.

Philip immediately went looking for O'Toole. "Sergeant, we've got orders to ride."

O'Toole brightened. He was eager to talk to Brand and find out what happened. "I can be ready in less than half an hour."

"It's not what you think. You'll need supplies."

At his tone, the sergeant cast him a curious glance. "What's wrong?"

"Some time last night Brand broke out of jail. Colonel Hancock wants us to take some scouts with us and find the posse that's riding out with Sheriff Warren. We're to help them find Brand and bring him in."

"But why did he run?" O'Toole was baffled.

"Ask him when you find him. All it does is make him look guilty as hell," Philip said angrily. "I guess he must have done it after all."

"I can't believe that. Brand's no killer."

"Whatever the case, we've been given our orders, so get ready to move out. I don't know how long it will take. He won't make it easy for us, that's for sure."

O'Toole was miserable. He had raised Brand from a boy. He knew him better than anyone, and he knew that he was not a murderer. He did not want to hunt down a friend—especially not Brand. "I'll get the scouts," he said reluctantly. "We'll be ready whenever you are."

It was late afternoon and the horses were near exhaustion, yet Brand kept urging them on. They couldn't stop yet. Ominous clouds were gathering to the north and west. A gully-washer would help them by erasing much of their trail, but it could also prove dangerous and deadly in these mountains. They would have to be in a high, protected spot to stay out of harm's way if the rains came, as he sensed they would.

Thunder was rumbling around them and black clouds were roiling above when Brand finally found a place for them to camp. It was high among the rocks, making it virtually impossible for anyone to reach them from below without being seen. There was just enough of an overhang to offer shelter from the rain that was to come, and he knew there was little time before the storm broke.

"We'll camp here. I'll take care of the horses," he announced as he reined in and quickly dismounted.

"I'll get the rest." She climbed down slowly, every inch of her body aching, but she wasn't about to say a word of complaint. She wanted to keep Brand alive. She hurried to stow their belongings beneath the overhang.

Lightning flashed nearby, and the boom of thunder that followed sent a shiver down her spine. Usually, she liked thunderstorms, but she'd never been out in one in the middle of the desert before.

"I thought it didn't rain in the desert!" she called to Brand.

"It doesn't—very often," he told her as he rushed to unsaddle their mounts and made sure they would be safe during the storm.

Another crack of lightning sent Sheri under the overhang. She had the rifle, the saddlebags, and their bedrolls, so there was nothing left to do but get comfortable. The downpour erupted before Brand had finished.

"It broke faster than I thought it would," he said when he finally came to join her. He was soaked

from the storm and his shirt was drenched and clinging to him. He immediately stripped it off.

Sheri watched as he tugged off the shirt. He was
hard and tanned, and as she watched the play of
muscles across his back, she couldn't help remembering how it had felt to touch him. She shivered at
the memory.

"Are you cold?" Brand saw her tremble as he
looked over at her. He was aware of everything about
her. It seemed he had been ever since he'd seen her
on the stage that day in town. He had tried to fight
the attraction. He hadn't wanted to care for her, but
she had stolen into his thoughts, and then into his
heart. And now into his soul.

"No . . ." she answered softly.

She lifted her gaze to his just as lightning split the
sky and thunder crashed around them, and it seemed
an omen to her. From their first encounter, he had
created a storm of emotions within her that she had
been struggling to deal with ever since. She had not
known for certain that she loved him until he'd come
to her in town, but now, as she gazed at him in the
dimness of their hideaway, she knew that she
couldn't bear to be without him. Though they would
have to fight for their love, she would withstand any
battle to be with him. She would never regret saving
him from a possible hanging in town, and if ulti-
mately she had to answer for what she'd done in
breaking him out, she would do so gladly.

Brand saw the depth of emotion mirrored in her
gaze. He did not know how he had come to be fortunate enough to have Sheri in his life, but he was
not going to deny himself the joy of loving her any
longer.

He reached out for her, and she went to him without hesitation. The fear that had driven them eased, and they found the haven they'd sought in each other's arms. The weariness they'd felt disappeared as his mouth settled over hers in a possessive claim. She clung to him, melting against him, needing the strength of him, needing to be closer. . . .

Her encouragement was all the invitation he needed. He drew back to undress her, his touch almost worshipful as he helped her strip away her clothes. Then he drew her to him, his hands upon her, sculpting the silken curves that so enticed him.

Around them the storm raged. Lightning rent the sky and thunder shook the land, but no force of nature was more powerful than their need for each other. Brand wanted Sheri more than he'd ever wanted any woman. She had saved his life twice, and now he knew she was saving his soul. Without her, his life had been barren and meaningless. With her, he had hope, and dreams, and love.

He moved away only long enough to shed the rest of his own clothing and then returned to her. She opened to him, wanting him near. There was no time to waste. They needed one another now, quickly. The desperation to be one overwhelmed them. Passion drove them together. Their bodies melded in a torrid embrace.

Brand's hands were never still as he traced paths of fire over her creamy flesh, cupping her hips, holding her to him as he sought the depths of her love. Sheri clasped him to her, holding him to her heart as she moved in that most sensual rhythm. She explored his body with intimate caresses that a short time before would have left her blushing. But no more. She wanted to please Brand, to make him want her as she wanted him. Being with him was heaven. She could imagine no greater ecstasy than to love and be loved by him.

They strained together, each seeking to give to the other that most perfect pleasure. And then it was upon them, that crest of ecstasy that swept them into desire's delight. Sheri surrendered to the glory of Brand's domination even as she conquered him. They soared to the heights together, hearts as one.

In the aftermath, there was no need to speak. Their bodies had spoken for them with devotion and joy. Brand sought her lips for a tender kiss, and they lay quietly, limbs entwined, in rapturous union.

Beyond their shelter, the rain continued. The lightning had ended, but thunder still echoed from afar.

Sheri rested against him, her head nestled against his shoulder. She could hear the steady, powerful beat of his heart beneath her, and it gave her the strength she needed to keep going. As long as she was with Brand, she knew nothing could ruin her happiness.

She had often written of love. Certainly, she had taken care of bringing Buck and the schoolmarm together, but that had all been fiction. She had never dreamed that loving a real man could be so wonderful or so frightening. She had almost lost Brand twice now, and knowing that there was a posse chasing them even as they lay together terrified her. He had to stay safe. Now that she had finally found him, she couldn't bear to think of her life without him.

Sheri started to tell him of her love, then hesitated, unsure as to his reaction. He might reject her. After a moment's consideration, though, she knew it didn't matter. She had to be honest. She had to tell him the truth of how she felt.

"I love you, Brand," she finally whispered.

Her softly spoken words fell upon his lonely soul like water on arid ground. His arms tightened around her, but he could not speak the words he knew she longed to hear.

Sheri rose on one elbow to gaze down at him. She studied his features, lovingly memorizing the strong lines of his face. It hurt that he did not profess to love her, but she had known it might happen. Loving him as she did, she would just take what he could give her, and hope that some day . . . some day he would be able to tell her he loved her, too. Gently, she bent to him and pressed her lips to his.

His arms came up around her and drew her down to him as he deepened the exchange. "You are one special woman," he said quietly.

She just smiled. "No, I'm just a woman in love for the first time in her life."

He kissed her, a soft, gentle exploration.

"What are we going to do?" she asked when they had ended the kiss, and she was curled up beside him.

He gave a low chuckle as his hands swept over her in an arousing caress. "I can think of quite a few things."

"Mmmm . . ."

It was some time later that they lay together, sated. The glory of their lovemaking had once again left them breathless with wonder.

Outside, the rain was slowing, its soft rhythm a seductive background to their loving.

"The rain's stopping. They'll be coming after us

now, won't they?" she asked, stirring in his embrace. Night had fallen, but her fears for the days to come were still very real.

"They'll try," was all he answered. Then he turned quiet again, lost in thought.

"What can we do? I told the sheriff the truth, but he didn't believe me. We've got to find out who killed Hale and let the authorities know. I've been trying to figure out who it could have been, but I'm not having any luck. It could have been someone in town who'd just been passing through, but if that's the case, then we'll never know who the killer was."

When Brand spoke, his voice was steely. "I know who did it. I just can't prove it."

"You do?" She sat up in shock to stare down at him. "Who did it? How do you know?"

"It was Hancock," he said flatly.

"The colonel?" She gasped in horror. "Why would he kill Hale?"

"For the same reason I wanted to kill him, and one more . . ."

"I don't understand."

"Hancock had just walked into the saloon when Hale made his remark about Becky and you. I'm sure the colonel heard every word the man said."

"So he would have been furious about him insulting his daughter . . ." She looked at Brand in astonishment as understanding dawned.

"Yes, and he hates me enough that if he thought he could frame me for murder and get away with it, he'd do it."

"You really think he hates you that much?"

Brand's gaze caught and held hers. "When he came in to see me at the jail, he told me in so many words

287

that he'd seen me going to you that night. His exact words were 'I wonder what Becky would think of you now, locked up like an animal after spending the night with another white woman. Last night was interesting. I saw a lot of things. But today is most satisfying'."

Sheri gasped at the revelation. "What else did he see?"

"What else did he do, is the real question. I've got a good idea, but I can't prove anything while I'm out here."

"Maybe Maureen and Charles will be able to find something out. They told me they'd go out to the fort and talk to O'Toole if they learned anything that could help. I knew he was the one person who would be on your side no matter what."

Brand nodded, his expression serious as he considered what they could do to prove his innocence. "Until we can offer them proof of my innocence, we'll just have to lie low and keep an eye out for trouble."

Sheri knew she had to change the subject before her worries took over completely. "I like the 'lie low' part of that," she said huskily as she curled up in his arms again. "As long as I've got you to lie low with."

His kiss was her answer.

It took O'Toole, Philip, and the three scouts who accompanied them the rest of the day to find the posse. Sheriff Warren was surprised by their offer of help, but quickly accepted. He knew that there weren't any better trackers than the ones from the fort.

Their efforts paid off for a while, leading them toward the mountains they dreaded. Brand knew the

Superstitions better than just about any man alive, and following him there would be hellish. Their luck turned from bad to worse when the storm broke, and they knew it would be a long day the next day trying to find any trace of the fugitives' trail after the gully-washer.

O'Toole was soggy, but actually half-smiling as he waited for the rain to end. Philip came to sit with him in the small shelter he'd erected for himself.

"You look too happy, O'Toole," the lieutenant complained. He was wet, tired, and irritated.

"Sorry."

"For some reason I don't believe you."

"We're going to have one helluva time picking up his trail in the morning."

"And that pleases you?"

"I'd hate to see an innocent man hang, lieutenant."

Philip was quiet for a long while, thinking about Sheri and her involvement in this. "So would I, but everything points to his guilt."

"Brand didn't do it." There was no room for doubt in his statement.

"What about Sheri? I can't understand why she got herself involved in this."

"Maybe she believed he was innocent, too."

The two shared a look, then sat in companionable silence, waiting for the rain to end and morning to come.

It was a dreary dawn, but there were clearer skies to the west. They were up and saddled and ready to ride, but theirs was a difficult job that morning. All traces of the tracks had been wiped out by the storm, and they were forced to guess at Brand's direction. They knew it was going to be a long day.

* * *

Maureen and Charles had arrived at the fort late the day before, only to find that O'Toole and Lieutenant Long had already gone. They'd tried to meet with the colonel, but he had sent word that he was too busy to see them that day. They managed to get rooms for the night and were eagerly awaiting the opportunity to speak with him that morning.

Maureen was standing outside waiting for Charles to join her, when she caught sight of Cecelia Whitmore and several of the other women she'd met at the parties. She decided to talk with them and see if they'd heard anything about Brand or Sheri.

"Why, Maureen, we didn't know you would be coming back to our fort," Cecelia greeted her.

"I didn't either, but so much has happened in the last few days that Charles and I though we should make some inquiries."

"We just heard the news about Brand's escape. This is terrible . . . A vicious killer on the loose . . ." Dora clearly meant every word.

"Brand is innocent, and Charles and I are here to help prove it."

"Innocent? A half-breed?" Dora scoffed. "How can you even think that?"

"Because I know he is. Sheri told me he was."

"Ah . . . your cousin . . ." The ladies exchanged a knowing look. "She's the one who broke him out, isn't she? Does she realize what the penalty is for jailbreak?"

"Do you realize an innocent man might have been hanged the other night by a lynch mob?" Maureen demanded.

"Well, the colonel's never trusted Brand, and I'm sure with good reason."

"His daughter trusted him," Maureen countered.

"And she's dead, as you well know," Dora remarked tightly. "Colonel Hancock has every reason to believe the worst of Brand. Why, it was his fault Becky was killed!"

"Dora!" This time it was Cecelia who was outraged. "How can you say such mean things?"

"You don't want to hear the truth? Really, Cecelia, sometimes you are so sheltered. If the half-breed had never married her, Becky would be alive and well today."

"Don't you think Brand knows that?" Maureen defended him. "Don't you think he's lived with that pain every day since she was murdered in the attack? He loved her and she loved him."

"My dear, you are romanticizing everything, just like your cousin," Dora scoffed. "Although I don't know this for certain, I would say the girl probably married him just to spite her father."

"She loved him, Dora," Cecelia corrected sternly. She had known and cared for Becky, and she remembered how desperately the young girl had agonized before deciding to go through with her marriage to Brand over her father's objections. "She knew her father would be upset, but she loved Brand more than life itself."

"And a lot of good it did her," the other woman sneered. "Now he's dragged Sheri into his life, and mark my words, she'd going to end up dead just like Becky, in spite of all her good intentions of saving him. She should have just let the mob have him and been done with it. He's no good, I tell you. Just ask

Colonel Hancock if you don't believe me."

"Dora, I knew you didn't like Indians, but I never had any idea you hated them this much," Cecelia said, amazed.

"After what we've seen out here? They're worse than animals. Animals only kill to eat. These Apache seem to kill for the pure enjoyment of it. I've heard the men talk about the torture and murder. I know what goes on out there."

Maureen was furious and barely held on to her temper. "If you will excuse me, I have to go find Charles."

"Of course, my dear," Cecelia said kindly. "Let us know if you hear anything."

Maureen only smiled faintly at her as she quickly moved away. They would be the last people she would tell anything to. She hoped Charles had an appointment with Colonel Hancock. She wanted some answers and she wanted them now.

Chapter Eighteen

Brand, the Half-Breed Scout, or Trail of the Renegade
Meanwhile, Back at the Fort . . .

Rachel lay in the bed in the hospital, her fever raging. Mercy stayed with her, pressing cool cloths to her forehead in a desperate attempt to bring her temperature down.

Rachel opened her eyes to look at Mercy. "Brand . . . How is he? Have they found him yet?"

"No. They haven't come back yet, but they will. Clark will find him. Everything will be all right," Mercy reassured her.

"I hope so . . . He saved us, Mercy . . ."

Mercy nodded as Rachel lost awareness again.

The doctor said there wasn't much that could be done other than to wait it out.

As soon as they'd returned to the fort, Mercy had sent word to Rachel's fiancé in Sacramento about what had happened. She hoped Carl would be coming soon to take care of her. Rachel certainly loved him, and Mercy believed he would want to be with her, as sick as she was.

"I just got word that he will see us now," Charles told Maureen as he sought her out.

"I'm more than ready. No wonder Sheri was so desperate to save Brand. You should hear all the ugly things people are saying. They're convinced that he's guilty, even though we all know that he's not."

"Prejudice is a terrible thing. It looks like it's up to us to find some kind of proof that Brand is innocent."

"Well, let's see what the colonel says. He was there that night. Maybe he'll remember something that will help us."

"And maybe he won't. Judging from what I've been hearing from the women, he had no use for Brand at all—none." Maureen's gaze met Charles's and they were both quiet.

"The man we really need to talk to is Philip. He could tell us what really went on that night, but from what I've found out, Hancock sent him, along with O'Toole and several scouts, off to help the posse track Brand."

"His own friends are hunting him down?" Maureen paled at the news and was truly frightened now.

"At least, they won't shoot first and ask questions

later, and you know how good Brand is. If anybody can outsmart O'Toole and Long, it's Brand."

"I know, but I was hoping O'Toole would be here to help us."

"It's better that he's out there, keeping the gun-happy men from town from shooting on sight."

"You're right. I just wish we could get to the bottom of this. The thought that Brand might be shot before we can prove he didn't do it scares me."

"It scares me, too," Charles agreed. "Let's go see if the colonel can help us."

"How do you want to handle this?"

"We'll just pretend innocence and ignorance and see what happens."

They headed for his office, hoping to learn some bit of information that might save Brand.

Hancock was not pleased that the pair had come to McDowell. In fact, he had stalled this meeting deliberately, hoping they would pack up and go back to town. When they'd stayed, waiting patiently to speak with him, he realized that he should have known better. Brennan was a good journalist. He had a way of digging at a story until he got everything he wanted. The colonel had to make sure that this time, the reporter didn't get anything except what he wanted him to know.

"Brennan, Miss Cleaver, come in and have a seat." He stood as he welcomed them and gestured them toward two chairs before his desk. He then sat back down and smiled encouragingly. "What can I help you with?"

"We're here because of Brand. So much has happened that we're very concerned about his safety and about Sheri's," Maureen began, playing upon his sympathies, hoping concern for Sheri would move him to help them.

"Why are you concerned about the safety of a flee-ing killer?"

"We are convinced Brand is innocent," Charles of-fered.

Maureen went on, "We think that's why Sheri dared to break him out of jail. There was talk of a lynch mob that night. She must have been afraid he was going to be hanged without a fair trial—a trial that would have set him free."

"Your cousin is a stupid woman," Hancock said harshly.

Maureen gasped at his words.

He went on without pause. "The penalty for break-ing someone out of jail is severe."

"What was she supposed to do, sir?" Charles pressed, sensing Hancock had overreacted to the re-mark. "Wait for him to be hanged before she took action? If a gang had come after him that night, there was no way Sheriff Warren and Deputy Sulli-van could have stopped them."

"So? The world would be a better place now if that had happened!" Hancock fought to control his tem-per. He was furious with the St. John woman for interfering. He slowly brought his rage under con-trol.

"Colonel, I can't believe you said that," Maureen said, aghast. "Sheri is a woman of principle. She could never have stood by and watched Brand hang for a crime he didn't commit."

Hancock wanted to scream that she had only freed him because she wanted the half-breed in her bed, but he didn't. He smiled thinly. "How can Miss St.

John and the two of you be so confident that Brand didn't kill Marcus Hale? I was in the bar when I heard Brand say he was going to kill him. If Lieutenant Long and I hadn't pulled him off of Hale then, he might have murdered him right before our very eyes, and then we wouldn't be having this ridiculous conversation. The breed said he was going to do it, and he did it. What more is there to know?"

Maureen heard the deadly edge to the colonel's voice and was intimidated by it. Charles, however, was puzzled and intrigued. He didn't understand why the man was so intent on seeing Brand hang for murder.

"Colonel Hancock, there were no eyewitnesses. No one saw Brand anywhere near Hale after he left the bar. The murder weapon was not found."

"Hale's throat was slit. Isn't that enough proof?"

"Anyone could have done that. Even you, sir," Charles said with feigned innocence.

"Me!" Hancock exploded, standing in a near-violent movement. "You dare to accuse me of this heinous crime? The half-breed's as guilty as hell, and your cousin is just as guilty for breaking him out. The authorities will deal with them appropriately when they find them, and I hope for justice's sake, it's soon!"

Charles stared at the colonel, taking care to keep his expression neutral. It would never do for Hancock to suspect what he was thinking. There was something very wrong here . . . very wrong. And Charles wanted to talk to the lieutenant right away.

"Colonel Hancock, do you have any idea when the lieutenant and Sergeant O'Toole will be returning?"

Hancock was shaken by his own display of temper,

and he struggled to appear calm as he walked around the desk, all but ushering them from the room. "When they find the breed. Not before. Now, if you'll excuse me, I do have other pressing matters to deal with."

Maureen rose, as did Charles. They thanked the colonel for taking the time to talk to them.

"If you hear anything from the posse, will you let us know?"

"Of course," Hancock said quickly, anxious to get them out of his office.

"We'd appreciate it."

As they passed through the office door, he shut it firmly behind them. Hancock turned away from the portal and went to the small cabinet next to his desk. He took out his whiskey bottle and poured himself a double shot in a tumbler. Without hesitation, he downed it.

"There," he said with satisfaction as he felt his nerves steady. Finally, as the wild anger within him calmed, he smiled. Now he could go on with his day.

Charles and Maureen didn't say anything until they were a distance away from the office and sure that they were alone so no one could overhear them.

"That was interesting," Charles said, glancing back toward the office, his expression thoughtful.

"Interesting? I'd call it more than interesting. The man is horrible! How can he believe that Brand is guilty? Why did he get so furious with us?"

He smiled slightly. "Sometimes, if you get too close to the truth, people try to scare you off by getting belligerent and accusing. You just saw a perfect example."

"You mean, you think . . ." Her expression was shocked.

"Exactly."

"But why? What possible motive could the man have for killing Hale and then letting Brand go to jail for it?"

"Didn't you just hear the women talking about how much he disapproved of his daughter's marriage to Brand?"

"But that was years ago."

"It doesn't matter. His daughter disobeyed him and is now dead. There's only one person he can blame for her death, and that's Brand."

"Do you think he hates him so much that he would have killed a man for no reason and then framed Brand for it?"

Charles looked thoughtful. "You have to remember what Hale was saying when Brand attacked him. He was insulting Becky and Sheri. As demented as Hancock seems to be, it makes perfect sense. Brand was heard threatening the man. The man ends up dead. Brand is guilty. Why would anyone suspect him? He thinks he's planned the perfect murder. He's exacted his revenge upon Hale, and now he's finally going to see Brand pay for what happened to his daughter."

"And he's going to get away with it," Maureen said sadly, seeing no way to prove Hancock's guilt. "There were no clues or witnesses. How can we prove he did it?"

"We'll think of something. We have to. Let's just hope Brand and Sheri can stay away from the posse long enough to give us time."

"Time to do what?"

"I want to go back into town for a while. There are a few other people I need to ask questions. Coming with me?"

"If it will help Sheri and Brand, you couldn't leave me behind."

The rains had provided one blessing for Sheri. When she arose early the next morning, there was a pool of water in an indentation in the rocks near the cave that was deep enough for her to bathe in. Brand stood guard, allowing her that short time of feminine privacy. He caught one glimpse of a slender thigh while he was trying not to look, and it took a major effort of will on his part to keep himself from joining her in the water. Under any other circumstances, he would have indulged himself in the sweetness of loving her in the morning, but the threat of danger was too real. He had to keep her safe. That was more important than anything else.

His thoughts drifted to the night before as his hawk-like gaze continually swept the valley below. He had never known love could be so beautiful and so giving. She was a passionate, tender lover. Just thinking of the hours he'd passed in her arms brought heat pounding back through his body, settling low in his loins, and he had to force his thoughts away from the night just past. He had to concentrate on keeping them alive, so there could be more nights like the last one. He wanted to spend the rest of his life loving her. But right now that was just a dream. He couldn't think of the future at all until his innocence was proven.

Sheri was refreshed and as ready as she would ever be to ride out when she finished dressing. She was thankful that she'd gotten the opportunity to bathe, for she knew how serious their situation was and how any small delay might cause trouble for them later.

"Are you ready?" she asked, as she found Brand keeping careful watch over the valley below.

He nodded. "The horses are saddled. Let's go."

"Where are we going?"

"Wherever they're not."

She knew she had to be satisfied with his response. She mounted up, prepared to follow him anywhere. She believed in him and trusted him, and she loved him with all her heart. Nothing else mattered.

Sheriff Warren was frustrated. "I sure am glad the colonel sent you to help us," he told Philip late that afternoon. "If it wasn't for you and your scouts, we'd have had to turn back hours ago."

"We still haven't picked up a new trail yet. The rain pretty much wiped everything out. It may take us until tomorrow to find it."

"That's all right. It will be worth every minute to bring the breed and the girl in."

"Speaking of the girl, what do you intend to do with her?"

"I'm going to arrest her and throw her in jail. It's what she deserves. She broke a killer out of jail!"

"Is there any possibility that she didn't do it? That maybe he kidnapped her and took her along for a hostage?"

Warren frowned. "No. She was in my office twice that day wanting to make sure he was all right. Why, she even . . ." He suddenly shut up as he realized what he'd almost told the lieutenant.

"She even what?"

"Nothing. She was making up all kinds of stories trying to get the breed released, but I told her I didn't have time to listen to her. I told her to go back to the hotel and stay out of the way because trouble was brewing down at the saloon."

"So she thought the crowd might try to hang him that night?"

"I was afraid they'd try. They were all drunked up and acting crazy, but Sullivan and I got them calmed down. When I got back, though, the breed was gone." He shook his head in disgust as he remembered his frustration that night.

Philip was intrigued by Warren's mention of Sheri "making up stories," and he couldn't resist asking, "Just what kind of stories was she making up about Brand?"

"I shouldn't have said anything. Just forget that I did."

"No, I'm serious," he pressed. "Maybe she was telling the truth. Maybe what she had to tell you wasn't a story."

"It had to be a lie. . . ." Warren cut himself off.

"What did?"

"She said Brand had spent the night with her," the sheriff blurted out, and immediately regretted it when he saw the lieutenant's shocked expression.

"I see." Philip went silent for a minute, digesting this news. Jealousy ate at him; he hated to think that Sheri and Brand were lovers. Still, as he thought about her and the kind of woman she was, he knew she was no liar. With much regret, Philip realized she had been telling the sheriff the truth, even at the risk of sacrificing herself. "Why did you think she wasn't telling the truth?"

"Well . . ." Warren looked at the officer and knew he was serious. "Well, it seemed so farfetched. I mean, she had a lot to gain by keeping him alive, what with her writing a book about him and all. It wouldn't look too good if the man she'd picked to be the hero got strung up for murder, now would it?"

"We're not talking about a novel here, sheriff. We're talking about a man's life."

"I didn't know you cared about the breed."

"I care about justice and truth. If Miss St. John came to you and told you in no uncertain terms that she could vouch for his whereabouts all night, and you refused to listen, I'd say she was desperate to save his life. And knowing her as I do . . . Well, she's the type of woman who will go to any lengths to achieve her goals if she believes in them."

Sheriff Warren heard the censure in the lieutenant's tone and suddenly realized that he might have been wrong about dismissing Sheri's tale as a lie. "But what does that make her, if she did spend the night with him?"

Philip shot the sheriff a cold look as he defended Sheri's honor. "A woman in love."

He put his heels to his horse and rode away. He'd heard enough from Warren for now.

But as they continued the search the rest of that day, Philip began to think about the night of the murder again. He had to admit to himself that he had automatically assumed that Brand was guilty. Now, he saw things in a different light. If Brand had been with Sheri, who else would have had the opportunity and the reason to kill Hale? The rest of that night in the bar replayed in Philip's mind as he tried to remember just what everyone had done. Colonel Hancock had left almost half an hour before he had, claiming fatigue. He'd stayed on and had had another two drinks before going back to his room. Hale had staggered out of the saloon sometime shortly before he had.

Philip frowned. Something was nagging at him that he couldn't quite put his finger on, and then he remembered. He had knocked on the colonel's door that night when he'd returned to the hotel, and there had been no answer. At the time, he'd just thought that Hancock had been sleeping soundly, but now he recalled that just as he had been falling asleep, he'd heard the colonel return to his room. He remembered thinking at the time that it was strange that the colonel had been gone longer from the saloon than he had and yet was just now getting back to their lodging.

Philip tensed as he tried to think things through. If Colonel Hancock hated Brand as much as he suspected he did, did he hate him enough to frame him for a murder that he himself had committed? The possibility was chilling.

They had to find Brand and bring him in alive. Only then could they get at the truth.

Just before dusk, one of the scouts signaled the posse that he'd picked up the fugitives' trail. They rode as quickly as they could to join him and then followed the trail until darkness forced them to quit for the night.

After they had made camp, O'Toole moved away from the others to stand alone and stare off into the distance. He wondered where in the massive mountain range his friend had taken refuge. He had been pleased with the rain the night before, but now that they had found Brand's trail, they would be closing on him. In his heart, O'Toole wanted Brand to remain free, but logically he knew his friend would never be free again until he'd been proven innocent.

He turned away from the view and went to bed down for the night. His thoughts were of Brand as he started to fall asleep.

Sheri settled in at their new campsite the second night and quickly ate the cold meal that was her dinner. It wasn't much, but she was too tired to care. As soon as Brand joined her, she moved to sit beside him. They were camped in the open this night, but they were still in a high, rocky location that would be impregnable after dark. They would be able to rest well again. After he'd eaten, Brand spread out their bedrolls. It took no encouragement to get Sheri to lie down.

"Tired?" he asked, stretching out next to her.

"Exhausted," she told him.

He lay back and folded his arms under his head as he stared up at the sky. "It's a beautiful night. You can see your stars tonight."

Sheri had had her eyes closed, but at his words, she looked up. There, overhead, was the most magnificent canopy of stars she'd ever seen. The moon had not risen yet, and the stars were all the brighter because of it.

"It's beautiful," she breathed, gazing up at the star-spangled sky. As she was watching, a meteor streaked across the heavens, and she gasped in surprise. "Brand! Did you see it?"

He smiled at her delight. As sophisticated as she was, she still took childlike pleasure in some things. "Yes."

"It was wonderful! I've never seen one before!"

"Be sure to use it in the book," he said, chuckling.

"If there is a book," she said softly. "When this started out, the trip was to be fun, an adventure for Maureen and me. But now it's become a matter of life and death, of survival, and I don't like it. I don't like it at all."

"That's what I was trying to tell you early on. Life out here isn't fiction. Sometimes it's harsh and cruel and ugly."

"I know that now, but even so, I won't write that in my stories. My stories have to have happy endings. I won't even think about writing them unless they do."

He turned serious as his gaze caught and held hers in the night. "What about our story, Sheri? Will we have a happy ending?"

Sheri gazed up at him and lifted one hand to caress his cheek. "Oh, yes. We're going to live happily ever after."

"I hope you're right."

"I am." She sighed as she pulled him down to her. "In fact, I can think of the scene I want to happen next. . . ."

"You can?" he asked with a devilish chuckle. "What scene is that?"

"It's the scene where Brand makes love to the heroine out in the open under the stars."

"Do you think that's a good idea?"

"I think it's a wonderful idea. . . ." she whispered as she kissed him hungrily.

"I do, too," he agreed, losing himself in the beauty of her embrace.

It was a long time later that they finally slept, sated and smiling in each other's arms.

Chapter Nineteen

Brand, the Half-Breed Scout, or Trail of the Renegade
Savage Protector

The troopers returned late the next day. Brand was safe and unhurt, and the renegades had all been killed. Things would be safe now in the Territory for a little while.

As soon as Brand had had the chance to clean up, he sought out Mercy to see how she was and to learn about Rachel.

"She's running a terribly high fever, and she's been asking for you," she told him. "Would you want me to go with you to the hospital? The doctor might let you in to see her."

"Yes. I want to make sure she's all right."

Brand hadn't been able to get Rachel out of his thoughts the whole time he'd been fighting the renegades. Every time he'd remembered the warrior attacking her that night, he had battled harder against them. Rachel was a beautiful, spirited woman, and he hoped she recovered soon. He wanted her to be safe and well. . . .

Hancock was in a vile mood. He grew angrier and more desperate as the days passed and no word came from the posse. He wanted the fugitives dead . . . both of them.

He had been pleased to hear that the reporter and the Cleaver woman had gone back to town the day before. They were thorns in his side that he didn't need. He just wanted to maintain a normal demeanor as he waited anxiously for word of Brand's fate. The rain had slowed the posse down, but now that the weather had been clear for several days, he kept expecting to see Philip and his scouts riding back into McDowell at any time. Each hour that they didn't, he grew more and more tense. The longer it took, the more concerned he became. He didn't like this. He didn't like this at all.

O'Toole knew Brand and Sheri were close. He just wasn't sure how close. He didn't know quite how he was so certain . . . a feeling, a sixth sense that told him they were near. But he knew, and he had to be prepared. He sat on his horse, his gaze scanning the horizon searching for some sign of Brand. He had to be the one to find his friend. That was the only way he could ensure Brand's safety.

Far above O'Toole, Brand hunkered down behind

a boulder with Sheri by his side, watching all that transpired below. He had deliberately doubled back to confuse them, and now he waited and watched as they sought the right trail to follow. They were good. There was no doubt about that. Brand had expected the posse to give up. He had not anticipated that O'Toole, Long, and several scouts from the fort would join in the effort, but it made sense. How better to catch them? And who better to order that they lead the posse than Hancock, the real murderer?

Brand glanced over at Sheri and gave her a slight nod of approval. She had impressed him more than he'd ever thought possible over the last few days. She had been tough on their first run from the Apache, but she had been even better this time. Never once had she uttered a complaint or sought to rest more than was necessary. If anything, her readiness to keep on the move kept him going. But this was the critical moment. If they could get behind their pursuers and head back the way the posse had come, they could pick up a good half day's lead on them, and that would give them time to rest their horses.

A shout went out from below, and Brand turned his attention back to O'Toole. One of the scouts had signaled for them to head farther down the canyon, and that was just what Brand had been hoping for. He watched with grim satisfaction as they headed in the opposite direction from where Brand and Sheri were in hiding. Sheri shot him a wide, victorious smile, and he smiled back. He didn't want to tell her it was just a temporary reprieve. There was no reason to dull her happiness. There was little enough of that.

They remained hidden where they were, watching

and waiting until the posse had disappeared from sight. Only then did they dare to move out.

"How long do you think it will take them to discover they went the wrong way?" Sheri asked once she was sure it was safe to talk.

"A long time, I hope. But they're good. They're real good. The best we can hope for is a few hours."

"Then we'd better hurry." She kneed her horse to a quicker pace.

They had ridden for almost half an hour when they heard it. Gunfire erupted. Volleys of shots and the echoing sounds of men's screams.

Brand reined in and stared back the way they'd come.

"What is it?" Sheri asked, terrified.

Brand listened, trying to judge the guns in use, trying to understand what had happened. But in his gut, he knew what had happened. Turning back as he'd done had been the most important thing he'd done in all their days of running, for by turning back when he had, he'd avoided running head-on into a raiding party of Apache.

"Apache," he said, his tone flat.

"They're attacking the posse?"

He nodded tightly, torn. It took him only an instant to make his decision. "I've got to go help them."

"No! They'll shoot you on sight!"

"If I don't go, they may all be killed! I can't leave them to be slaughtered. Not if I can help!"

"But Brand—those are the same men who want to see you hang."

"I know, but some of them are my friends. I have to help them. You stay here. You have the revolver?"

"Yes."

"Then I want you to ride up there." He indicated a locale with a good view of the area that would be impossible to attack with ease. "And stay there. I'm going to help O'Toole."

"I want to come with you!"

"No! Stay where I know you'll be safe. I'll be better able to fight if I know that you're out of harm's way."

"But . . ."

"Promise me," he said darkly, his gaze boring into hers as he sought her word.

"All right. I'll stay here."

The look on her face was so distraught at the thought that she might lose him that he wheeled his horse around close to hers and pulled her to him for a fast kiss.

"I'll be back," he vowed. With that, he drew his rifle from its scabbard and raced back the way they'd come, heading toward the sound of the fighting.

Sheri watched him for only a minute, then did as she'd been told. Carefully guiding her horse up the treacherous hillside, she sought safety in the rocks above. She would wait for him. He had promised he would come back to her. She believed him.

Dismounting, and then hobbling her horse the way Brand had taught her to, she settled in to await his return. As the sound of the fighting continued to echo through the mountains, she said a fervent prayer that he would be safe.

O'Toole and Philip were pinned down close together, covering each other as best they could. At least three men of the posse had been shot, and one they knew for sure was dead.

"Where the hell did they come from?" Philip asked,

furious that they'd been caught unaware.

"Hell is exactly it," O'Toole answered, returning fire with the renegades who had them pinned down.

"How many do you see? I can pinpoint five, but that's just on this side."

"There are at least four more over here, and they've got the high ground."

"Where's Sheriff Warren?"

"He's pinned down to your left about a hundred yards."

Philip paused in his firing to reload. "How did we walk right into this one?"

"Remind me to ask one of the scouts when we get out of here," O'Toole said sarcastically, wondering how they'd missed the signs of the raiding party. He ducked down and muttered an expletive when a shot came too close.

Philip responded to the shot with a round of his own, but he was driven back behind the boulder when a warrior high above fired again. "I think we're in trouble."

"I always did think you were one helluva smart officer," O'Toole growled, firing carefully, picking his shots so as not to waste ammunition.

More shots rang out, and they heard another of the posse cry out in pain. The hail of bullets from the Indians continued, and the posse was helpless to do more than stay under cover.

"We've got to do something. We can't just sit here and wait for them to slaughter us!" Philip was angry and determined not to die this way.

"We need to get someone up above."

"I don't know how we're going to do that if we're all pinned down!" O'Toole snapped. The plan was good, but executing it was impossible.

"There's got to be some way. . . ."

The sun beat down unmercifully as the raiding party continued its assault. They had already scared off the white men's horses and were now taking pleasure in picking off their helpless victims one by one. Their confidence was great. They had won. It was just a matter of time before the whites were all dead.

Brand left his horse a distance back and crept undetected above the scene of the ambush. With great care, he took his time, selecting the best spot from which to fire on the attackers. When he had counted them and knew their hiding places, he began shooting, making every shot count.

The first shot that rang out brought a scream from one of the Apache and startled the pinned-down posse.

"What the hell . . . ?"

"It's Brand!" O'Toole shouted, catching a glimpse of him high above. "There's your man up on top, lieutenant. We got 'em now!"

Brand's position was perfect, and the renegades began to scatter. As they ran from their positions, the posse below began to shoot at them. Screams of fury erupted from the Indians as they fled.

O'Toole had shifted his position and was getting ready to shoot at one of the braves running past him when he took a bullet in the arm. He fell heavily and struggled to get up. Brand saw him go down and felt a wave of fury go through him. With cold, deadly precision, he picked off the fleeing braves. When it was all over, only three of the Apache had made it to their horses.

When all was quiet and they knew it was safe, Philip ran to O'Toole.

"Where are you wounded, sergeant?"

"Just in the arm," he groaned. "I'll be all right once we get back to the fort. Signal Brand. Let him know that it's over."

Philip stood up and raised his hand. Brand saw the gesture and rushed to climb down the rocks to see if he could help O'Toole. He had seen him go down, but he hadn't seen him get back up. He was filled with a terrible dread that his friend was mortally wounded.

"He's coming down here," Philip told O'Toole in amazement. "If that had been me, I would have run again."

"Brand's a special kind of man, lieutenant," O'Toole said quietly as he braced himself against the rocks and watched his friend come toward him.

"Ain't that the half-breed?" one of the posse yelled, lifting his weapon to fire.

Philip turned on him, his own revolver aimed at the man's chest. "That 'half-breed' just saved your miserable life. Put the damned gun down or I'll shoot you on the spot."

O'Toole couldn't believe what he was hearing, but he heartily agreed with the sentiment. The man from town turned gray at the threat and quickly did as he was told.

"Sheriff Warren, Brand's coming down! He just saved all our miserable hides, so tell your men to hold their fire."

The sheriff quickly did as he was told, and they turned their attention to tending to the wounded.

Brand was carrying his rifle at the ready, but when

he saw that they were welcoming him, he relaxed a bit and went straight to O'Toole.

"O'Toole?" He dropped down beside him on one knee.

"You're a sight for sore eyes," the sergeant told him, relieved that Brand was uninjured.

"You hurt bad?" Brand asked, keeping an eye on Philip, who was coming toward them.

"I'll be fine. A couple of the men from town are shot up pretty bad, though."

Brand nodded.

"Brand?"

He looked over at the officer, skeptical of what he was about to say.

"We appreciate your coming to our aid. Thanks."

His thanks surprised Brand, and he only nodded again.

"And Brand?"

Their eyes met.

"Where's Sheri?"

"I left her back up the trail. She's waiting there for me."

"You know we have to take you in, don't you?" Philip said, his revolver aimed at Brand. "I don't want to do this, but I've got no choice. Not until we can prove you're innocent."

"Lieutenant!" O'Toole protested, furious with the man.

"He's accused of murder and breaking out of jail. We are bound to take him in. It'll go better for you if you just come with us without a fight."

Brand thought about running again. He thought about fighting his way out of there. He thought about Sheri. "All right, but give me your word that Sheri will not be charged with any crime."

"I can't do that."

"I can." Sheriff Warren spoke up from where he was doctoring one of his men.

Across the distance, the sheriff's gaze met Brand's in silent understanding.

"Let's get the horses and head for the fort. These men need attention. I don't think they can make it all the way to town."

Brand helped treat O'Toole's wound. When the men returned with the horses, they were ready to ride. It would be slow going, but they would make it.

Brand was eager to return to Sheri. He could just imagine how anxious she was, especially since the shooting had stopped. It was the longest ride of his life, for he worried that something might have happened to her while he'd been gone.

Philip had taken his weapons, but had not bothered to bind him. He rode next to Brand on the trek.

"You're a contradiction, Brand." At the scout's look, Philip went on, "You're accused of cold-blooded murder, yet you rode back into the middle of an ambush to save the very men who were hunting you down. You don't find that kind of self-sacrifice in most men."

"I didn't kill Hale, Lieutenant," Brand said stiffly.

"I'm coming to believe you," Philip answered, looking at him with respect.

"I just don't know how to prove it," Brand went on. "Do you remember anything unusual that happened that night after you got me out of the saloon?"

"Colonel Hancock left before I did. I stayed around and had a few more drinks. The strangest thing I

317

remember is that when I got back to the hotel, I knocked on the colonel's door and there was no answer. Then later, when I was falling asleep, I heard him come in. I have no idea where he was during those hours we weren't together, and I left before he got up the next morning, so I didn't get the chance to ask him."

"It all fits. I just can't prove anything."

"What fits?"

"Hancock told me when he came to see me in jail that he knew I wasn't guilty, but he said I wouldn't be able to prove it." Brand smiled tightly. "He knew he had me even then."

"That was before I remembered what happened that night," Philip put in. "He's going to have some explaining to do once we get back. It will be interesting to see what he has to say for himself."

Sheriff Warren had been riding nearby, listening to their conversation. "You know, what you just said reminded me of something. . . ."

The two men looked at him quickly, wondering if he knew anything that could help them.

"That day when the colonel came to the jail to see Brand, I spoke with him first. The way he talked about the time you spent at the saloon, he made it sound like the two of you left the bar and returned to your hotel together." He was speaking to Philip as he explained.

Philip's eyes narrowed at this news. He had served with the colonel for some time now. He respected and admired him. The thought that his commander might have done something so deliberately savage was deeply troubling. It didn't fit with the man he knew. "It seems our colonel has quite a few things to straighten out when we get back."

"But we still can't prove anything." Sheriff Warren was still worried.

"We will," Philip said with confidence, looking over at Brand and seeing a friend now instead of a half-breed scout.

Sheri had kept her word to Brand. It hadn't been easy. There had been any number of times when she'd wanted to get on her horse and chase after him, but she'd controlled the urge. She had promised to stay, and she did.

Her nerves were stretched taut. The sounds of the gun battle had seemed to go on forever, and then suddenly they had stopped. The silence that followed had seemed deafening, and Sheri had been left wanting to scream in frustration. She wanted to know where Brand was and that he was safe. Her heart ached with the knowledge that he might be wounded somewhere, needing her. Desperate for something to keep her busy, she had dragged out a few pieces of paper and a pencil and had started writing. She knew it was crazy to be writing in the middle of the real wild West with Indians and posses having a shoot-out nearby, but it was the only way to save her sanity. Without her story right then, she would have gone mad. It was far easier to lose herself in Rachel and Brand's story than it was to deal with the reality that the real Brand might be in trouble.

Sheri wrote furiously. Pages flowed from her thoughts. Pages of worry and heartbreak, of longing and of love. She wrote a heart-wrenching scene in which Rachel had to make the most important decision of her life. If Sheri had written the scene a month before, sitting at her desk at home, it would have been sterile—one-dimensional characters walking through the plot line. This scene was so real, it brought tears to her eyes when she reread it. She was smiling a watery smile when she finished.

Drained of emotion, yet still worrying about Brand, she stowed her writing materials and crept forward to look down the canyon for some sign that he was returning. It seemed an eternity since he'd left her. For certain, more than two hours had passed, and yet there was no sign of him. She wondered what she should do, but she remembered his promise. He had said he would be back, and he never lied to her.

Sheri settled back down on the hard ground to wait even longer. It wasn't easy being patient, but she would do it. Brand was coming back. He'd said he was, and she believed him.

Another hour passed before she heard the sound of horses coming. Her first instinct was to jump up immediately and start yelling. Then common sense took over as it occurred to her that it might not be Brand returning. Ever so cautiously, she drew the revolver he'd given her and moved to get a look at the area below.

Sheri saw them immediately. Brand, Philip, and Sheriff Warren were in the lead. The others were following, several who looked as if they were grievously wounded. Even Sergeant O'Toole seemed slumped in the saddle. Brand looked up her way then, and she stood, revealing her position.

"Brand!" she shouted, holstering the gun and then waving at him excitedly. Her heart was pounding a frantic rhythm as she realized that he was unhurt.

Brand was thrilled to see that she had kept her

word to him and had stayed put. He urged his horse forward and scrambled up the steep hillside to reach her. As he neared her, he dismounted and she came into his arms, throwing hers around his neck and kissing him full on the lips right in front of everyone.

"Thank God you're all right!" she cried, hugging him close.

"I told you I'd come back for you," he said in a low voice for her ears only.

Philip and the sheriff were coming up right behind him, but the others had waited below.

Brand and Sheri broke apart, aware of the other two men nearby.

"Sheri," Philip greeted her with a smile. "It's good to see that you're unhurt."

"I did exactly what Brand told me to do. I stayed put."

"Good advice. It got ugly down there," he told her. "Brand was a hero. He saved us all."

She gazed up at Brand with love shining in her eyes. "I know."

"Let's get your horse," Brand said, uncomfortable with the praise. "Some of the others were shot, and we've got to get back to the fort as quickly as we can."

"The fort?"

"It's closer. There's a doctor there. He'll be able to take care of them," Philip explained. "And we've got the guardhouse where . . ."

"Where what?" Sheri demanded, suddenly outraged by what she realized was going to happen. "You're not planning on locking Brand up again, are you?"

"Sheri, he's been arrested on murder charges and escaped from jail. We have to take him back in."

"But I'm the one who broke him out! Arrest me!"

"I made arrangements with Sheriff Warren," Brand told her. "You're not going to be charged with any crime."

"And you shouldn't be either!"

"Until we can prove his innocence, we have to keep him locked up."

"But he didn't do it!" she protested, wondering why no one would believe her. "I already told you, sheriff, that Brand was with me that night." She went to stand before the two of them, where they still sat on their mounts. "Why won't you believe me?"

Both men looked at Brand for confirmation.

"Sheri can't vouch for me that night," Brand said tersely.

"What?" She gasped and spun around to glare at him, thinking that he was crazy.

But Brand wasn't looking at her. He was looking straight at Philip, who was returning his regard, a very serious expression on his face.

"This is absurd! Why are you doing this?" Sheri asked Brand.

"We aren't certain of Brand's whereabouts that night, so we'll keep him locked up until we can arrest the real killer," Philip said. He had seen the truth in the other man's eyes and knew Brand would rather die than disgrace Sheri. He would protect her virtue with his life. Philip's admiration for him grew even more, and he wondered how he could have been so prejudiced against him. Brand was a good soldier and a gentleman.

"I'll get your horse, Sheri. We need to get back to McDowell," Brand told her, then walked away.

Frustration filled her. She didn't understand why

he was doing this. If only they would listen to her, everything would be fine. He would be a free man. She rushed to Philip's side.

"Philip, you have to understand. Brand and I were together that night. I don't know what he's doing by denying it . . ."

"I do," Philip answered seriously. "He's protecting you. Don't worry, Sheri. We're going to get the man who murdered Hale, and when we do, Brand will be proven innocent."

Sheriff Warren wanted to reassure her, too. "Things will be quieter when we get back to town. There won't be any lynch mobs. I'll make sure he's safe, and as soon as we find the real killer, he'll be released."

Tears burned in Sheri's eyes. She'd known she would be ruining her reputation by publicly admitting that she and Brand had spent the night together, but that hadn't seemed to matter. She wanted Brand free. The men, however, were determined to keep her out of it. Even on his way to jail, Brand was keeping her safe.

Chapter Twenty

Brand, the Half-Breed Scout, or Trail of the Renegade
Love's Sacrifice

Brand gazed down at Rachel's fever-flushed features and felt a stirring of emotion deep inside him. She was beautiful. The most beautiful woman he'd ever seen. He had never known anyone like her. She was brave. She had fought him when she'd thought he was the enemy. She had saved his life and been wounded for her effort. She had never complained throughout the whole ordeal of returning to the fort, and now she lay seriously ill, and he could do nothing more to help her.

"Rachel . . . I brought Brand to see you, just like you asked," Mercy said quietly.

Her eyes fluttered open and she gazed up at him. "Brand . . ." His name was a whisper. "Brand . . . you're safe now. . . ."

"We just rode back in. I wanted to see you and make sure you were all right."

"You saved our lives. . . . Thank you . . ."

He was amazed that, as sick as she was, she was thanking him. She was the one who had saved his life. He bent down closer to her. "I'm the one who should be thanking you. You saved me."

She managed a weak smile, then drifted off into a feverish sleep.

"We'd better go and let her rest," Mercy said softly. "The doctor says there's nothing more we can do but to keep her as cool as possible and wait for this to pass."

"Let me know how she does, all right?" he asked, his concern very real.

Brand cared about her, though he knew he shouldn't. He knew nothing would ever come of it. She was a white woman, and he was a half-breed. But even though he was fighting against the attraction he felt for her with all his being, there could be no denying that Rachel had won a place in his heart.

Charles was frustrated. He'd spent the whole day trying to track down the maid who'd been working at the hotel where the colonel and the lieutenant had stayed the night of Hale's murder. It had been her day off and finding her had proven to be impossible. He had to wait until the next afternoon for her to show up at the hotel before he could question her. He hoped his hunch proved right, but he wouldn't be able to find out for another day.

He was taking Maureen to dinner and was looking forward to it. She was definitely going to be the bright spot in his day. Knocking on the door to her room, he was pleased to find she was ready to go. She looked lovely in a dark blue gown that highlighted her pale complexion and the fairness of her hair.

"You look beautiful," he complimented her, his eyes warm upon her as they settled in at the restaurant.

"Why, thank you," she told him with a smile. "I was looking forward to seeing you tonight. It's been a long, lonely day."

"I understand, believe me."

"Why? What happened? Did you talk to the maid yet?"

"No. She's gone until tomorrow, and no one knew where to find her. I checked in about four different places before I gave up. The only good news is that the posse isn't back yet, so I'm hoping Brand and Sheri are still safe."

"I hope so. I'm so frustrated and scared. It seems all I do is worry about Sheri. She could be killed out there! You heard the colonel. The way he sounded, he didn't care if they were brought back dead or alive."

"I know. I'm just hoping, since O'Toole and Lieutenant Long are with them, that they won't shoot first and ask questions later."

Maureen shuddered at the thought. "There are times when I wish we'd never come to this godforsaken place! We've had nothing but heartache since we got here."

Charles had been feeling good about the way their relationship was developing. He'd even hoped that she might have come to change the way she felt about the Territory, but everything that had happened just seemed to make things worse for her. He didn't blame her one bit for feeling that way. She'd had a rough trip West.

"I'm sorry it's been so difficult for you. This is a tough, untamed place, but what you and Sheri have experienced is unusual."

She saw the shadow of disappointment in his eyes and realized that something she'd said had hurt him. "There have been some good things, too. I got to meet you."

He smiled slightly, then said derisively, "And a lot of good I've done you. First, I get shot by the raiding party when we're out on the scout and you're stuck nursing me back to health, and now I think I know how to identify Hale's killer and save Brand and Sheri, yet there's no one way to interview the witness. And even if I did, there's no one around to tell."

"But you're trying to help," she said. "That's more than most people have done. Everyone else has been ready to lynch Brand."

"It did look bad in the beginning. I don't blame Sheri for wanting to break him out. I'm not sure Sheriff Warren really could have kept them away if they'd decided to storm the jail that night."

"It was very brave of her. She's a remarkable woman."

"I just hope she comes through this all right."

"So do I. I love her a lot. If it hadn't been for Sheri,

I would still be back in New York. She's the one who brings out the best in me."

"She is a rare woman, but then, so are you," he told her, gazing at her across the table. In the candlelight, she looked even lovelier than usual, and he remembered collecting his winnings and wondered if she was up to another hand of poker. He would certainly enjoy winning again.

"Thank you." She smiled at him. She had come to care for Charles a great deal. When the time came for her to go back to New York with Sheri, she was going to miss him a lot.

"No need to thank me. I'm the newspaperman, remember? I just tell the who, what, when, where, and why of things. Journalists don't lie."

"I'm going to miss you, Charles."

"And I'm going to miss you." He wanted to say more, to tell her that he loved her and wanted to be with her always, but he held himself back. She was too worried about Sheri to be able to think clearly about anything else right now. He would wait until the time was right to speak to her of love and commitment. "Well, we'd better enjoy what time we have together, then, shouldn't we?"

And they did. They had a delicious meal that night and then he accompanied her back to her hotel room.

"I'll see you tomorrow?"

"Of course. Do you know when you're supposed to meet with the maid?"

"In the afternoon some time. I have to check back at that hotel and find out when the woman's coming in."

"Can I go with you?"

328

"I'd like that."

She started to go inside her room, but Charles touched her arm to stop her.

"Maureen . . . ?"

"Yes, Charles?" She turned to glance at him and saw the heat in his gaze. It took no more encouragement than that for her to take a step toward him.

Charles took her in his embrace and in the silence of the hallway, he kissed her. His lips moved hungrily over hers, letting her know without words how much she was coming to mean to him, and Maureen responded with equal eagerness.

"Good night," he said quietly, when they finally broke apart and he had to force himself to leave.

"Good night."

They parted sweetly. Maureen went inside and retired for the night. As she lay in bed, thoughts of Charles's kiss kept her awake. She wondered if he cared about her. She wondered, too, how she was going to bear to leave him when the time came for them to return home. Rest was long in coming.

Charles found that Marguerite Sanchez had been worth the wait. He and Maureen sought her out at the hotel the following afternoon, and she seemed nervous that he wanted to talk to her.

"Have I done something wrong, sir?" she asked, fearful of losing her job.

"No, nothing like that. I just have a few questions for you. That's all."

"All right . . ." She was tentative, but agreed to talk to him.

"Do you remember the night when Marcus Hale was killed?"

"Oh, yes, sir."

"It was a terrible thing, him being killed that way."

"I know . . . I heard them talking about it." Her color faded and she swallowed nervously. "But what does that have to do with me?"

"What I'm interested in finding out . . ."

She waited, her eyes wide, her manner nervous.

"When you were cleaning the rooms the following morning, did you find anything unusual in any of them?"

"Unusual?" She frowned, not understanding what he was looking for. "I don't understand."

"Blood, for example. Did you find anything bloody in any of the rooms?"

"Oh . . ." She looked really frightened now. "Yes, sir. There was, but I didn't think anything of it."

"What did you find?"

"Well, sir, in one room, there was a towel with some blood smeared on it, and the water in the washstand was bloody."

Maureen gasped at the revelation. "Didn't you think that was strange?"

"No. I just thought the colonel cut himself shaving or something. . . ."

"So, it was in Colonel Hancock's room?"

"Yes, sir."

Charles felt triumphant at her answer. "Marguerite, you're wonderful. Thank you."

"That's all you wanted?"

"That's all for now, but stay close to town. As soon as the sheriff gets back, I want you to talk to him. Your story could help to free an innocent man."

"Good. I will, sir. I will stay close."

"Thanks."

With that she disappeared to go back to work, leaving Charles and Maureen alone. In a spontaneous act of excitement, Charles grabbed Maureen around the waist and spun her around in a complete circle.

"That's it! We've done it! Once we tell the sheriff of her testimony, he'll have something to go after Hancock with!"

Maureen felt like celebrating, too, and she looped her arms around his neck and kissed him firmly on the mouth.

"What was that for?" He was shocked.

"Because I think you're wonderful, Charles Brennan!" She looked up at him in awe, admiring his hard work and brilliance.

He actually blushed.

"You know, when Sheri gets back here, I may just have her change her hero's name to Charles! How would you like being the hero in a novel?"

"I'd love it . . . As long as you were my heroine . . ." He hadn't meant to say it so soon, but it was too late to take the words back now. He drew her closer to him, seeking her lips with his in a poignant, breathless kiss.

A noise down the hall jarred them apart and they were laughing as they left the hotel.

"Now, if only the posse would get back," he said worriedly.

Hancock had been drinking steadily for days. No one had caught him in the act, but those who had dealings with him had said that the smell of whiskey on his breath was unmistakable and that his temper was hotter than ever. Most elected to stay out of his way, or if called upon to do duty, did it as quickly and quietly as possible. They had seen his rages before and knew how ugly they could be.

"The posse's coming!" the shout went out.

An enlisted man hastened to knock on Hancock's door. "Sir!"

"What is it?" he bellowed.

The man opened the door to tell him the news. "The posse is on its way into the fort, sir."

Hancock's expression had been black, but hearing this, he suddenly smiled. It was not a smile of happiness, though. It was a smile of cunning. He rose from his desk.

"Thank you, corporal."

The corporal quickly closed the door and resumed his duties.

Hancock strode to his window and stared out, watching as the straggling group rode in. From this distance, he couldn't recognize anyone. He saw one body thrown over a horse's back and hoped it was Brand's. Nothing would please him more today than to see the bastard dead. As far as the woman went, he didn't care what had happened to her. He straightened his uniform and started from his office. He was more than ready to greet the sheriff and to speak with Long and O'Toole.

The first person he saw when he strode toward the exhausted riders was Brand, riding in next to Long. A vile curse rose in his throat, but he choked it back. He fought down the fury that threatened to erupt. The man was obviously under arrest. He would have to be satisfied with that.

"Lieutenant Long!" he called out. "I see it was very wise of me to send you and the others along with the sheriff. You found them."

Long was careful to keep his expression from revealing what he was thinking. "Yes, sir. We found them both."

"Is he the one who ambushed you and shot the others?" He was almost gleeful at the prospect. All the more reason to rush the breed to the gallows. They could string him up tonight, if they wanted to.

Long tensed at Hancock's words. He slowly dismounted, casting a quick glance toward Brand and Sheri, who were riding up behind him. "No, sir. Actually, we were ambushed by an Apache raiding party. Brand came to our rescue. If it hadn't been for him, we'd probably all be dead."

Hancock went still at the news, and his regard was icy with hatred as he looked at Brand. "Whether he helped you or not, he still killed Hale. Take him to the guardhouse now, lieutenant, and I want a guard posted on him at all times. You can't trust him."

Long wanted to tell his colonel that he trusted Brand more than he would ever trust him, but he said nothing. This was not the right time for the confrontation. He swung back up in the saddle. "Yes, sir. I'll see to it. We also have injured men from the posse. They need to be taken to the hospital."

"I'll give the orders," Hancock said tersely.

Long and Brand rode off toward the guardhouse. Both men were glad to be away from the commanding officer.

Sheri was angrier than she'd ever been in her life as she watched them go. She wanted to jump down off her horse and slap the colonel as hard as she could. It was bad enough that Brand was going to be locked up and under guard, but to listen to the colonel and his insults was almost too much for her to bear.

"You!" Hancock saw her then, and for just an instant, his facade dropped and his face turned red with rage.

"Miss St. John is free to do as she pleases," Sheriff Warren explained as he rode up and dismounted before the colonel.

"Isn't she the one who broke the breed out of jail?"

"There are conflicting stories about the incident, so we're giving her the benefit of the doubt, especially since Brand came to our rescue and then surrendered to us peacefully," he said.

"I see," Hancock ground out. "Very well. I'll have the captain see to accommodations for you for the night. Take your wounded to the hospital, and I'll make sure the doctor is ready to see them. You have one dead?"

"Yes, only one, thank God. If it hadn't been for Brand, we all would have been killed."

"Don't let that influence your judgment, Sheriff Warren. You know the man's a killer."

"We'll let a judge and a jury decide that, colonel. If you'll excuse me? I'll tend to my men." After the discussion they'd had on the ride back, he wanted to say as little as possible to the man until they were ready to question him extensively.

Hancock was infuriated by his answer, but bit back what he was going to say. He couldn't lose his temper here with so many people watching. Later there would be time for that. He took one last look around, saw that everything was under control, and turned and strolled off. He went back to his office.

He needed another drink. This wasn't going the way he'd planned.

Sheri couldn't believe that the men from the posse weren't confronting the colonel right then and there. She was livid at the prospect of his getting away with Hale's murder and blaming it on Brand, and she was more than ready to confront the arrogant officer. All the way back, she'd been thinking about what she wanted to say to the man, and it wasn't pretty.

She dismounted and was thinking about following Hancock, when Cecelia appeared.

"Sheri, dear, thank heavens, you're back safe!" she said, hurrying to her like a mother hen. "Maureen was here trying to find out something about you the other day, but there was nothing to be learned. She's gone back to town now with that nice newspaperman. I understand you need quarters for the night, and the rooms you had on your last trip are all ready for you. Come with me, and we'll get you all settled in."

"Thank you, Cecelia. Would it be possible to send word to Maureen that we're back and safe here at the fort?" Sheri was relieved to know that her cousin was fine.

"Of course, my dear. I'll see to it as soon as I take you to your rooms."

She allowed the older woman to lead her off, but her gaze was fastened on the retreating, ramrod-straight back of the colonel. As soon as she got cleaned up, she was going to see the man. Philip might not be ready to confront him, but she was feeling no such constraints. She had a few things to say to the man, and she was going to say them.

* * *

Hancock was cold inside. Fear was gripping his soul. He didn't like this. He didn't like this at all. Bits of the conversations he'd had with the lieutenant and the sheriff were haunting him. Had Brand really saved them? Did they really suspect now that he wasn't guilty? He drank straight from his bottle of whiskey. The knock at his office door surprised him.

"Who is it?"

"Sheridan St. John, Colonel Hancock. I wonder if I could talk to you for a few minutes?" Sheri said through the door.

"Yes . . . Just a minute . . ." He quickly put the top back on the bottle and shoved it into his drawer. "All right. Come in."

Sheri had taken the time to wash up and was feeling much more in control as she ventured into his office. She despised this man for what he was trying to do to Brand, and she was determined to get to the bottom of it, even if the lieutenant and the others weren't.

"Thank you for seeing me," she said with a sweetness she wasn't feeling.

"Of course, it's my pleasure," he replied graciously, all the while grinding his teeth in fury at her presence. "Please have a seat."

"I will, thank you."

"What can I do for you, Miss St. John?"

"I know we're going to be heading back to town just as quickly as we possibly can, so I wanted to take the opportunity to speak with you privately and thank you for all your help."

"You're more than welcome," he said, caught a little off guard. He didn't know what he'd been expecting, but it wasn't this.

"Yes, it will be a pleasure to let my cousin James in Washington know just how much help you were." She deliberately used James's name to remind the colonel of her political connections.

"I appreciate that. So you've done all your research and you're ready to write your book?"

"Oh, sir, I've been writing it the whole time we've been here."

"But won't you need to make some changes? You can't possibly use Brand for your hero now that he's going to hang for murder, can you?" Had he been sober, he would never have said what he was thinking, but he wanted to remind her that Brand was a filthy, no-good renegade, just like the ones who'd attacked them out in the mountains.

Sheri had known the conversation was going too smoothly, and she was glad for this crack in his armor. Her championing of Brand was his weak spot, and she knew that if she was going to get him to reveal anything, that was the way.

"Brand's not going to hang. He's innocent, and we're going to prove it," she said simply.

"We?" he asked quickly.

"Why, Lieutenant Long, Sheriff Warren, and me. And as for my book, well, there will be no problem there at all. You see, though the Brand in my book is framed for murder, the truth comes out in the end. . . ."

"What truth?" Hancock went still behind his desk as he watched her like a predator.

Sheri sensed that he was growing angry, but she did not waver in her determination to confront him in the only way she knew—through her fiction. "Oh, yes. You see, in my book, Brand, of course, is innocent. He couldn't have done the crime, for he was with my heroine, Rachel. The problem was finding the one who did do it and making sure there was enough evidence to convict." She lifted her gaze to his and did not flinch before the murderous look in his eyes. "I decided the perfect villain was Brand's commanding officer at the fort. He had the motive and the opportunity, and he had long wanted Brand out of the way."

Never in all her years had Sheri seen any expression like the one that flickered across Hancock's face. It was evil . . . pure evil. But as soon as she'd caught a glimpse of it, it was gone. She fought down a shiver.

"What do you think of my plot line?" she asked sweetly, taking care to keep her expression as innocent as possible. "Do you think it's believable?"

Hancock's smile was tight. "I think it's very creative fiction, Miss St. John, but that's what you're paid to do, right? Make up stories?"

"Ah, but sometimes my stories are based on the truth. That's why I'm here researching. My publisher wanted my work to be more authentic, you know." Sheri saw his hands clench into fists so tightly that his knuckles were white. She rose smoothly, sensing the need to make a quick exit. She felt a sudden fear for her life, and she was glad it was daylight and there were lots of people around outside. "Well, again, thank you for everything. I'll be going now."

She did not wait, but started from the room. She moved as slowly as she could make herself walk, for she didn't want him to know how scared she was. It wasn't easy, though, for she felt his deadly regard on her the whole time she was crossing the room to the door.

"Miss St. John?"

His voice stopped her as she reached for the door knob. She glanced back, and this time she did tremble. He looked like a vicious predator watching her.

"Yes?"

"I'm sure I'll see you again before you go. Thanks for stopping by."

She nodded, then left, wondering if she had done any good at all. She had wanted to shake his control, to taunt him into losing his temper, but now she feared she'd failed miserably and had possibly ruined things for the lieutenant. She hoped not. Disappointed, she returned to her room, and when she got there, she instinctively locked the door behind her. Only then did she feel she was reasonably safe.

Hancock stared at the closed office door. He did not know how he'd controlled himself, but he'd done it and he was proud of himself. He'd wanted to kill her, to wrap his hands around her throat and silence her for eternity. Her and her half-breed hero!

Rage roared through him. He stood up to pace the office. If what she was saying was true, then she knew the truth—and it would only be a matter of time before they came for him. He broke out in a cold sweat. They must have some clue to his killing Hale, but he didn't know what. He'd been so careful about it.

He sat back down at the desk to think. He had to take action. He had to do something! He wanted Brand dead, along with the St. John girl. If only he could think of a way. . . . He got out his bottle and took another deep drink. He had little time to waste.

He had to come up with a plan.

Sheri hadn't been gone long when there was another knock at his door.

"Who is it?" he demanded, outraged by another interruption.

"Lieutenant Long, sir. I wanted to report in."

Hancock thought for a moment, then called for him to come in. "How are the wounded, lieutenant?"

"They should all make it, sir. I just spoke with the doctor and they're doing as well as can be expected. He thinks they should stay on for a few more days before trying to make the trip back to town."

The colonel nodded. "That will be fine. Anything else?"

"Yes, sir. There is one other thing I'd like to broach with you . . ."

"Speak your mind, lieutenant. What is it? Are you worried about the breed escaping? I've posted a guard on him."

"No, that's the least of my worries, sir. The truth is, colonel, I've become convinced that the sheriff has arrested the wrong man."

"What? Everyone in the saloon heard Brand threaten Hale! You heard him, too! Everyone knows he did it!" Hancock raged, nearly out of control at the thought of his plan failing. They had to hang the breed; it was what he deserved.

"Not everyone," Philip said coolly, watching the change in his commanding officer and amazed by it. It looked like their hunch was right. Everything did fit. "You see, I spoke with the sheriff and with Brand. It seems you told the sheriff that we left the Gold Bar Saloon together that night, and you know that's not true. Also, when you spoke to Brand when he was in the cell, you told him that you knew he was innocent. Yet, when you speak to anyone else, you say you are certain he did it."

"I was trying to give him some moral support," Hancock lied, his color fading as he faced the younger officer. "And what I said to the sheriff, exactly, I have no idea. He asked me if I remembered anything unusual about that night, and I told him that we'd left about the same time."

"I see."

"I don't understand your point, lieutenant. Are you trying to accuse me of something?" Hancock challenged, wanting to back him down. He'd never known Long to have much backbone before, and he'd never had any trouble controlling him.

"No, sir. There was just one other thing. You left the saloon before I did, but when I returned to my room at the hotel, you were not there yet. I knocked on your door, thinking you'd retired for the night, but there was no answer. Later, as I was falling asleep, I heard you come in."

Hancock flushed as his rage grew. He was being trapped! He knew it! "I was otherwise occupied that night."

"Otherwise occupied, sir?" Philip pressed, sensing he had stumbled upon something important here.

"I . . . uh . . . I paid a visit to Miss Loretta's," he blurted out. "I spent some time with one of the girls."

"Which one, sir?"

"What the hell difference does it make?" he roared.

"I was just going to follow up on your story and see if everything checked out."

Hancock rose to his feet, towering over the younger man. "Are you calling me a liar? I have no reason to lie. I'm the commanding officer of this fort! When I give orders, they are obeyed!"

"Absolutely, sir."

"Then what are you trying to do here?"

"I'm trying to find the truth about a murder." Philip stood, looking Hancock in the eye. He saw the bloodlust there and had the distinct, chilling impression that the man was quite insane. "If you'll excuse me, sir? I have some other things to attend to." He walked out.

Hancock was in a deadly rage. First, they brought Brand back in alive! Then, that St. John woman showed up and all but accused him of the murder! And now! Now! His lieutenant was questioning his very authority! His world was coming apart, and he knew the reason it was happening! He knew the one who had caused all his troubles! It was Brand!

Brand was the one who was responsible for all this! Brand deserved to die, and if he had to be the one to execute him, he would! The hell with the rest of them if they couldn't see the truth that was right before their eyes!

Hancock took out his revolver and checked to make sure it was loaded. He drank again from his bottle and looked out the window. It would be dark soon, and then he would make his move. Until dusk, he would just sit and wait. The time for justice was near at hand.

Chapter Twenty-one

**Brand, the Half-Breed Scout, or Trail of the
Renegade
The Revelation**

Rachel began a slow recovery, and she was
thrilled when Brand came to see her. She found
herself eagerly waiting for him and anticipating
his daily visits.

"You have a visitor," the doctor announced.

Rachel looked up, expecting Brand. She was eager to hear about his day and to just be with him.
But she was jarred to the depths of her soul when
her fiancé, Carl, walked in.

"Carl!" she said in surprise.

He thought she was thrilled and he went to her

and took her in his arms. "Thank heaven you're all right. I came as soon as Mrs. Stewart sent word."

Carl was sitting next to her, telling her of his love and how much he was worried about her, when Brand came to the doorway.

"Who's that with her?" he asked the doctor.

"That's her fiancé," the physician explained.

Brand's expression hardened and he backed from the room without Rachel being aware that he'd ever come to see her.

Rachel had truly thought she loved Carl and that he truly loved her. When she told him how she and Mercy had been captured and how Brand had rescued them, though, his reaction shocked her. He withdrew from her emotionally, suddenly treating her as if she were somehow tainted from the experience. It was then that she realized that she had never loved him. Brand was the man who made her heart sing. Brand was the man who had risked his very life to keep her safe. Brand was the man she dreamed about at night and longed to be with all day.

Hancock waited until it was late. He didn't want any interruptions. He wanted to be alone with Brand. He had a few things to say to him in private.

A deadly calm settled over him. At last he was going to do it. He was going to make the bastard pay. Moving with slow deliberation, he put the top back on his bottle and stowed it back in the drawer. The next drink he took would be one of celebration.

Hancock met no one as he crossed the parade ground on his way to the guardhouse. As he neared the building, he was pleased to see that a guard was posted. At least someone was following his orders.

"Good evening, private," he said smoothly to the man standing guard.

"Colonel." He saluted.

"I need to speak with our prisoner for a moment. Why don't you take a break? I'll stay with him until you get back."

"Thank you, sir." The private was pleased to have some time off. It had been boring standing guard there tonight. No one was going to bother Brand. He was as safe as he could be locked up there at Mc-Dowell. He handed his commanding officer the keys and moved off to get something to eat.

Hancock was smiling. Everything was going so well. Now, all he had to do was get Brand out of that cell. . . .

"Hello, Brand," Hancock said smoothly as he stepped inside the guardhouse.

Brand jumped to his feet at the sight of the colonel. He did not speak, but watched him cautiously. He knew how evil the man was, and he didn't trust him.

"Glad to see me, are you?" Hancock asked with a cold smile as he advanced toward the cell door. "I should think you would be. I've come to release you."

"Release me? Why?" Now Brand was shocked. He hadn't seen or spoken to Sheriff Warren or Lieutenant Long since he'd been locked up here, and he found it difficult to believe that they would send the colonel to free him if they'd finally found proof that he was innocent.

"I spoke at length with the sheriff and Long, and all agreed that a terrible mistake was made in arresting you. Obviously, they jumped to conclusions

345

about your guilt. So . . ." Hancock paused as he unlocked the cell door and opened it. "You are free to go."

Brand would have liked nothing better than to walk out of the guardhouse a free man, but he hesitated. There was something in the colonel's manner that gave him pause. He knew this man too well, and he suspected that if he was really being freed, Sheriff Warren would have been there with Hancock. "Where's the sheriff? Shouldn't he be here, too? It seems awfully late to be letting me go."

Hancock gritted his teeth as he responded, "I spoke with him at length. In fact, he was the one who told me to let you go tonight. We had talked about waiting until morning, but I thought you'd probably had enough nights in jail cells already."

Brand smiled slightly. "Why didn't he come with you? I'm his prisoner."

"He was tired." Hancock's eyes narrowed as he watched and waited for Brand's next move. "He said he'd speak to you in the morning."

Had it been anyone but Hancock saying these things to him, Brand might have believed him. But this was Hancock, the very man who had framed him for the murder. Why would he suddenly be so sympathetic to him and want to see him freed?

"If it's all the same to you, colonel, I think I'll just stay here until the sheriff comes by tomorrow," Brand said easily, stepping back and sitting down on the cot.

Hancock was ready to explode. He wanted the son of a bitch out of that cell! His plan was perfect. All he had to do was get Brand to step through that door and then he was going to shoot him point-blank in the back and claim he was trying to escape. It was perfect. All he needed was for Brand to walk out of there, and the man was refusing!

"You don't understand, Brand. You are free to go. There's no reason for you to stay here. Everyone knows you didn't kill Hale."

"But if I didn't do it, colonel, who did?" Brand countered, deliberately taunting him.

Hancock knew then that Brand suspected he had other plans for him than giving him his freedom. "You filthy Indian scum . . . Get out of that cell!" His hand hovered over his revolver.

"If you want me dead, colonel, you're going to have to come into this cell and kill me here. And I won't make it easy for you."

Sheri had taken a bath and had gone to bed, but she couldn't sleep. All she could think of was Brand locked up, all alone in that guardhouse. Having slept in his arms these last nights, she missed him and wanted to be with him. Her solitary bed held no appeal.

She thought about just sitting up all night, but realized that was ridiculous. They were at the fort and they were safe. There was no reason why she couldn't take a walk out to the guardhouse to see how Brand was doing. She'd heard them say that they had put a round-the-clock guard on him, so she would be in no danger at all. Slipping out of the gown that Cecelia had lent her, she got dressed and quietly crept from her quarters.

Sheri made her way to the guardhouse without incident. When she reached the building, she was surprised to find there was no guard posted outside and the door was standing ajar. It puzzled her, but she thought she'd find the guard inside with Brand when she walked in. Instead, she found terror. . . .

Hancock had heard someone coming and had prepared for the worst. He'd drawn his gun and was ready to claim that he'd caught Brand trying to break out. Instead, he found himself face-to-face with Sheri.

"You!" he roared in mindless fury, grabbing her in a bruising grip.

Sheri had no time to call for help as he wrapped a choking arm around her neck and pinned her helplessly against him.

Brand was on his feet in an instant. He had heard someone coming, too, but had never suspected it was Sheri. "Let her go, Hancock!" he said in a steely, threatening voice.

Hancock gave a maniacal laugh. "Oh, no. I'm not about to let her go. This is the moment I've been waiting for for years. I've got you where I want you now, you murdering bastard!"

"Whatever hatred you have for me has nothing to do with Sheri," Brand said in a flat tone as he tried to plan his next move. He could not, would not, see her hurt because of him. "Let her go, and I'll do whatever you want."

"It's too late!" he declared, his eyes glowing with power. He could make Brand grovel now before he killed him! The thought was exhilarating. "You ruined my dreams when you married my daughter and you destroyed my life when you killed her!"

"I didn't kill Becky," Brand answered, pain searing him at the vicious words.

"You killed her as plainly as if you'd stabbed her

348

yourself! And now I'm going to kill you! But first I think I'll let Miss St. John here have a taste of what Becky suffered."

"Don't do this, Hancock. Sheri has nothing to do with what's between you and me. Sheri's an innocent in all this."

"An innocent? So was my Becky when you took her away from me! You forced her to marry you! You forced her to leave me! And then you left her all alone out in the wilderness to be sliced to pieces by your own people!" Hancock was crazed as he snarled at the man he'd hated with an undying passion for all these years.

"Walk out of the cell, Brand, or so help me, I'll shoot her right now while you're watching."

Brand knew from the look on Hancock's face that he would do exactly what he'd said. "All right. I'll do whatever you want. Just let Sheri go."

"Do you think I'm that big a fool?" Hancock sneered. "She's mine, just as you are, right now. Start moving."

"What do you think Becky would say about you right now, colonel? Don't you think she'd be ashamed of you and what you've become?"

Hancock's expression turned even more deranged. "How dare you even bring up my daughter? You aren't fit to speak her name!"

Brand was suddenly afraid the man was going to go completely crazy. He looked at Sheri and saw tears in her eyes. He glanced around, searching for some way to help her, some weapon he could use to free her, but there was nothing close at hand. He was helpless.

"Move faster! I don't like that look in your eyes.

You try anything—anything at all—and she's dead."

Sheri couldn't stop herself from trembling, and Hancock laughed, feeling invincible.

"She's real scared, so you'd better not make any sudden moves if you want to keep her alive."

Sheri knew she had to do something. There was no way in the world that she was going to let Hancock shoot Brand down in cold blood just because he was holding her hostage. She knew from what had transpired in the mountains that he would put her life and well-being ahead of his own.

Hancock pressured her to take a step forward as Brand cautiously began to emerge from the cell. Brand was watching the man's every move, waiting for the opportunity to attack him. He would let no harm come to Sheri. He loved her, and just the sight of Hancock's hands on her infuriated him. He looked at Sheri and his eyes met hers. He saw the terror in the depths of her gaze, along with her love, and it tore at him. He would save her, no matter what.

Hancock positioned himself close to the open cell door, but out of Brand's reach. He wanted a clear shot at Brand's back as he walked out of the cell.

"Where do you want me to go?" Brand asked.

"Toward the front of the building," he instructed. "I caught your woman here trying to break you out of jail again, and that's when I shot you. You were obviously running again because you knew you were guilty and were afraid you were going to hang."

"What's going to happen to Sheri after you kill me?" Brand asked tightly, taking one step outside the cell to face his mortal enemy. "How will you get her to go along with your story?"

"If she wants to stay alive, she'll go along with my

story. Otherwise, I'll just have to shoot her, too, and claim she was helping you run." He tightened his hold on her throat.

It was in that minute that Sheri could stand no more. She knew little about fighting, but she did know that if she could jar her captor and make him turn her loose, she might be able to knock the gun away. With all the force she could muster, she suddenly jammed her elbow into his stomach as she tried to jerk herself free. Brand saw her move and dove toward Hancock.

Sheri's attack stunned Hancock. He had never expected her to fight back. At her sudden movement, he fired. He wanted Brand dead . . . and then he would kill her.

Philip had been deeply disturbed by his conversation with Colonel Hancock. The man was obviously hiding something. He had talked to Sheriff Warren, and first thing in the morning the sheriff was going to ride back into town and have a long talk with Miss Loretta. Philip had a feeling that in another day Brand would be a free man again.

He had never thought that he would come to like and admire Brand, but he admitted to himself now that he did. Brand had proven himself to be brave and honest. He was a rare man, indeed, and Philip felt honored to know him. Brand had suffered a lot in his life, and it was time that something went right for him. Philip was going to make sure it did.

Leaving his quarters, Philip went to stand outside and enjoy a breath of fresh night air. It was then that he saw Sheri heading toward the guardhouse across the parade ground some distance away. He understood her need to see Brand, and he decided to follow her to make sure everything was all right.

He moved at a leisurely pace, in no hurry after the long days in the saddle. It felt good just to be back at McDowell.

It was then, as he watched Sheri enter the guardhouse, that he heard the colonel's voice boom "You!" Philip was startled and wondered what the colonel was doing there. He looked around quickly for the private who was supposed to be on guard. When he saw no sign of him, he knew something was wrong.

Philip drew his sidearm and approached the guardhouse cautiously, listening, trying to hear what was going on inside. The voices came to him indistinctly at first, but as he got closer he could make out what they were saying.

"What's going to happen to Sheri after you kill me?"

"If she wants to stay alive, she'll go along with my story. Otherwise, I'll just have to shoot her, too, and claim she was helping you run."

"Lieutenant? Is something wrong?" A corporal saw him lurking there in the shadows and came up behind him.

Philip jumped, startled by the interruption. In a low voice, he quickly instructed, "There's trouble in the guardhouse. Keep quiet and go get Captain Whitmore right now! Be quick about it." He had informed the captain earlier that evening of all that had transpired with Colonel Hancock and he wanted him there, too.

"Yes, sir!" the enlisted man said as he rushed off to do as he'd been ordered.

His gun held at the ready, Philip moved forward to position himself at the front door. He knew timing would be everything in this. If he waited too long to make a move, Brand and Sheri might end up dead. He took a deep breath, girding himself for what was to come. Then he made his move. Philip burst through the door, just as Sheri tried to break free and Hancock fired.

Brand has moved the instant Sheri had tried to break free. As the gunshot exploded, arousing the whole fort, he threw himself bodily at the colonel, tackling him and throwing him to the ground. As they crashed to the floor, locked in a savage struggle, Philip came charging through the door with his gun drawn.

"Hold it right there!" Philip shouted.

"Shoot him, lieutenant!" Hancock ordered as he continued to struggle with Brand, refusing to let him go. "He was trying to escape! She was helping him! Shoot them! Shoot them both!"

"Brand, Sheri—get up and move away from him!" Philip told them.

Brand and Hancock broke apart. Brand rushed to Sheri to make sure she was all right, while Hancock quickly stood and reached for his weapon where it lay on the floor. He thought the lieutenant was there to help him.

"Don't touch that gun, colonel."

"What?" Hancock looked up at Philip in shock.

"You heard me. Just stay right where you are. Brand, Sheri, are you all right?"

"We're fine."

"Good. Take a look outside and see if Captain Whitmore's coming. I think we have a few things to tell our new commander."

"What are you talking about?" Hancock demanded, assuming his usual confident demeanor. "I'm the commanding officer here."

"Not anymore. Not after what I just overheard."

"You're crazy. You didn't hear anything," the colonel scoffed arrogantly.

"I heard you threaten to kill two people in cold blood. Is that how you killed Hale, too? I want you relieved of duty and thrown in this guardhouse!"

"What is it, lieutenant?" Captain Whitmore appeared behind him in the doorway and was startled to see that the lieutenant had his gun on the colonel. "What's happened?"

"I was coming to the guardhouse to check on things, when I heard Colonel Hancock telling Brand to walk out of the jail cell so he could shoot him in the back and tell everyone that he'd caught him breaking out. He was planning on shooting Miss St. John, too."

Whitmore looked at Hancock. "Sir, you are under arrest for attempted murder. Lieutenant, lock him up."

The sheriff had heard the commotion and had come running. "What happened?"

"I'd like your permission to release Brand, Sheriff Warren. I believe Colonel Hancock is the man you're looking for in connection with the death of Marcus Hale."

"Absolutely," the sheriff agreed. "Brand, you're free to go."

Sheri was so happy, she threw herself into Brand's arms. He hugged her close, unable to believe that it was really over.

The sheriff's pronouncement sent Hancock over the edge. As Long came toward him, he let out a scream of pure rage and dove for his gun. Snatching it up, he began firing blindly in Brand's direction. If he was going to die, then Brand was going to be waiting for him in hell!

Whitmore and Long both fired at him at the same time, and Hancock collapsed, dead, on the guardhouse floor. They ran to his side, kicking away the gun that he'd dropped and checking to make sure he was dead. They were both speechless with the horror of what had just happened. Only after their quick examination did they look up. They stared in torment at the vision of Brand clasping Sheri's limp form in his arms; blood was dripping from a wound in her head.

"Dear God, man, let's get her to the hospital!" Philip said, rushing to help him.

Philip ran ahead and alerted the doctor, then helped prepare a bed for her in a private area, away from the men who'd been brought in with the posse.

Brand came in after him, carrying Sheri as if she were his most precious treasure.

"Over here, Brand!" Philip called.

Brand hurried to where the doctor was waiting and laid her gently on the bed before him.

"You two go wait outside. I'll call you as soon as I know something."

"I'm staying," Brand declared.

But the doctor needed to work without interruption. He looked at Philip, who urged Brand to go with him.

"He needs to do his work, Brand. He'll call us in as soon as he's through. Come with me. I'll stay with you."

Brand took one last look at his love, and then reluctantly went with Philip. O'Toole had heard all the ruckus and had tracked Brand down to find out what was going on.

"I saw Captain Whitmore. He said you were here with Sheri—that she was shot. What happened, boy?" His gaze searched Brand's pain-filled face for answers.

"I thought it was over. She was hugging me. . . ." His iron control, so fierce for so long, shattered. "Hancock shot her while I was holding her. . . ."

"Is she going to make it?" O'Toole pressed.

"I don't know . . ." Brand lifted his tortured gaze toward the hospital and wondered what was happening within.

"What are they doing with Hancock?" O'Toole was ready to take care of the colonel himself.

"I shot him. He's dead," Philip admitted with deep regret. Unfortunately, there had been no other way. He, too, was staring back toward the building, wondering if Sheri was going to live, wishing he'd moved sooner . . . faster . . .

"Good," O'Toole declared with conviction. "I'm glad he's dead. He deserved killing."

O'Toole stayed with the two men, trying to keep them talking to distract them and help the time to pass, but neither Brand nor Philip wanted to talk. All they wanted was word of Sheri's condition.

Nearly an hour passed and no word came. Things were tense and quiet within the building. Then, finally, the doctor emerged.

Brand was there instantly. He felt certain that Sheri had died and that it was all his fault—just as it had been with Becky. Sheri had even been in his arms, and he had been unable to protect her. He waited for the doctor's announcement, his hands clenched into fists, his jaw locked in a rugged fight for control. "How is she?"

The silence that followed only lasted a second, but to Brand it seemed an eternity.

"She's going to be fine," the doctor said.

Brand could only stare at him. The news was so wonderful that he couldn't believe it. "She is?"

"The bullet just grazed her. She was unconscious for a while, but she's awake now. She's going to have a terrible headache for a day or two, but she should recover fully."

Brand stood unmoving, his jaw working furiously to control the emotions that were churning within him. *Sheri was going to live . . . Sheri was going to live . . .* He drew a ragged breath and tried to ignore the tears that burned in his eyes.

"Thank you." He started to turn away.

"Where are you going, Brand? She asked specifically to see you."

He stopped and squared his shoulders. He took one glance at O'Toole, who smiled at him, and then started after the doctor.

Philip stood with O'Toole, smiling, too. "Thank God she's all right. She is one special woman."

"That she is, and she's got herself one special man."

The two shared a look of camaraderie and moved off into the night together.

Brand walked quietly into Sheri's room. She was deathly pale, and there was a white bandage on her forehead. Her eyes were closed and he took a moment just to watch her. It wasn't often that he prayed, but he did now, thanking God that her life had been spared. After a long, silent moment, he was tempted to leave. He didn't want to disturb her if she was resting, but it was almost as if she sensed his thoughts. Her eyes opened and she managed a weak smile.

"Brand . . ." She said his name softly. It took all her strength to lift her hand to him.

He was by her side in an instant, clasping her hand in his, feeling how delicate and fragile she was.

"I love you, Brand," she whispered.

He raised her hand to his lips and pressed a kiss to it. He bowed his head, averting his gaze, so she couldn't see that the possibility of losing her had nearly destroyed him. He drew a shuddering breath.

He realized after a moment that she was still. He looked up, suddenly worried, only to find that she'd drifted off. Even in slumber, though, her face was turned toward him and her smile was softly serene.

"You'd better go now," the doctor told him quietly. "Come back tomorrow whenever you'd like."

"Thank you."

The doctor moved away to give him a moment of privacy, and Brand took the opportunity to press one gentle kiss to her cheek. Sheri did not stir as Brand gazed down at her for a long moment, then turned and walked away, out of her life.

Brand returned to his quarters to find O'Toole waiting for him.

"How was she?"

"The doctor says she'll be fine. She fell asleep right away, so I didn't stay long." As he was speaking, he took out his saddlebags and was packing things in them.

"What are you doing, boy?" O'Toole demanded, wondering at his actions.

"I'm leaving."

"You're what?"

"I'm leaving, O'Toole. I don't know when I'll be back."

He frowned. "What about that little girl lying in there who loves you?"

Brand stopped in mid-motion and turned to look at his best friend. "She's the reason I'm going. She could have been killed today . . ."

"But she wasn't."

"She could have been, O'Toole, don't you see? It could have been just like Becky . . ." He stopped, the words catching in his throat.

"So you love her."

"It's better this way. If she goes back to New York, I'll know she's safe." He turned away to finish packing.

"What do I tell her if she asks for you?"

"Tell her I said good-bye . . . and that I want her to be safe and to be happy."

He said no more, but picked up his saddlebags and rifle and left the room.

O'Toole stared after him, understanding Brand's heartbreak yet wishing there was some way he could fix things for him. He knew there wasn't.

Chapter Twenty-two

Brand, the Half-Breed Scout, or Trail of the Renegade
The Parting

Rachel stared at the doctor. "Well? Do you know where he is? Or do I have to go find him myself?"

"He came to see you that day, when your fiancé . . ."

"My ex-fiancé," she corrected.

"Yes—er, when your ex-fiancé arrived. When Brand saw that he was here, he left."

"And he hasn't been back since?"

"No. I haven't seen him around the fort either."

"I need my clothes."

"But you're not fully recovered yet," he protested.

"I don't care. I have to find Brand. I have to talk to him."

Over the doctor's objections, she left the hospital and sought out Captain Stewart in his office. If anyone could help her find Brand, he could.

"You need to find him? Why?"

"It's personal, sir. But I will be forever indebted to you if you would help me."

"Wait right here."

A short time later, he was back. "He's left the fort. The chief of scouts said that he wasn't sure when he'd be back."

Rachel was devastated, but refused to give up. She loved Brand and she was going to tell him so the next time she saw him.

The days passed slowly for Rachel. Mercy helped her find a place to stay at the fort, and she kept her company as Rachel waited for the return of the only man she would ever love.

Maureen and Charles made the trip to the fort early the next morning. They were relieved to know that the posse was back so they could tell the sheriff what Charles had learned in his investigation. When they reached McDowell, Philip met them.

"I'm glad you're here," Philip told Maureen.

She looked up at him, sensing that there was something very different about him. A new strength of character . . . an awareness of others . . . something she couldn't quite put her finger on. At the same time, his serious tone alarmed her.

Charles spoke first. "We got Sheri's message late

yesterday that you were back, so we came as soon as we could. I have information—"

"Later." Philip cut him off, looking at Maureen, his expression at once sympathetic and pained. "Maureen, Sheri's at the hospital."

"She's what? Yesterday she was. . . ." She knew a moment of panic and grabbed Philip's arm.

"She was injured, but she's going to be fine." He covered her hand in a gesture of sympathy.

"Oh, God! I have to see her!" Tears flooded her eyes. "How did this happen?"

"Come on." He drew her along. "I'll tell you both everything while I walk you over there."

Maureen looked frantically at Charles, and he was instantly by her side.

Philip glanced at Charles. "I don't know what information you found out about Hale's murderer, but last night we discovered who the real killer was."

"Colonel Hancock?" Charles asked.

Philip nodded. "What did you learn?"

Charles told him what the maid had described.

The officer's smile was grim. "So even if last night hadn't happened, we would have had him today. Good work."

"What did happen last night?" Maureen interrupted, desperate to know.

"Brand was being kept in the guardhouse, and Hancock went out there under the pretense of freeing him. The colonel really wanted him to walk out of the cell so he could shoot him and claim that he'd caught him escaping. Sheri showed up in the middle of it. I was lucky enough to be going there myself to check on Brand, and I walked in on the whole scene right after Sheri did. Brand and I managed to stop

Hancock, and we thought it was all over, but he went for his gun. He wanted Brand dead." Philip tensed as he remembered that horrible moment. "Sheri was with Brand. Hancock's shot missed him and hit her."

Maureen actually felt faint. Charles saw her sudden unsteadiness and quickly slipped an arm about her waist to help support her.

"Are you all right?" he asked, concerned.

She was ashen, but the look in her eyes was fierce. "Where's Hancock now?"

"He's dead. I shot him."

Maureen looked up at Philip with new respect and admiration. "Thank you."

"He must have been crazy to think he could get away with all this," Charles remarked.

"He was insane. He hated Brand so much that he risked everything just to see him dead."

"Brand . . . Where is he? How is he? Was he hurt?"

"He wasn't hurt. I haven't seen him since last night, but I'm sure he's around somewhere."

They reached the hospital, and Maureen hurried ahead of them. Dr. Aldridge saw her coming and showed her where Sheri was.

Sheri was sitting up in the hospital bed, sedately clad in a gown and wrapper that Cecelia had given the doctor for her. She was nursing a vicious headache. Dr. Aldridge had warned her that she might have one for a few days, and he'd been right.

At the sound of frantic voices, she looked up to find Maureen rushing into the room. Charles and Philip remained respectfully behind with the doctor.

"Sheri! Are you all right? Philip met us and told us what happened!" Maureen ran to Sheri's bedside. The bandage on her forehead was testimony to how close she'd come to death. Maureen quickly hugged her. "You could have been killed!"

They hugged for a long moment, then broke apart. Maureen settled in the chair next to the bed, her expression still shaken.

"How do you feel?"

"I've got a terrible headache, but Dr. Aldridge had warned me about that. Otherwise, I'm fine."

"I can't believe everything that's happened to you since we came out here."

"It has been an adventure, hasn't it?" Sheri tried to laugh, but it hurt too much.

"How's Brand?"

"He was with me last night, but I haven't seen him yet this morning. Would you help me fix my hair so I look nice when he comes in?"

"Of course. You might feel better, too, if we get you freshened up a bit."

"I just want him to know that I'm going to be fine. It must have been horrible for him. . . . I was hugging him when Hancock shot at us."

"Dear lord . . ." Maureen could well imagine Brand's horror in that moment. "Poor Brand. . . ."

"I know. I can't wait to see him today. I miss him already." She looked up at Maureen. "I love him so much. . . . When I thought Hancock was going to shoot him yesterday . . ." She shivered as she remembered the confrontation.

"I understand. But all that ugliness is over now. The real killer is dead, and you're in love."

Sheri managed a grin. "We have done some good research, haven't we?"

"Yes, we have." Maureen brushed out Sheri's hair gently so it fell about her shoulders in a tumble of soft curls. "There now, you look beautiful."

"All I need is for Brand to show up."

"Well, Charles and Philip are out with the doctor. Would you like to see them?"

"Yes, please. Philip saved our lives last night. I just may make him a hero in a book yet. He's certainly earned it."

"I'll go get them. I know they'd like to see you."

A short time later, she returned with the two.

"Sheri, I am so glad that you're going to be all right," Philip told her.

"If it hadn't been for you, Brand and I might both be dead today, Philip. Thank you. You were wonderful."

He actually blushed at her compliment. "I'm just glad I was there."

"How are you doing?" Charles asked, seeing the bandage and realizing just how close she'd come to dying.

"I've got a terrible headache, but I'll live, and that's the most important thing."

"Charles did some investigating in town. We were coming out here this morning to tell the sheriff what he'd learned so we could free Brand. I think I would have liked seeing him get out of jail that way, rather than the way it happened," Maureen said.

"So would I." Sheri said. "But it's all over now. Brand's out of jail and the real killer is dead. Sometimes life really can be like one of my books." It was a happy thought.

They all laughed.

"Did the doctor say how soon you could leave the hospital?" Maureen asked.

"Not yet, but I don't want to plan anything until I

talk to Brand again. He should be coming by soon, I hope."

"I can go see if I can find him for you, if you'd like?" Philip offered.

"Thanks."

"I'll go with you," Charles volunteered, and the two men went in search of Brand.

It was only a short time after they'd gone to find him that Sergeant O'Toole came to see her. He greeted both Sheri and Maureen warmly, but seemed a bit nervous about being there.

"Hello, sergeant. It's good to see you," Sheri said, beaming at him. "How's your arm doing?"

"It was just a flesh wound," he responded. "The doc says I have to keep in it this sling for a while, but it feels better already."

"Good."

"But what about you? You're all right?"

"Yes. I'm going to be fine."

"Do you feel up to talking for a moment?"

"Of course. Pull up another chair."

"No, ma'am. I won't be staying that long."

He was suddenly so serious that Sheri sensed something was wrong. She glanced at Maureen, who looked apprehensive, too.

"What is it, Sergeant?"

"It's Brand. He asked me to give you a message from him."

"Well, why didn't he just come here and give me the message himself?" Sheri asked with a smile. She was anxiously anticipating his visit and could hardly wait to see him.

"That's just it . . ." He paused, wondering how to phrase what he had to say, and knowing there was no easy way to break her heart. "You see, Brand's gone. He left last night."

"He's gone?" Sheri repeated, staring at him in disbelief.

"Yes, ma'am. He left some time after midnight. But before he rode out, he asked me to come see you this morning and give you a message from him."

She looked up at him expectantly. "What was it?"

"Brand said to tell you that he wants you to go back to New York and be safe . . . and happy."

Sheri felt as if her world came to an end in that moment. She had been filled with a great sense of warmth and love since falling asleep with Brand by her side the night before. She'd been waiting joyously for him to return to her. She'd wanted to see his smile, to kiss him . . . to touch him . . . "I don't understand. Doesn't he want me to wait for him to return?"

"He didn't know if he was going to return."

"So you don't know when he's coming back?"

O'Toole met her gaze. He saw the confusion in her eyes. "He didn't say. I'm sorry."

Sheri looked away as she struggled not to cry in front of him. "Thank you, sergeant, for delivering his message." When Sheri looked up at him again, all that was revealed in her eyes was loneliness and despair.

He saw the sadness in her and silently cursed Brand for the pain he'd caused her. "I'll be going now."

As he left the room, he didn't look back.

"Sheri, I'm so sorry. . . ." Maureen said softly.

She went to her cousin and sat on the edge of the bed next to her, then took her in her arms and held her while she cried. It was a wrenching cry from the depths of her soul. After a while, Sheri became strangely silent.

"Are you going to be all right?" Maureen asked gently, knowing how devastated she was.

"I'll be fine," she answered flatly. "Or at least, I will be once this headache goes away."

"Do you want to stay here and rest up?"

"No!" Sheri's answer was quick and sharp. "If the doctor thinks I can travel, then I want to go back into town and stay there until we can leave for home."

"You're done with your research? You're ready to go back to New York?" Maureen was asking as much for herself as she was for Sheri.

"Yes. I want to go home."

"I'll talk to the doctor and find out how soon you can travel." Maureen stood up to go find him.

"Maureen . . . ?"

She turned back to see that Sheri was looking up at her, trying to smile. "What? Do you need something?"

"No . . . I just wanted you to know that I'm glad you came with me. I don't know what I would have done without you."

Maureen gave her an impulsive hug. "I'm glad I was here with you."

A short time later, Dr. Aldridge completed another examination of Sheri and pronounced that she could leave for town the following day.

Sheri could hardly wait to depart. She was miserable there, even though as the day progressed, she had a steady stream of visitors. The ladies from the fort dropped by with food and conversation, but Sheri barely heard what they were saying. All she could think about was Brand. Everywhere she looked she was reminded of him. If she was going to keep her sanity, she had to get away from the fort. She had to go home. *Go home and be safe . . . and happy . . .*

Maureen left her alone to rest after the other women had gone. She went outside to find Charles waiting for her.

When Charles and Philip had returned to tell Sheri that they'd learned Brand had left the fort, they'd discovered that Sergeant O'Toole had already been there. They'd made a strategic exit, and Charles had been waiting for Maureen ever since.

"How is she doing?"

"It may take a little while, but she'll be all right," she told him as they walked out across the parade ground.

"I'm sorry things have turned out this way for her."

"So am I. I've been close to Sheri my whole life, and she's never cared for any man the way she cares for Brand. She really loves him."

"What does she want to do?"

"Dr. Aldridge said she would be able to travel tomorrow, so she wants to go back into town. We'll see how she feels after that, and then we'll know how soon we can start our trip home."

Hearing her say that they would be leaving for New York jarred Charles. He'd known it was coming. He'd known that Maureen would have to return home one day. He just hadn't wanted it to be this soon.

The thought of never seeing her again forced him to action. There wasn't much time left. If he was going to tell her the way he felt, he had to do it now.

He directed their walk toward a shady spot away from other people. He wanted a moment alone with her. What he had to say was important.

"Maureen . . ." he began. "Maureen, I . . ."

She looked at him strangely. "You sound so serious all of a sudden."

"I know. That's because I am." He paused, then began again. "Maureen, I know you're eager to get back home. I know how much you miss New York. . . ."

"It will be nice to see civilization again." She sighed.

Charles tensed. She wasn't making this easy for him, but he could not let this moment pass. "Maureen . . ."

She looked at him and frowned, wondering what was bothering him.

"Do you think you could ever be happy here?" He knew he was doing a miserable job of this. He was good at writing things, not talking about his feelings. But he had to make her understand. He had to tell her now that he loved her and wanted to marry her, or risk losing her. He feared, though, that no matter how much he cared for her, she wouldn't be able to stand living in the Territory.

She gazed up at him, seeing his fierce, determined expression. "What are you asking me, Charles?"

"Maureen . . ." He hated being so nervous. He was a man who did things logically and methodically. He didn't like this uncertainty. He cleared his throat to try again. "Maureen, I wish you didn't have to go back." When Charles realized how totally inane he'd sounded, he could have groaned out loud.

"That's sweet of you to say, but I have to go with

370

Sheri. She's really going to need me now . . . after Brand." For a moment there, Maureen had thought Charles was going to sweep her off her feet with a proposal. She sighed to herself in disappointment.

Charles was not about to let his own romantic ineptitude stop him. He wanted this woman, and he meant to have her. He girded himself. He was going to be sophisticated and say all the right things. He was going to impress her with his way with words. After all, that was how he made his living. He would woo her gently and then propose and then . . . "I love you, Maureen."

The disappointment that had haunted her vanished instantly at his declaration. "You do?" she asked, startled, delighted, ecstatic.

"Yes."

They were very aware that they were standing right where everyone could see them, yet Maureen didn't care. Without a thought to propriety, she launched herself into his arms.

"I love you, too!" she cried.

Now it was Charles's turn to be shocked.

"Really?" He took her by the arms and held her away from him to look down at her.

Maureen was gazing up at him, her expression adoring. "Really."

"Will you marry me?"

"Yes. I would be honored to marry you, Charles Brennan."

He found himself standing there looking down at her, a lopsided grin on his face. She'd just said yes!

It hadn't been so difficult after all, he thought with manly pride. *His sophisticated way with words had*

371

worked! He probably should have asked her ages ago.

Emboldened by his success, he lifted one hand to tenderly touch her cheek. "Now? Tomorrow? This weekend?"

Maureen started laughing. "I'd love to marry you this very minute, but . . ." Her gaze drifted back toward the hospital. The happiness in her expression faltered at the thought of her cousin. "I have to help Sheri . . . Would you mind very much getting married in New York?"

"Not at all. I still have some family back in Cleveland, and they could come. But, Maureen, afterward, will you be happy living here?" he asked, posing the question that had been troubling him for days now. He knew how she felt about the West. "I know it won't be easy for you, because you're used to living in the city. But I promise you that I will do everything in my power to make you happy, and though we'll probably never be rich, no one will ever love you more than I do."

His declaration touched her heart, and tears shone in her eyes. "As long as we're together, Charles, I'll be happy wherever we live."

Charles was elated. He had been prepared for her to ask him to return back East permanently. Her response thrilled him. He hadn't thought he could be any happier, but he was. Unable to stop, he drew her to him and kissed her.

"I love you, Maureen, and I'll spend the rest of my life proving it."

"Thank you for being so patient with me. These next few months are going to be difficult for Sheri. I don't think I'll tell her about us for a while. Not until she's had time to deal with her disappointment."

"Do what you have to do to help her. We can set the wedding date later. As long as I know you're mine, nothing else matters. I'll wait forever for you, if I have to."

"You won't," she said with an enticing smile guaranteed to set his heart to racing with the promise of love to come. "I'll be missing you too much to delay very long. As soon as everything settles down, I'll let you know. By this time next year, I predict we will be an old married couple."

"I like the sound of that."

Sheri and Maureen were packed and ready to return to town the next morning. As they made their way to where the stage was waiting, they stopped to thank everyone who'd come to see them off. The Whitmores were there, along with most of the ladies. Cecelia had come straight out and told Dora to stay home, that she didn't want to listen to her meanness today.

"Thank you for everything, Cecelia," Sheri told her, giving her a hug. "You and Laura were wonderful."

"It was our pleasure, believe me. I'm just glad everything turned out so well. Good luck with your writing."

They thanked the captain, too, and then saw O'Toole standing back a little, watching them go.

"I'll be right back," Sheri told Maureen. She sought him out, wanting to speak with him alone.

"You have a safe trip," he said as she came to him.

"We will. Maureen and I thank you for everything

you've done. It was the adventure of a lifetime for me. I'll never forget any of it. . . ." She lifted her gaze to his. "Ever."

O'Toole saw the pain in the depths of her regard, but knew there was nothing more he could say.

"Good-bye, sergeant."

Sheri turned and walked back to join Maureen. She saw Philip standing near the stage and went straight to him.

"You were wonderful," she told him.

"I'm going to miss you. Having you here was quite exciting."

"Maybe a little too exciting, don't you think?"

"You'll take care of yourself?"

"Yes, and you do the same."

He nodded.

Impulsively, Sheri stood on tiptoe and pressed a kiss to his cheek. "You saved my life, Philip Long. You are a true hero."

He smiled down at her, admiring her, wishing things could have been different between them. "Thank you."

She started to climb aboard the stage, and he stepped forward to help her up. When she turned to look at him one last time, he said, "I wish you well, Sheri."

She gave him a bittersweet smile as she settled into the coach. Maureen and Charles followed her in, and it was time to go.

As they rumbled out of Fort McDowell headed for town, Maureen gave Sheri's hand a reassuring pat. She knew how painful this departure had to be for her, and she just wished there was something more she could do.

Behind them at McDowell, Philip stayed where he was, watching the stagecoach until it was out of sight.

Sheri weathered the trip to town fairly well, but as tired as she was when they arrived, she knew she was in no shape to start the long trip home. They agreed to spend a few days resting in Phoenix before heading east.

Sheri spent the next two days in her room at the hotel, only coming out to eat. Maureen had planned to stay with her and try to entertain her, but Sheri announced that she was going to use the time to write. She encouraged Maureen to spend what time she could with Charles.

And so, during the day, Sheri did work, turning out page after page in the drama of Brand, the Half-Breed Scout, and his beloved Rachel. But at night, when she should have been sleeping, she sat by the window, watching and waiting as she remembered another night.

Brand had come to her before. She felt certain that he would come to her again. She stayed there gazing out into the darkness, looking for her love. She fell asleep each night just before dawn, her heart aching. The day of their departure came, and Sheri was ready. Her hopes had died. There would be no happy ending for her here. Brand was not coming after her. Her life was not a novel.

She knew Maureen was concerned about her, and she tried to allay her worries as she put on a smile and acted excited about returning home.

"So you're ready to go? Charles is downstairs waiting to see us off."

"I'm more than ready. Let's go home."

They met him in the lobby, and Sheri could sense the heartache he felt at Maureen's departure.

"I'll write to you," he promised as he walked them out to the stage.

"You'd better," Maureen countered.

"When are you coming to New York to marry her?" Sheri asked, perceptively. Though Maureen hadn't said a word about their plans, she sensed they cared deeply for one another.

They both looked at her, a bit shocked, and then laughed.

"We're that obvious, are we?"

"I write love stories for a living," she countered, smiling at him. "And I think you two are definitely in love."

"I have proposed," he told her.

"And I've accepted. We were thinking of a late fall wedding."

"It sounds wonderful," Sheri said as she went ahead and climbed aboard the stage to give them some time without her. "I wouldn't miss it."

Unmindful that others were watching, Charles swept Maureen into his arms and kissed her thoroughly.

"I'll see you soon," he promised.

Maureen was crying as she got on the stage and sat down next to Sheri. As the stagecoach lurched to a start and headed off, she leaned out the window and waved to Charles until she could no longer see him. Only then did she sit back and give Sheri a watery smile.

"It's going to be a long trip home, isn't it?"

"Don't worry. Charles loves you very much," Sheri told her. "The fall will be here before you know."

Chapter Twenty-three

**Brand, the Half-Breed Scout, or Trail of the
Renegade
Happily Ever After**

Rachel couldn't believe she was doing this. She couldn't believe that she was getting on the stage bound for Sacramento.

Tears burned in her eyes, but she refused to cry. She was leaving. Brand had sent her away from him. She cast one last longing glance around, hoping to see him, but there was no sign of her scout.

When he'd finally returned to the fort, she had sought him out. She loved him, and she wanted him to know it. His reaction had stunned her, *though, for he'd told her that there could be no future for them. Rachel had been heartbroken by his rejection and was now on her way to start a new life.*

She boarded the stage and sat by a window. Memories of the trip to the fort came to her then—thoughts of Mercy and Jenny and the horrible Indian attack. With those memories also came images of Brand.

As the stage rolled away, Rachel knew she would never forget him. She knew, too, that she would never love another man as she loved him.

Brand tried to tell himself it didn't matter if Rachel left. It was true that he loved her, and she had come to him and told him that she loved him, but it couldn't be. Their worlds were too different . . . too far apart. He kept busy all day, deliberately not going to see her off. It was better this way.

As the hours passed, though, and he knew the stage had gone, the ache in his heart drove him to desperation. He loved her as he'd never loved any woman, and he wondered how he'd ever thought he could let her go. Cursing himself for being a fool, he quickly got his horse and started after her. It might be dangerous living out West, but at least they would be together . . . if she would still have him.

"Where are you going, Brand?" one of the other scouts shouted at him as he rode off.

"To get my woman!" he called back, and he disappeared down the trail after the stage.

The stage driver saw what looked like an Indian sitting on his horse in the middle of the rode ahead. He was a little frightened until he drew near enough to recognize him as one of the scouts from the fort. He halted the team to see what the fellow wanted.

"I need to talk to one of your passengers," Brand told him, riding around to the side.

Rachel had been wondering why the stage had stopped, and at the sight of Brand on horseback looking for her, her spirits soared.

"Brand?" she cried. She quickly got up and opened the stage door.

He held out his hand to her. Without stepping down from the coach, she took Brand's hand and he lifted her onto his horse before him.

"I'll never let you go again," he promised.

"Oh, Brand . . ." she sighed. "I love you."

They rode off into the sunset together.

The End

Sheri was excited as she entered Carroll and Condon, carrying her new manuscript with her. In the months since she'd returned from Fort McDowell, she had remained secluded in her office, working diligently for long hours to finish the book on time. She'd made it, and, according to Maureen, *Brand, the Half-Breed Scout, or Trail of the Renegade* was better than anything she'd ever done before. Sheri hoped it was. She had put her heart and her soul into this book, and she could hardly wait to see what Mr. DeYoung was going to say after he'd read it.

"Miss St. John! It's good to see you again," Joanna greeted her as she came through the front door.

"It's good to see you again, too," Sheri answered. "I've got my new story for Mr. DeYoung. Is he ready for me yet?"

"Yes, he is. Harvey Karpf and Don D'Auria are with him right now, but he said to send you right in when you arrived."

"Thanks."

Sheri went to Tim DeYoung's door and knocked once softly. At his bid to enter, she opened the door and walked in.

"Sheri! You're right on time as usual," Tim said, standing to welcome her. "You know Harvey and Don, don't you?"

"Yes, we've met before." She smiled at the two men who also worked for Carroll and Condon.

They exchanged pleasantries and when they'd gone, Tim gestured toward the chair opposite his desk. "Come, sit down, and let me see what you've got."

She handed him the manuscript as she took a seat.

"What do you think of it?" he asked. "Did the trip out West help with your writing?"

"The trip was a great help with research," she said.

"And how was Brand, the half-breed scout? I was really curious how the time you spent with him went." He settled back in his chair, expecting her to regale him with tales of her adventures at the fort.

"Brand was a very nice man. He helped me a lot. So did Charles Brennan, the reporter who'd written the original article, and a lieutenant named Philip Long out at the fort."

Her editor was frustrated by her lack of specifics. "Tell me all about it. How was the fort? What did that town look like? What was the name again . . . Phoenix? Did you run into any Indians?"

"It was the most exciting time of my life. I'd never dreamed the West was so vast or so untamed. But you'll get all the answers to your questions when you read the book. I'd hate to spoil anything for you."

"So you're glad you went?"

Sheri paused. For just a fleeting instant, there was a shadow of pain in her expression. She masked it so quickly that Tim was left wondering if he'd imagined it.

"Yes," she finally answered. "I wouldn't have missed it for the world."

"This is going to be very interesting reading. I'm looking forward to it."

"I'll be waiting to hear from you."

She stood to go, and he walked her to the outer office.

"I'll let you know as soon as I'm done."

Sheri thanked him and then went upstairs to visit with Cathy Goellner. She wanted to tell her friend that the book was done. As she crossed the readers' room, she was greeted warmly by Kathy Carlon, Brooke Borneman, and Bari-Leigh Buiso, some of the other women who worked there.

"So you've finally finished, have you?" Cathy asked as Sheri came to sit by her desk.

"I just left the manuscript with Mr. DeYoung. He said he'd get back to me right away."

"Do you think it's good?"

"I know it's good."

"I want to know everything about Brand. Tell me, what was he like?"

"Well, he was tall, dark-haired, and broad-shouldered. The first time I saw him, he was riding with some other Indian scouts, and the only way I could tell he was a half-breed was by his blue eyes."

"Blue eyes?" Cathy was surprised, and then she

sighed. "I bet he was handsome . . ."

"Very."

"Did you like him?"

Sheri nodded, unable to say what she really wanted to. "He taught me a lot."

"What did he think about having a book written about him?"

She gave a little laugh as she remembered their initial meetings. "He was not the most cooperative in the beginning."

"He didn't like the idea?" Cathy was surprised.

"No. In fact, I had the distinct impression that he thought I was wasting his time."

"That must have been difficult for you."

"It was at first, but then . . ." Sheri saw in her mind's eye the raiding party attacking and that first terrifying ride with Brand to the cave.

"Then, what?"

"Then we started to get along. It was a very exciting trip. I'm glad I went. My cousin, Maureen, went along with me, and she is going to marry the reporter who wrote that article you gave me."

"You mean Charles Brennan? Really? That is so romantic! When's the wedding?"

"Next month. Charles is coming back here for the wedding, and then they're going to be living in Phoenix."

"Is he a nice man?"

"He's wonderful. He was a great help to us while we were out there. I don't know what we would have done without him."

"You know, I've been watching for articles written by him ever since you took that first one about Brand."

"Did you find any?" Sheri asked.

"As a matter of fact, we did. I had Thea, Mira, and Gwen keeping an eye out, and we found four." Cathy pulled out an envelope that was in her bottom desk drawer and handed it to Sheri. "I thought you might like to see these."

Sheri sifted through the four articles. She was smiling as she began. The first one was a short note about her research trip, "Novelist Visits The Area." As she looked through the others, her smile faltered.

"Scout From McDowell Arrested For Murder." "Scout Escapes From Jail." "Scout Released, Was Innocent of Charges."

All the memories she'd been trying so hard to forget surged back to life within her. Their first night of lovemaking . . . Her desperate plan to save Brand from the lynch mob . . . Their flight into the mountains . . . The confrontation with Colonel Hancock . . . Her hands were trembling as she laid the articles back down on Cathy's desk.

"It sounds like it was a very exciting trip," Cathy said with a slight smile. "How did you ever survive it?"

Sheri's happy mask almost slipped, but she forced herself to be professional. "As I said, it was exciting."

"Thank heaven he didn't kill that man."

"Brand may be half-Indian, but he's not a murderer," Sheri retorted fiercely.

"Are you ever going to see him again?" Cathy could tell that Sheri cared about the scout.

"No."

"Too bad. He sounds fascinating. Let's just hope he's a bestseller, what do you say?"

"I'd like that. I'd like that a lot."

"Have you got an idea for the next book?"

"Not yet. I was going to wait until I heard from Mr. DeYoung. I wanted to make sure he liked this first *Brand, the Half-Breed Scout* book before I plot a second one."

"I'm sure it's wonderful."

"We'll see."

The door to Carroll and Condon opened, and Joanna looked up to find the most handsome man she'd ever seen coming toward her. He was over six feet tall, and he moved with an easy grace unusual in a man his size. She was mesmerized and found she could only stare at him. His hair was black and long, but he wore it tied back. Joanna thought his features were as perfect as God could make them, and his eyes were a brilliant, almost hypnotizing blue. She had the distinct impression that he missed nothing with that penetrating gaze. He was wearing dark pants that fit him like a second skin, polished boots, a white shirt open at the throat, and a jacket. She could not imagine who he could be, and right then she didn't care. She was just enjoying the view.

"Can I help you?" she managed, gazing up at him wide-eyed when he stopped before her desk.

"Yes, I'm looking for someone. . . . Miss Sheridan St. John. I was told that she was here this afternoon."

"Er . . . uh, yes. Miss St. John is in the building. If you'd like to have a seat, I'll see if I can find her for you. May I tell her who's looking for her?"

"No. I'd like to tell her myself. Could you just show me where she is?"

"This is highly unusual . . ." Joanna stammered, unable to look away from him. And then he smiled at her and her resistance vanished. He could have whatever he wanted.

"Miss . . . ?"

"Joanna," she said dreamily.

"Joanna, I've traveled over more than half the country to find Sheri. Will you take me to her?"

"I'd love to." She stood up and started off toward the stairs with her mysterious visitor following.

Tim DeYoung was in a meeting with Kevin St. John, Thomas Nicholson, Mira Son, and Chris Keeslar when he heard Joanna talking to someone. He excused himself and stepped out of his office just as she walked by.

"Joanna? Do we have a visitor?"

"This gentleman's here to see Miss St. John, sir. I was just taking him upstairs. She's with Cathy Goellner right now."

"I see."

Tim did not try to stop them, but watched as they walked away. The man was impressive. He had a certain Western look about him, and he wondered at his connection to Sheri. As the stranger disappeared up the steps, Tim had an inspired thought. If this new book of Sheri's was any good, he might ask that man to pose for the cover. He certainly appealed to the ladies, if Joanna was any judge. Tim made a mental note, as he went back into his office, to ask Sheri who her visitor was and if he'd be interested in being on the cover of a dime novel. The cover art for *Seth Jones* had made a big difference in the sales of that book, and he was willing to do whatever was necessary to help profits at Carroll and Condon. It was worth a try.

"She should be right in here. . . ." Joanna led him

through the door to the room where the readers worked.

As they entered the room, it seemed that almost everyone looked up. Everyone, that was, but Sheri, who was seated next to Cathy's desk with her back to the door.

"She's over there," Joanna told him.

"Thanks." He moved toward Sheri like a predator stalking its prey. He had found her, and he was never going to let her get away from him again.

Something in his manner was so intense that Joanna felt a shiver go up her spine. She wished she were the one he was after.

Cathy and Sheri had been talking for quite a while when Cathy noticed Joanna coming through the door. She thought nothing of it at first—and then he walked in. Her expression suddenly changed, and she lost track of what she'd been saying.

"Cathy, are you all right?" Sheri asked, puzzled by the look on her face.

"I'm just fine," she answered with a grin. "And I'll be even finer when I find out who that is. . . ."

"Who who is?" Sheri frowned.

"Him!"

Sheri started to turn in her seat to see what Cathy was talking about.

Brand had been hard put not to run across the room and sweep Sheri up in his arms. He was focused only on getting to her, on being with her. He'd made a terrible mistake that night at McDowell. The horror of her being shot while he'd been holding her had torn him to shreds. It had taken him weeks to come to grips with the terror of it all. Only then had he come to realize that a life without Sheri would be meaningless for him.

He had fought the idea of searching for her. He had told himself that he should stay out of her life, that she was no doubt glad to be rid of him. But then he'd returned to the fort and had talked to O'Toole and to the lieutenant. O'Toole had told him how Sheri had reacted to his message that day, and then he'd run into Philip. He had not respected the man much until that day with the posse in the mountains, but now, as he came to know him better, he found he actually liked him.

Especially that day, after Philip had come straight out and told him what a fool he'd been for letting Sheri go.

It had taken Brand a while longer to come to understand his feelings completely. He could not face another day without Sheri by his side. He loved her. He had missed her, and he would spend the rest of his life making up for the pain he'd caused her—if only she would give him the chance.

As he strode toward Sheri now, his heart was thundering in his chest. He wouldn't blame her if she told him to leave and never come back, but it was a chance he had to take. He would tell her that he loved her, and he would let her decide the rest.

"Sheri?" he said softly as she looked his way.

Sheri stared at him in shock as he made his way toward her.

It was Brand. . . . He was there. . . .

She couldn't move. Night after night, she had dreamed of this moment, but in the light of day she'd never imagined that he'd really come for her . . . not after all this time. Her gaze met his and she slowly stood up.

"Brand . . ." she whispered.

And then he was there, standing over her, looking down at her, aching to touch her, yet holding himself back.

"I shouldn't have let you go," he said solemnly. "I'm sorry if I hurt you."

Tears filled her eyes as she lifted one hand to his cheek. "I've missed you. . . ."

"Not nearly as much as I missed you," he said, still holding himself under steely control. He wanted to hold her, to crush her to him and never let her go. He had been waiting a long time to say the words to her he could no longer deny. "I love you, Sheri."

It was all that she'd ever dreamed of and more. With an exultant cry, she went into his arms, and right there in front of everyone, she kissed him.

A collective romantic sigh went up from the room full of women. Cathy looked over at Kathy, Brooke, and Bari-Leigh.

"It's Brand," she whispered.

They all smiled, each secretly wishing some handsome man would come into their lives and kiss them that way.

When Sheri and Brand finally broke apart, Sheri's cheeks were flushed and her eyes were shining with love for him.

"Will you marry me?" he asked, his voice hoarse with emotion.

"Oh, yes." Her answer was heartfelt.

The office of women erupted in cheers and applause. Sheri fell back into Brand's arms, laughing and crying at the same time. Never had she known joy so sweet.

"Everyone," Sheri announced, "this is my Brand. The fictional hero of my new book and the true hero of my heart."

The women were smiling as they watched the happy couple make their way from the office. Joanna watched with envy from her desk as they left the building. She hoped some day the man of her dreams would come and take her away, too.

"What was all the commotion about?" Tim De Young demanded, coming out of his office after Sheri and Brand had disappeared through the door.

"That man who was just here . . ."

"Yes?"

"That was Brand, the hero of Sheri's new book."

"That was Brand, the half-breed scout?" He was startled. "He came all the way to New York?"

"Yes. He just proposed to Sheri, and she accepted."

Tim frowned thoughtfully. "I'd better read that book today."

He hurried back into his office and shut the door. He had a lot of reading to do.

Sheri lay in her husband's arms, delighting in the joy of being with him again.

"I love you," Brand told her. He would never regret his decision to come after her. He loved her more than life itself, and together they would have a wonderful future.

"I love you, too. You know what?"

"What?"

"My life is just like one of my books," she declared. "We're going to live happily ever after."

Bobbi Smith

"You're sure about that?" he teased.

"I'm positive." She rose over him to kiss him.

He gathered her close to him, his hands restless upon her silken curves. Now that she was his in all ways, he was certain that he would never get enough of her. Sheri melted against him, surrendering to his masterful touch. When he came to her, she welcomed him, taking him deep within her. They moved together in perfect union, each offering to the other the gift of total self. Ecstasy was theirs. They had never known that love could be so sweet.

Epilogue

Eighteen Months Later

"Sheri!" Jeremiah Wayne, the postmaster, called out to her as she entered the post office. "You've got a letter here all the way from New York City!"

Sheri was excited. She had come into town with Brand and the baby to get supplies. Her first stop was always the post office . . . just in case. Today, her wishes had come true. Today, she had a letter. She hurried back to the desk to see what he had for her.

"Who's it from?" she asked.

"Looks like your publisher," Jeremiah told her. "I'll just bet it's good news."

"I hope so. Thanks!" She was smiling brightly as she left.

Jeremiah was disappointed that she hadn't read it right there in front of him. He wondered what was in it, and he hoped he'd been right when he'd told her that it was good news. He'd certainly enjoyed her book.

Sheri headed back to the newspaper office to meet Brand. Tearing open the envelope, she began to read on the way.

"I got some mail, and wait until you hear this!" Her eyes were aglow as she entered the newspaper office.

Maureen, Charles, and Brand, who was standing holding their six-month-old daughter, Becky, in his arms, all looked up expectantly when she came in.

"What does it say? Is *Brand, The Half-Breed Scout* selling well?" Maureen asked. They had heard nothing from Carroll and Condon since the book had come out a few months before, and they were eager to know.

"It says, Dear Sheri, We are pleased to inform you that sales of *Brand, The Half-Breed Scout*, or *Trail of the Renegade* have been phenomenal, with sales rivaling those of *Seth Jones*. Please contact us about writing a sequel as soon as possible. Sincerely, Tim DeYoung."

"Sheri, that's wonderful!" Charles said.

The very pregnant Maureen went to hug her. "I knew you could do it! I knew you could write a bestseller!"

"Yes, but I needed my inspiration. I needed my husband," she said, looking at Brand with love in her eyes.

Brand slanted her a wicked grin. "Any time you're ready to do some research, just let me know!"

"Maybe we should head back to the ranch right now, then, what do you say? If Mr. DeYoung wants this next manuscript in less than six months, I'm going to have to work real hard on it. I might need a lot of inspiration."

"It would be my pleasure," he told her as he came to her side and pressed a soft kiss on her lips. "Congratulations. You earned it."

Sheri looked up at Brand with all the love she felt for him mirrored in her gaze. "I couldn't have done it without you."

PATRICIA GAFFNEY — Fortune's Lady

"Like moonspun magic...one of the best historical romances I have read in a decade!"
—Cassie Edwards

They are natural enemies—traitor's daughter and zealous patriot—yet the moment he sees Cassandra Merlin at her father's graveside, Riordan knows he will never be free of her. She is the key to stopping a heinous plot against the king's life, yet he senses she has her own secret reasons for aiding his cause. Her reputation is in shreds, yet he finds himself believing she is a woman wronged. Her mission is to seduce another man, yet he burns to take her luscious body for himself. She is a ravishing temptress, a woman of mystery, yet he has no choice but to gamble his heart on fortune's lady.

_4153-7 $5.99 US/$6.99 CAN

Dorchester Publishing Co., Inc.
65 Commerce Road
Stamford, CT 06902

Please add $1.75 for shipping and handling for the first book and $.50 for each book thereafter. NY, NYC, PA and CT residents, please add appropriate sales tax. No cash, stamps, or C.O.D.s. All orders shipped within 6 weeks via postal service book rate. Canadian orders require $2.00 extra postage and must be paid in U.S. dollars through a U.S. banking facility.

Name _____

Address _____

City _____ State _____ Zip _____

I have enclosed $_____ in payment for the checked book(s).
Payment <u>must</u> accompany all orders. ☐ Please send a free catalog.

FLAME
CONNIE MASON

"Each new Connie Mason book is a prize!"
—Heather Graham

When her brother is accused of murder, Ashley Webster heads west to clear his name. Although the proud Yankee is prepared to face any hardship on her journey to Fort Bridger, she is horrified to learn that single women aren't welcome on any wagon train. Desperate to cross the plains, Ashley decides to pay the first bachelor willing to pose as her husband. Then the fiery redhead comes across a former Johnny Reb in the St. Joe's jail, and she can't think of any man she'd rather marry in name only. But out on the rugged trail Tanner MacTavish quickly proves too intense, too virile, too dangerous for her peace of mind. And after Tanner steals a passionate kiss, Ashley knows that, even though the Civil War is over, a new battle is brewing—a battle for the heart that she may be only too happy to lose.

_4150-2 $5.99 US/$6.99 CAN

Pure Temptation

Connie Mason

"Each new Connie Mason book is a prize!"
—Heather Graham

Spirits can be so bloody unpredictable, and the specter of Lady Amelia is the worst of all. Just when one of her ne'er-do-well descendents thought he could go astray in peace, the phantom lady always appears to change his wicked ways.

A rogue without peer, Jackson Graystoke wants to make gaming and carousing in London society his life's work. And the penniless baronet would gladly curse himself with wine and women—if Lady Amelia would give him a ghost of a chance.

Fresh off the boat from Ireland, Moira O'Toole isn't fool enough to believe in legends or naive enough to trust a rake. Yet after an accident lands her in Graystoke Manor, she finds herself haunted, harried, and hopelessly charmed by Black Jack Graystoke and his exquisite promise of pure temptation.

_4041-7 $5.99 US/$6.99 CAN

Dorchester Publishing Co., Inc.
65 Commerce Road
Stamford, CT 06902

Please add $1.75 for shipping and handling for the first book and $.50 for each book thereafter. NY, NYC, PA and CT residents, please add appropriate sales tax. No cash, stamps, or C.O.D.s. All orders shipped within 6 weeks via postal service book rate. Canadian orders require $2.00 extra postage and must be paid in U.S. dollars through a U.S. banking facility.

Name _____

Address _____

City _____ State _____ Zip _____

I have enclosed $_____ in payment for the checked book(s).

Payment <u>must</u> accompany all orders.☐ Please send a free catalog.

Winner of the *Romantic Times* Storyteller Of The Year Award!

Lord Lyon of Normandy has saved William the Conqueror from certain death on the battlefield, yet neither his strength nor his skill can defend him against the defiant beauty the king chooses for his wife.

Ariana of Cragmere has lost her lands and her virtue to the mighty warrior, but the willful beauty swears never to surrender her heart.

Saxon countess and Norman knight, Ariana and Lyon are born enemies. And in a land rent asunder by bloody wars and shifting loyalties, they are doomed to misery unless they can vanquish the hatred that divides them—and unite in glorious love.

_3884-6 $5.99 US/$7.99 CAN